Scandal's Heiress

a Regency Romance

D1607744

AMELIA SMITH

ISBN: 1-941334-01-6

ISBN-13: 978-1-941334-01-0

Table of Contents

CHAPTER ONE: AFTER TRAFALGAR

Gibraltar, 28 October 1805

George! George!" Hyacinth called. How could he? He should know better than to run away like that. She ought to have taught him better.

Out on the bay, ships limped in, their sails black with soot, drenched with rain and saltwater. Broken spars littered their decks. The *Belleisle* had brought news of the victory a few days before, but Admiral Nelson had fallen, so any celebration was tempered with mourning. It was like a pole star had gone out. Other women paced the shore, too, hoping to see a familiar face among the sailors.

"George!" Hyacinth shouted again, as one of the *Victory*'s boats approached. A wisp of her hair escaped its bonnet, curling in the moist air. She tucked it back in resolutely.

"Hallo, Miss," one of the sailors called. His shipmates hooted and whistled. "My name's George!"

"Not you!" Hyacinth said. The man was wounded. He shouldn't be flirting.

"I'm looking for a boy," she clarified. "He's only ten years old, but tall, with black hair. He wouldn't be part of the ship's regular crew."

The sailors muttered among themselves as they lifted their wounded shipmate onto the sand, wincing even as he winked at her. Hyacinth Grey's young half-brother, George, had stolen away on a ship which was carrying dispatches just as soon as he'd gotten wind of the coming battle. She had tried to help him with his studies, and to stand in for his mother as well as she could, but it hadn't been enough. Their father, Captain Grey, wouldn't be able to bear losing him, not after losing Hyacinth's mother, his wife and the love of his life, then losing the mistress who had consoled him, too. Hyacinth looked at the sailors, hoping they would have some news.

"Aye," one of them said after a moment. "He made a fine powder monkey."

A powder monkey. Hyacinth took a deep breath. Captain Grey would have his head. "Is he alive?" she asked.

"I believe so, Miss."

"Don't you worry, Miss," said another sailor, "he'll be along in good time."

"Thank you," Hyacinth said. "If you see him, tell him to report to Captain Grey immediately."

"Aye aye," the man called George grinned. "Could you not spare me a kiss and forget your young rapscallion?"

Hyacinth shook her head and walked away, back towards her father's offices. Then she turned to search the harbor one more time.

❧

Thomas Pently, alias Smithson, sighted the rock of Gibraltar on the horizon, the starting point of the final leg of his journey, a journey he would rather not have made at all. Spent storm clouds stretched raggedly across the sky, showing streaks of the clear blue sky above. The sea churned, but they had a fair wind behind them at last, after days of being tossed hither and yon by a storm.

Thomas had negotiated passage with the captain of an Arab trader in Alexandria, and the man had agreed to set him down at

Gibraltar. From there, he'd thought that it would be easy to arrange passage back to England, but now he wasn't so sure. Dismasted ships crowded the bay. Perhaps he should sail on to Cadiz with the Arabs and avoid his countrymen a few weeks longer. He could creep his way up the Atlantic coast, one port at a time, stretching his journey.

No, it would be better to get it over with. Even in this dilapidated state, the Navy's fleet would be more efficient than rag-tag merchants. He had expected to find Gibraltar peaceful and well-ordered, but whatever had driven all these broken ships to shore was more than just a storm.

"What is this?" he asked one of the Arab sailors.

"This?" the man answered. "This… there has been a battle, a mighty sea battle."

That didn't tell him what he needed to know: Who had won? And when would he be able to find a ship to carry him onwards?

"That's a Spanish ship," another of the sailors said. "I have a cousin who sails with them."

Thomas pulled out his telescope and clicked the cylinders together until they reached their full, functional length. He'd won the piece from a Turkish sailor in a card game. On the rare occasions when he sat at the gaming table, he played to win.

He could make out the names of the ships, French, Spanish, and English, too. All in all, it looked as though the British had emerged victorious, but the flags flying at half-mast worried him.

Half an hour later, Thomas strode along the sands with his bag slung over his shoulder. His trunks had gone ahead on an East Indiaman and were probably already waiting for him in London. Boat after boat nosed up onto the sands as he walked, discharging sailors and officers in every state of body and dress. Some looked hale and hearty, but most bore wounds in one degree or another.

"The Admiral…" he heard, muttered over and over again. Slowly, from the crossing currents of conversation around him, he gathered the news that Admiral Nelson had died in the battle and that his body would be returning to England to lie in state. Ships would sail north soon, then, whatever their current state. The challenge would be to get himself aboard one of them, when half the Navy no doubt wanted to sail home, too.

Thomas carried a letter of introduction addressed to Admiral Nelson, in case he'd needed passage with the Navy. One of the older men at the East India Company's factory in Trivandrum had penned it for him: now he would need to figure out who to deliver it to, or attempt to rely on his family name alone to leverage passage. That, or a reasonable amount of gold coin, would sway most captains.

Ahead, a young woman walked up the beach with unladylike vigor, soft brown curls clinging to the pale skin of her neck.

"George!" she screamed. Thomas saw her dart forward and grab her target, a dark-haired, powder-blackened boy. He looked as if he might break free, then grinned at the young woman.

"It was grand!" he said.

"Captain Grey won't think so," she chided. "Off we go!"

She wore a drab but respectable gown. A governess, Thomas concluded. Then she turned and he saw her face. Governesses had gotten prettier since he left England. He lingered where he stood, watching her lead the boy up Gibraltar's muddy streets.

❧

Hyacinth tried not to show how relieved she was.

"Father will not be happy," she said, once the oddly-dressed stranger was out of earshot.

"I don't care," George said, trying to worm out of her grip.

The man wasn't dressed like an Englishman, certainly not like any kind of Navy man. He wore a long Indian blouse over vaguely English trousers. He wouldn't be Indian, though, not with that fair hair and those piercing blue eyes. Maybe Turkish? Whatever nation he belonged to, he exuded arrogance, carrying himself aloft from the chaos of the battle's aftermath, as if he'd come through the storm unscathed. He had smirked at her, amused by her efforts to recapture George. She straightened her back and kept walking.

Then she noticed a brown patch on the side of George's grimy shirt, a whisper of fresh blood turning it dark red in the middle.

"What is that?" Hyacinth said, turning him to face her.

"Nothing," said George.

"Were you hit?"

George pulled away from her and started walking towards home. He seemed to be in good spirits, so it could hardly be life-threatening, but she wanted to see for herself.

"Is it serious?" Hyacinth asked him, tucking her hand into her skirts to stop herself from prying.

"It's just a scratch, see?" George lifted up his shirt. The bandage was old and dirty, but the scab had broken, making it bleed again. Hyacinth couldn't help but imagine how much worse it might have been.

"I'm glad you're back in one piece," she grumbled.

"I can't wait to go to sea again!" George said. He was impossible.

ঽ

Hyacinth waited in the parlor with her embroidery on her lap. Embroidery was her best ladylike accomplishment, but today she'd only managed to create a tangle of mismatched threads. At least it gave her something to do with her hands while she waited for her father to return, probably after dark. She was startled by the sound of the door opening, hours before he would usually come home. Captain Grey walked in without so much as removing his coat, shaking the raindrops from his beard and hat. He took out a sealed letter and passed it from hand to hand, worrying its edges.

"He's all right," Hyacinth said quietly.

"George? Yes, I received your message an hour ago," her father

5

said distractedly.

"Shall I fetch him?" Hyacinth glanced towards the kitchen, anxious to get George's scolding and punishment over with.

"No, no," Captain Grey shook his head and looked out the window. "I have to speak with you first."

"I know I should have kept closer watch on him," Hyacinth apologized.

"I never should have asked you to mind the boy," he said, as if not hearing her, "not for so long, not to be his governess and half a mother, when you needed a mother, too..."

"But he's my brother, too," Hyacinth protested. She hadn't minded. At the very least, it had kept her occupied.

Her father slumped into an armchair and looked at his daughter, his only legitimate child. "You've done a fine job trying to raise the boy. I don't know how he would have managed without you, or with Rosa's people. He's been happy here, happy enough, I thought, until this escapade. He's a fine, spirited lad."

"Too spirited?" Hyacinth said.

Captain Grey shrugged. "A boy *should* be spirited at his age. If we were home in England, I wouldn't worry, but..." He stared out the window, north, towards Spain.

"You're not thinking of sending him to them now, are you?" Hyacinth said. George's mother had been a kind, gentle woman, but she'd never expressed a wish to return to her family. Rosa had entrusted Hyacinth with looking after George, even if she'd never said so directly.

"No, certainly not. This last trouble has only steeled me to do what I ought to have done long ago. I want both of you as far from this war as possible."

"To England? London?" Hyacinth had heard tales of London, dazzling tales told by Lady Hamilton and others. She had sometimes dreamed of going there herself, but hadn't wanted to abandon her father and brother.

Captain Grey nodded. His face was tense, lips pressed together. "I've arranged a place for George at a school in Portsmouth, Mr. Portnoy's school. There will be lots of other officers' sons there, born one side of the blanket or the other. He will manage, even if he doesn't like the idea at first."

"But who will look after you?" Hyacinth asked.

"I have work to keep me busy," he said, "and there will be plenty of it. I should be in the offices now, portioning out wood for repairs. I should have sent you to stay with Celia years ago, but when your mother died, I couldn't bear to let you go, and when the yellow fever came again and Rosa..."

"It's all right," Hyacinth said. She had been to England once, the summer after her mother died. She'd been eleven years old and lost in grief. Aunt Celia had swept her into a world of pretty dresses and children's parties. Her father was too wrapped up in mourning to care for her, or her grief at losing her mother, not until after he'd set up a new household, at another navy outpost. Aunt Celia never once mentioned Hyacinth's mother, all summer long.

Captain Grey brought Hyacinth back to Gibraltar, where he'd been stationed after Malta. Their housekeeper was a dark-skinned Andalusian woman, and Captain Grey's mistress. About a year after Hyacinth returned from England, George was born. Their home wasn't the aristocratic world Celia would have introduced Hyacinth to, but Captain Grey tutored her in the evenings, teaching her Greek, Latin and mathematics. After George's mother died, Hyacinth taught George in his turn. She lived a quiet life, socializing with the few of the younger officers' wives who lived at the garrison. She didn't wish for more.

"I should have sent you to London years ago," her father repeated. "I want you to have all of that... those things Celia always writes about, the dinners and socials and balls." He waved his hand vaguely. "It's not too late. If you could just look after George for the journey. I think he will do well at school. You've done an admirable job. I couldn't write Greek half so well at his age, but he needs to be with other boys."

"But then what will I do?" Hyacinth asked.

"What all young ladies do, I suppose," her father said vaguely. "You're a lovely young woman, and I'm sure there will be gentlemen clever enough for you in London."

Hyacinth shook her head. Surely, she was too awkward and provincial for any London gentlemen.

"And there's also this," her father said. He had been holding the letter close to his chest, but now he handed it to her. "It came almost a month ago."

Hyacinth took the letter, embossed in an elegant hand which she didn't recognize.

"It's from your grandmother's solicitor," he explained.

"But weren't all her affairs settled by Lord Grey?" Her father's mother had died only five years before, and her grandfather soon after. Her uncle had inherited their small estate, near Brighton.

"Your other grandmother, Mrs. Miller."

"Oh." Hyacinth's maternal grandmother had been the mistress of a wealthy earl, and was not at all respectable, though as successful as that sort of woman could ever expect to become. Violet Miller Grey, Hyacinth's mother, had been illegitimate. That was why her parents had never mingled in high society, or even returned to England. The Navy wasn't as high in the instep as the *haute ton*.

"I believe there is a cottage near Windcastle, and some jewelry," her father said. "They're yours, now."

"I see."

"Your mother was a greater lady than any woman I've ever met," he said, looking out the window. "Never mind what side of the blanket she was born on. If anyone tries to brush you with that old scandal, remember that you're a gentleman's daughter, and no matter what your grandmother was, you're a lady.

"And now," he said, "I'd best see to that young rapscallion. You'll want to read the letter."

He strode out towards the kitchen, leaving Hyacinth staring at the envelope, wondering about the grandmother she'd never known. She could hear voices from the kitchen, a calm rebuke, a muttered apology, then only the ordinary prattle of the housekeeper and Maria, her maid, preparing supper.

Hyacinth cracked the seal and unfolded the letter, smoothing it on the table before her.

Dear Miss Grey,

I extend my heartfelt condolences on the loss of your grandmother. She was a friend as well as an esteemed client and will be sorely missed.

Mrs. Miller left nearly all of her property to you, apart from a few small bequests. This includes a manor house near the Welsh border, some ten thousand in stocks and funds, and a collection of valuable jewelry. They are to be yours until you marry, at which point you will become trustee of the estate until your own daughter, should you have one, comes of age. She wished for me to relay the details of these matters to you directly, in person, but as you are overseas, I feel that you should know the general situation before you undertake the long journey home. She also asked me to advise you to keep your own council on the subject of your inheritance, so as not to be swayed by any erstwhile friends who might seek to use it for their own ends.

In keeping with her wishes, I respectfully advise you to come to London and meet with me at your earliest convenience.

Yours Sincerely,

John Butler, Esq.
Lincoln's Inn
London

Hyacinth sat back and read the letter again. Ten thousand? And a manor house? It was dizzying. She managed the house in Gibraltar quite comfortably on three hundred a year. She doubted that her father had ever had ten thousand pounds of his own together in one place. She hoped that her grandmother's warnings were unnecessary. She had always been sensible with money. If she were a different sort of young lady, she might be tempted to spend it all on fripperies, but as it was, she wouldn't know what to do with it. She would certainly not yield it to any "erstwhile friends." She must think of something to do with it, some purpose.

With George in school, and her father's household far away, she would have nothing to occupy her, but with her own means, she might accomplish something, but what?

She did not worry overly about a husband's influence. Even in the rocky outpost of Gibraltar, with very few eligible young ladies, the officers scarcely seemed to notice her. She attracted the occasional compliment, but no earnest suitors. She was plain, plainly dressed, and would be entirely unremarkable in the sophisticated society that Aunt Celia might introduce her to. What on earth would she do with herself in England?

፨

Thomas found an inn. The sturdy-looking man behind the desk was sharp enough to see through Thomas's eastern attire, and escorted him directly to one of the better rooms. It was adequately clean, looked out over the bay, and had a sturdy lock on the door.

"Yes, thank you," Thomas said. "I believe this will do."

The man named a price.

"That is rather more than I thought..." Thomas began.

"I can show you another room if you like," the man offered.

"No, never mind. This will do."

"Dinner was served at three. We keep ship times here," the man said apologetically, "but you can find something along the harbor, I'm sure."

"I'm sure," Thomas said, dropping his bag onto a chair.

"Let me know if I can be of any further assistance," the man said.

"Just one thing," said Thomas. "Would you be so kind as to direct me to the naval offices?"

"But surely you know where they are already? You can hardly have missed them. They're in the three buildings next door," he gestured to the left of the building.

"Thank you," Thomas said. He paused on his way out to ask one more question. "Do you know of any ships sailing for London in the next day or two?" he asked.

The man behind the desk laughed. "Not so soon as that. Have you seen the state of the fleet? There's hardly a fully masted warship among them. And you'll have to talk to the officers next door if you want to get on board a navy boat. The local merchant ships won't take you farther than Cadiz."

"I suppose I'll go next door then," Thomas said. He hadn't spoken to a bureaucrat since he'd left India. He had a dread of them. It would have been so much simpler if he could have walked up to Lord Nelson, chatted a bit about his grandfather, and been sent off in style. He decided to try his luck at the offices before he fell into bed.

Outdoors, balmy evening air drifted in off the sea. Men shouted to each other, singing and drinking as they walked home along the strand. Thomas felt uneasy in his skin. Perhaps he should go back to the inn and change into more English garb. Bureaucrats were sensitive to that kind of thing.

He was just about to return to his lodgings when he spotted a ginger-haired clerk scurrying up to an office building with a key in his hand.

"Excuse me, Sir," Thomas said, stopping him. "Is this where I would make an inquiry about passage on a ship?"

The clerk looked him over, suspicious. "Are y-you an Englishman?" he asked.

"I am," he said, "Thomas Pently, of the Windcastle Pentlys."

"I see. The n-Windcastle Pentlys, is it?"

Thomas could see the clerk calculating his standing, figuring it in to what he should do next.

"You should speak to my superior officer, Captain Grey," the clerk said briskly. "He will be here first thing in the morning, and I've just been making inquiries for him on the subject. I'm sure he'll be happy to help you."

"Thank you," Thomas said, "but might I ask what ships might have a berth available?"

"I... t-think you should address yours-self to Captain g-Grey, Sir," the clerk said, managing to sound officious even with his stutter. He turned his back to Thomas and entered the offices, locking the door firmly behind him.

❧

Thomas woke at dawn to bathe. He trimmed his beard himself,

peering in the mirror, and put on his best suit. He had carried it all the way to Trivandrum and back, and had had it altered to fit once, a few years ago, but hadn't worn it since his first month in India. His servants had managed to keep it free of insects all these years, and though it wasn't in the latest fashion, it was still impeccably English – even if Thomas himself wasn't.

The shoulders were too tight, though they'd been let out as far as the fabric would go. A bit of thread trailed from the left leg cuff. He cut it off and sucked in his gut. He was by no means stout, but he wasn't the slender youth of sixteen he'd been when he set out. Still, the wool was good, and he could put on his best aristocratic mien for this Captain Grey. He did remember how, didn't he?

The letter summoning him home had informed him of his brother Richard's untimely and much-lamented death. Thomas was now his father's heir. A few years before, he might have torn up those summons and left it all to his younger brother, to let them think he was dead, but matters in India had grown complicated.

Thomas checked his pocket one more time for the letter to Admiral Nelson. A minute later, he stood at the door of a busy office. Files filled the tables and shelves and piled in corners of the floor, but a sense of order dominated despite the clutter. A middle-aged man with a neatly trimmed beard stood behind the largest desk, reviewing a list. He looked up at Thomas's entry, frowning.

"Mr. Pently, I presume," he said.

Thomas bowed. "You must be Captain Grey. Your clerk told me that you had information about which ships might be bound for London."

Captain Grey looked back to his list. "You can see the condition of our fleet for yourself," he said. "Anything fit to sail through the straits is full."

Thomas crossed the room to stand before him. Although he stood a good inch taller than Captain Grey, he could feel the bureaucrat's indifference to his presence. Hostility, even.

"I have a letter here, of introduction," Thomas said. "It was meant to be given to Lord Nelson, to speed my passage…"

"Let me see it." Captain Grey reached out for the letter and broke the seal with a swift flick of his thumb. Thomas's hand had hardly returned to his side before the captain looked up from the letter.

"This letter, Sir, is hardly a glowing recommendation. You were dismissed from the company for dueling?"

"Many men duel, and few with better cause than I had," Thomas said. The man was needling him. He had no idea why, but he refused to be drawn in.

Captain Grey threw the letter down on the table. "I'm afraid I can't help you."

"My uncle…" Thomas began. His uncle was a tyrant. He did not want to invoke such a spectre. "I beg your pardon, Captain. I'm sorry to have wasted your time." He picked up the letter from the table and bowed to Captain Grey, then left. He would have to walk the shores and address himself to each ship's captain individually, but first, he was going to read that letter and see what slander it contained.

Thomas stopped on the steps outside of the office and read the letter. He had to read it twice to see how Captain Grey might have read between the lines to deduce that he'd dueled. The letter was worded politely, with all the correct salutations. It detailed his social standing and the urgency of his safe return to England to preserve the Windcastle line. There was no overt mention of dueling in India, only disagreements. His estrangement from his family was only implied by the fact that he'd been so long away. He crumpled the letter and put it in his pocket. He resolved to carry on as Mr. Smithson again, the name he'd gone by in the Company, until the Pently family tightened their noose around him in person. They certainly hadn't given him any advantage with Captain Grey.

≥

The morning of their departure dawned still and foggy. The household woke before first light to breakfast together one last time. Captain Grey sat at the head of the table, looking from one of his children to the other.

"Hyacinth," he said. "I believe that Celia will guide you well. You should marry, or at least have the chance to."

"Father?" she said.

He nodded for her to continue.

"Would you mind if I didn't marry?" Hyacinth said. "You see, I was thinking that with Grandmother Miller's inheritance, I might start a school. For girls."

Captain Grey took a deep breath. "If that is what you wish to do, of course you may," he said, "but marriage... I thought you would want to be married. Young ladies generally do, and I thought you were only hoping for a more suitable match than the few gentlemen you've met here. I wish you could be as happy as I was with your mother and... I believe she was happy with me, too."

George swung his legs under the table and rolled his eyes. Hyacinth would have kicked him if she could. He usually yawned loudly when anyone said anything about love. Part of it might have been his illegitimate birth, but mostly it was because he was a boy, and boys his age never thought much of romance.

Their father was too wrapped up in his own thoughts to notice.

"I won't marry for the sake of convention," Hyacinth said. "If I do, it will be for love."

"There's my girl," he said absently. "I wish your mother could see you now." He took a deep breath, then turned to his younger child.

"Now, George," he said in a firm, brisk voice. "Things won't be so easy for you."

"Then why are you sending me?" George said. He pushed his eggs around the plate and had torn his bread into crumbs. He made hills and craters with his food as their father spoke.

"Because, with a good education you'll be able to do better than be a simple sailor."

"But I want to be a navy man!" George said. "I want to fight!"

"George. Listen to me. Even those of us who wield pens and ledgers do our part."

"Yes, Sir," George mumbled.

❧

A quarter of an hour later, Hyacinth stepped onto the boat which would row them out to the *Whistler*. Hyacinth's maid, Maria, sat in the prow beside George. George looked more like Maria's younger brother than Hyacinth's – George took after his mother's half-Moorish family. Maria had joined their household as a maid of all work when Hyacinth first came to Gibraltar. She was only a year older than Hyacinth and had been her closest confidante, though that wasn't saying much. Maria would help to chaperone George on the journey and then stay on as Hyacinth's lady's maid, unless she chose to return to Spain. Hyacinth and Captain Grey sat at the stern of the boat, looking out at the fleet before them.

The sailors bent to their oars, weaving in and out among the warships. The flotilla departing for England included the *Victory*, which carried the body of Admiral Nelson. Hyacinth crossed herself as they passed under its shadow.

"Captain Grey!" A man on the decks shouted. It was the *Victory's* purser. "We're short a barrel of tar!"

Captain Grey acknowledged him. "I'll see to it shortly," he called back.

When they'd rowed on a few strokes past the *Victory's* bowsprit, Captain Grey turned to Hyacinth.

"I'm afraid I won't be able to stay with you until you set sail, as I'd hoped. I'll have to make the rounds of the other ships, as well."

"That's all right," Hyacinth said. She felt the slight bob of the boat underneath them and hoped that the knot in her stomach was only nerves, not seasickness. She had never been seasick as a girl, and there was no reason to think she would start now. Up ahead, she could see the *Whistler*, so much smaller than the gunships around it.

"Celia will no doubt help you select a fashionable wardrobe when you reach London," Captain Grey said. "She's always been a paragon of style, if nothing else." He sighed.

Hyacinth had gathered that relations between her father and his sister had been strained since her father had married, but they were still family, so the letters came and went while the old disagreement – whatever it was – simmered under the surface.

"I've made arrangements for George to have an allowance," her father continued. "I'll leave you with some of it, here," he said, passing Hyacinth a heavy purse. "You can also draw on my account at Seaman's Trust." He handed her a worn deposit book. "There's enough there to cover his school fees, with a little left over. I've left a hundred pounds there for you, in case you need it, but Celia will most likely see to all your needs."

"If I remember, she was very generous," Hyacinth said as she fit the coin-filled purse into her reticule. "Besides," she added, "there'll be the accounts I have from Grandmother Miller."

Captain Grey sighed. "Celia's a stickler for other people's propriety and will interpret that whatever way she pleases. Take care of George."

"Of course I will," Hyacinth promised. "I hope we won't give you too much to worry about."

Her father chuckled. "I believe it won't be long until you find a husband to handle your affairs. In the meantime, you have a sensible head on your shoulders."

The boat was sliding abreast of the *Whistler* already. She would have liked to tell her father again that she was not so intent on marriage, to remind him of her plans for a school. There were probably hundreds of girls forced onto the streets as her grandmother must have been. If she could help a few of them, maybe it would help redeem her grandmother's memory. Besides, her inheritance promised independence, and she would not throw it away. Marriage, even courtship, would surely be an impediment. Beginning a school seemed like a better adventure than courting young gentlemen under Aunt Celia's guidance.

The boat pulled up to a ladder and their baggage was handed up. They didn't have much, just a small chest of books and a slightly larger trunk of clothes apiece. As they waited to climb aboard, another boat approached, oars dipping in and out of the water in a steady rhythm. A tall, light-haired passenger sat in its stern and tipped his hat to Hyacinth.

"That…" Captain Grey frowned. "Have you met that man, Hyacinth?"

"No," she said. "I might have seen him in the town this past week, though."

Her father's frown deepened. "That man's family has left a string of neglected bastards across the west of England, and I doubt he's an exception. To be a black sheep in that lot…"

Hyacinth's father rarely shared his opinions so forcefully. She wondered what the man had done to earn his ire.

The man had turned his head away, avoiding Captain Grey's gaze.

"Did you grant him passage on this ship, then?" Hyacinth asked under her breath.

"I did not," Captain Grey said. "I will speak to Captain Hotham, but..." Up on deck, the captain had come to the rail. He shouted a greeting to the approaching boats. At his orders, a second ladder coiled down, so that both boats could discharge their passengers at once.

"I may be too late." Captain Grey frowned. "I'll see if other arrangements can be made, but steer clear of that man, if he is to be your fellow passenger."

"Certainly," Hyacinth said, but even as she promised, she had a hard time keeping her eyes off the man. He scaled the ladder as if he'd lived his whole life on the sea. She turned away and picked up her reticule, checking it once more for the solicitor's letter, the bank notes, and her other papers. She stole another glance at her fellow passenger as he disappeared onto the deck above.

"Steer clear of that man, I say," her father repeated.

❧

CHAPTER TWO: THE WHISTLER

Hyacinth bunched her skirts and climbed up the ladder to the deck. It had been years since she'd set foot on a ship of any size, years since she'd left Gibraltar. This ship, the *Whistler*, felt smaller and busier than the last one she'd been on, years ago, drifting back from England the summer after her mother had died, before George was born.

"Excuse me a moment, Hyacinth," her father said, setting a hand on her shoulder. "I'll go find the captain." Captain Grey's eyes narrowed as he spotted the captain greeting the windswept passenger from the other boat. He muttered something under his breath and strode away.

George sprang onto the deck and dashed to the fo'c'sle before Hyacinth could catch him. Maria was still in the boat, clinging to the ladder with her hands but refusing to put her feet on its rungs.

"What's the trouble?" Hyacinth asked her.

Maria bit her lip and shot a glare at one of the sailors, who gave her a teasing prod.

"Leave her alone!" Hyacinth said.

Maria still looked uneasy.

"You have to get up on the ship one way or another, and this is easier than hanging onto a basket while they hoist you up."

"Possibly," Maria said.

"We'll turn our backs if you like," the sailor offered.

Hyacinth nodded. "That would help, yes," she said. "Thank you."

Without the sailor's eyes on her, Maria put a tentative toe up.

"You can do it," Hyacinth said. "It's no worse than going up to the attic."

"The attic doesn't rock, and there's the floor to catch me, not the sea," Maria complained, but she set her foot onto the next rung and reached Hyacinth a moment later.

"You'll get used to it," Hyacinth said, trying to cheer her. "Besides, we should reach England in a fortnight. It's not for long, and then we'll live in a fine house."

Maria smoothed her skirts and nodded stoically.

"I see all the ladies are aboard, then?" Captain Grey said as he returned. "May I present Captain Hotham."

"Good morning, Miss Grey." The captain was middle-aged, his hair so bleached and grizzled that it was impossible to determine its original color, though it might have been auburn. He shared Captain Grey's calm, upright demeanor and air of command, but they stood a long arm's length apart, measuring each other. Hyacinth's father kept the other passenger in his sights.

Captain Hotham spoke to the first mate. "Mr. Bromley, would you please show Mr. Smithson to his quarters?"

Captain Grey narrowed his eyes. "Mr. Smithson, is it?" he said. "Hmm. He said he was..."

"Said he was what?" Hyacinth asked.

Her father shook his head. "Never mind, but I won't have you compromised before Celia can toss you out into the social whirl."

"Yes, Father," Hyacinth said, "I should hope I have more sense than that!"

Captain Hotham returned his attention to them.

"I trust you're well-provisioned," Captain Grey said.

"Tolerably well," Captain Hotham said, "but our supplies of wine are only adequate to half this journey, and we have no spare mid-weight line for the rigging. Of course, we can make do with other line, if need be, but…"

"I took special care with this ship, you understand, but we're operating under quite a shortage." Captain Grey sighed. "When I'm back on shore I'll see if I can requisition another reel for you and a barrel of Madeira for the galley."

"We would appreciate it," Captain Hotham said.

As the men discussed provisioning, Hyacinth looked around. The ship was only a frigate, so it had been at the edges of the battle and escaped the worst damage. The passengers' and officers' cabins sat at the rear of the vessel, where the ship's motion would be smoothest. The guns were tucked away and locked in place, but they could be ready for a skirmish in a moment, if it came to that. Sailors hurried around, checking the lines and sails for wear and giving the brass rails a final polish before setting sail.

"I trust you have breakfasted?" Captain Hotham asked Hyacinth as they walked toward the stern.

"Yes, thank you, very well," Hyacinth said. Maria hovered at her shoulder, but George was on the far side of the deck, leaning over the rails.

"George!" Captain Grey barked.

George sprang to attention and scurried to join them as they reached their cabins.

"Here is your cabin," Captain Hotham said, opening a small door. "Your maid and the boy will be in the next one to starboard."

The cabin was cozy, so small that Hyacinth could touch both walls with her arms outstretched, and neatly furnished in varnished oak. A carefully made berth lay along one side and a small writing desk stood opposite. A high window in the door out to the deck let in a little light.

"That door leads to my wife's parlor," Captain Hotham explained, indicating a small door at the side of the cabin. "She is particularly looking forward to having another lady aboard. She is also fond of embroidery."

"I had no idea that your wife was aboard," Hyacinth said.

"How nice for you." She wasn't so sure it would be nice for the wife, though, to be surrounded by sailors all the time.

Captain Grey smiled. "I hope that Mrs. Hotham will be able to inform you of all the latest news from England, as well as keeping you company," he said.

Hyacinth blushed. "Thank you, Father. I'm sure I'll be glad of some company," she said, although she would have been content with only Maria and George as companions. She wouldn't even know how to gossip about the news from England.

"We dine at three, weather permitting," the captain said, stepping back from the cabin door. "I hope to see you then."

"Thank you, Captain Hotham," Hyacinth said. "I'm sure I will be quite comfortable here."

Her father inspected the cabin again to assure himself that it was clean and its fixtures secure. He looked askance when he saw the other passenger out on deck again, chatting with the first mate.

"Your mother would have wanted you to have a Season in London, so that you could mingle with society as she never could," he said to Hyacinth. "I believe that your fellow passenger would think nothing of ruining you before you even arrived."

Hyacinth eyed her father curiously. He rarely maligned anyone, so he must have had good cause, but what? The man had only recently arrived in Gibraltar; she was sure of it. "What do you know of him?" she asked.

"Enough," he said. "A black sheep in his family he must be dark indeed. Also, he was dismissed from the East India Company for dueling with a fellow officer, over a matter which caused a scandal even in that permissive territory."

"I see," Hyacinth said. "I'll be careful." Even as she spoke, she found herself wondering what had prompted the duel, and how this man had gained passage on the ship, in the face of her father's formidable opposition.

࿏

Thomas watched as Captain Grey escorted the young woman, or lady, to her cabin, then walked off with the *Whistler*'s captain. For whatever reason, Captain Grey had taken a strong dislike to him, that much he could tell. If it had anything to do with the family connections he'd mentioned, he could hardly blame the man. Also, some officers took an exception to dueling. He didn't think much of it, himself, as a general rule, but there were times when it seemed the only honorable way forward.

In any case, Captain Grey would not be aboard, and Thomas didn't expect to meet him again. If the young lady had some connection to him, that was no concern of his.

He lay back in his bunk and opened one of the books he'd purchased in Gibraltar, a copy of Aristotle's *Poetics*. If the seas were calm, he would have plenty of time to read, and if they were rough, he would make do.

Thomas held the book in front of him, but found that he couldn't concentrate. Captain Grey's animosity irked him. From the neighboring cabin, he could hear the young lady chattering to her maid in Spanish while the boy ran in and out, announcing his discoveries. Thomas spoke only a few words of Spanish, though, so he heard nothing but musical babble in the sounds he strained to understand, despite himself.

He opened his Aristotle again and renewed his efforts to read.

࿏

A bell rang and a shout went out. With a luff of sails and a gurgle of water under the bow, the *Whistler* was underway. Hyacinth came on deck to watch Gibraltar slip away to the stern. Maria stood beside her, biting back tears. She seemed determined to greet her future in England with a frown on her face.

"You can return any time you like, you know," Hyacinth said.

"Ah, but then you will be all alone, in England," Maria replied. "Besides, it will be an adventure for me, too."

"I will have Aunt Celia and my cousin Sophie," Hyacinth said, "and of course there's always George."

"Yes, George." Maria sighed. "He has run off already."

Hyacinth looked up and down the deck. George was nowhere to be seen. She wondered if he had stolen away on the last tender back to Gibraltar, but then a flurry of motion in the rigging caught her attention. A shout sounded from the quarterdeck. There he was, halfway up the mizzen mast, climbing as fast as he could.

"George!" Hyacinth shouted.

"Haloo!" he echoed back. She could barely hear him over the creak of the ropes and rigging. Maria stood agape.

"*Dios mio*," she said.

"He'll get himself killed before we reach England at that rate." Hyacinth muttered. She hurried over to the foot of the mast while Maria waved her hands ineffectually. The first mate, Mr. Bromley, held the wheel.

"Mr. Bromley?" Hyacinth said, trying to catch his attention.

Bromley smiled at her. "Good afternoon, Miss Grey. It's a pleasure to have a lady aboard," he said, as if nothing were amiss.

"George is up in the rigging," Hyacinth said. "He has no business there, and he's likely to fall."

Bromley looked up and considered the situation. "Umm. Very tight grip that boy has. Not likely he'll fall in this light breeze."

Hyacinth turned at the sound of a soft chuckle. Her fellow passenger stood just behind her, now clad only in breeches and a light shirt, which revealed a lean, muscled chest underneath. He, too, smiled at her as if all were well.

"It isn't funny," Hyacinth said. "I am responsible…"

"You can't keep a boy like that tied to your apron strings, Miss," he said.

"Pardon me, but I don't believe we've been introduced,"

Hyacinth said. He had no business telling her how to mind George.

The man was going to say something cutting, she was sure, but Mr. Bromley stepped in first.

"Allow me to rectify that" he said. "Miss Grey, whose beauty needs no introduction, I present Mr. Smithson of..." he knit his brows. "Where was it that you said your family hailed from?"

"I am going to London after we reach England," he said, which was no sort of answer at all.

"London, then," Mr. Bromley said.

"I've spent over a decade in Trivandrum, though," Mr. Smithson said, "so I suppose that makes me a colonial."

"Hardly," Mr. Bromley said. "And where is it you're bound to?" he asked Hyacinth.

"I will be staying with my aunt," Hyacinth answered.

The man, Mr. Smithson, winked at her and laughed. "That's as bad as saying you're going to London."

Hyacinth frowned. She should be keeping her distance. He looked striking enough at first glance, with no particular expression on his face, but when he smiled, he looked so charming that she didn't want to remember her father's warnings.

"And your name is Miss Grey?" he said. "Are you by chance a relation of Captain Grey?"

"I am his daughter," Hyacinth said.

"I see." Mr. Smithson's smile evaporated, which made it easier for Hyacinth to step away and look up to the rigging again. "How unfortunate. I never would have guessed that your beauty had such a dour sire."

Hyacinth stiffened. Before she could think of a retort, Mr. Bromley cut in with a laugh.

"Goodness, Mr. Smithson! You mustn't insult Captain Grey. Without him we'd have no rum or oakum. He's one of the most efficient officers in the navy."

"I'm sure he is," Mr. Smithson grumbled.

Hyacinth wondered again what quarrel her father had with

the man.

"What errand carries you to England, then, Miss Grey?" Mr. Smithson asked.

"It's no affair of yours." Hyacinth had no intention of telling him anything about herself. She didn't want to be embroiled in a shipboard romance when she had her whole future ahead of her. Gibraltar, her past, was fading fast in the ship's wake, and the rest of the fleet sailed beside them, bound for that dark, cold land.

She peered up through the rigging, hoping to catch another glimpse of George as he climbed. He had reached the crow's nest.

"That is far enough, George!" she shouted.

George ignored her. He hadn't even heard her above the creak of the rigging and the sound of the wind, but Mr. Smithson was laughing at her again.

"You are minding that young boy then?" he asked.

"I am to deliver him to a school in England," Hyacinth said, blushing. "Preferably in one piece."

"I'm coming down!" George shouted from the cross-trees. He began a hesitant descent, slower and less graceful than the climb. Hyacinth watched every twitch of his muscles as he reached down from one foothold to the next, praying that he wouldn't slip, and that he'd have the good sense to stay out of the rigging in the future.

"I can go collect him if you'd like, Miss Grey," Mr. Smithson offered. She glanced over at him.

"That will be quite all right, Mr. Smithson," Hyacinth said. "We do not need your assistance."

She turned away from the men at the wheel and strode back towards her cabin. George was low enough in the ropes now that a fall would most likely take him to the deck in safety. It was going to be impossible to avoid that man. The ship was simply too small to skirt around him.

Maria was still standing in the same place, clutching the rail.

"Come, Maria," Hyacinth said. "It won't do us any good to

watch. He'll only be more tempted to show off. Let's set up the embroidery frame."

❧

Thomas waited until the boy was safely back on deck then took himself off to his cabin. He lay in his bunk, watching the bright light dance across the ceiling above him. With the ship underway to England, he felt that he ought to be thinking ahead, but there was nothing there which bore contemplating – Richard's death, his father's tireless philandering, the net of marital schemes and dynastic responsibilities which would tighten around him the moment he stepped on shore.

India was no better. There, the memories were simply too painful, full of layers of deception and naked ambition, glittering, empty wealth, and his one hope of happiness snuffed out before her time. Brutally, shamelessly.

No, neither the past nor the future held anything worth contemplating. All he had was this ship, this fortnight or so of idleness between one form of hell and another.

❧

Hyacinth found a note on her desk from Mrs. Hotham, an invitation to join her for a cup of tea. She asked Maria to help George settle in, then stepped through the inner door to her hostess's cabin.

"Come in!" The voice was light and lilting. Mrs. Hotham lay on a settee, or, rather, a bunk, with a handkerchief in one hand, a bucket by her side, and a swelling belly under her dress. No wonder she hadn't been out on deck. The cabin's tall windows faced the stern of the ship, but with chintz-covered cushions and an embroidery frame hung on one wall, it felt like being in a parlor.

"Mrs. Hotham." Hyacinth curtsied. Outside, she could see the *Belleisle* and the frigate *Boadicea* sailing in their wake. The other frigate, like the *Whistler*, retained her masts and rigging, but the massive gunship limped along with half its spars patched together.

"Please, Miss Grey, make yourself at home. I'll ring for tea," said Mrs. Hotham. She rested a hand on her belly and smiled to herself.

"That sounds lovely." Hyacinth hoped that was the right thing to say. She'd never been out to tea much with other ladies, and knew next to nothing about pregnancy, or babies. She probably should say something about how well Mrs. Hotham looked, but she wasn't sure. Mrs. Hotham appeared to be only a little older than herself, but much more at ease.

"It's so good to have you aboard, Miss Grey," Mrs. Hotham said. "I am never quite well on the sea and in this condition..."

"I admire your fortitude," Hyacinth said. "It must be difficult to make such a long sea journey with such an important..." A baby on the way could only make seasickness worse.

"The journey will pass quickly, I hope," Mrs. Hotham said. "I must say I look forward to getting back home to my sisters."

There was an awkward pause.

"Have you been away long?" Hyacinth asked.

"Oh no," Mrs. Hotham said. "I left only last year, right after marrying Captain Hotham. I had no knowledge of life in the navy, but I didn't want to be left at home alone before Henry and I had had some time to get to know each other. I'm glad we've had this time together, now that the baby is coming so soon. I don't think I can risk going to sea with a little baby."

The ship heeled, and Mrs. Hotham held her handkerchief up to her face. She clutched the side of her settee.

"Are you all right?" Hyacinth asked, jumping up.

She took a deep breath. "Yes I'm fine. Just a moment. Please, do sit."

Hyacinth perched on a bench, and when tea arrived, and her hostess had recovered, she made some polite inquiries about life in England. Although Mrs. Hotham protested that she was hardly aware of London fashion, she was much better informed than Hyacinth.

"You are going for the Season, aren't you?" Mrs. Hotham

asked.

"I think I will be there," Hyacinth said. "My aunt is always in London during the season, and I presume that I will go with her while George is in school."

"George... Is that the boy who came with you?" Mrs. Hotham asked.

Even Mrs. Hotham, who didn't seem at all high in the instep, would see how unorthodox Hyacinth's situation was; a legitimate daughter being given charge of an illegitimate son. It would seem even more peculiar in England.

"He's been in our household since he was an infant," Hyacinth explained. "Our former housekeeper was his mother, and my father has taken charge of George's upbringing."

Mrs. Hotham raised an eyebrow. "His natural son. Oh!"

"Father hopes for George to be educated in England, and to become more than just a common sailor. He's quite an intelligent boy," Hyacinth said.

Mrs. Hotham covered a yawn.

"I should leave you to rest," Hyacinth said, getting up. "Will I see you at dinner?"

"I will come tonight, before we reach heavier seas," Mrs. Hotham said, "but I often take meals here. You must go to the captain's table, though. The officers are delighted to have you on board, and your fellow passenger must be looking forward to a bit of feminine influence after his time in the colonies."

Hyacinth blushed. "I really don't think that's..."

Mrs. Hotham giggled. "The officers are gentlemanly enough, too. Who knows, maybe we can make a match for you before you even set foot in London!"

"I'm in no hurry," Hyacinth said.

"Oh, you might say so, but I was in your shoes not much more than a year ago. I remember what it's like. Mother had nearly given up on me, twenty-three and not a single offer!"

"But you did – "

"I was so fortunate to meet Captain Hotham. I knew right away. I think you might know, too," she said with a wink.

Hyacinth shook her head more firmly. "I believe I've been introduced to all the officers already. I didn't hear wedding bells."

"But I heard you were talking with Mr. Smithson?"

Hyacinth looked towards the door of her own cabin, transparently wishing to escape Mrs. Hotham's matchmaking.

"I don't mean to pry," Mrs. Hotham said, "or prod, or any of that, but..." She trailed off and smiled gently. "I only want to help. Do let me know if I can, in any way, and if all the male company is too much for you, you may dine with me."

"I appreciate your offer very much, thank you," Hyacinth said. "But tonight, you say you will dine with the officers?"

"I will, Miss Grey, and so will you."

❧

That evening, Mrs. Hotham sat at the head of the table, for all the world as if they were in a respectable English manor house on shore. Hyacinth sat at her right hand with Mr. Smithson seated immediately across from her, his blue eyes distant. She wondered, again, what had turned her father against him.

"Good evening, Miss Grey," Mr. Smithson said.

"Good evening, Mr. Smithson," she replied. She could at least extend simple courtesy to him – that wouldn't strike anyone amiss, or cause a scandal, no matter what her father thought.

"Do tell me more about the ship, Captain Hotham," Hyacinth prompted as they began the first course.

"I'd be much obliged," he said. "She's a fine frigate, and the navy has kept me out of the main line of fire this past year, for Mrs. Hotham's sake. Before my marriage, I was a mate on the *Bellerophon*." He gestured out the window to the *Victory* and the *Bellerophon* lumbering beside them through the Strait of Gibraltar.

"I am also grateful that you didn't see the heat of that battle," his wife said.

Captain Hotham chuckled. "Not with you aboard, dear, but the time will come when I'll sail on a ship of the line again." He turned to Mr. Smithson. "This is my first command," he explained, "and I'm delighted to have such a fine ship. Last spring we made the journey from Portsmouth in only three weeks, despite being becalmed for five days straight off the coast of France."

"That is quite good time," Hyacinth said. "Even with fair winds, few ships would make that journey so quickly against the trades."

"I haven't had the pleasure of meeting many ladies in my recent travels," Mr. Smithson said. "Is it usual now, in England, for young ladies to be knowledgeable about such matters?"

Hyacinth straightened in her seat. "I would hardly know," she said. "I am not entirely familiar with customs at home, having lived my life here in the Mediterranean."

At the foot of the table Mrs. Hotham giggled. "Mr. Smithson! You must apologize to Miss Grey. That had every hint of a set-down."

"There's no need," Hyacinth said hurriedly. She had gotten things off on the wrong foot, but at least Mrs. Hotham would see that there was no budding affection between them. "I understand that you, Mr. Smithson, have been in the colonies and cannot be expected to move faultlessly into polite society."

That was too much. The men around the table exchanged uncomfortable glances and Mrs. Hotham covered her mouth with a delicate hand, her eyes going wide. Hyacinth wished the floor would swallow her up.

"It's I that have gone too far now," Hyacinth said. "Please, Mr. Smithson. Do accept my fervent apologies."

He looked at her, his eyes an intense blue, so pale that they almost made her shiver. Then a smile spread across his face for the second time that day and he laughed.

"Not at all," he said. "It is quite true that I have been in India for many years, but although I was a callow youth when I was last in England I was familiar enough with society then. I have not entirely forgotten how to speak to a lady, though it might seem so at the moment. I don't mind being reminded."

Hyacinth blushed. The closest she'd come to society had been that summer with Aunt Celia, when she was too young to learn the finer points of social ritual, and too steeped in mourning to care. If they continued this banter of unveiled set-downs she would certainly lose.

The navigator, Mr. James, came to her rescue. "Do tell us, Mr. Smithson, what you know about the ships of the east," he said. Hyacinth's father had spoken well of Mr. James. She was relieved that he had stepped in to save her, even if his oiled hair smelled of too much pomade and he leered a bit.

"I would be glad to, though it is not a subject I've studied in great detail," Mr. Smithson said. He leaned back and cast his eyes around the table. The officers were listening politely.

"Perhaps instead, I might tell you about their interpretation of the stars," he suggested.

"Oh!" Mrs. Hotham said. "That would be delightful!"

"Astrology?" Mr. James's eyebrows shot up. He was in his middle thirties, but had a serious demeanor which made him seem older. "That's hardly a topic for rational conversation."

"Well," Mr. Smithson said, "the natives of India consider astrology a serious matter, and hold its practitioners in high regard. I cannot even begin to broach that subject. It is far too arcane for me. However, I did learn how they class the stars and group them into constellations, which are quite different from the ones we know here. Would that subject be more palatable?"

Mrs. Hotham sighed. "I would have liked to learn you could tell fortunes, Mr. Smithson, but I will be content with constellations."

"And you, Miss Grey?"

Hyacinth blushed. The talk of stars had made her think of her father's lessons in navigation. "I have always been interested in navigation," she said. "I am sure there is much to learn from these other constellations."

"Interested in navigation?" Mr. James said. "How very unusual for a young lady." He leaned towards her with an insipid smile.

Hyacinth smiled back, lips tight.

"Well then," Mr. Smithson said, leaning in front of the navigator. "If the ladies are content, I will tell how the Hindus named the star we call Aquila after one of their gods, Garuda."

❧

Hyacinth returned to her cabin that night dazzled by tales of the East, of gods she had never heard of whose stories rivaled the legends of the Greeks. She tried to think of those tales, not the man who told them, as she lay in her bunk rocked by the gentle haw of the ship, sailing north, on to the country she was supposed to call home.

❧

Thomas couldn't settle to sleep, that first night aboard the *Whistler*. Every time he was about to drift off to sleep, a whistle of wind in the rigging sounded like a woman's sigh and his whole body tensed as if she were still out there somewhere.

He had chosen to tell the story of Garuda largely because it was a rollicking adventure with hardly even a hint of sex about it, unlike so many Hindu epics. It would not offend the ladies – if that stern Miss Grey could be offended at all after living her life in navy outposts – and more importantly, it would not make him think too much of what he'd left behind.

But even Garuda's exploits were too close to the tropical hills of his adopted home. He'd been sixteen when he'd gone out to India, older than some young men who signed on to the Company, and had felt like a grown man beside them. Looking back, he'd been little more than a boy. He had planned to stay forever in the East. He should have known that his childhood world would summon him back someday.

England would be new to him, governed by the once-familiar rules Miss Grey had alluded to. He wondered if society's matrons would still wag their tongues at him as they had over his youthful escapades. Still, he thought, even without his parents' title and estate, the fortune he'd amassed in the east would smooth over his inevitable missteps. Although his mother was Baroness of Lawton in her own right, his father was brother to the Duke of Windcastle, and it was his father who had always ruled Lawton, for as long as he could remember. The letter had told him in no uncertain terms that he was to take his father's place, both at Lawton and as his uncle's heir.

The Lawton estate would tie him to England, and it seemed that he was to be heir to the duchy of Windcastle, too. The thought of stepping into his uncle's shoes sickened him. It didn't bear thinking about. He turned over again in his bunk and watched the moonlight until, after what felt like many hours, he drifted off to sleep.

❧

Every night at dinner, Mr. Smithson told tales of India: of things that he'd seen himself, and of legends. Hyacinth noted that his tales never touched on his own life, and she began to watch for hints of what had led him to these places. She found almost nothing. Even when he had been present at an event, he downplayed his own role, making it impossible to discern much, except that the man could spin a yarn and was an astute observer.

It was easy enough to stay away from him at other times. Hyacinth established a routine which kept her occupied for most of the day. She could command George's attention at his books for a few hours after breakfast, then he would scramble off to help raise the sails and hear old sailors' tales. In the afternoon, she and Mrs. Hotham embroidered or read to each other.

The seas stayed calm, with scarcely a breath of wind to speed them north. A week into their journey, they were still creeping up the coast of Portugal when they ought to have been approaching Brittany. Mrs. Hotham had recounted every scrap of society gossip she could remember, and Hyacinth scoured her memory for any tales of interest from Gibraltar. She finished embroidering a border that she'd been working on since spring, and resorted to empty chatter about the weather. There was little occasion to dawdle on deck where she might cross paths with Mr. Smithson, but she began to wish for something to relieve the monotony.

Then, one afternoon off the coast of northwest Spain, the seas grew rough.

❧

CHAPTER 3: THE STORM

Thunderheads blew in from the south, whipping up the waves and dimming the midday sun.

George threw down his books. "A storm!" he exclaimed. "Finally, some adventure."

Hyacinth tucked the books into their cubby. They'd finished the day's lesson. George hoped to join the sailors for the afternoon, doing whatever bits of work they could find for him, but Hyacinth worried that he would be in the way or worse, with a real threat on the horizon. She reminded herself that George had weathered another storm at sea recently, so perhaps it would be all right.

Crackling energy hung in the air, lightning waiting in the thunderheads. Hyacinth's pulse quickened in anticipation. She could hardly blame George for his excitement. On deck, the sailors scurried, checking latches, tightening knots.

"Can I help reef the sails, Hy?" George asked.

"The storm could be dangerous," Hyacinth said. "You must stay out of the sailors' way. We could all be smashed on the rocks."

As George sulked off, Hyacinth observed that they were closer to the rocky shore than usual. The *Whistler* sailed at the rear of the flotilla. Up ahead, the ships of the line turned their courses away from the coast.

Hyacinth wondered how Mrs. Hotham was faring in the rough weather, and went to look in on her. She found her in her bunk, holding a basin.

"How are you?" Hyacinth asked. The ship's motion had already changed. It heaved erratically, no longer moving with the steady sway they'd grown accustomed to.

"I am holding on," Mrs. Hotham said. "The sickness isn't so bad yet. You ought to go on deck and take the air while you can."

"But I'd be happy to sit here with you, Mrs. Hotham," Hyacinth offered.

"It's quite all right. If you're concerned, though, perhaps you could send your maid in to me," she suggested.

Hyacinth considered that. "Maria might welcome the change from keeping George company."

Mrs. Hotham smiled. "I suspected as much. She can mind the invalid while you make sure your young charge doesn't do anything foolish," she said.

"It will be refreshing if I don't get blown overboard," Hyacinth said. Although prudence might have kept her inside, she was glad of the excuse to be out in the air, instead of inside the stuffy, storm-tossed cabin.

Hyacinth wrapped on her woolen cloak. The weather had been unseasonably warm since they'd left Gibraltar, and the storm had blown up from the tropics, bringing more warm air with it. She didn't want the cloak's warmth, but it would keep her dry through anything but a true downpour.

Out on deck, the breeze had stiffened into a brisk wind and the storm clouds were closing the gap between themselves and the *Whistler*. Hyacinth knocked on the door of George and Maria's cabin.

"Maria?"

"Yes?" Maria said. "That George…"

"Don't worry about him. I'll watch out for him. Mrs. Hotham asked if you would sit with her through the storm. I think she misses having a maid of her own, and she's not in the mood to talk."

Maria nodded. "I will go there. You will find George?" She was making an effort to speak English more often, but she still wasn't entirely comfortable with the language.

"Yes, and I'll lock him in the cabin if he doesn't behave!"

She startled at the sound of a laugh just behind her. It was Mr. Smithson. He hadn't really crept up on her; it was only that his cabin was next to George and Maria's cabin, and the door must have been open when she arrived. "Do you always keep the boy so close?" he asked.

"I didn't until recently," Hyacinth bristled. "He stowed away into that battle, though. It became clear to me that he had no sense at all. I think it best that he be kept out of harm's way."

"I believe I might have done the same if I were a boy," Mr. Smithson said, as if it were all quite amusing.

"I had the impression you were more fond of self-preservation than that," Hyacinth said, wondering where the thought had come from.

"You are mistaken, Miss Grey. But then, boys never linger long over the choice between safety and adventure."

"I have to go find my…" Hyacinth started, "to go find George. Excuse me, Sir."

Mr. Smithson stepped aside, bowing in a way that Hyacinth felt sure was meant to be satirical.

❧

Thomas watched Miss Grey storm off as the thunderheads closed in around them. Her skirts swayed briskly and she held her dark blue cloak tight around her shoulders, arms locked over her chest. She was quite pretty. It was a shame she wore such dour colors. Seated across from her at the dinner table, he'd stolen many glances when she wasn't busy glaring at him. Her eyes would look much more lively set off by one of the colorful scarves or saris that the women of India draped…

He stopped himself. There was no point comparing her to

them. She was, as he'd observed from the first, far too slender to match their ideals of feminine beauty. He wondered what Sarita would be doing now, if she had lived. She might be braiding her hair, or walking in the garden, or eating ripe mangoes, sliced on a silver platter.

"Sir!" Captain Hotham said, snapping Thomas out of his reverie. "If you would go to your cabin! The storm will be on us in minutes."

"My cabin?" Thomas said. He looked at the approaching storm. "Might I not be of use?"

"I don't see what you can do, Mr. Smithson," the captain said. "My men have the ship well in hand." He nodded to Thomas then started to walk away towards the bridge. He turned back suddenly. "I presume that the other passengers are safely inside?"

Thomas's answer came clear on his face.

"Where the deuce are they, then?"

"I don't know, Captain."

"Well find out then! And lock them in when you catch them!" He strode away, no doubt cursing the young boy, and perhaps the lady, too.

❧

The ship bucked under Hyacinth's feet. She clutched a nearby rail for balance. The wind made the lines snap against the masts. A sailor clutched at his cap as he ran to secure a loose rope.

"Get below!" he yelled as he passed her.

Hyacinth shook her head. "George!" she called.

She crept the length of the upper deck, moving towards the bow. The waves grew, crashing into the sides of the ship. A spray of foam flew over the rail. She was drenched. Hyacinth moved hand-to-hand along the deck, never letting more than one limb move at a time.

"Get below!"

She didn't even turn to see who shouted. A sail was coming down on the upper cross-trees of the foremast. The sailors scampered, lashing sails to their booms and holding on for their lives. Hyacinth looked aloft between them. George was nowhere to be seen. Gritting her teeth, she descended to the gun deck.

She could scarcely see for all the swinging hammocks and crowding of men and guns. She worked her way aft, back towards their cabins, hoping that George had seen sense for once and gone inside. Then she saw him.

&

"George!" Miss Grey screeched.

Well, he'd found one of them, Thomas thought. He hurried down the deck. A wave broke over the rail, sending a river across the boards. Thomas grabbed onto a bit of line that wavered from the beams above, praying it would hold. Then he saw the boy.

George balanced at the rail, stripped to the waist and barefoot.

"What are you doing?" Miss Grey shouted.

"Going back to Spain!" the boy replied. With that, he crouched and jumped out through the gun port, into a crashing sea.

The gunners' jaws dropped. None of them had ever seen anything so foolish in their lives.

Thomas pushed and sprinted to the end of the deck. He grabbed Miss Grey roughly by the arm. "Can the lad swim?" he asked.

"Yes, very well," she answered, "but in this…"

Thomas didn't wait to hear more. He stripped off his own shirt and shoes and leaped overboard, strong strokes bearing him towards the disappearing boy, whose thin brown shoulders were dwarfed by the white-capped waves.

Thomas kicked forward and looked ahead from the crest of the next wave. He wondered if this were some kind of suicide, but he saw that the boy could swim, probably better than any of the sailors back on the ship. The coast lay at most a half-mile away. It would be an easy enough swim – in calmer seas. With the storm coming down, it was another matter. Whatever had prompted the boy to dive off the ship? Could the fate that awaited him in England seem that bad?

His own fate there was none too inviting, Thomas thought. Then a wave crashed over his head, driving him under, driving the air from his lungs and all thought out of his head. Only the search for the surface could command his attention now.

He came up, gasped for air, and dove again. He had no idea where the boy was. He'd been a fool to leap in. A wave carried him up to a point where he could see around. He glimpsed the last of the sails being reefed in another notch, and the captain storming the deck. Over his other shoulder, the small dark speck of the boy's head disappeared behind another wave.

Then he was in the valley of the waves again and the rain poured down harder, hard as an early monsoon rain, driving up the seawater like dust into his eyes. He swam on, on towards the boy, not along the more sensible course, back to the ship with its bells clanging the alarm: man overboard.

The captain would do well to leave them there, Thomas thought. The lad had risked the ship by making it change course this close to shore, but he wouldn't have thought of that. He must have some childish delusion of freedom, or worse, some kind of perverse loyalty to Spain.

Thomas came up a wave and spotted his quarry. Three more strong strokes would bring him to the boy.

George seemed to sense him and turned around mid-stroke. "Leave me alone!" he hollered.

A huge wave swept up behind the boy.

"No!" Thomas shouted. The wave crashed down, swamping George in its turbulence, dragging him under, mouth open. Thomas dove.

The waters off the coast of Spain were by no means cold, by English standards, but they were chilly after the seas off the Malabar coast. Thomas questioned his own sanity again, but he was in the drink now and there was nothing to do but swim on. He ducked his head under the churning surface and pulled towards the boy. One, two, three long strokes and he sensed the depth of water above him change. He came up for air just in time to take in a lungful before diving under the next crashing wave. The boy was just beside him, flailing aimlessly, no longer moving forward with the strong, certain strokes he'd taken before.

Under the surface of the water, under the next wave, Thomas grabbed the boy around the middle. A moment later, George was clinging to him like a piece of driftwood. At the next valley between waves Thomas grasped him more firmly.

"Be still or you'll pull us both under!" he said.

The boy nodded mutely, eyes wide, as the next wave descended.

They came through that one, and then another smaller swell rolled up without any treacherous churning foam on the top. Thomas rode up it, holding the boy and looking around for help, if any were coming. The ship was barely visible now through the lashing rain, but a boat had gone over the side and a small crew rowed towards them. Thomas shouted, hoping against hope that they would hear him, then another wave dragged them down.

Wave upon wave crashed down, bearing them closer and closer to the rocky coast, but they'd been sighted.

"You're a damn fool!" Thomas said – whether to himself or the young George, he wasn't sure. They weren't through it yet. The men in the boat might as well turn tail and leave them to crash on the rocks, save their own skins. Thomas kicked, hoping to reach the boat, moving them farther out into the ocean, away from the shore.

It could have been a lifetime, but probably no more than twenty minutes had passed when the boat reached them and Thomas threw his free arm around the ring buoy.

"Up you come!" The second mate himself was in the boat. His name was Mr. Green, Thomas remembered. The man helped him over the gunwales while the sailors hitched a rope under the boy's arms and shifted him into the boat.

Despite everything, despite Thomas's daring or foolhardy

rescue, the lad looked back once more to the coast of Spain, as if wishing he were being washed up on those unforgiving rocks. Thomas grabbed him by the arm.

"Don't even think it!" he growled.

As Thomas was bundled into a relatively dry wool blanket, the men in the boat clanged their bell, signaling to the *Whistler*. They left George lumped between rowers in the middle of the boat, shivering. Thomas was helped to the stern and handed a flask of brandy.

"M-may I have a blanket?" George stammered after the men had set to oars.

Mr. Green frowned at the boy.

"You may, only if you swear on your mother's grave never to pull another stunt like that while you're passenger on this ship, or any other ship, for that matter."

George shivered. The mention of his mother's grave had made his Mediterranean complexion go paler than sea foam for a moment. He sat very still as the oars splashed in and out of the water, bearing them closer to the ship, which sat with its sails furled, waiting for them.

"All right then, I swear it. On my mother's grave." George's teeth chattered.

Mr. Green tossed him a blanket and the boy huddled down, holding his head between his knees. Thomas and the second mate sat at the far end of the boat, far enough away to talk without being overheard by the boy.

"You're a strong swimmer," the mate commented.

"Hmm." Thomas had learned to swim in India, where the surf could rise high, but at least the water provided some respite from the crushing heat.

Mr. Green shook his head. "I forgot that the boy was an orphan," he said.

"Is that how he came to be in Captain Grey's, ah, household?" Thomas asked. He was in no fit condition for idle talk, but the brandy was warming him already.

"In a manner of speaking," the mate said. "I understand he's a bastard. His mother was the captain's housekeeper."

"Ah!" Thomas shielded his face from a line of rain with the blanket. He puzzled it out. The young lady, then, was the boy's half sister. Quite unorthodox. If Thomas recalled correctly, gently bred young ladies were usually ignorant of their father's bastard children. In the event that they knew of them, they certainly didn't take charge of their educations.

"Not an entirely respectable family then?" Thomas queried.

"On the contrary," the mate said. "Captain Grey is the second son of a marchioness and his sister wed an earl. Besides which, as I'm sure you've heard, he's possibly the most efficient supply line officer in the navy. A little eccentric, though. He will be forever in your debt for rescuing the lad."

The prospect of having Captain Grey in his debt mollified Thomas's sense of his own foolishness. The thought warmed his stomach, helped along by a deep gulp of brandy. The rains and wind seemed to ease a bit. From the relative safety of the boat, he was free to contemplate what had driven him to leap in after the boy. He didn't have to think far.

It wasn't the boy himself, though he felt sorry for the lad, with those two interfering females hovering over him. No, it was Miss Grey. The look of despair in her eyes had goaded him to dive out of a perfectly safe ship into a very high chance of immediate and merciful death.

Thomas had no desire to engage in idle chatter with the second mate. He kept himself warm with occasional sips of brandy as they made their slow journey back to the ship. He would have volunteered to help row or bail to keep warm, but it was too much effort to speak. Besides, the men worked well together, far better than they would if he tried to put his shaking hands to the oars.

The irregular swells and whitecaps made slow going, and it was nearly evening by the time the boat nosed alongside the *Whistler* again. The downpour had slowed to a steady rain which fell more straight down than sideways, as it had when the wind was at its height.

The rope ladder came down and a slender white hand reached out alongside it. Miss Grey's face shone out of the gloomy evening air like a beacon. Her eyes were damp with tears, luminous blue-grey, like the shining clouds brightened by a few last rays of sunlight. She bit her lip and leaned forward, revealing more bosom than he'd seen in... well, at least since Gibraltar. Blood rushed to parts of Thomas's anatomy that had resisted the brandy's effects.

He stepped onto the ladder first and scrambled towards her. When she was just before him, he took her delicate fingers in his wet, salty hand.

"My lady," he said and kissed the back of her hand. He smiled up at her. Droplets of water shone like diamonds in her hair. That once-severe cloak hung wet around her shoulders, clinging to her curves. Her eyes had all the intensity of the sea and none of its chill.

One of the sailors pursed his lips to whistle, but another elbowed him broadly before he made a sound. They all raised their eyebrows at the little tableau of Mr. Smithson bowing to the young lady. Miss Grey's blush deepened and she pulled her hand away. Thomas relinquished it reluctantly and climbed the last rung onto the deck.

George was pushed up the ladder next, to be greeted not by his half-sister, but by the more forbidding face of Captain Hotham.

"Alive, I see," the captain observed. "It's better than you deserve." He turned to the first mate, who waited beside him. "Mr. Bromley. Lock the lad in his cabin."

"But I…" George started.

"There's no excuse for what you've done."

George choked back a genuine sob. He was still shivering – the long row back had chilled him even more than the swim. "I know Captain," he said. "I'm sorry."

Captain Hotham grunted. "That's as may be. I am sure you are, having seen what the Atlantic surf can be like. Nonetheless, I think it best if you spend the remainder of our journey firmly inside your cabin."

"And you will translate Homer and work sums until your tongue comes out of your ears!" Miss Grey added. Her voice cracked, sounding almost hysterical. "But I am glad to see you alive," she added more quietly.

The captain nodded to the first mate, who marched George off to his imprisonment.

"Do make sure he's well, Miss Grey," Captain Hotham whispered. "And don't hesitate to send for the surgeon if you need him."

"I will," she promised. "I certainly will."

Thomas still stood at the rail. She turned to him and he realized that he'd been staring at her throughout the whole, heated exchange.

"Thank you, Mr. Smithson" she said. "I don't know how we can ever repay you."

Thomas thought of a few things, none of which would bear mentioning to a lady with any hint of respectability. The brandy had gone to his head.

"I assure you, Miss Grey, I am always glad to come to a lady's aid in her moment of distress." It was a platitude, but it was the best he could manage. His toes weren't gripping the deck properly, and he stumbled, but managed to catch himself on the rail before losing his balance.

"That is most gentlemanly of you," she said, with no idea of all the un-gentlemanly thoughts in his mind. "We are in your debt," she continued. "You have my sincerest thanks, as well as Captain Hotham's."

"Indeed," the captain said. "I might not have judged it worth the risk to the *Whistler* to rescue the boy alone, especially with young George making so surely for the Spanish coast. However with you in the drink too, Mr. Smithson…"

"I thank you, too, Captain Hotham," Miss Grey said, looking back and forth between the two men, as if unsure who was really responsible for her brother's rescue. "I really must go see to George now." With that, she hurried away down the deck.

Thomas watched her go, shaking the sea water from her cloak.

"She was here at the rail the whole time," the captain said to him. "She was sick with worry, and not all of it was for the boy, I think." He winked, and Thomas felt like... it would be better if he stepped away and into his cabin before he made a further fool of himself.

"You ought to have stayed on board," the captain said.

"I thought that," Thomas said, "especially when I realized that the lad was trying to go over to Spain."

"Perhaps he thought his mother's people would let him run wilder than his English relations."

"Relations who are unlikely to even acknowledge him," Thomas said, "on either side." He shivered.

"I will walk with you back to your cabin and see that a hot brazier is brought," the captain said. He looked back at the fading coast of Spain. On the main deck, the men were raising the sails, preparing to get underway again.

"You will, of course, not mention this to the ladies when you return to England," the captain said as they walked. "It will go better for Miss Grey if she isn't beset by this scandal, too. Common enough to have a bastard in the family, but you know..."

"Indeed, I do," Thomas said. He could well remember the furor that had been raised when his uncle had taken up too openly with his mistress and left every un-entailed scrap of his property to his bastard son. "But do tell, what other scandal can already be afoot regarding the girl if she's spent her life in obscure Gibraltar, studying Latin and Maths?"

"Ach, I assumed you knew. It's a tired old matter of her ancestry, though as you can clearly see, Miss Grey is a lady to the bone, no matter what her grandmother might have been."

The wind, which had grown slack, picked up again, blowing from the north. The ships ahead of them faltered in their course.

"Curse this wind!" the captain said. "Reef the sails again!" he shouted. "At this rate it will be a month before we reach

England," he complained to Thomas.

"That long?" Thomas wasn't sure if he were glad of the delay, or if he wished the journey already done. At least his cabin was before him, its door opening in his hand, the brazier sitting ready on the deck outside.

"Perhaps not quite so long," Captain Hotham said, "but we should have cleared Spain days ago. Please, pardon me for rattling on. You are in no state to stand out here in the wind. Go inside and warm yourself. I'll have one of the boys check in on you shortly."

With that, Captain Hotham marched away, leaving Thomas wondering what other mysteries Miss Grey harbored.

❧

"Good gracious, Hyacinth, you must be soaked to the bone!" Mrs. Hotham exclaimed as Hyacinth came into her parlor.

Hyacinth unclenched her fingers from the sodden cloak to warm them at the freshly lit brazier, while Maria prepared one in her own cabin. Mrs. Hotham looked well enough, considering the storm that had just passed.

"I am rather damp," Hyacinth said, "but it's Mr. Smithson who is truly drenched."

"And young George, I imagine," Mrs. Hotham added.

Hyacinth shook her head. True, George was wet to the bone, but that was the least of her worries. What worried her was what would become of him, how he could have done such a foolish thing, and how their father would take the news when it inevitably reached him. The boy was a fool and a reckless, thoughtless one at that, despite all the Greek and mathematics she'd managed to work into him. He had not a whit of common sense.

She'd stood at the rail all afternoon, rain, wind, and all. They couldn't budge her from her vigil. It was all she could do for George, and it was nothing. Captain Hotham ought to have left him to his foolhardy swim. If Mr. Smithson hadn't jumped in, too, they might have sailed on, and she would never have heard from George again, most likely, or known whether he'd lived or died. That would have been worse, she supposed, than this feeling of helplessness, of uselessness in the face of George's ill-timed rebellion.

She must have muttered something in comment, because Mrs. Hotham was talking again.

"Your father is more than usually generous with the boy."

"He always has been," Hyacinth said, "but now I don't know what he'll do. He might cut George off entirely. I wouldn't blame him. I don't much feel like speaking to him, myself."

"And Mr. Smithson!" Mrs. Hotham exclaimed, as if she hadn't heard a thing Hyacinth was saying. "How valiant!"

Mr. Smithson had plunged through the sea like Poseidon. Hyacinth had thought her heart would burn right through her chest at the sight of him. She turned back to the fire to hide her blush as she thought about him. Hyacinth looked up, but Mrs. Hotham hadn't guessed the direction of her thoughts. She was only indulging her own admiration of the man.

"Do you think it was on your account?" Mrs. Hotham asked teasingly.

"No. Never," Hyacinth said. "Although he did say as much, some nonsense about doing anything to ease a lady's distress. To be honest, I think it was the only excuse he could muster. He must have been half-mad to jump in like that. And George was worse than foolish. He at least has the excuse of being still a boy, but Mr. Smithson is a grown man…"

Mrs. Hotham giggled. "My dear!" she exclaimed. "I thought you would have noticed that before!"

Hyacinth's blush ran all the way up to her hairline. She avoided looking at herself in the bit of mirror beside the fire, but she could feel the heat of it on her brow. "I had known that he was a man, of course, but I suppose I hadn't truly appreciated it until this afternoon. He took his shirt off. It was all most…"

"Scandalous, I should say!" Mrs. Hotham tittered.

Hyacinth wished that Mrs. Hotham would be serious. She might be trying to be cheerful, but it wasn't helping. It was so deeply embarrassing that Mr. Smithson had leapt to her aid, to George's aid, when she'd been able to do nothing but stand in the way while the sailors lowered the boat to try to save the swimmers.

"It's hardly a scandal," Hyacinth said. "If I hadn't been present, a shirtless man would have been completely commonplace. We are at sea, after all. They can hardly be expected to go about in full evening dress."

"I still say it is all very thrilling," Mrs. Hotham said. "I am only sorry I wasn't well enough to see him half-naked on the deck!"

"You are?" Hyacinth was frankly shocked. She tried to laugh. "But you're a married woman," she said, "and in your condition, too!"

Mrs. Hotham pursed her lips. "I am happily married, but my condition doesn't blind me to the charms of a handsome and daring man. You'll see soon enough, after you catch yourself a husband in London this season."

Hyacinth shook her head. To think of finding a husband, at a time like this? She had her responsibilities to George first, and then she would have to sort out her inheritance. Finding a husband would only be a hindrance and a distraction.

"I don't know," Hyacinth said after a pause. "Did you manage any embroidery this morning, before the storm?"

Hyacinth managed to direct the conversation away from herself and more towards embroidery until the ship was steady enough for the cook to ladle out a simple supper. She excused herself as soon as they had eaten and went to see to George in his imprisonment.

≈

CHAPTER 4: NIGHT

Thomas huddled over his brazier until feeling returned to his limbs. He lay down on his bunk to rest for a moment, and woke hours later, with a clear night sky outside and the full moon shining through his porthole. A covered dinner sat beside him, gone almost cold, but he didn't mind that. He devoured it and poured himself a glass of wine.

With a full belly and relatively calm seas, he should have fallen asleep again almost immediately. Instead, he sat on his bunk and felt the minutes drag by. Lingering discomfort from his afternoon's swim needled him. His muscles, unaccustomed to so much exertion, were starting to ache despite the wine, and he couldn't help but think how close to death they'd been out there, he and the boy. He hadn't minded the danger. What happiness did he have to lose? All of that had been destroyed.

Thomas gave up trying to sleep and got out of his bunk. Thoughts of India kept churning to the surface, needling him awake again and again.

On deck, all was quiet. The first mate, Mr. Bromley, stood at the helm. A few sailors were on duty to trim the sails if needed, but they sat in a group around the skuttle-butt, talking amongst themselves. They scarcely seemed to notice Thomas leaving his cabin. The ship's prow lapped through the water. Thomas took his bottle of wine and walked to the stern. The ship's wake bubbled behind them in the moonlight.

A chill was in the air, reminding him of England – not an entirely sunless country, but nothing like the tropical climate he'd grown accustomed to. If Sarita had lived, he would have ignored that summons home, surely he would have ignored it.

He had first met Sarita a year after his arrival in India, in Trivandrum. She came from a respectable family that had fallen on hard times – the same sort of story that might be told anywhere in the world. She was never one of those women who could be had just for money or costly gifts. He'd courted her much as he would have wooed an English lady, but of course it had been different, and far more complicated as time wore on.

At the start, their relationship caused no comment. Many of his fellow recruits, and almost all of the veteran company men, had taken up with local women at some point, often with many at once. Thomas had always felt that his relationship with Sarita was different. He had loved her. He refused to set her up in the shabby conditions that most men considered adequate for their mistresses, and he didn't hide his relationship with her, either.

They lived together happily for eight good, long years. Every now and again, he would think of home in passing, but he had adapted so well to life in India that he never seriously thought about returning to England. He had survived that first hard year when half his peers had succumbed to tropical fevers. His northern constitution proved more robust than those of his fellows, too, and so he rose in the ranks and began to amass a fortune that even his father, a blue-blooded miser if ever there was one, would have found noteworthy.

Sarita's family had been scandalized by her decision to become his mistress. He would never have isolated her further by leaving her behind, or by taking her to England, either. He had heard that a few Indian women had made the transition to life in London in decades past, but they had been fairer-skinned, from the north, and in a different generation. As his years in the subcontinent wore on, company policy turned against the native women who had for so long been the companions of the men who set out to make their fortunes in the East. Against a rising tide of prejudice, Thomas had begun to think of Sarita as being almost his wife, although actual marriage was impossible because she would not convert to Christianity and he could not become a Hindu, even if he had wished to do so.

One day, not so many months ago, she had come to tell him that they might be expecting a happy event. He was terrified and delighted, and felt that at last things were certain. He would stay in India until he died. It would be his home and his children's home. The murmurs of unrest from the sepoy camps did not scratch his resolve. There had been disputes before, and there would be again. He'd thought it could not touch his domestic bliss. Better still, Sarita had gone to her sister's house to help while a new baby was being born. He rejoiced at this sign of reconciliation with her family, and looked forward to her return in a few days' time.

The very next day, a letter arrived from England, from his father. Ordinarily, he would have torn it up unread, but the prospect of becoming a father had roused some kind of nostalgia in him. The letter informed him that his elder brother had died, making him his father's heir. Further, his cousin, who had always been a sickly boy, was next in line to become Duke of Windcastle. If he died, and that could only be expected given his frailty, Thomas's elderly father would become next in line for the duchy, with Thomas after him. The letter demanded that he return to England. He tore the letter up and tucked its scraps into the back of his desk.

The following morning, a riot broke out in town. Thomas was kept busy all morning with one thing and another, trying to keep the factory running in the midst of the upheaval. He thought little of it, in fact. The Company had put down riots before and this one showed no signs of being serious, as riots went. It was only one small company of sepoys who had objected to a change of uniform, and negotiations were underway, being handled by one of Thomas's junior officers, a man who had been in India for five years, who showed every sign of competence. Even when shots were fired, Thomas did not leave his work. When they continued, escalating into the early evening, he began to worry. He did not worry much for Sarita. She was supposed to be at her sister's house, and had planned to stay there another day, so he'd thought she was safe, far away from the trouble.

Two soldiers accompanied him back to his bungalow. Though shots had been fired, only a few pieces of broken wood and torn cloth littered the ground to tell of the disturbance. Two of the company's men were reported killed. Thomas was sorry for that, but it could have been much worse. No one had told him of any injuries in the populace at large, and all appeared well until he'd seen her, slumped on the corner.

He recognized her sari at once. The men with him knew it, too.

"Is she sleeping, and so close to home?" he'd said, stupidly. He walked up to her, reaching down to the dusty ground. A lazy fly circled away from his hand and settled on her arm. She did not flinch, or twitch. He saw the stain of blood, dark on the ground beneath her heart, the hole the bullet had made in her back. He touched her hand, cold like the ground. No one had told him.

The street around her looked much as it usually did, but it was there, a few hours earlier, that the riots had been at their height. Surely someone would have seen her? How had she come to be here? He knelt on the ground, and touched her face.

The soldiers urged him on. Dumb with shock, he had carried her home, and from there to the muddy riverbank, where he saw her burned in the rites she would have asked for. He sent a servant to tell her family. He should have gone himself. They did not come. He didn't think he could have faced them. He stood all night beside her pyre, through the first lick of flame in the timbers, the cloth lighting, the ashes spiraling in the air and settling down to coals. They were raking away its remains when he stumbled home.

The days after that passed in a fog. He drank local whiskey, which burned away his senses. He avoided work and society. A fellow officer came to admonish him for shirking his duties, and he'd decked the fellow. Then he'd gone to the officer's mess, and someone had said something, he couldn't remember what, but through that slip of an utterance he discovered who had shot Sarita.

Her murderer was a young officer. He was as arrogant as any of the rest, but Thomas had thought him no worse than most. He had met Sarita. He should have recognized her, should have known. Instead, he had gunned her down just as if she'd been any other native, and not even bothered to send in a report that he'd killed an innocent bystander, the possible mother of Thomas's son.

Thomas had challenged him to a duel and killed him the following morning. He was summarily dismissed. He left his servants to pack his trunks, not caring what they stole, and took himself, a few books, and his old English clothes down to the docks where he boarded an Arabian vessel bound for the Gulf. He was determined never to have traffic with John Company again... and that meant leaving India, at once.

In the moonlight, the *Whistler* felt like a phantom, as if only his dreams were bearing him away, and somewhere in the south of India his body lay sweating on fevered sheets, dying like so many had before him, dying far from home.

He took another drink, emptying his mind. Then he heard a footfall and a rustle of skirts. Miss Grey stood there, leaning on the rail, gazing astern as if she, too, left heartbreak behind.

≈

As soon as Hyacinth lay down to sleep, her thoughts started racing. What *would* their father do when he discovered what had happened? Would he disown George? She chided herself for not keeping him close enough, for not allowing for his discontent. Was Mr. Smithson right? Did she keep George too close to her apron-strings? Had George jumped overboard to escape the confines of his female-directed world? What should she have done?

Some hours passed before she finally gave up trying to sleep.

She put on her second cloak, an old grey one, lighter wool, soft and wearing at the hem, but not drenched with seawater. She stepped out on deck, covering her head. A soft breeze blew from the south, a favorable wind at last. She paced forward along the deck, nodding to the navigator as she passed the helm. The ship's prow whispered through the water, turning up bright eddies, which bubbled away into the night.

England lay only another two weeks' journey or so ahead, less if the wind stayed fair. She'd been born there, as had all her ancestors, and so the place was called "home," but it wasn't a place that she knew. Home was a story that other people lived in. How could she ever be truly comfortable in England? Maybe Mrs. Hotham was right, and she would adapt, even if George refused to give the place a chance.

She drifted back along the deck towards the stern, hoping to summon happy memories of the world she was leaving behind. There wasn't much there, apart from managing her father's house and tutoring George. It had been a quiet life. She hardly went out in what little society there was. Once, a young officer had courted her, but after his ship left port, he'd only written her one poor letter, not even covering the paper. She wrote back to him, but there was little to say, and perhaps the letter had gone astray. Then the fever came, taking Rosa, and she'd had more important things to do than worry over being slighted in love. Her past few years had revolved entirely around her own studies and teaching George. On the rare occasions when she did go out in Gibraltar's small society, her father glared at any man who approached her, driving most of them away before they were even properly introduced.

She couldn't summon much regret at leaving that life behind, especially because now, after the afternoon's misadventures, she saw how she had failed George. Whatever direction she had given him wasn't enough, could never be enough.

Only on Malta, when she was a very young, had she known any real happiness. Hyacinth's hand went to the locket at her throat. She didn't need to look inside to summon the tiny image of her mother. She held onto it as she leaned on the rail, watching the wake roll away behind them like a road.

Then Hyacinth heard a breath behind her, and with a shift of the wind she smelled the wine. There was a man on the deck. For a moment, she thought it must be one of the sailors, but then the sails swung around, letting in the moonlight. Mr. Smithson crouched there, between the after-mast and a deckhouse, his cheeks wet with tears.

She should have ignored him, a man in the darkness, weeping, but instead she stared at him, slouched there, so unlike his usual, arrogant self. He must have been deeply in his cups. Even after her mother and Rosa died, her father had only cried when he'd drunk far more than he was accustomed to, and then only once – well, only once for Rosa. She didn't know how long or loudly he'd grieved for Violet Grey, her mother, his only wife.

Mr. Smithson looked up, appearing as startled as if he'd seen a ghost.

"I couldn't sleep," Hyacinth said hurriedly. "We were so close to losing George," she added, as if that excused her from intruding on his private grief. She turned her back to him and fixed her eyes on the receding wake, embarrassed for him, and for herself.

Mr. Smithson grunted, as if dragging himself out of a reverie. "Close enough," he said, "though he is a strong swimmer."

"In calmer waters he is," Hyacinth said, attempting a normal conversational tone, "but we don't have anything like this surf in the bay at Gibraltar. I'm afraid he was out of his depth."

"He has a will to live, though," he said. "You're very attached to the boy," Mr. Smithson observed.

"Of course I am. He's…" Hyacinth supposed she shouldn't actually say what he was to her, even though nearly everyone knew.

"Your brother," Mr. Smithson finished for her.

The moonlight rippled across the waves. Hyacinth thought she saw a dolphin's fin, far away behind them, but she wasn't sure. She fixed her eyes on the sea near where it had disappeared.

"Why were you made responsible for him?" Mr Smithson asked after a while. "It's unusual."

"Maybe," Hyacinth said. She leaned against the rail, still not looking back at him. "I mostly raised him after his mother died. I suppose it's just that there was no one else."

"You must have been little more than a child yourself, then," Mr. Smithson said.

"I was nineteen," Hyacinth said. "Old enough, and George was only six."

"And that was how long ago?"

"A bit more than four years." They'd been long years, though, a lifetime.

"Ha. I'd have thought a young lady like you…" He trailed off.

"Thought what?" Hyacinth said.

"I don't know what I was going to say," he said. His face fell into shadow as the sails shifted above them.

"Why do you ask me these things? My life cannot possibly interest you, and you reveal nothing about yourself," Hyacinth remarked. "You're quite a mystery."

"On the contrary, every man on this ship knows all about me."

"Do they?"

"They believe they do. That is all that matters. They believe I'm a man who was lucky in the East. That tells them I'm rich because I worked for it. Ha. And was lucky. Sailors set great store by luck. That's enough for them." The ship swung slightly, letting the moonlight fall on his face again. The tears were gone. He must have wiped them away while her back was turned, but the sadness was still there, deep, impenetrable sadness. Not the look of a rogue at all, unless he were very good at crocodile tears.

"Is it who you are, though?" Hyacinth felt that she should return to her cabin, sleep or no. In the moonlight, Mr. Smithson's eyes entranced her. She'd avoided looking at him, she realized.

She didn't want to be taken in too much by his tales.

"How are you different then from what they suppose?" she asked, stepping closer. She sank down to the deck to look at him and leaned against the deckhouse beside him.

"Oh, there are a thousand things," he said. "I have..." he sighed. "Somewhere on a company ship, or in London now, I have chests bursting with treasures from India, the kind of thing poor boys hope for when they sign on to the company. Usually they get death instead, some dreadful thing like malaria, or cholera. I should have had that. I think maybe I would have preferred death, rather than face my family in England. Today, too."

Hyacinth shook her head slowly. "But you and George both lived."

Mr. Smithson took another long drink from his bottle, then passed it to Hyacinth.

She had never drunk straight from the bottle before. She tried it, tentatively. Drops of wine splashed onto her chin and cloak. She took another drink, more successful than that last, a deep, numbing, thirst-quenching drink. Belatedly, she rubbed at the stain on her pale cloak. She had to say something.

"Father said you dueled."

"That's another thing the sailors don't know. I suppose your father said I was a rogue, too?"

"He did."

"He doesn't like me; I know that much."

"And are you a rogue?" Hyacinth asked.

"I was in love," he said. "That was what they could not forgive. All the men there kept mistresses... or most did. Those few who didn't spent their time entirely with each other. I shouldn't be saying these things. You're still a young lady, delicate, but I'm past caring. Death is close all the time, but not close enough for me. I'd rather it had taken me already."

He was staring at the receding horizon.

"Was it love?" Hyacinth prompted. "The duel?"

"Well, a strong affection at any rate," he said. "I regarded her as my wife, but the distance between us... we came from very different worlds."

"And now where is she?"

"Dead. And I killed the bastard who did it."

"Oh." Hyacinth shrank back.

Mr. Smithson straightened up against the deckhouse, but he didn't stand. Hyacinth passed him the almost-empty bottle. He drained it, then held the empty bottle with its neck pointing astern, like the barrel of a gun.

"What else did your father say about me?" he asked.

"Only that you were a dueler and a... a black sheep even in your family, he said, and that such a feat beggars imagination."

Thomas laughed at that until tears rolled from his eyes. The laugh turned hysterical.

Hyacinth looked up towards the area amidships where the night watch were gathered. What if they saw her? What if Mr. Smithson really were deranged? Would they hear her if she screamed? Would they defend her honor?

She looked back at Mr. Smithson, clutching his stomach and weeping, and felt a strange yearning, with no fear or reasonable trepidation at all. She felt a reckless urge to cast her lot with this man. The sea hadn't swallowed him, had spared him and George, and here he was, looking as if he might just leap in again to give the Atlantic another chance to drag him under. He was hysterical and mad, or broken, but certainly not the kind of bounder her father had warned her about, not if he would risk his life for a boy he barely knew. She reached towards him.

At the touch of her hand on his arm, he fell silent and looked into her eyes. "I'm sorry," he said.

"Don't jump."

He shook his head, and then he reached for her, fell into her arms. He leaned his head on her shoulder as though she were stronger than he. She held him there, and had a last, fleeting thought of calling for help, then forgot it. If she were compromised, what of it? George could be going to the gallows. This could hardly be worse, to hold onto a man who wanted to drown.

He drew back a fraction, his eyes running over her face as his arms loosened. She did not relinquish her grip. He gazed at her slack-jawed then suddenly his lips were on hers, hungry, pushing them open.

Hyacinth let go of everything else, even with her mind, and sank into his embrace, warm and hard at the same time. She reached for him, into him, though they were already touching. She felt the boards of the deck she sat on, heard the gurgle of the sea behind them and the creak of the rigging and felt him there upon her, so strong and slender and unlikely in his barely-concealed grief. She opened her lips to him, shutting her eyes tight against the reality of what they were doing.

He kissed her. It was more, other than she had thought a kiss would be. All the blood in her body seemed to rush to her lips. His hand ran along her arm, up to her shoulder, rippled down the small of her back. He cupped her buttocks and hoisted her closer. He held her tightly against his groin, hard angles and heat and the smell of wine on his breath. He pulled away, turned her over, and was on top of her, plunging his tongue into her mouth, pushing his hand up into her hair, undoing her.

And Hyacinth dug her hands into his back and pulled him closer, crushing herself into the deck, wanting more.

He reached down and began to draw up her skirts, so the warm breeze circled her thighs. He grunted. Far away, a bell tolled.

Abruptly, he pushed himself away. "I can't," he said. "I'm so sorry. Your father had the right of it, at least with regards to most of my family. I had hoped not to become like them." He stood up and turned his back to her.

"Goodnight, Miss Grey," he said, and stumbled off to his cabin, not so much as offering to help her to her feet.

Hyacinth lay there on the deck, frozen in place, for a long time after he had gone. The storm turning inside her would have swallowed up the afternoon's squall whole and made it look like nothing, nothing at all, she thought. She had not known what it would feel like, had not guessed. She had been kissed before, once, briefly, coldly, indifferently. She'd had no idea.

Eventually, she stirred herself up to a crouch on the rolling deck and rested her head on her arms. She hid from herself, and from the sailors making their rounds, until she began to shiver in her light cloak. At last she went back to her cabin, finding the oblivion of sleep as dawn streaked the sky.

꙳

He would have to marry her, Thomas thought, waking up to the clamor of midday. It was the only honorable course. The prim Miss Grey, with all her prying, schoolmarmish questions, had more than curiosity bottled up inside her tall, slender form. The memory of her lithe body underneath his sent his blood coursing, as if he had no more self-control than Captain Grey had credited him with.

Whatever had prompted Captain Grey's censure, he'd just earned every speck of it. Worse, he'd begun to like the girl. If she'd been a man, he could have admired her wit at the dinner table, and probably would have found much to laugh about in the similarity of their circumstances. As it was, she was a lady, and a particularly pretty one at that, even if her clothes were not.

She was nothing like Sarita, of course. Sarita had been round and warm, always smiling, easily pleased. She was everything a man would want in a mistress. And she had been his mistress, not his wife. There was no changing that in death.

He rolled over onto his other side, as if he still might sleep. Miss Grey was nothing like Sarita, and she was an English gentlewoman, even if she didn't entirely realize what that meant. Everyone on the ship treated her as such, with the exception of young George. And himself. She would have to marry him. As he drifted off to sleep, he found that prospect strangely comforting.

꙳

"You seem a little pale today," Mrs. Hotham said. "Are you

quite well?"

"I am fine," Hyacinth lied, staring out the window at their wake. She had been on the deck just above last night. The planks in the ceiling stared down at her accusingly. Her head pounded as if she'd spent most of the night drinking old wine instead of just that one, deep drink from the bottle. In the night, the trade wind had carried them up into the Bay of Biscay, nearly to France. "I suppose it's just that I'm worried," Hyacinth said.

"Dear, Hyacinth." Mrs. Hotham set down her embroidery and got up to rest her hands on Hyacinth's shoulders. "You mustn't trouble yourself about the boy. He will be fine. You said yourself that he's only a little chilled."

Hyacinth smiled wanly. "Oh, he'll be hale enough soon," she said. "It's only that there's Father to contend with, and whether Captain Hotham... what the captain will decide to do when we reach Portsmouth." She felt sick just thinking of it. "He threatened George with a trial in England, if the law allowed it."

Mrs. Hotham shook her head firmly. "He most certainly will not be sent to trial. Henry doesn't have the heart for it. We admire and rely on your father, and the boy scarcely knows his own mind. Henry might threaten a trial, but I believe that every sailor on this ship will say that any falling overboard was purely an accident."

"Will they?" Hyacinth asked. It gave her a little hope for George, even if though where she herself was concerned, all was lost, if Mr. Smithson said anything. "Will the men really say that it was an accident?"

"Of course they will!" Mrs. Hotham assured her. "No one with any sense at all would jump off a good, safe ship! Especially not into rough seas like that. They're already saying so. They likely think it quite harsh that the Captain is keeping him confined with his schoolbooks."

Hyacinth's smile was still weak.

"I might be confined to my parlor all day and night, but in the past year I've come to know this boat and these men as well as I ever knew my own brothers," Mrs. Hotham said. "They're fair, and soft on the young ones. They will give your George the benefit of the doubt, and he'll be grateful to them for it."

"Yes," Hyacinth said, "I'm sure he will be grateful, to all of you."

"And especially to Mr. Smithson, I would think," Mrs. Hotham said, her eyes twinkling. She turned to face Hyacinth, looking into her eyes. "I do hope you're softening towards him, dear," she said.

Hyacinth's blush was so deep that she felt sure it told every detail of her night's misadventures. She bit her lip and evaded Mrs. Hotham's gaze until she mastered herself.

"He is quite brave," she conceded. He was more than that, too, not just a dashing adventurer. He was also a man whose passions… but it really wouldn't do to think of that, not with Mrs. Hotham watching every twitch of her eyelashes. Hyacinth bent resolutely back over her embroidery.

Fortunately, Mrs. Hotham was taken up in her own flights of fancy, so she barely noticed Hyacinth's discomfiture. "Brave, and so handsome," she sighed, smiling as if she were praising a pretty garden on a sunny day, and nothing more.

Mr. Smithson had spoken of the woman he'd left behind far more tenderly than Hyacinth would have expected him to, but he could not be loyal to his mistress's memory, not if he was kissing her on the darkened deck. Maybe her father had been right about him after all. He might speak of his love for his mistress, but he was already a traitor to her memory. He had kissed her, Hyacinth Grey. He had taken her into his arms instead of that woman, wherever she was, far away in a lonely grave on the subcontinent. She couldn't shake the image from her mind, a woman gunned down in the street, left to lie there in her own blood until the tropical flies circled her, and her lover carried her home.

"Dear?" Mrs. Hotham's voice cut through her reverie. "Are you sure you're quite all right?"

Hyacinth looked down at her embroidery. Her stitches had gone awry, overlapping each other in all the wrong directions.

She shook her head.

"I should go look in on George," she said. She put down her needle and tucked her work away as quickly as she could. "He should have done his calculations by now."

"Have a rest instead!" Mrs. Hotham said. "You are quite grey around the gills. I'll have cook send you a posset. Don't worry yourself so much over that boy," she said. "It won't do to have you arrive in England looking tired and worn out already! You have a whole Season ahead of you."

"A season, yes," Hyacinth sighed. "I suppose I should look forward to it. The prospect of a posset is far more appealing to me today."

"I'll have it sent along," Mrs. Hotham said, reaching for her bell. "You go straight to bed, Miss Grey."

Hyacinth agreed, and gratefully closed the door behind her. In her own cabin, she leaned against the bulkhead and shut her eyes. Mrs. Hotham knew nothing. No one knew anything. If Mr. Smithson were any kind of gentleman, he would say nothing, either, and she would not be ruined. She would only be deeply ashamed... and hungry, longing as she never had before for a touch she shouldn't even have tasted. She must not let it happen again.

She would have to stay away from him, even more so than before. Her father had done well to warn her. She didn't want to arrive in England leg-shackled already, before she'd had a taste of the freedom her grandmother had bequeathed to her.

❧

Late that afternoon, after a few hours' rest, Hyacinth was awoken by a knock on her door.

"Miss Grey?" Maria said.

"Come in," Hyacinth said, sitting up in her bunk and straightening her shawl.

Maria slipped in. When she saw that Hyacinth was in her bunk she hurriedly closed the door. "Are you well?" she asked.

Hyacinth shook her head ambiguously. "I am... I did not

sleep well," she said.

Maria looked over her shoulder. "The man, Mr. Smithson. He has just come to our cabin to see George. He wants your permission to see how the boy fares."

Hyacinth put her fingers to her temples. She was going to get a headache. "I don't know. What do you think, Maria?"

"It's for you to decide," Maria said, "George will be happy to see him."

Hyacinth frowned. "Too pleased, I think. He should be made to see that what he did was no good, no good at all. Tell Mr. Smithson to go away."

"Are you quite sure?" Maria asked. "You don't seem well."

"I think I have a headache."

"But you never get headaches! This is very serious!"

"It is only a headache," Hyacinth said. "Do tell Mr. Smithson to go away. George cannot see him today. Perhaps tomorrow."

"Yes, Miss Grey," Maria said. She slipped out the door.

Then Hyacinth, despite her better judgment, got out of bed and tiptoed to the door. She leaned against it, listening.

"And may I see Miss Grey?" he was asking.

"No! You may not," Maria said, a little too emphatically. "She is not well. Head ache. You can come tomorrow, and ask again."

"I will," he said. "Give my regards to Miss Grey, and if there is anything I can do…"

"We have everything we need, thank you," Maria said icily.

Hyacinth slumped to the floor at the sound of his footsteps walking away down the deck.

The knock came at her door again and Hyacinth leaped back into bed, turning her face to the wall before Maria came in.

"He will come tomorrow," Maria said.

"I know," Hyacinth groaned. "I heard."

"He is a very handsome man," Maria said.

"Yes. Mrs. Hotham says so, too, at every chance she gets. It is a pity."

"And Captain Grey?" Maria hesitated. "He told you something, when he saw that Mr. Smithson was on this ship.

What did he say?"

"To cut him a wide berth," Hyacinth would never be able to think of Mr. Smithson again without remembering him huddled against the deckhouse, hiding from his future, mourning his past.

"You look very pale," Maria said. "The ship's surgeon can come?"

Hyacinth shook her head. "People have headaches all the time. We are at sea, after all. I simply took a slight chill. But..."

"Yes, miss?"

"Would you send word that I'd prefer to have my dinner here tonight? I don't think I'm well enough for company."

"Of course!" Maria said.

"And bring George's books in to me when he's done with his sums. I will see him in the morning."

&

Small wonder she wasn't feeling well, Thomas thought. She had stood out in the rain all afternoon, and probably hadn't slept a wink longer than he had, though she hadn't had nearly as much wine as he had. He had that to blame for his fuzzy vision and pounding head, never mind his battle with the waves the afternoon before.

If he were a different man, he might have blamed the wine for making a cad of him, but he knew himself better than that. Men blamed drink for the secret desires of their hearts, but his passions were his own. If he had drunk enough to unleash them, it was his own fault, though he hadn't thought Miss Grey was their object. He had thought that he would return to his cabin and be tormented again by dreams of a shady bungalow under coconut palms, with his mistress's familiar hands massaging away his cares. After all, he had dreamed of her through his whole long journey across the Indian Ocean, across Arabia and the Mediterranean.

But that was not what had happened after he staggered out of the moonlit night. Instead, he'd lain back on his bunk only to replay the last half-hour, over and over again – especially the way she had looked, standing at the rail in the moonlight, like a ghost of things yet to come. He could not fathom what had compelled him to reach for her. Was it loneliness? That wasn't justification enough. Affection? Perhaps, but it was misplaced affection, affection that belonged to a woman who was dead and in her grave. He would never feel Sarita's touch again.

When he reached for those happy memories, as he always did on waking in the morning, he found that they had grown slippery in his thoughts. Her face had blurred. He could not remember where, exactly, the mole on her neck had sat, or how it had felt. Thomas's journey of exile, back to his homeland, had taken the better part of three months already. He would have thought that those years would stay with him for at least as long, a decade, at least. It had all seemed clearer than the daylight until yesterday, but now the images of his life in India took on the quality of a dream, slipping away in the morning light.

❧

Miss Grey did not come to the table for dinner that night. In the absence of the ladies, the men's talk turned to coarser subjects.

"So tell us, Mr. Smithson," the navigator said, "about the ladies in India."

"Mr. French!" the first mate exclaimed. "I've been waiting ever since Cadiz for those tales. Do tell, Mr. Smithson."

Thomas bit his lower lip. "The ladies do have a civilizing influence on proceedings, do they not?"

"Indeed they do," Captain Hotham chimed in. "Though I confess, I don't mind it."

"Nor do I," Thomas said, breathing a quiet sigh of relief. "I have been on far too many ships in recent months with nothing but a lot of scurvy Arabs to look at. It's quite refreshing to see a pretty female across the table instead of a man in a turban who'd sooner kill you than take a drink."

"Aye, so it is," the second mate agreed. "Those Arabs are odd ones, aren't they?"

With that, the talk turned mercifully to the strange customs of foreign sailors, and if Thomas pecked at his meal like an invalid, no one saw fit to comment.

≈

CHAPTER 5: SAILING ON

Thomas knocked at George's cabin the next morning, and again he was turned away.

"And how is Miss Grey this morning?" he asked the maid.

The maid put on such a sour look that Thomas almost laughed.

"I suppose it's none of my business, but do send her my rega..." He stopped himself. It would not do to simply send his regards. He could do better than that. He excused himself and returned to his cabin, where he rummaged around in his trunk until he found what he was looking for. He took out a piece of good writing paper and composed a short note, then tied a piece of twine around the lot and considered it ready to deliver.

❧

After a day's rest, Hyacinth felt well enough, physically, but she still couldn't bear the thought of going out on deck. Mr. Smithson had been in and out of his cabin a dozen times already. She could hear him coming and going, every creak of the hinge and click of the latch. He went so often that she hadn't even dared go over to George's cabin to give him his lessons. She thought of slipping through into Mrs. Hotham's sitting room, but then she would know that she was better, and urge her to go to dinner with the officers and Mr. Smithson.

So she waited. She re-read a bit of Ovid that she was thinking of having George work on. She unpicked a bit of her disgraceful embroidery from the previous afternoon. The sun crept slowly up the sky. She felt as if Mr. Smithson were hovering outside her door. Perhaps he wanted to apologize, she thought, but that would mean a word in private, which in itself might be a compromising situation, and besides, she wasn't at all sure what *she* would do in that situation. She might throw herself straight back into his arms, which wouldn't do at all. No, it wouldn't do at all. She picked up the book again. She would memorize a poem, that's what she would do.

Maria knocked at the door, interrupting Hyacinth's self-imposed studies. She was sure that it wasn't time for luncheon yet.

"Come in," Hyacinth said.

Maria entered with a stern frown on her face and a square bundle in her hands.

"Miss Grey," she said, "that Mr. Smithson came and asked about you. I didn't say anything, then he ran off into his cabin. He brought this out and said to give it to you."

Maria held out the bundle, string tied around cloth, with a note attached. Even before she touched it, Hyacinth could tell that the purple-grey fabric would be meltingly soft. She sat up and took it in both hands, letting her fingers sink into the incomparably fine wool.

"It's so soft!" she couldn't help but say.

"Yes, but do you think…" Maria began. "To accept a gift from a man."

"Well…" Hyacinth felt a twinge of doubt, but not enough to stop her from untying the strings. "It's not jewelry, though it is very fine, and he did say he was concerned about my health. It's only a shawl after all," she said. "I hardly see how it could make us more indebted to him than we already are."

Maria frowned and nodded as Hyacinth unwrapped the

shawl. The long center length of it was as plain as could be, but at the ends the sombre, half-mourning color was broken by a band of rich embroidery, paisleys and abstract flowers in all the hues of the rainbow, with tiny bright glass beads knotted into the fringe.

"*Que bella!*" Maria remarked, despite her disapproval.

"It's stunning!" Hyacinth said. She wondered if it had been very expensive, but didn't voice the question. It wasn't jewelry, that was the important thing, even if the fringes were as bright as some necklaces. "I don't know…"

"But no, you can't return it!" Maria said. "It's too pretty to give back."

Hyacinth laughed at Maria's sudden change of heart. "And I suppose I'd better read the note," she said. She didn't want to do that with anyone looking on, not even Maria. "Will you ask George to get his books out and open to his lesson?" she said. "I believe we have time to translate a page of Homer before luncheon."

As soon as the door closed behind Maria, Hyacinth had the note in her hands. She hesitated a moment before breaking the hastily-applied seal. What would he say? Would she have to respond? She supposed she would.

The sound of George opening and closing his lockers came through the partition between their cabins. She didn't have much time. She snapped the seal and unfolded the paper.

My dear Miss Grey,

No apology can excuse my behavior. I have lapsed in my manners as a gentleman.

Would you do me the great honour of accepting my hand in marriage?

Yours,

Thomas Smithson Pently

Hyacinth froze, slack-jawed, with the paper dangling out of her hand. Did he not even use his real name? What did that last name signify? Was that what her father had alluded to? If so...

The door of the neighboring cabin slammed shut and she tucked the note into the nearest hiding place: her bosom. As her own door swung open and George walked in, she fervently wished she'd found someplace else to hide it. The paper might have been a burning ember.

"What news, Hyacinth?" George grinned, oblivious to the lumpish paper burrowing between her breasts.

Her mouth moved but no sound came out.

"Cat got your tongue?" George continued cheerily. "That should be me, I'm the one who nearly drowned and has the gallows waiting for him in England."

He was only a boy, Hyacinth reminded herself, and he was trying to put a brave face on things. He could have no idea what she was drowning in now. She forced herself to say something.

"Well, we'd best get on with the translation, then. Here." She took his book and opened it at random.

Some time later, George looked at her with concern.

"Hy, we did this passage three days ago. Are you all right?"

"I am perfectly fine. Your brush with death and the threat of the law seems to have tired me more than it did you. Perhaps we'd better leave it, after all. Do a new passage, I'll come check it before dinner."

George looked at her as if he wanted to ask something else, but then he shrugged. "All right. I'll go then. Should I have Maria bring you luncheon?"

That would only give her more time to sit alone and stare at the note.

"No. Tell her that I will go sit with Mrs. Hotham."

"I'll tell her," George said. He closed the door, leaving her alone with her new torment.

Hyacinth sat down heavily on her bunk and clutched her knees to her chest. She didn't know what to think. She would have to answer, but she would delay it as long as possible.

❧

Unfortunately, "as long as possible," was only the space of an afternoon. Having spent the midday hours with Mrs. Hotham, Hyacinth couldn't see a way to excuse herself from dinner again. Besides, she was going to have to see Mr. Smithson eventually, and she didn't think she could spend another day cooped up in her cabin. George was next to insane with restlessness already, and she felt it, too.

As afternoon stretched the ship's shadow across the waves, Hyacinth donned her best traveling gown. Like her other dresses, it was plain, but it had been made for her by Lady Hamilton's own dressmaker, from Naples. The fine, dark blue wool fit her perfectly. She called Maria in to put her hair up.

"Maria?" she said, inspecting herself in the small looking glass. "Do I look all right?" Her hair had been brushed to a sheen and swept up into a tidy roll. Her eyes seemed bright, and she hoped no one would notice if she bit her lip more than usual.

"Of course! You look beautiful as always!" Maria said.

"I mean, do you think I might still be ill?" Hyacinth asked hopefully. Her stomach felt unsettled. Perhaps she would be nauseous soon, though the seas had been dispiritingly calm all day.

Maria frowned. "Why would you be ill? You were only a little tired and overwrought. You will feel better after a good meal, not just these possets the cook sends you when you're in your cabin."

"I suppose you're right," Hyacinth sighed.

"Of course I am right. Go to dinner and don't let that man frighten you."

Hyacinth suppressed a deep sigh. "It was a lovely gift, wasn't it, though perhaps not entirely appropriate."

"He is a wealthy man, they say. You were right when you said that it is nothing, compared to rescuing George."

"Yes, yes of course. The shawl is nothing to him," Hyacinth said, hoping it was true. What if it had belonged to his lover, the woman who had been shot? What if he had given her that leftover thing, too, as well as his misplaced kisses? One thing at least was clear to her – his note had been written out of a sense of obligation, and foolish obligation, too. He could not love her, even if he pretended to hold some regard for her, or felt the tug of propriety enough to compel a proposal.

Besides, Hyacinth reminded herself, she had no intention of marrying, especially not someone she scarcely knew, who used a different name as it suited him. She was going to use her inheritance from Grandmother Miller to start a school.

"Stop looking in the mirror!" Maria chided. "Off to your dinner!"

Hyacinth nodded and stood up, keeping her spine straight and her shoulders squared. Whatever happened, she would not show how much she feared seeing him again. And the others must not guess what had happened, not ever.

❧

Thomas watched Hyacinth glide into the room, steady on her feet and tall, looking everywhere but at him. She looked elegant, graceful, and perhaps not as prim as he'd thought her, before. She certainly hadn't been shattered by what had passed between them two nights before, at least not if her demeanor were any indication.

Her hand trembled ever so slightly as she sat down opposite him, but she quickly mastered it and looked up, as if she were addressing him directly. Her eyes were focused on his chin, so that they would not risk locking gazes.

"Good evening," she said to everyone, "and good evening to you Mr. Smithson. I must thank you again for your daring rescue the other day. We are all most obliged."

Her gaze had drifted down to the table as she spoke.

Thomas's heart raced. He let a long moment pass and the captain coughed, prompting him to reply.

"It was nothing, Miss Grey, nothing at all. Please, think no more of it."

"But I cannot..." She bit her lip and looked up, then quickly glanced away again. "It was an admirable feat," she said. "We are very much in your debt."

"I assure you, Miss Grey, it was my pleasure," Thomas said, wondering what he would have thought of those words when he was under the waves, fighting for a chance to breathe. He hoped that she didn't feel the debt too keenly. He had not intended to do anything that would prompt such feelings. He had not intended anything at all, in fact, not when he dove in.

The first mate, Mr. Bromley, was speaking. "Mr. Smithson swims like a porpoise!" he said. "I never saw such a feat in all my years at sea."

"Well," Thomas said, "the waters here are quite chilly. The waters off the coast of India are warmer, and it's worth braving the surf there to get some relief from the heat."

Thomas hoped that Hyacinth's stammering "I cannot" was not intended as an answer to his proposal, though something told him that it might be. It would be an absurd way of replying.

Surely, she must feel at least some of the awkwardness which made him fidget in his seat like a schoolboy. She was no maharani with an army at her back. Surely, he'd faced more fearsome prospects than protecting a young woman, who had possibly overstepped the bounds of propriety. Maybe he shouldn't have proposed. Maybe the sailors hadn't seen, and even if they had, none of the officers seemed to have heard anything. Even if the officers knew, would their gossip reach society? Still, he felt an urge to protect her, if she would have him. If she would have him?

Any respectable young lady who knew who his uncle was would snap up his offer, regardless of their personal feelings. At least, that was what he'd been told when he was younger, and that was when his much-loved elder brother, as well as his sickly cousin, had stood between him and the duchy. Of course, she couldn't be expected to know his family, even if her father did. That certainly hadn't worked to his advantage. She might not be impressed, either. It was better if she came to know him as only himself, as a man returning from the subcontinent with health intact and a decent fortune to his name. He felt that said more of his true self than his aristocratic ancestry.

Thomas's thoughts drifted as the conversation continued around him. Mr. French, the navigator, was speaking to Hyacinth, exchanging pleasantries. There had been English ladies in India, too. About a half-dozen. He'd met three of them over the course of his decade there. Hyacinth was far prettier than any of them, and he imagined her holding court among them, in conditions that would make most of her peers faint away.

The sound of Hyacinth's laugh snapped him back to the present. The navigator was leaning close, as if to whisper something in her ear. Thomas straightened up and leaned across the table, knife in hand.

"I say, man!" the navigator said suddenly. "You look rather alarming."

"I… excuse me, Mr. French. I was thinking of India."

"Always thinking of India, aren't you?" Hyacinth said. It would be an innocent enough question if he hadn't told her about Sarita, but he had. He hoped that no one else around the table detected the undercurrents in their conversation.

"I do think of India often," Thomas said. "After all, I lived my whole life as an independent man on its shores."

Mr. French's skin had an oily look, as if he drank too heavily. Thomas wondered why he'd never noticed it before. He was sitting entirely too close to the lady.

"I do think often of India, but not constantly," he continued, ignoring the navigator. "Since my recent swim I find myself thinking more and more of home, of England, and of the future. The past is gone."

He looked over at her, affecting a conversational smile. She didn't seem quite her usual self, did she? She sat very still in her seat, unnaturally so.

"Is it?" she asked.

"But of course," Thomas smiled weakly. "By definition, the

past is gone."

"And yet it haunts some men," the first mate, Mr. Bromley, cut in. "My own grandfather even had a ghost in his house."

"Really?" Thomas said. "Do tell us, what was its story?"

"As to that, I really know only a little," the mate said.

"Do tell, Mr. Bromley," Captain Hotham said. "And don't neglect the embellishments!"

"No, indeed, don't!" Mr. French added.

Thus, the conversation turned to another man's haunting, and Thomas could sit back and listen to the story, keeping one eye always on Miss Grey. Once, when she thought she was unobserved, she cast a glance in his direction. She blushed, then quickly turned her attention back to her plate.

Thomas had no further occasion to talk to her until they were rising from the table. "Please, Miss Grey," he said. "May I escort you back to your cabin?"

She bit her lip again, a gesture which made her look younger and less self-assured than usual.

"That w…would be lovely, thank you," she said.

℀

That won't be necessary. That was what she'd meant to say! But he was already walking over to her and taking her arm. There was no way to refuse his offer without drawing attention to herself, which was the last thing she wanted. She looked back at Captain Hotham and his officers. They had already turned away, taking no notice as Mr. Smithson offered her his arm.

"Allow me, Miss Grey," he said.

She smiled at him through gritted teeth and nodded a brief goodnight to the assembled company. Mr. Smithson touched her elbow, and all the blood in her body rushed to that lone point of contact. It left her head empty and light, dizzy. She tried to shift away, but the passage was too narrow. She steadied her breathing as they walked out onto the open deck.

Sails billowed above them like swan's wings in the light of the rising moon. Hyacinth took a deep breath of the chilly air.

"It's quite a brisk night," she commented.

"Miss Grey?" Mr. Smithson lightened his grip on her arm. She could feel the warm spots left behind where he'd clutched her in the dark. His touch still lingered lightly on her forearm as he turned her to face him.

She looked up at him. He was tall, and his hair shone silvery in the moonlight. His eyes lay in impenetrable shadow.

"Would you answer me?"

Ahead of them on the deck, the second mate stood at the wheel. He nodded a greeting to them, but with the sound of creaking blocks and lines, the whisper of the wind and the gurgle of the passing waters, he would be able to hear nothing of the words that passed between them.

"No," Hyacinth said at last. "I cannot."

"Cannot answer?"

"I can answer well enough," she said. "And my answer is no. I cannot accept your offer."

"I have behaved most dishonorably," he said. "I must rectify the situation."

"It is not the only way. No one saw. We may easily go on as if nothing has happened. I am not a child lost at sea needing rescue."

"But we are at sea, if not lost," he said, "and something has happened. You cannot deny that. And I confess I cannot see you the same way since." A plea colored his voice.

Hyacinth jerked her arm away. "Have you lost all respect for me, then? Is that any grounds for..." she couldn't bring herself to say the word marriage, it was all too preposterous. They scarcely knew each other, she told herself, no matter what drunken confessions he'd made in the night.

"Not at all," he said. He looked anxiously towards the wheelhouse and reached out as if to take Hyacinth's arm again. She backed away. "I retain the utmost respect for you. I am the one who is at fault."

"And you would not think me... improper for staying there with you?" Hyacinth said. "I should have left the moment I saw you there. I should not even have been out on deck at all." Her throat felt tight, constricted. She swallowed, trying to keep breathing normally.

"But you did stay," he said. "Do you think me such a rogue?"

Hyacinth closed her eyes lightly and shook her head, feeling the night wind tease a curl of hair out of her chignon.

"I don't know," she said at last. "My father warned me against you."

"Yes, he seemed to form quite a firm opinion of me on very brief acquaintance," Mr. Smithson said, a note of bitterness in his voice.

"I have seen nothing to confirm his appraisal of you, except that you seem to change your name at a whim."

"It..." he stammered. "Forget that. It means nothing. I've been Mr. Smithson for all these years. I don't even know if I'll go back to being a Pently at all."

Hyacinth peered at him. "Well," she said, "there was also your rescue of George. That was heroic. Whoever you say you are."

"Heroic?" Mr. Smithson laughed. "More the foolhardy act of a man who thought nothing of throwing his life away."

Hyacinth shrugged. "It remains that your life is still with you, and maybe you are a rogue. You may not see yourself as such, but you as much as said that you ruined a woman in India, then let yourself be carried away by misplaced passion to the point of killing a man, a man who might have made an honest mistake."

"I did not ruin her. It is different there. Not altogether different, but different. And I do not believe my passions were misplaced," Mr. Smithson said. "Besides, he could not have done what he did innocently. He may not have recognized her, but she was, beyond doubt, a woman, and unarmed." He closed his eyes and took a deep breath before continuing.

"Believe me, Miss Grey, I am well aware of the disservices I did her over the years, making her a stranger to her family for the sake of their pride, making her so much more alone than she might have been otherwise, but we had each other, and at the time it seemed it would be enough. She had her own house, and wasn't kept in a harem with half a dozen other women, as some of the British officers kept their mistresses. No, I did the best I could. I ask you to believe that, at least. Can you?"

Hyacinth paced to the side of the boat and looked over the rail at the water gurgling slowly past. There was very little wind that night. She wondered again if perhaps it would be better to simply leave, to not continue this conversation. After a long minute of reflection, she answered.

"Yes," she said, "I believe you, of course I believe you. You have no reason to lie to me, do you? We are strangers. We will probably never see each other again after we dock in Portsmouth. I certainly believe that you meant her no harm, and could have done worse. It isn't enough, though."

"I know," he answered. "It never was enough. I suppose I'm beginning to see that now," he said, as if that meant anything. "I felt deep affection for her."

"I thought that you had left your heart in the Indies."

"I thought I had," he said, "and I thought that I loved her, too."

"Let's say no more about it," Hyacinth said. She was suddenly sick to death of hearing of Mr. Smithson's mistress, and she didn't even know the woman's name. What he said next was worse, though.

"Will you have my heart, what's left of it, Miss Grey?"

It sounded so like a plea that she was half-tempted to relent and say yes, but he was only asking in order to fulfill his half-forgotten sense of propriety.

"No," Hyacinth said again. "I do not mean to be coy or cruel, but I do not think the fragments of your heart are enough. For one thing, my father would hardly grant his permission, rescue or no."

"I doubt that would be true, if he knew everything." Mr. Smithson frowned and leaned against the cabin wall, gazing ahead. He straightened a little as a sailor approached, making the rounds, checking lines as he went along the deck.

"Well, I don't know everything, either," Hyacinth said, "but what I do know is that I don't wish to marry now, even if..." She took a deep breath and steered herself back to practicalities, away from the thoughts of kissing and more, which threatened to cloud her senses.

"I expect to receive an inheritance when I reach England," she continued. "I intend to live on it if I can. I intend to enjoy my independence."

Mr. Smithson snorted. Snorted!

"I am afraid you'll find that difficult. Independence, for a woman, is elusive, especially in England, if I recall correctly. Men will judge you as either a bluestocking or a light-skirt, and respectable women... well, they would suspect that you were not one of their kind and would keep you at arm's length, or shut you out entirely."

Hyacinth looked at him, wishing she could see the thoughts that lay behind those words.

"Are you so familiar with the world of respectable women, then?"

"I knew my mother, and my girl cousins. We were young, but some things became clear to me, looking back from the safety of thousands of miles' distance."

"I wouldn't know any better, myself," Hyacinth said, "but I mean it. I intend to enjoy my independence, and we know nothing of each other, do we?"

Mr. Smithson turned his gaze away from the northern horizon and looked at her.

"Many go to the altar knowing less," he said. "I would..." He trailed off and took a deep breath. "May I kiss you again?"

Hyacinth's whole self flushed. She shook her head.

"I must go to my cabin," she said. "The sailors will think it strange that we are standing here so long."

"But Miss Grey, please," he said. "I would be greatly honored."

He gazed at her so longingly, so admiringly that for a moment, she thought that perhaps he was proposing in earnest, but he had only lately declared that their shared world, life aboard the *Whistler*, was little more than a waking dream to him.

"It doesn't matter," Hyacinth said. "I do not wish to make any kind of permanent arrangement without knowing the details of my own situation in England, even if you truly are so inclined. Which I am not sure of."

"But I have no one," he blurted out.

"You have family in England, as I do," Hyacinth reasoned. His lost mistress could hardly have been his first confidante, just as Hyacinth herself was unlikely to be his last.

Just then, a slight turn of the wind brought the ship sideways against a wave and the deck rocked farther than usual, unbalancing Hyacinth. Mr. Smithson caught her, and she found herself wrapped once more in his arms. For a moment, she would have gladly lost herself in them again, if only to taste another kiss, another useless, world-spinning kiss.

The mate at the wheel stood only a short distance away. He could turn around at any moment, and besides, the sailor who had been making his rounds was approaching again, whistling "Blow Ye Winds," a popular new tune from America. Hyacinth pulled herself away.

"I cannot accept," she repeated, "but you are the most daring man of my acquaintance, Mr. Smithson, and among the handsomest."

She pulled away. In two long steps, she covered the distance to her own cabin door. She heard Mr. Smithson's steps behind her.

"Please, Miss Grey," he said, "may I ask you one favor?"

She hesitated. "I suppose. Yes, you may ask."

"Please, call me Thomas. Or even Tommy. It is the only name I feel is really my own. In India, I went by Mr. Smithson, wishing to be rid of my family name. When we land, I may have to go by Pently again, much as I'd rather not. I don't feel it's truly my name any more. So please, Miss Grey, would you call me Thomas?"

Hyacinth let go of the handle and leaned against the door,

looking up at this stupidly brave and handsome man. It seemed a small thing to ask, under the circumstances.

"I will call you Thomas, then," she said, "but not in company." That would incite comment, as both of them knew. "You may call me Hyacinth," she added, surprising herself. "When we are alone. Which had better not happen again on this journey."

"No?" he asked. Then he nodded. "You are correct, as always, Miss... Hyacinth. Hyacinth. Thank you."

"It is nothing, Thomas," she said, but it was something, far more than she ought to have given up, but it was done now, like the fiery kiss they'd shared.

A round of ribald laughter sounded out of the captain's salon.

"You had better go," Hyacinth said. "They will wonder what is keeping you."

"Let them wonder," he said, catching her hand in his. Then he released it. "No, you're right. I'd better not."

Hyacinth unlatched her door. "Good night, Thomas," she said, and closed the door behind her. She locked it, fell onto her bunk, and cried.

❧

CHAPTER 6: ENGLAND

Thomas knew, in the cold light of day, that everything Hyacinth had told him was perfectly reasonable, but she was the prettiest English lady he'd met in ten years, which made her reasoning seem weaker, somehow. They could marry now, and be spared their families' scheming. He knew that his family, at least, would have plans for him which had nothing to do with his own wishes, or even his character. He would rather marry a woman who had no interest in his possible title. That argument would not be likely to sway her. He had forgotten much about the ladies at home in his decade of self-imposed exile, but he did know that Hyacinth was sensible and practical, the sort of woman who could help her husband manage an estate, if it came to that. Not that he wanted it to come to that, but his father could not survive on bile forever. Thomas would need a wife. Why not Hyacinth, instead of some society miss who knew nothing of the world outside of a ballroom?

He would not really know what awaited him until he arrived in London, at the very earliest. It seemed a long time to wait. As he contemplated the possibilities, he wished that he would be free to return to India, even though his mistress would not be there to greet him.

The ships sailed on, creeping north through the chilly

Atlantic waves. Thomas spent part of every day on deck, looking at the warships they traveled with. They sailed close enough to the coast of France that sometimes he could see the green countryside. He almost wished he'd chosen to travel by some other means, some place where he was not confined to a creeping ship with the same ten men at the table every night, their conversation becoming insipid and repetitive as the weeks wore on and the rations grew short. The captain had hoped to make the journey in a fortnight. Between light winds and foul weather, it threatened to stretch to a month or more. England would at least offer some relief from the tedium of months of sea travel and hard tack.

Except that once he had arrived, he would no longer sit opposite Miss Grey over a meager dinner every afternoon. He would miss the sight of her, even if she had avoided any intimate conversation with him for over a week. They could not help but exchange a few polite words, and sometimes at the table she forgot her reserve and proved a more entertaining conversationalist than any of the *Whistler's* officers. She was alluring, and she reminded him that England might hold some good things, even though they both sailed back as strangers to the land of their birth.

Even with the thinning rations, Thomas half-wished that the journey would go on forever.

ﺭ

Hyacinth kept herself busy tutoring George and embroidering with Mrs. Hotham when the seas were calm and the ship idled in its maddeningly slow journey to England. George studied because it was the only form of distraction available to him, but no amount of calculation and translation and study could keep him from feeling the effects of his imprisonment. The threat of the gallows seemed to sharpen his mind, although Hyacinth felt that their studies seemed futile in its shadow. Despite Mrs. Hotham's assurances, she worried that her brother would be hanged for a traitor.

Three and a half weeks after they'd left Gibraltar, Captain Hotham called her aside one night after dinner.

"Miss Grey," he said, "you must not worry yourself. My wife has tried to reassure you, but I want you to know that Mr. Bromley and I have concluded that young George's confinement is punishment enough. He will hardly turn Spaniard once he's settled in England, I think."

Hyacinth realized then how worried she'd been about the threat of a formal charge against George.

"I hope that you are right, Captain," she said.

"I am quite confident of it. He has your father's blood, after all."

Hyacinth looked over her shoulder. Mr. Smithson – she still couldn't really think of him as Thomas – and the officers were engaged in a loud, dull debate over the dubious merits of the port they were drinking, from the last cask on board. They were paying no attention to her, for once. She felt so exposed, some nights, with Mr. Smithson stealing glances in her direction and Mr. French flirting so clumsily, but never to the point of giving offense. Besides, Mr. French knew better than to try to speak with her in private, as Mr. Smithson, Thomas, would if he had the chance.

Hyacinth avoided walking on the deck after dinner, when she knew that Thomas would be there, but as they approached the coast of England she couldn't contain her restlessness. First, she stopped in to George's cabin.

"I've translated that bit of Horace," he reported dispiritedly. The sight of the English coast seemed to have dampened his spirits. He'd been mad with boredom during the weeks of his imprisonment, but he'd been petulant, rather than dull.

Hyacinth glanced at the paper he'd handed her. It was neat and, at first glance, appeared nearly perfect.

"You've done well with this, George," Hyacinth said. "You'll be ready for school I'm sure."

George sat up straighter. "You think I will go to school after all?" he asked hopefully.

"Yes," Hyacinth said, "of course you will."

"They won't try me for treason?"

Hyacinth bit her lower lip and glanced at Maria.

"Well, he should know it was serious!" Maria said.

"It's not?" George said. "They're not going to hang me?"

Hyacinth found herself wanting to laugh as George's relief turned to anger, but she kept a stern countenance.

"Why didn't you tell me?" He stomped his feet on the floor, just as if he were a much younger child.

Hyacinth calmed herself. "It was not at all frivolous," she said, "but Captain Hotham and his crew have concluded that you fell overboard quite by accident. He only told me recently. I didn't know, either. The seas were rough, after all, and no sensible man would make that leap by choice. You must not do or say anything to suggest otherwise. Ever. Do you understand?"

"Yes," George answered. "Do you think I'll do all right in maths, too?" he asked.

"You'll do brilliantly," Hyacinth assured him. "Now collect your things. You'll be at that school tomorrow, if all goes well."

Hyacinth bade George goodnight and stepped out onto the deck feeling lighter of heart than she'd been since leaving Gibraltar. Soon George would be in a place with other boys, and she would be free to uncover her mysterious inheritance and to... to do whatever it was that young ladies did, as her father had put it.

The breeze carried the ships along at a steady clip, steering a course parallel to the coast. Hyacinth was tired of the sight of the other ships, their constant, silent companions on the journey. Although the captains communicated with each other as needed, she'd only spoken to the officers and her fellow passengers on the *Whistler*. At least England would provide a fresh set of companions. Whether she liked them or not remained to be seen. She leaned on the rail, peering out at the low, dark outline of the shore. Here and there, the dim yellow light of candles and fires shone through cottage windows in the gathering dusk. This was the land called home, she thought, this dark silhouette of a country.

"Good evening, Hyacinth." Mr. Smithson's voice startled her, close at her side.

"Good evening... Thomas," Hyacinth said, trying to sound cheerful. She smiled nervously at him.

"Ominous, isn't it?" he said with a nod to the coastline.

"Pardon?" Hyacinth said. Then she laughed nervously. "England, ominous? Maybe dawn will improve the view."

"I expect it will still be gray and dark," Mr. Smithson, Thomas, said. "It tends to be, this time of year."

"I've only been here in summer, at least, so far as I can remember, and that was ten years ago. I might have seen a winter here as an infant, but I don't recall any of that," Hyacinth said. "I don't have any idea what it will be like."

Thomas shrugged. "Cold, like this, and a little less dark in the daytime. At least, that's what I remember from when I was a boy. Not a cheerful climate."

"I see," Hyacinth said. "I will probably make good use of your gift in that case. It is a fine piece. I don't think I thanked you for it properly."

"No, you did not, but I'm glad you like it."

Hyacinth wasn't sure, but she thought for a moment that Mr. Smithson was blushing.

"It's nothing," he said. "In fact, if you wear it in company, it could be considered a favor to me."

"How so?" Hyacinth asked.

"Well, I bought a bundle of them before I left India, shawls like that. They'll do as gifts to female relatives, but if I don't have to return to the family estate after all, then I might sell them, and return to India for more."

Hyacinth was dumbfounded. "Go into trade, you mean? In ladies' fashions? Even though your family has an estate?"

"Several, actually."

"Surely you can't be serious!" Hyacinth said.

"Oh, but I am," Thomas said.

"Could you go into trade, independent of the East India Company?" she asked.

"I have a few ideas, and it's possible that I'd be able to arrange something," he said.

"But your family," Hyacinth said. "Would they approve?"

Thomas laughed. "Never. They would never approve and that makes me all the more determined. It would amuse me to rankle them again, and I must have something to occupy my time. I was never well suited to the life of an idle younger son, and even if... Never mind."

He turned away from her, but Hyacinth thought she detected a hint of sadness in his voice. Why was he so angry with his family, after all these years?

"I do not want to be tied to any of my family's estates, but if I'm saddled with it, I suppose I'll be obliged to stay among my insufferable relations, most of whom can't see past the end of their own long noses."

"I confess, I do not understand you," Hyacinth said. "Most men would be happy to inherit an estate, I think."

Thomas shook his head. "Not really," he said. "My elder brother, everyone loved him. He died after a hunting accident. And you're right; I was a black sheep in my family. I won't be loved as he was. Maybe better than my father, but still, I don't think I'll like my family any more than I did when I left, more likely less. They'll be insufferable. I probably will be, too."

Hyacinth pondered that for a moment. "I'm not at all sure that I'll like my aunt, either. What I remember of her... But it doesn't matter. I wouldn't go out of my way to annoy her. It could only make life more difficult, don't you think?"

Thomas shrugged. "It may be, but I can't see going about things any other way. I quarreled with my father. I thought as a second son I ought to have some freedom, and there were other things… but I don't want to think about them until I have to," he said. "I'd rather think of you, while we are both here."

Hyacinth blushed, but there was nothing to say. In the dim light of the lanterns, he wouldn't see her cheeks color.

"I will miss you," Thomas said. "I do not think the other young ladies of England will have half your wit or charm."

"Charm? I don't think I've ever been called charming before," Hyacinth said. "I expect the ladies will surprise you." Then again, Hyacinth thought, he himself would probably be quite an oddity among gentlemen, with his preference for India over England, and his lack of family feeling. "I cannot imagine that most gentlemen in England share your qualities, either," she said.

"Qualities?" Thomas said. "What qualities would those be?"

"Recklessness?" Hyacinth proposed, searching for something not too damning. "And wit," she said, "far more wit than most men." Hyacinth looked down at the deck. A moment later she felt his hand on her arm.

"Please, Miss Grey," Thomas said. "Would you consider my suit again?"

She shook her head. "No. It will not do, anymore than it would have before. We are still adrift, besides which I think you are merely passing the time. Would we have even spoken to each other if we'd only met on the shore at Gibraltar, and not been confined together to this one small ship on the ocean these four weeks?"

He must know that she was right, she thought.

"I like to think that we would have met, in any case," Thomas said, "and become friends, or... I don't know. You are probably right, but I have before me only the lonely prospect of returning to a land I never got along with. I would rather face it with you by my side."

"With me?" Hyacinth said. "Again, no. I still have my own affairs to attend to and I am not at all sure that I wish to be married, ever."

"No? It would be a shame to see you a spinster."

"If I have independent means, it would be better than many marriages," Hyacinth said. He was probably thinking about that kiss, that ill-advised kiss they'd shared. The night was cool, but the sailors were all out on deck, looking towards the shore. Even if she gave in to her desire to touch those lips again, she couldn't do so with all the men looking on.

"Some marriages are happy," Thomas said. "Our captain and his wife, for example."

"They are," Hyacinth said. "I think my father and mother were happy too, but then, she died young, and… it cannot last." Her father had been devastated. Whatever his affair had been with George's mother, it had not been love. They had lost too much when her mother died. She had lost too much.

"You don't speak of her often," Thomas said.

"No, but I was only ten years old when she died."

"Were you lonely?" he asked.

"Of course I was. Wouldn't you have been lonely if your mother had died?"

"No, I don't think I would have missed her so much."

"How ever not?" She could not imagine not missing a mother. She did not understand him. If he had seemed passionate, that night in the dark, it was probably an illusion, or an effect of wine and moonlight.

"I rarely saw her," Thomas said, after a pause. "She was always in London or visiting friends when I was young, and knowing what I later learned about my father, I can understand why. I would have been sad at her passing, but it wouldn't have made much difference in my day-to-day life. I would still have had the same nursemaids, tutors, schools. No. It would have made little difference to me."

He shrugged when he finished, as if his words didn't mean much to him, but they puzzled Hyacinth, and saddened her. "She must love you, in her way?" she said.

"Perhaps. I'll see her soon, along with the rest of them, whoever is left."

The ship slid on through the channel, past a clanging bell-buoy.

"It is all very close now, isn't it?" Hyacinth said.

"Yes, but…" Thomas reached out, touching Hyacinth's elbow. There, in the dark, with the last miles of their journey fast slipping into their wake, his touch sent a ripple of alarm straight to her heart. She turned to face him.

"I would prize your friendship," he said.

"Friendship?" Hyacinth said. How could he be a friend? She had had friends in Gibraltar, when she was a girl, and before George's mother had died. She certainly didn't count any men among her friends. "We have so little in common," she said.

"We do, though," Thomas said. "We are both returning exiles, and reluctant ones, too. My old friends, never mind my family, wouldn't understand how that feels. You would."

Hyacinth shook her head. "We cannot meet in clubs or converse in private, or even have correspondence without causing comment," she said, but she realized that he was right, he was like her, in some ways. She would be lonely in London. Aunt Celia was unlikely to approve of all her intellectual interests, never mind her ambition to establish a school. It would be good to have a confidant, however unlikely their friendship. "I will consider you a friend," she said, "for what little that's worth."

"We will meet again, I know it," he said. He ran his hand down her forearm and settled it over her own hand on the rail, as if he would have embraced more of her if he could. They both stared out to the horizon. The silence between them was only heightened by the small noises of the ship under sail, and the far-away murmur of sailors talking over a game of cards.

"I really must return to my cabin," Hyacinth said. "I have much to prepare for tomorrow."

"So do I," Thomas said. "Adieu, my friend."

With that, he squeezed her hand and broke away, while the coastline closed in like a cloud.

❧

It was late in the short December daylight when the *Whistler* finally weighed anchor in Portsmouth. With the ship steady in the harbor, Hyacinth penned a short message to Aunt Celia to be posted immediately to her residence in Brighton, along with a note to Mr. Portnoy's school, informing the schoolmaster of their arrival. George was bursting to escape his cabin. Hyacinth felt like the confines of the ship would drive her mad, too, now that they were almost free of it.

She checked over her trunks one last time, then a tentative knock sounded on the door. Hyacinth opened it quickly to see the captain's wife dressed for travel.

"Mrs. Hotham!" Hyacinth exclaimed. "Are you leaving already?"

Mrs. Hotham took a deep breath and smiled. "Yes. I'm quite ready to be off this ship with its rations of hard tack and salt cod. Would you accompany me to shore? The captain has arranged a suite of rooms at an inn for us, but he won't be able to leave the ship until tomorrow noon at the earliest. You and Maria are most welcome to spend the night there with me."

"I'd be delighted to," Hyacinth said, hesitating.

"We can arrange a room for George, too, if needed. Are you ready?"

"Yes! I certainly am." With that, she left her cabin behind at last.

George jumped out onto deck, one boot half on, the other dangling from his teeth by its laces.

One of the sailors saw him and suppressed a grin. "Be orderly there, lad!" he said.

George grinned back and paused only long enough to finish putting on his boot before sprinting across the deck to the waiting boat. Maria breathed a deep sigh of relief.

"Come," Hyacinth told her. "We'll have proper beds and a good hot dinner tonight."

Captain Hotham came to help his wife down the ladder into the boat, and to bid Hyacinth a safe journey onwards. Hyacinth thanked him for his hospitality, and George, relieved to be in the open air again, thanked him too.

"I'm so sorry, Captain Hotham, for the trouble I caused you," he said.

The captain winked at him. "Just don't let it happen again."

"And Captain?" George said. "Would you please... please don't tell my father."

"I'll do my best," the captain promised, "as long as he doesn't catch wind of it through others, if you take my meaning."

"I do, Captain," George said. "Thank you."

The captain consulted with the second mate, said farewell to his wife for the evening, and then they were skimming across the harbor, bound for shore. Swarms of local navy boats had come out to meet the warships. It was different from the bay at Gibraltar. A dull, English city wrapped all around it and the steely dark clouds hung overhead. Hyacinth shivered.

"I wonder that Mr. Smithson didn't come to bid you farewell, Miss Grey," Mrs. Hotham remarked.

"He couldn't've come, ma'am," one of the sailors said. "He was off with the first boat."

"Was he so eager to get away from us then?" Mrs. Hotham tutted. "Oh well, I daresay he had important business to attend to."

"I'm sure he did," Hyacinth said. There had only been one boat set down when they first reached their mooring. Most of the sailors were needed to put the ship in order before the crew could go ashore, and it was a long row in to the docks. A piece of dull-colored seaweed floated by. She had said her farewells to him the night before, but now she wished she could have seen him one last time by daylight. She was sorry to see him go.

The oars lapped in and out of the water, punctuating the growing noise of the approaching shore, the calls of fishmongers on the docks, the noise of horses and dogs and so many men and women and children crowded together. By the time they reached shore, it was dark enough that the vendors and inns were lighting their lamps.

Maria and Hyacinth helped Mrs. Hotham to shore, their feet wobbly underneath them. George nearly fell over as he leaped out of the boat, and the sailors laughed at his clumsiness.

"You'll get your land legs by morning," one of them said.

George blushed.

"Come on," Hyacinth said. "If we old ladies can walk, you can, too." She looked around, trying to get her bearings, but in the dusk it was hard to see enough to get a true sense of the place, so huge, compared to the ship, and far bigger than the little outpost at Gibraltar, the only town she really knew.

"It is so good to be home again," Mrs. Hotham said, urging her on.

"Home again," Hyacinth said. "I will have to get to know it as if from nothing, even though I was born here."

"Were you born here in Portsmouth?" Mrs. Hotham asked. "I should have thought you would have told me a thing like that."

"I suppose it slipped my mind," Hyacinth said.

One of the sailors hailed a wagon to carry their trunks to the inn, and she was spared further conversation by the confusion of getting through the unfamiliar streets. Maria and George stuck to her skirts, afraid to get lost in the crowds. George did look very thin, Hyacinth thought, comparing him to a group of boys standing on a corner playing with marbles. She hoped he would recover quickly from his imprisonment in the cabin. The chill and damp of night closed in like walls, as if England would be just as confining as close quarters on a ship had been.

They arrived at the inn and were whisked up to Mrs. Hotham's suite by the innkeeper himself.

"Your dinner will be along shortly, ladies," he said. "If you have need of anything, the bell is here."

He was halfway out the door before Hyacinth realized he was going.

"Wait!" she said.

The innkeeper returned his attention to her impatiently.

"Could you please give us the directions to Mr. Portnoy's school?"

"Mr. Portnoy's?" the innkeeper knit his brow. "Surely you know! It's just across the square, here."

"Can I go tonight, Hy?" George chimed in.

"I..." Hyacinth stammered. "I'd hoped you would stay tonight, but I don't see why not, if they're still up and about."

"Oh, they will be," the innkeeper said. "It's early yet. The boys there usually have games after dark, this time of year. I hear them shouting at all hours."

"All hours?" Hyacinth said. "That doesn't sound very orderly."

The innkeeper shook his head. "They're as good a school as any, send boys up to Cambridge sometimes. Just out the front door, cross the square, can't miss it. Green shutters. Big old place, almost as big as my inn."

George was at the door.

"Eat your dinner with us, at least," Hyacinth said.

"He'll be fed well enough there," the innkeeper said. "I'll tell the kitchen to send dinner for three ladies, then."

With that, he left. George shouldered his bag and looked pleadingly at Maria, who sighed. Mrs. Hotham raised her eyebrows, then swept off into one of the suite's two small bedchambers. Hyacinth gave in.

"I suppose Maria and I can carry your trunk between us," she said.

"Be back in time for dinner," Mrs. Hotham called from the other room. "Captain Hotham says this inn has the best beef stew in Portsmouth." George hesitated for a moment at the mention of beef stew, but then he opened the door.

"Thank you, Mrs. Hotham, and tell the captain thank you again," George said, one foot in the hall.

"I will, dear," Mrs. Hotham said. "Off you go!"

CHAPTER 7: WINDCASTLE HOUSE

The moment Portsmouth came into view, over a month after they'd left Gibraltar, Thomas was possessed by a fevered desire to be on shore again, to face his family before he turned tail and jumped onto a ship for the Indies instead. He tried to put Miss Grey out of his mind. He half regretted leaving her without a final good-bye, but England was staring at him with its cold rainy eye, inspecting him and finding him a disgrace to his lineage. Miss Grey, Hyacinth, knew him as just a man, coming home from a successful foray into the subcontinent. She did not know him as an aristocrat, and he was glad of that. If she liked him at all, it wasn't for his family, or even his wealth.

What had he seen reflected in Sarita's eyes? He had no idea. The whole decade seemed a bit like a fevered dream against the rain and mud and the gathering dark around him. For now, he was just a man in an old, ill-fitting suit, on a voyage which could not end well. He would remember Sarita again someday.

The coachman barked at a cart blocking the road, jolting Thomas back to the present. He tried not to fall into the passenger beside him, an elderly gentleman who was somehow managing to snore despite the constant jerk and sway of the coach. England was just as he had left it: the stink, the shouting, the cold misty rain. Maybe the young ladies in London would manage to make him forget Hyacinth, standing at the stern of the ship, looking back at the watery road they traveled together.

❧

An hour before midnight, a hackney deposited Thomas and his two small trunks in front of Windcastle House, the ancient London residence of his extended family.

He hesitated at the gate. The house loomed, ghostly in the flickering lamplight. A few lights shone from inside, which was probably only a sign that some servants were about. With any luck, he would be the only member of the family there, and he could gather news from the servants before having to face his relations. With a little more luck, he would escape inheriting any cumbersome estates and walk away a free man. But he doubted it.

At least it wasn't the castle at Windcastle. Thomas wouldn't have liked to storm those gates at midnight. He walked across the street and rang.

A sleepy porter appeared moments later, keys clinking on a heavy iron ring. He regarded Thomas through the bars of the gate.

"May I help you, Sir?" The porter's tone communicated contempt. Thomas's trunks were mud-spattered, his cuffs ragged and dusty. He straightened his posture.

"Are any of the family in residence?" he asked.

The porter raised his eyebrows. "And who might you be, Sir?"

"Thomas Smithson Pently."

The man was clearly racking his brains, trying to ascertain where Thomas fit into the family, if at all.

"Algernon's son," Thomas clarified.

"His second son?" the man said, a note of panic creeping into his voice.

Thomas nodded.

"Pardon me for holding you up, Sir Pently! I'll ring for Mr. Jones right away!" He tugged the bell-pull twice, hurriedly, and dropped the keys in his attempt to unlock the gate. He finally got the key in and turned it, dropping into an apologetic bow as Thomas entered.

"I take it my father is still alive?" he asked.

The man sucked in his breath. "Oh, yes. Quite alive, I believe, though they say there was a fever last summer. Quite a fever."

"And Marquess Gravely?"

The man looked puzzled.

"My cousin Gregory," Thomas clarified.

The man shifted back and forth, then finally swallowed and answered. "Mr. Jones had... he had better tell you about it. I... "

"Never mind," Thomas said. "I've been this long without knowing, I can wait a few minutes more." He looked at the house and wondered what twists and turns it had in store for him. It would be a mercy for everyone but himself if Gregory, Marquess Gravely, had died. Gregory had been sickly all his young life, and his father had hated him for it, wishing aloud more than once that Georgina had been a son, instead of a useless daughter. She was headstrong, but she was strong in other ways, too, and her father had doted on her in his cold, angry way. Thomas might have asked the porter about Gregory again, but a flurry of movement from inside the great house drew his attention away.

"Your younger brother is in town," the porter said, clearing his throat. "Maybe he can tell you the rest."

The main door swung open, as if on cue, silhouetting a man with polished boots and a well-tailored coat that did not quite disguise the growing paunch at his middle.

"Harry! Where is my gig?" he slurred.

Thomas stood back.

"Sir, the groom will have it around directly," the porter said.

The man was frowning as if he was about to launch into a tirade about the porter's slowness when he spotted Thomas, where he stood at the base of the steps.

"And what poor relation of yours is this?" he demanded, looking askance at Thomas's tattered attire.

"He says that he is *your* brother, Sir." The porter shuffled his feet and looked over his shoulder to Thomas, who was starting to laugh.

"Good evening, Nate!" he said. "Are you drunk already?"

Nathan scratched his head as Thomas stepped forward into the light. "Thomas?" he said.

"The same," he confirmed.

"Whatever possessed you to grow all that muck on your face?" Nathan asked.

"Try shaving yourself on a sailing ship someday," Thomas said.

Nathan's gig, an extravagant, high construction, built for show as much as for speed, rolled into the courtyard. Nathan looked back and forth between it and his long lost brother, favoring the gig. "I didn't think you would come back," he said. He sounded put out.

Thomas shrugged. "I might not have, but Father's summons came and I was beginning to... let's just say it came at just the right time. He's still hale and hearty?"

"As much as I am," Nathan chuckled, "not that that's any great claim." He walked closer to Thomas and peered into his eyes. "He's old though. Tough, not like poor Gregory there."

"What happened?"

"Pneumonia, of course. What else? Least Richard had a hunting accident. Damned more manly way to go than in a sickbed all your life."

"So Father..."

"Is learning the ropes up at Windcastle, or will be as soon as he's well enough to travel. I'm s'posed to go there, too, but now you're here."

Thomas's heart sank.

"Don't look so cheerful, man. It's the richest estate in half of England!" Nathan said, squinting at Thomas's beard. "I was just about to step out to my club. Care to come along?"

Nathan's horse snorted and stomped on the cobblestones. The gig looked as if it would be even faster than the mail coach, and not much more comfortable.

"I've just come up from Portsmouth," Thomas said. "I thought I'd have a quiet drink here and collapse into a well-stuffed bed for the first time in a few months."

Nathan shook his head. "Shame, it's a very good club. I s'pose you can come another night?"

"I could," Thomas said.

Nathan paused, looking less than pleased. "Harry, be a good man and hold the horse there for a moment." He nodded to Thomas. "Come on in, then, Tom, if that really is who you are, and we'll have a drink here."

Thomas laughed. "I assure you, I am. And there's no need to stay to greet me if you don't want to. I'll still be here in the morning."

Nathan followed him into the grand entry hall, where lamplight cast its sallow glow on Nathan's face. He was recognizable, but when Thomas had left England, Nate was a boy of fifteen who scarcely needed his chin shaved. He'd always had a tendency to make mischief, without the wit or guile to get away with it. None of that seemed to have changed, nor had his taste for drink slackened any with age. He had the same blondish hair, a little darker now, or maybe it was the light, the same green eyes, a little bloodshot already, maybe from the previous night's outing. He'd grown into an indolent drunkard, a perfect model of the Pently family's men.

"You do look quite dark, I do say," Nate commented as they came inside. "I don't remember Tom being so dark."

Thomas sighed. "Of course I wasn't. I hadn't been four months on ships then, after a decade in the tropics. Even you would be darker after all that, if you weren't cooked outright."

"Sorry, old man," Nathan said. "I didn't mean it that way." He looked Thomas up and down. "You do look different, though."

"Well, you look a good bit different, too. Heavier, for one," Thomas said.

"I suppose I do," Nathan said. "Come on into the library," he invited. He tried the handle of a massive oak door, and, finding it locked, looked about for the man with the key.

"Where is that confounded Harry when I need him?" he said.

"Outside, holding your horse, I believe," Thomas said.

"Oh, confound it!" Nathan said. "I really didn't expect you tonight. I suppose I knew you were coming back sometime, since Jones mentioned that your trunks had arrived…"

"They're here, then?" Thomas said. "Well, that's one bit of good news."

Nathan stood awkwardly in front of the library doors, the massive house looming around them. Portraits and carpets lined long corridors stretching into the far reaches of the house. A light bobbed up from the servants' stairs.

"Look," Thomas said, "I'm sure the servants will be able to look after me tonight, and I'll see you at breakfast."

"Ha," Nathan said. "I don't breakfast. But tea. We'll have tea tomorrow." He was halfway out the door before he finished speaking, but hesitated there until the man carrying the light had bustled up the hallway and bowed to Thomas.

Mr. Samuel Jones was a bit greyer around the temples than when Thomas had last seen him, but his suit was as impeccable as ever, even at this late hour.

The butler smiled. "You return at last, Sir Thomas," he said.

"I was told I might have pressing business here," Thomas answered.

"I've called for a room to be prepared for you. Have you dined?"

"No," Thomas said, "but I won't want much. Bread, maybe."

"Bread?" Nathan snorted.

Jones looked enquiringly at Nathan. "Would you like it here in the library?"

"No," Thomas cut in. "Nate was just about to step out to his club, I believe."

Nathan nodded. "So I was. Good night, Mr. Jones, Tom." He nodded again to each of them and hurried to his gig.

Thomas tried to remember if he'd crossed swords with Nathan before he left, too. If he had, he'd forgotten it in the shadow of his quarrel with their father. He didn't expect a gushing welcome, but Nate had been nearly rude. No, he *had* been rude. But he was drunk. The morning would tell.

"Sir?" Mr. Jones said.

"Yes?"

"You must be very tired from your journey."

"I am," Thomas said. "And I'm sorry to have roused you from your rest."

"It's no trouble at all, I assure you," the butler said. "We're glad to have you back, Sir."

"It is quiet here, now," Thomas said.

"It always is, this time of year. We don't expect your father or the duke to return until the season, but now that you're here... Will you be going to Windcastle?"

Thomas considered his options. If he wanted to play the part of the dutiful son, it would be best to go straight up to Windcastle, but it was four days' journey in summer, likelier six at this time of year, and he could justify a week's rest in London. By that time it would be nearly Christmas, and by the time he reached Windcastle, his father and uncle could be on their way to London, depending on Parliament.

"I'll write them a letter in the morning," he said, "but for now, a good night's rest is all I can think of."

"Excellent. I'll show you to your room."

Thomas followed the butler up the once-familiar stairs to the second floor.

The butler paused at the top of the stairs and looked Thomas over. "Do you have a valet?" he asked.

"No, I come quite unencumbered," Thomas said.

"I will send one of the men to you in the morning, and help you to make more permanent arrangements. I'll have the tailor call before nuncheon, with your permission."

"I'm not up to standard, am I?" Thomas said.

The butler shrugged. "You can hardly have been expected to keep up in India, but you're back in London now."

"Yes," Thomas said, "I suppose I am." Jones would bring him

up to scratch, and make sure he had the attire to uphold the family name, even if he went and forgot all his manners, like Nate had. The thought of a few new suits of clothes did have some appeal, after living out of one small trunk for months.

He slumped onto the sofa in front of the fire and sipped a glass of port. By the time the butler returned from the kitchen with a platter of bread and cheese, Thomas was snoring, his barely-touched drink at his side.

❧

Aunt Celia's carriage collected Hyacinth and Maria late the next morning. They set off for Brighton after a quick farewell to Mrs. Hotham and a last glance in at Mr. Portnoy's school. The school was as promised; a decent establishment, clean but cheerful, and full of boys. George disappeared into their midst, emerging only for a quick goodbye. Mr. Portnoy proclaimed himself satisfied with George's intelligence and deportment and promised to send Hyacinth word if there was any need for her help, and to compel George to write to her fortnightly.

That was all. Hyacinth felt... empty. There was nothing for her to do. She didn't have to take care of George and she scarcely knew what would be expected of her at Aunt Celia's. Besides, Thomas was gone. She missed him. She shouldn't have, but she'd been kissed, if only that once. The other time, when she was younger, that hardly counted, now that she knew what a real kiss could be like, even if it did happen under cover of night, and for all the wrong reasons.

She watched the countryside roll by while Maria dozed beside her.

"It's so bleak, isn't it?" Hyacinth said, when Maria roused a little.

"It will be beautiful in springtime, Mrs. Hotham said," Maria mumbled, unconvinced.

They reached the outskirts of Brighton at early dusk. It was a smaller town that Portsmouth, but had more grand-looking houses than Hyacinth had ever seen all together.

The carriage drew up in front of a perfectly symmetrical brick house with gleaming white pilasters and an impeccably maintained front garden. The door swung open at their approach. By the time the coachman had set out a step for Hyacinth, Aunt Celia had emerged to greet her.

"My dear Hyacinth," she exclaimed as she rushed to the carriage. "How are you?" She paused to look Hyacinth up and down, narrowing her eyes slightly. "You've grown into a rather beautiful young lady, I see."

Hyacinth blushed and shook her head.

"You must be exhausted from your journey," Aunt Celia said.

Although she was widowed and near forty, Aunt Celia was still rosy-cheeked and ebullient, clad in a trim-fitting gown with a low neckline, even when at home for an evening. A very young lady in a pink gown trailed her, and it took Hyacinth a moment to realize that this was her cousin Sophie, who she'd last seen as a toddling baby.

"I confess I am a little tired, but we had a good rest at Portsmouth last night," Hyacinth said as Maria climbed down behind her.

"We?" Aunt Celia said.

"This is my maid, Maria," Hyacinth explained.

Aunt Celia frowned. "We may have a spare bed in the servant's quarters. Does she speak English?"

"I do, M'um," Maria said, curtsying awkwardly.

"Harold! Take the Spanish girl to the kitchens and have Mrs. Murphy find her a place to sleep." Maria glanced briefly at Aunt Celia then retreated with the servants. Harold, the coachman, shouldered her trunk and led her off without so much as a smile. Hyacinth looked after them until they rounded the corner of the house, then her attention was drawn back to the young lady in the pink gown, hovering behind her mother.

Celia allowed her daughter to step forward.

"Cousin Sophie!" Hyacinth said. "You've grown so much. I wouldn't have known you."

Sophie blushed. "I don't remember when you were here before, but I've heard so much about you that I am quite looking forward to getting to know you better."

"And I am glad to meet you again, too," Hyacinth said. "You're only a few years older than George, but you're certainly much more grown-up!"

"Who's George?" Sophie asked.

Aunt Celia froze, frowned, then glared at Hyacinth.

"Sophie," she said quietly, "would you please step inside and tell Mrs. Murphy that your cousin has arrived?"

"But she already knows that!" Sophie protested.

"Sophie!" Aunt Celia raised her eyebrows.

Sophie's shoulders slumped and she gave Hyacinth a timid smile before dragging her feet back up the steps and closing the door behind her.

Aunt Celia took Hyacinth by the arm and led her towards the house, one slow step at a time.

"My dear," she said, "you are always welcome in my house, and it is understandable that you would want to bring your maid along, but please do not mention that... boy. I'm afraid I cannot countenance it."

"He's your nephew," Hyacinth said.

Aunt Celia raised her left eyebrow again and shooed the servants away. "That is beside the point. He is none of my business."

"Well, he is mine," Hyacinth said. "Father charged me with the task of seeing George settled in a school here. I've been looking after him since his mother died four years ago."

Aunt Celia shook her head. "Well, maybe you have developed some attachment to him, but I simply can't have people talking about it. I have mentioned to several acquaintances that you are coming, and it was hard enough to distract them from the old scandals, not to mention your... mother's name, which is still remembered."

"I'm glad to hear it," Hyacinth said.

"You shouldn't be," Aunt Celia said with a frown. "You'll

see, if you're not careful, but I hope to shelter you from all that. It will be quite impossible if people, the right people, the people you ought to be on the best of terms with, learn that my brother's Spanish by-blow has come to roost in England."

"I'm sorry that you feel that way," Hyacinth said. Surely her aunt knew that half the men in the Navy, not to mention merchants and seamen, left children scattered around the globe, and it didn't seem to bother them in the slightest? Of course women, especially society women, were held to a different standard, but George was still her brother, and she cared more for him than she did for Society's opinion. Clearly, Aunt Celia had other ideas.

"I have only your best interests at heart, Hyacinth," Aunt Celia said. "I presume your father sent funds to provide for his by-blow?"

"For George. Yes, he did," Hyacinth said. "And it is a good school."

"Well." Aunt Celia hesitated at the door of the house. "Well, you had better just leave it at that, then, and do not mention the boy in polite society. Which includes my house."

"I suppose," Hyacinth said.

"Good." Aunt Celia took a deep breath. "Now, let's go in and prepare for supper. Mrs. Murphy will show you to your room and your maid will be along shortly, I'm sure," she said. She had a tone of voice which suggested a suspicion of all things foreign, especially foreign maids. Harold had re-appeared from the direction of the kitchen and picked up Hyacinth's trunk.

Hyacinth was halfway up the stairs when Aunt Celia called to her again.

"Oh, and dear?" she said cheerily. "There's a letter that came for you last week. I've left it on your table. A Mr. Butler. I hope you don't have an *understanding* with him. You have all the eligible bachelors in London still to meet. Wouldn't do to make your choice too soon!"

Mr. Butler? Hyacinth thought. Oh! Her grandmother's solicitor. She laughed, but fortunately Aunt Celia was already halfway down to the kitchen. She didn't need to reply to her aunt's concerns about Mr. Butler. Yet. Whatever he was, he certainly wasn't a suitor.

ঌ

The letter was a curt note asking her to send word once she had arrived in England, and saying that Mr. Butler would not be able to make the journey to Brighton to meet her, and could she come to London at her earliest convenience. Hyacinth wondered, for the first time since coming to shore, what her grandmother had left her, and why.

She had hardly even met her maternal grandmother. Although her grandmother had visited them often when she was an infant, she remembered nothing from those years in Portsmouth. Hyacinth's earliest memories were of playing beside her mother in their walled garden on Malta, with the bright sunshine bouncing off the whitewash and cheerful bougainvillea climbing up the walls.

There was one memory, though. It came from that summer she had spent with Aunt Celia, after her mother had died.

From the nursery window at the Talbot estate, Hyacinth saw a post-chaise drive in through the gates. A tall lady sat at the reigns, and a pair of grooms followed on horseback. It was a curious sight, so Hyacinth dropped her book and ran to the top of the stairs, where she could observe without being seen.

The butler opened the door.

"Please inform Lady Talbot that I am here to see my granddaughter," the woman said.

"I hardly think that would be a…" the butler stopped in mid-sentence. There was a long silence before Hyacinth heard his heels click down the corridor to the breakfast room.

She peered over the banister, but only managed to see the lady's purply-blue gown. Aunt Celia had been teaching her about fashion, and she could tell that it was exquisite, just the kind of thing Aunt Celia would praise, and yet the butler had been practically uncivil to the visitor. It was all quite curious.

At the sound of Aunt Celia's footsteps on the carpet below, Hyacinth darted back from the edge.

"I should think you would know better than to come here," Aunt Celia said, without preamble.

Hyacinth was shocked. She'd never heard Aunt Celia be so rude.

"I was merely passing," the woman said, her voice clear and calm. "I would like to see my granddaughter."

"Well. This is my house, and it's up to me to decide whom Hyacinth sees when she's in my charge. I hardly think it would be appropriate…"

Hyacinth's pulse thumped in her ears. She could hardly believe it. Was this her other grandmother, the one her mother had told her so much about? She froze for a moment, torn between fear of Aunt Celia's displeasure and curiosity. Curiosity won.

Hyacinth, who was small for her age but quick, dashed down the stairs and ran for the door.

"Hyacinth!" Aunt Celia screeched.

The other lady turned to Hyacinth and smiled as Aunt Celia reached out to restrain her niece. The visitor raised her eyebrows. Aunt Celia stepped back.

Hyacinth's Grandmother Miller was tall for a lady. She powdered her hair in the fashion of her youth, and she might have worn paint, but none that was obvious to Hyacinth's untutored eye.

"You are the image of your mother when she was a girl," the old lady said.

"But with her father's nose," Aunt Celia said coldly. "I beg you, leave at once! If you do not, I will have you bodily removed."

Grandmother Miller knelt down so that she was at eye level with Hyacinth. "I am glad that I have had a chance to see you, if only for a moment, but it appears I am not welcome to stay," she said. "Send my regards to your father. I hope we may meet again some day."

"So do I," Hyacinth said.

Grandmother Miller squeezed her hand and left without a word, taking up the reins and driving straight-backed away from the Talbot house.

Aunt Celia was in a high temper after that, but did not punish Hyacinth except to give her a stern warning:

"You will not speak of that woman again, not in this house, and above all not with my neighbors. Is that understood?"

Hyacinth had nodded, not understanding why her aunt's wrath was so dire. She was not prepared to face it again, not now, when she was only just setting foot in England.

≈

Hyacinth came down to supper feeling not at all at ease. Aunt Celia would not look kindly on her desire to discover her inheritance. Hyacinth was sure of it. She hoped, though, that her aunt would eventually see the sense in claiming it and putting it to good, charitable use, rather than letting it fester in a banker's vault.

Aunt Celia sat at the end of the table, keeping a sharp eye on every detail of the supper.

"Sophie, do sit up. Your posture is very important," she said, regarding her daughter coolly.

"Yes, Mother," Sophie said, fiddling with her napkin. She seemed like a very quiet girl, Hyacinth thought. Aunt Celia dominated the conversation with instructions to the younger ladies about fashion and the latest styles in London. She strayed from the topic only long enough to ask Hyacinth who this Mr. Butler was.

"Oh," Hyacinth said. "Just an acquaintance, a business associate of sorts."

"Business? Well, that won't do. But at least he's not a suitor. I think we can find a knight for you, or perhaps even a Sir Pently. A plain Mister just won't do. Unless he's very well-connected, of course. Is this Mr. Butler well-connected?" she asked.

"I'm afraid I have no idea," Hyacinth said.

Aunt Celia just shook her head. "I do think we should add some trim to that gown," she said to Sophie, and went back to talking about one dress and another.

In between courses, the evening post arrived. The butler laid it beside Aunt Celia's plate and she snatched it up immediately.

"Excellent!" she proclaimed. "Here's *The Lady's Magazine*. I'll see if there are any new styles here which would especially suit Hyacinth. I can have one of my old gowns made over to look very like this one here," she said. She turned the pages, searching for illustrations. She was so intent on the engravings that she didn't notice the letter underneath the magazine until her plate was removed. She squinted at it.

"Another letter for you!" she handed it to Hyacinth. "You are very much in demand already!"

Hyacinth glanced at the letter. "It's from Father," she said.

Aunt Celia frowned. "Well, that's not very thrilling, is it? You can open it later."

Hyacinth had already broken the seal. She glanced down. Like most of her father's dispatches, it was short and to the point.

"I'm sorry, I'm afraid I've read it already."

"That's Horatio," Aunt Celia sighed. "Too busy to take the time to write a proper letter."

"I don't mind," Hyacinth said. "It's just asking me to attend Admiral Nelson's funeral. It's to be held on the sixth of January at Saint Paul's."

Aunt Celia set down her fork and wove her fingers together for a moment, thinking.

"Yes," she said at last. "I had heard something about that. Admiral Nelson himself was hardly high ton, but everyone is talking about it, even here. It will be something of an event. Ordinarily, no one would be in Town at that time of year, but perhaps we should consider going. I hear that all of the right people will be there."

Sophie brightened at the mention of London.

"Oh, can we go, Mother?" she asked. "It is so quiet here.

There's hardly anything to do."

Aunt Celia favored her daughter with an indulgent smile. "Very well, dear, but you must promise not to ruin your eyes with too much reading from that lending library. Reading can ruin a girl's looks."

Hyacinth frowned. "I quite like reading, myself," she said.

"I do, too," Sophie said, "though Mother thinks it's dull. Have you read Shakespeare's sonnets, Cousin Hyacinth?"

"Of course I have," Hyacinth answered. "Which is your favorite?" The conversation turned to poetry for a few minutes, until Aunt Celia recovered the reins to discuss what color dress Hyacinth should wear, if they went to the funeral.

"Lilac could complement your eyes," she said, "with a little dark trim. Yes, that would do nicely."

"I don't believe I have a gown in that shade," Hyacinth said. "I prefer blue."

"Like that dark thing?" Aunt Celia said. "Of course that won't do. We will have to have gowns made for you, as soon as possible."

As they were pushing their chairs back from the table a little while later, Aunt Celia announced that she had made up her mind.

"We will travel to London just after Christmas," she said. "That will give us time to see Hyacinth fashionably attired for the event."

"But Aunt Celia," Hyacinth said, "it's a funeral. I hardly think I'll need to be dressed at the height of fashion."

"Nonsense," Aunt Celia said, "it will be your first appearance in London. Besides, the Admiral deserves to be sent off in style. Even if *all* the right people aren't there, *some* of them will be, and I insist that you make the most of it."

"Very well, Aunt," Hyacinth said. "I will defer to your judgment." *In matters of fashion only*, she added to herself.

❧

CHAPTER 8: THE FUNERAL

Mourning clothes," Thomas directed.

"Begging your pardon," Jones said, "but your brother has been gone nearly a year now, and you have responsibilities, as you know."

Thomas lifted the cup of coffee and stared into it. The gilded glory of Windcastle House's breakfast room brought back memories of the years before he'd sailed away, years when he'd been on the verge of becoming a fashionable gentleman, but was still stuck in boyhood. Mostly, though, it made him aware of his own travel-worn clothes. The butler, good old Mr. Jones, was treating him as if he were still a boy. Thomas didn't really mind. It was going to take him a while to get his land-legs.

"I haven't mourned Richard properly," he said.

The butler nodded.

"And there's Gregory."

"Marquess Gravely succumbed two months ago, and as dear as he was to all of us, he's only your cousin."

Thomas set his coffee down with a clatter.

"So his death makes me heir presumptive, is that it?" He did not want to be heir presumptive.

"No," the butler clarified, "that would be your father."

"My father is sixty if he's a day, and the duke hasn't fathered a child in twenty years."

"Certainly not a legitimate heir," the butler agreed. "Also, Marquess Gravely left a widow."

"Gregory married? He can't have been old enough." Thomas's cousin had been such a sickly boy that it was hard to imagine him fathering a child, though. Impossible, in fact.

"He did, and he was twenty-two," the butler said. "Also, you will note that there are men in your family who have lived past ninety, and the Duke is not yet in his grave. Your fate is not assured, not at all, Sir Pently."

Thomas frowned. The thought of his father or his uncle living on in bitterness until ancient old age didn't comfort him in the least. And had Mr. Jones just called him Richard? No.

"What was it you just called me?" he said.

"Sir Pently," Jones answered. "It's your title now. And you are likely to outlive your mother, so you'd best be prepared to be a Sir Pently, too."

Thomas stood up, took a piece of toast, and walked out of the room.

"And should your father inherit the duchy before he passes, you'll be Marquess Gravely."

Thomas cursed under his breath and thought longingly of the Factory in Trivandrum.

"The tailor will be here in an hour," Mr. Jones said.

"Tell him to bring black," Thomas said. "Lots of black cloth."

❧

"If Sophie likes, we can have a few new dresses made up for her, too," Aunt Celia said the next day. They had just chosen two of Aunt Celia's old dresses to have the Brighton dressmaker make over for Hyacinth, which would supplement her wardrobe until they reached London.

Sophie nodded dispiritedly. "I hardly ever get an opportunity to wear them out." She slumped back in her seat. "It is so awkward! There is nothing for me to do! I am too old for children's things and not old enough for balls."

"Aren't there some young people's socials?" Hyacinth asked.

"Oh, certainly," Aunt Celia answered, "but I never enjoyed them myself."

"Really?" Hyacinth said.

"Well, I was never pretty," Aunt Celia said, "not like my dear Sophie."

"But you're such a paragon of fashion," Hyacinth said. It was hard to imagine that her aunt could ever have been a wallflower.

"That's a different matter," Aunt Celia said. She was buxom and red-cheeked, but her nose was a little too long to be called pretty, and her teeth were crooked.

"No one notices, now," she continued. "A good dressmaker can cover a multitude of faults, and the right hairstyle takes care of most of the rest. And that is why we will be going to London immediately after Christmas."

With that, Aunt Celia swept out, leaving Hyacinth and Sophie to themselves.

"Sophie?" Hyacinth said. "Are you really looking forward to going to London?"

Sophie nodded vigorously, which made her curls shake. "Yes, very much so, it's just that mother thinks…"

"Thinks you ought to be more like her?" Hyacinth whispered.

"No… I don't know, something like that. But I do wish she…" Sophie shook her head and would not continue, despite an encouraging nod from Hyacinth.

"Does the town house have a very good library?" Hyacinth asked, changing the subject. The shelves of Aunt Celia's Brighton library were filled with dummy books.

Sophie nodded. "It's better than this one, and there's the lending library, too," she said.

"Well, when we're in London, I would also very much like to go to the lending library. I'll go with you, if you like."

Sophie's face lit up. When she smiled, her youthful awkwardness faded away and hinted at her future beauty.

"Would you really?" she said. "Oh, Hyacinth, I'm so glad you've come."

"And I'm glad I've come, too," Hyacinth said. It was not entirely the truth, but poor Sophie did look lonely, and she was glad that there was someone she could help, if only by finding her something to read.

In Gibraltar, Hyacinth had been almost entirely her own mistress, although she'd had many responsibilities. Her aunt treated her like a child. She was not a child, but for now, there was nothing to do but write to the solicitor to let him know that she had arrived in England, and to give him her London address.

❧

Thomas leaned back into the soft leather upholstery of an armchair at Nathan's club, a snifter of brandy in his hand. It was a week after Christmas, and he had hardly left Windcastle house, except to come to the club a few times.

"What's the matter, Mr. Smithson?" a voice said. "You've been sitting with that same glass half an hour and not tasted a drop."

"Have I?" Thomas looked up to see a familiar-looking man he couldn't quite place. Who had called him Mr. Smithson. Thomas lifted his glass and racked his brains.

"Don't you recognize me?" the man said.

"I'm afraid I don't," Thomas admitted.

"Frank Churchill, from Darjeeling," he said, and it all clicked into place.

"Darjeeling. Of course," Thomas said. He'd spent the past weeks trying to re-build his childhood memories of who was who, and Nathan had been making a sport of bringing him up to snuff on knowledge of clubs and gaming hells. He was thankful that at least Nate hadn't brought him to any brothels. Yet. India was a world away. "India has completely gone out of my mind," Thomas apologized.

"Sorry to hear that," Mr. Churchill said. "You were a good

negotiator." He took the chair opposite Thomas. Frank Churchill had been in the Subcontinent long before Thomas arrived. He was stationed in the north, so Thomas hadn't seen too much of him, but they'd corresponded on trade matters once or twice, and had met in Calcutta. Mr. Churchill had a reputation as an intelligent man who stepped on people's toes when he was drunk, which was often, but Thomas had never had any quarrel with him.

"Maybe with the natives I could talk my way around things," Thomas said, "but I found it harder going within the Company."

"Ah, we all have our failings," Mr. Churchill said, pouring himself a drink. "What's brought you back to London? Business or pleasure?"

"Family," Thomas said, finally taking a sip of his drink. It was better brandy than they'd been able to get in India, that much was sure. "And you?"

Mr. Churchill tilted his head. "It's all a bit of one thing and another. I take it you've left the company?"

Thomas didn't answer.

"So have I," Mr. Churchill said. "I'm starting a small enterprise. Would you be interested in joining in on it?"

"I don't buy stock in other men's companies, as a rule," Thomas said.

"No, that's not at all what I meant," Frank said, in a way that made Thomas think that it was exactly what he'd been after. "The thing is, I have big plans, and at the moment I'm working virtually alone, just a pair of clerks in my offices here and in Calcutta. What I could use is another man, a man with your experience, to run the home office while I trade in India. I just thought of it now, seeing you here. I was just having a hard time working out how I'd do it without a business partner here, a man who knew India as well as you do."

Thomas emptied his glass. It was a refreshing change to be seen as his old self. "I'll think about it," he said, "but the family has me quite bound up with one thing and another. I might even have to leave London for the hinterlands."

"That's a pity," Mr. Churchill said. "Think on it, though. I could do with a partner in this venture. Just think, Sikkim!"

Thomas had half stood up to go, but he sat down again. "You think they'll open to trade with you?" he said incredulously. "When the Company can't crack in?"

Mr. Churchill winked. "Ah, but I haven't stepped on their toes, haven't stolen their jewels."

"Surely they'll just see you as another Englishman?"

"Not at all," Mr. Churchill said. "You see, I've married one of their women."

Thomas's face fell. "Married. Actually married?" He had always thought it was impossible. Sarita was a Hindu, of sorts, and to marry outside of her religion would have been in some ways worse than carrying on the affair that they'd shared. It had not been marriage, though; it had been an arrangement. As fond as he'd been of Sarita, he hadn't found a way to actually marry her, which he might have been able to do, if he had truly tried. If Mr. Churchill had found a way, then it must have been possible. It was too late, now. But at least he and Sarita had been happy together, if only for a little while.

Either Mr. Churchill didn't notice the effect his pronouncement had had on Thomas, or else he chose to ignore it. He also didn't mention whether or not his wife had traveled with him to London. He wasn't sure why, but Thomas suspected that she hadn't.

"We were married three years ago. I'm surprised you didn't hear anything of it," Mr. Churchill said.

"No one saw fit to tell me." Thomas considered pouring himself another drink, but his mind was addled enough by his old colleague's pronouncement that he didn't want to blur it any more.

"It would have been harder if she'd been a Hindu," Mr. Churchill said, "but she is a Buddhist, a niece of the king of Sikkim."

"You are well-placed, then," Thomas said.

"But not so well-positioned in London," Frank said, standing to go. "Do consider my offer."

Thomas nodded noncommittally and they said their goodbyes. He sat frozen in his chair for a long moment after, then walked back to his new fate: Windcastle House.

&

A week after Christmas, Aunt Celia's household was packed off to her London residence. The new Earl Talbot had built a house for himself in fashionable Mayfair, but had agreed to let his uncle's widow maintain the family's old Elizabethan manse in Bloomsbury as a sort of second dower house. Celia had made it her own.

"I hardly ever go to my actual dower house," she said as they rolled into London. "It is such a dreary place. I don't know how I endured that area when Charles was alive."

Hyacinth made polite listening noises.

"I quite like it there," Sophie ventured timidly.

"Of course you would," Celia said. "You were a child there, and your aged father doted on you."

"I remember it a little," Hyacinth said. "At least in summer, it was very pretty. And although it might not have been as lively as London society, the children's parties were quite entertaining."

Sophie's face lit up. "Oh, yes, they were! I remember…"

Aunt Celia laid her hand on her daughter's arm. "They were very nice, dear, but in a few years, you'll be able to come to balls, and you'll never think of them again."

Sophie slumped back in her seat, and they rode on in silence until they came at last to the old London residence of the Talbots.

&

On the morning of the funeral, Maria helped Hyacinth into her new lilac dress. It fit around her shoulders and bosom like a finely made glove, and Aunt Celia insisted that its high waist and low neckline were the height of fashion, and not at all inappropriate for a funeral.

"You look beautiful," Maria said.

Hyacinth felt half-dressed, and pulled the shawl closer. Her hair was done up tidily, as she'd asked, but not fussed with for hours as Aunt Celia's would be. The dress had cost more than she'd imagined a dress could possibly cost, but Aunt Celia insisted that it was worth it. She'd been too busy getting her bearings to put up much resistance. She hadn't heard from the solicitor, and was starting to worry about it, but they had only been in London for a week.

"I suppose it will have to do," Hyacinth said, looking at herself in the mirror one last time.

"Don't worry so much," Maria said. "I don't think the Admiral would have lost sleep over the fashion in necklines."

Hyacinth smiled. "No, you're right, but... I will just use my shawl. Besides, the weather is quite cold."

A knock on Hyacinth's door summoned her to the front of the house. Half an hour later, they were riding up to the cathedral through throngs of traffic. Boats crowded the Thames so thickly that a man might walk across their decks from one bank to the other, or so it looked from the shore. There were merchant ships as well as Navy vessels, all coming to pay their tribute.

Hyacinth blinked back tears. Captain Grey was still tending his post in Gibraltar. She knew that there were others like him, all around the empire, but the masses around the cathedral made it look like the entire navy was assembled there. Hyacinth and Aunt Celia made their way to the cathedral doors and slipped in as the funeral began. Sophie had been left at home.

The speeches and the hymns rolled on, hour after hour. Hyacinth looked up at the domed ceiling, wondering if Admiral Nelson could hear them singing his praises. About halfway through the service, she started to look around her at the other mourners. Some of them, like her aunt, seemed to be only interested in seeing and being seen, but many genuinely mourned Admiral Nelson, too, she was sure. Far away, near the front of the cathedral, but to one side, Hyacinth spotted Emma, Lady Hamilton, the admiral's lover. The admiral's widow sat in the front pew, assiduously keeping her head turned so that she would not see the disreputable Lady Hamilton.

Hyacinth watched for a while as the two women sat, pointedly not looking at each other. She wondered if Lady Hamilton would speak to her after the funeral. She certainly wouldn't meet her in Aunt Celia's all-too-proper social circles. Hyacinth glanced to one side. Her aunt was batting her eyes at a gentleman in the row behind them – a gentleman with ice blue eyes and the remnants of a tan, except where his beard had been shaved off.

It took her a moment to recognize him. It was Mr. Smithson! Hyacinth literally bit her tongue to keep from shouting out his name.

"What are you doing here?" she hissed as the congregation began another hymn.

"The same thing you are, Miss Grey," he answered.

Aunt Celia shot her a withering look. "Do you know this gentleman?" she asked.

"Yes, he was also aboard the *Whistler*. Do *you* know him?"

Celia whispered in her ear, "I do not, yet. I find he reminds me of someone I once knew, that is all."

"I see," Hyacinth said. Who did Thomas remind her aunt of? She could hardly have known him as a child, and he'd been little more than that when he'd left England. Aunt Celia was much younger than Captain Grey, but not nearly as young as Thomas.

Hyacinth glanced back to Thomas, who smiled at her. He did look very different, as if he, too, had been pressed into the mold of fashion. He looked quite elegant, in fact, without a trace remaining of the ruffian she'd first seen on the shores of Gibraltar.

She forced herself to face forward until the recessional hymn began, when she turned again to see the coffin go by, with half of the navy's officers in its wake.

As the people in the pews started to shift towards the aisles,

Hyacinth attempted to excuse herself.

"I would like to go pay my respects to a lady I know from Gibraltar," she said to her aunt.

"What lady is that?" Aunt Celia asked distractedly, as she waved to an acquaintance.

"I don't believe you'd know her," Hyacinth said.

Aunt Celia turned to look at Mr. Smithson, who had edged towards the aisle. "And who is this acquaintance of yours?"

"Mr. Smithson," Hyacinth said. "He's been in India."

Aunt Celia frowned, and looked around the cathedral. She nodded to another lady and to a gentleman in a yellow waistcoat. "Well, I don't know how the carriage will make it through the crush," she said. "You may as well go. Meet me by the baptismal font in a little while."

"Certainly," Hyacinth agreed, glad that her aunt was distracted. She made her way into the side aisle, then started forward, away from the official receiving lines and towards a more informal gathering near the pulpit.

"May I accompany you?" asked a deep voice at her elbow.

Hyacinth startled and turned to face Mr. Smithson.

"I suppose you may," she said, "though I barely recognized you."

Mr. Smithson stroked the place where his beard had been and shrugged.

"I see that you have been to the tailor's, too," Hyacinth added.

Mr. Smithson nodded. "Our family butler was adamant that I not besmirch his image by appearing in my shipboard attire."

"My aunt has insisted on kitting me out in more gowns than I've owned in my entire life," Hyacinth said. "This one was sewn up on her orders, and I think she has a half dozen more at the modiste's."

"Well, the effect is stunning," Thomas said.

"Thank you. Your new clothing is also… becoming." She looked up at him and felt as if she were at sea all over again.

Thomas chuckled. "I hardly care how I look, really, but I suppose Mr. Jones would be pleased to hear it."

"You may pass on my compliments to him, then," Hyacinth said. "I take it that is your family butler?"

Thomas nodded, but said nothing as the crush made it necessary for them walk one behind the other.

"Are your family in London, then?" Hyacinth asked. She knew nothing about him, she realized, not in terms of who he was, or where he came from, even if they had touched once. Even if she might have glimpsed his soul.

Thomas waited a little too long before answering. "I... No. Most of them are still in the country. They'll be here for the Season, of course, at least, some of them will."

There was something not quite right in the way he talked about his family, Hyacinth thought. He was happy enough to talk about the butler, but why would the butler be in London if the family were in the country? And why hadn't he gone to see his family?

"Who exactly is it you're going to speak to?" he asked her.

"Lady Hamilton," Hyacinth said.

Thomas sucked in his breath. "I hardly think your father would approve."

"There, you are wrong. She has been very kind to me, and Father has no quarrel with her."

"She is not quite respectable," Thomas said.

"Respectability is more my aunt's concern," Hyacinth said, glancing back over her shoulder. Aunt Celia had disappeared into the throngs.

Thomas shook his head, and led Hyacinth around a cluster of young men. The detour took them into a relatively quiet alcove. Hyacinth took a deep breath. It was strange that Mr. Smithson had found her there, she thought, in the midst of all those thousands of mourners.

"Were you looking for me?" she asked abruptly, then wished that she hadn't. Thankfully, the alcove was dark enough to hide her blush.

Thomas tipped his head to one side and looked out at the crowds for a moment before responding. "Not consciously, no," he said, "but I have missed you, I think, and life on the *Whistler*, cramped as it was. The journey would have been tedious without you. As it was, I'm not at all sorry it took as long as it did."

Hyacinth nodded. "Without you there I would only have had embroidery with Mrs. Hotham, and George to tutor... well, no, I wouldn't have, would I, if you hadn't been there."

"How is young George?" Thomas asked.

"He's in a school in Portsmouth," Hyacinth said. "I had a short letter from him a few days ago."

Thomas nodded. "The only boys who wrote long letters home from school were the ones we bullied," he said, "the ones who were most unhappy."

"Do you think?" Hyacinth said. "Were you away at school much, as a boy?"

"Yes," Thomas said. He opened his mouth as if to say more, but then took Hyacinth's elbow and drew her back out into the crowded aisle.

The crush was beginning to thin. It was strange and unsettling to remember that she had kissed him, or maybe it was he that had kissed her. There in the quiet alcove, she had wished for it to happen again. It was hard to imagine all that had been real, and that this fashionable but guarded gentleman was the same person who had wept so openly over his lost mistress on that ship in the moonlight.

"Miss Grey?" he asked gently. "Are you all right?"

Hyacinth pulled herself together. They were in a public place and there was nothing between her and this man, nothing but friendship, and it wouldn't do to have people speculating about them when they had only just arrived in London.

"I am quite all right," Hyacinth said. "Merely a bit overwhelmed by the crowds. I think it would be best to move on. We've lingered enough."

Thomas took her arm again, and she felt his touch through

the thin silk of her gown. She tried not to think of it too much. She was going to share her condolences with Lady Hamilton, that was all that she was doing. Mr. Smithson was simply a friend.

&

Thomas found Lady Hamilton's reputation for charm and beauty more than justified, even though she was no longer lithe or young. She seemed scarcely touched by the condolences offered to her. Considering it coldly, a man might think it was because she despaired of finding another protector as generous as Nelson, but Thomas hoped that she had genuinely loved him.

She also seemed fond of Hyacinth, who expressed sympathy for the courtesan, without worrying at all what people might think. If Captain Grey thought that the Pently clan, with its wealth and ancient lineage, was a den of vipers to be avoided, and yet he didn't mind his daughter speaking with a known woman of the demimonde, then he did march to a different drummer. So did Hyacinth. She seemed to steer herself by an almost masculine code of conduct, and yet it was charming. Perhaps it was because she had lost her mother at such a young age, and her father had raised her himself, and her father was possibly as different from his father as a man could be, based on his brief impressions.

"Thank you, Hyacinth," Lady Hamilton was saying. "You are always so gracious. It has been a delight knowing you."

"But surely we'll meet again," Hyacinth said. "I wanted to ask your advice. About a school. I'm thinking of starting a school for girls."

"I'm afraid I'm going to have to retire to the country, dear," Lady Hamilton said. "I don't know a thing about schools."

Hyacinth wanted to say more, he could tell, but there was a man tugging at Lady Hamilton's sleeve.

"Best wishes to you, and to your gentleman there," Lady Hamilton said, nodding to him.

Hyacinth blushed. Lord Nelson's famous mistress had

already turned to speak to another of her sympathizers.

"Come," Thomas said. "We should be moving along." He scanned the emptying cathedral for people he might still recognize from his youth. Although he'd been in London for over a month, he hadn't ventured out much beyond Nathan's club and a gaming hell or two. Nor had he gone to Windcastle. He was getting his bearings by sleeping more than he had in years, and by spending most of his days in the library of Windcastle House.

"Look!" Hyacinth tugged on his arm. "It's Captain Hotham!"

"Why, so it is!" Thomas smiled and waved at the man, who returned the greeting with ebullient enthusiasm, even though they were at a funeral.

"Miss Grey! Mr. Smithson!" Captain Hotham exclaimed. "Such a delight to see you both again." The captain looked as if he'd been drinking, more than he ever had on their journey together.

"How is Mrs. Hotham?" Hyacinth asked. Her hand tightened its grip on Thomas's arm – he hadn't realized how lightly her hand had rested there before.

The captain beamed, his cheeks rosy and shining, eyes twinkling. "She's in fine fiddle, so say the letters. And so is our son!"

"Congratulations!" Thomas clapped him on the back. "That is indeed good news."

"How wonderful!" Hyacinth said. "I must write to her immediately."

"I won't be able to carry the letter for you unless you write very quickly indeed," the captain said. "There's a stagecoach on its way west in half an hour, and I'm going to get on it."

"Send my regards to her," Hyacinth said. "I'll post a letter by tomorrow morning at the latest. It is so good to hear such happy news, even on this occasion."

"Yes, most of all for myself!" the captain said. "And now I'm away!" He hurried off, calling out to friends of his as he shouldered his way to the doors.

Thomas felt an odd tightness in his chest, watching the man go, like envy, or regret. He once could have had a son, too. He tried to imagine what that child might have looked like, impossible as his existence had become.

"I'm sorry," he said to Hyacinth, once he realized how long he'd been standing there, staring into nothingness. "I should see you to your rendezvous point."

She gave him a quizzical look. "Aren't you happy for him?"

"Happy?" Thomas said. "I am, I suppose. It's only..."

She put her arm on his hand. "Never mind. I'm sure he didn't notice. And your demeanor is appropriate for a funeral."

She was annoyed with him, but he was annoyed with himself, too, so much so that he couldn't muster an apology for his glum mood until they were almost to the back of the cathedral.

"I'm sorry I was so distracted," he said at last.

"It doesn't matter," Hyacinth said.

He desperately wanted to talk of something else, anything else, but he was hard pressed to think of anything. They'd reached the last pews by the time he thought of something to say, however inane.

"How have you passed your time here?" he asked.

"My aunt has kept me occupied with modistes and social calls, morning, noon and night," she sighed. "There's my cousin Sophie, too, who is only twelve. We embroider together a bit."

"And that is all?"

"No. I mean, that shouldn't be all. My grandmother left me an inheritance. I'm supposed to be claiming it, looking after it. I mean to start a school for girls."

"Ah. Yes. You mentioned something like that to Lady Hamilton," he said, trying to puzzle it out. "She's hardly headmistress material."

Hyacinth laughed. "Oh, no. It's just that it's... I thought... for girls, you know, who are in her situation. The situation she was in, as a girl. They could have an education. Become governesses or housekeepers, instead of..." She shook her head.

Thomas nodded. "That's ambitious. But why?"

"Because I think it would be the right thing to do with my inheritance."

"I see," Thomas said. "I suppose there's nothing to stop you."

"There is, though," Hyacinth sighed. "Aunt Celia wouldn't approve, and it's hard to get around her. I'm her guest, after all."

Thomas smiled. "Not her prisoner."

"Prisoner to her marriage schemes, maybe."

Hyacinth abruptly let go of his arm.

"I shouldn't have said that. It was ungrateful of me."

Thomas shrugged. "My family will have schemes for me, too. It's only natural to resent them."

"Is it?" Hyacinth asked.

"I think so," Thomas said. "But I can help. I mean, if you need any help, just let me know."

"But how will I find you?" Hyacinth asked.

Before Thomas could answer, the baptismal font came into view. There was Hyacinth's aunt, gossiping loudly with a woman about Thomas's age, a woman who could only be, by her green eyes and sharp looks, his own cousin, Georgiana. According to Mr. Jones, she was still unmarried despite better-than-ordinary looks and substantial property of her own near Windcastle.

"Thomas!" she called across the crowds. "I knew you at once by your terrible tan! Mr. Jones told me all about it. Are you acquainted with Lady Talbot?"

"Lady Georgiana," he said, ignoring Hyacinth's aunt for the moment. "So good to see you again. I believe I was seated behind Lady Talbot, but we weren't properly introduced."

"We certainly were, Mr. Smithson." Lady Talbot's lip curled momentarily into something like a snarl, but she turned her expression into a simper and a wink, so smoothly that most would not have noticed her momentary hostility.

"Mr. Smithson!" Georgiana laughed. She chortled so loudly, in fact, that people turned to look. "Surely... Why on earth were you using *that* name, Thomas?"

Thomas stiffened. Hyacinth pulled away, going to her aunt's side.

"It was the name I used in India, and on my way home."

"Well," Georgiana said, "Let me introduce you properly, then. This, Lady Talbot, is my long-lost cousin, Sir Pently, whose father is now heir presumptive to my father."

"Oh, my," Lady Talbot said stiffly. "I am pleased to make your acquaintance, Sir Pently."

Hyacinth looked puzzled.

"Miss Grey..." he started.

Georgiana cut him off. "And Lady Talbot, I have not yet been introduced to this young lady."

"This is my niece, Miss Hyacinth Grey," said Lady Talbot. "Hyacinth, may I present Lady Georgiana Pently."

"Delighted to meet you, Lady Pently." Hyacinth curtsied, ignoring Thomas.

"Miss Grey and I were aboard the same ship from Gibraltar," he explained to Georgiana.

"Oh, I see," Georgiana said. Thomas could practically see the wheels in her head turn as she calculated all the interrelationships. "Your brother's daughter?" she asked Lady Talbot.

"Yes," Lady Talbot said. "She is Horatio's only child."

Hyacinth's frown deepened into a scowl, then she remembered herself and plastered an insipid smile onto her face. Georgiana didn't seem to notice.

"Welcome to London, Miss Grey," Georgiana said. "I hope you will enjoy it here, even though we can't offer you much sunlight this time of year. I trust that at least some of our festivities will lighten the gloom. I'll be hosting a small soirée on Tuesday. I do hope you'll be able to attend, Miss Grey, and you too, Lady Talbot."

"We would be delighted," Lady Talbot answered for both of them. "And now I'm afraid we must go. My coach should be waiting. Do call some time!" She said the words to Georgiana, but she batted her eyelashes at Thomas as she turned away.

Thomas ignored the gesture. He found it distasteful, for some reason. It was as if she'd been deliberately needling Hyacinth.

"Goodbye, Miss Grey," he said composedly.

"Goodbye… Sir Pently," she said, turning away as quickly as she could.

"Will we see you at the soirée?" Lady Talbot called back to him.

"I don't know," Thomas said. "I haven't been invited yet, have I, Georgiana?"

Lady Talbot rolled her eyes. "How old-fashioned of you!" She did look better than most women her age. He had heard of her sort when he was young, widows angling for affairs with young men, but it was the first time he'd encountered one of these mythic creatures in the flesh, as a man. He preferred gaming hells – at least no one there pretended to be respectable.

He wished, for Hyacinth's sake, that her aunt were kinder, but he could hardly recommend his own family as better. Nathan had no hold over him, but that was his only redeeming quality. Still, he had always liked Georgiana when they were children. He hoped that she had not fallen so miserably into the old family vices as Nathan had.

"Thomas?" Georgiana said. Her voice reminded him that he would have to talk to all of them soon. "You seem quite taken with Countess Talbot. Or is it Miss Grey?"

Thomas shook his head. "Neither, actually, but they must have a very good dressmaker."

"Oh, they do!" Georgiana gasped. "And Lady Talbot won't give me the name. It's infuriating. If you could ferret out that information I would be *most* appreciative."

Thomas watched them walk down the steps of the cathedral. Hyacinth cast one last, frowning glance back at him, and then they were swallowed by the crowds. She was no more pleased with his family connections than her father had been, or maybe it was something else. Thomas turned his attention back to his cousin.

"I don't know that I could do that," he said, "if it's such a close secret that even you can't reach it."

"Nonsense, of course you can find it out. I remember that you were always quite persuasive."

Thomas laughed. He had gotten into a fair few places he wasn't allowed when he was younger. "That was when I was a boy," he said. "I save my energies for other things these days."

"Such as lingering around the library?" Georgiana said. "Or walking to Nathan's club and back, and only staying for one round of cards?"

"I usually win that round, though," Thomas said. "I see you've been gossiping the servants."

"Well of course I have!" Georgiana said. "It's been a very long time since we've seen you, and I've heard only the vaguest of rumors. You never wrote to anyone!"

"No one ever wrote to me," Thomas said.

"Nonsense. Nathan told me that he wrote you at least twice, and that your replies were most unsatisfactory."

"He was a prying pest of a younger brother when I left," Thomas said, taking Georgiana's arm and leading her towards the line of coaches. Men and women wandered out with them in groups and pairs, forming a slow-moving tide on the square in front of the cathedral.

"But is he not much improved now?" Georgiana said.

She was joking, of course. He'd forgotten that about her, always with a sharp word about those who left themselves open to her barbs.

"Well, I don't think he'd go telling tales of me to Father any more, but that's the best I can say for him."

Georgiana sighed. "I'm afraid that Uncle Algernon was never pleased with any of you boys."

"Except Richard," Thomas added. Everyone had loved Richard. "I should have been here," he said.

"For what?" Georgiana said.

"Richard's funeral, or before that. I am sorry I never saw him again."

"Have you met Elizabeth?" she asked.

"His wife? No."

"But of course you wouldn't have. You haven't deigned to come up to the country."

"I hardly think it necessary. Everyone would be here by the time I reached Windcastle."

"But you might inherit the duchy!" Georgiana said.

"Mr. Jones says that my father is in fine fettle, so I won't even be a Sir Pently anytime soon. I don't even like being Sir Pently. I might yet disappear back into the depths of Asia and leave it all to Nate to ruin at his leisure."

"You couldn't!" Georgiana said.

"I could," he said, as if he were joking, although he wasn't.

Georgiana laughed. "Has the east curdled your mind, 'Mr. Smithson'? You used to have such a good one. I don't believe you could live with yourself."

"I could drown myself in blissful ignorance," Thomas said. "Or start meditating under banyan trees."

Georgiana laughed. They had reached the line of coaches, and Thomas spotted one with the Windcastle coat of arms.

"You brought the coach?" he said to his cousin.

"Of course," Georgiana replied. "Why didn't you summon it yourself?"

"I was rather in the mood to walk, and besides, I didn't even know you were in London."

Georgiana sighed. "I think you will reach the house before me, if you walk back now."

Thomas agreed. "Shall I walk back, then? Would you rather not have the black sheep of the family in your coach?"

Georgina threw up her hands. "You are not the black sheep at all these days! I tell you, Nathan has that role firmly in hand."

"Then what am I?" Thomas asked.

"We don't know what to make of you," Georgiana said. "You've been away a long time. We hardly know you anymore."

"Can I be the black sheep again?" Thomas asked.

"Really!" Georgiana let Thomas hand her up into the

carriage. "I won't answer that. Will you ride back with me?" she asked.

The carriage in front of them had started to move forward, but it stopped again, started, stopped, creeping away from the steps.

"No, I'll walk back," Thomas said. "You could, too. It's only a mile."

"I think not," she said. "I have your dubious status to mull over, and I have a special affection for this dress. It's muddy today, as it always is. Do be a gentleman, though, and run along home to tell them I'll be back soon, and that I'm famished!"

Thomas bowed, a teasing glint in his eye. "Always pleased to fulfill an unladylike request," he said.

Georgiana swatted him with her fan. "Go on then! I'll see you there, and they'd better have the tea ready."

She closed the carriage door in his face and tapped on the ceiling. The driver nodded to Thomas, and they rolled off at a snail's pace into the London traffic.

Walking through the ebbing crowds, Thomas supposed that his family weren't all bad, but most of them were, most of the time. He'd almost forgotten about Georgiana in his years in India. She'd been a hellion in their youth, and from what he could see so far, she hadn't changed. In her case, that was just as well. Most of his family were high-handed wastrels or bitter, miserly old men and had remained so if Nathan were any indication. Thomas only hoped that his father and uncle would stay away from London for a while longer.

❧

CHAPTER 9: GRANDMOTHER MILLER'S STORY

The carriage moved so slowly that Hyacinth wished she'd gotten out and walked. Better to get lost in the city and be robbed blind by footpads than to stare across at her scowling aunt for another hour. Her toes went numb. The air in the carriage was stale. When her aunt's house finally came into view, she blurted out one of the many questions she'd been pondering.

"Why does Father dislike the Pentlys?"

Aunt Celia bared her teeth like a cornered cat. "I don't think that dislike is a strong enough word for how we feel about the Pentlys," she said. "I am shocked, but not entirely surprised, that you took up with that one."

"I did not 'take up' with him!" Hyacinth said. "Mr. Smithson, or Sir Pently, or whoever he is. He and I were shipmates on a long and tedious voyage. That is all."

Her aunt frowned more deeply, skepticism etching lines around her eyes.

"Besides," Hyacinth noted, "you seemed quite friendly with Lady Georgiana."

"That's different," said Aunt Celia. "She's a *Lady*. The men in that family are to be avoided at all costs." The carriage halted, and the coachman opened the door.

"We're here," Aunt Celia said. She lunged to the carriage door, but hesitated there.

"You will not mention them again," she said.

"Very well," Hyacinth said.

"But of course we will go to Lady Georgiana's soirée."

"But of course," Hyacinth echoed, as if that made any sense at all.

Her aunt stepped briskly up to the door, shutting out any further possibility of conversation. Hyacinth followed slowly, slowly enough that Maria appeared at the door, looking worried.

"Come inside, Miss! It is raining," Maria said.

The mist was, in fact, starting to turn to rain, but she'd hardly noticed. Maria looked at something behind Hyacinth, and her expression brightened. Hyacinth turned to see what it was. Harold the coachman ducked his head and wiped his mouth, an embarrassed gesture. When she turned back to the door, Maria was blushing.

She might have asked Maria about it, just a little, but when she got inside, something else commanded her attention.

"Hyacinth," Aunt Celia said, "you must send this back. At once." She held out a small package, at arm's length. It was wrapped in brown paper, and bore the handwriting of Mr. Butler, her grandmother's solicitor.

"You may say that this Mr. Butler is not a suitor, like that... other man you spoke with at the funeral, but this appears to be a gift, and men only send gifts to women they are courting."

Hyacinth took the package from her aunt. "I've never even met him," she fumed. "The notion that he's courting me is preposterous."

"Nonsense. You are quite innocent of the ways of men," she said. "Your father may have meant well, I don't know, but his unconventional views will not help you in courtship. You must send this package back."

Hyacinth glimpsed a small motion, a bit of pink ruffle through the gap at the bottom of the parlor door.

"That is my final word. We will have tea now." Aunt Celia

swept into the parlor. The bit of pink ruffle jumped away – Hyacinth hoped that Sophie had managed to compose herself before her mother noticed that she'd been eavesdropping.

"It must be only papers," Hyacinth said, handing the package reluctantly to Maria.

"What will I do with them?" Maria asked. "Will I send them back?"

Aunt Celia re-appeared at the parlor door.

"Send them back *immediately*," she said.

Hyacinth mouthed, "No." She hoped that Maria saw her, as she curtsied to Aunt Celia.

"How?" Maria asked Aunt Celia.

"Harold will take care of it," Aunt Celia said. "Take it to the stables. And send word with that package that I will not have any more such letters delivered to my niece." She waved Maria away and pulled Hyacinth into the parlor.

"Now," Aunt Celia said, sitting down on her favorite settee and smoothing her skirts, "we must get to work."

"To work, Mama?" Sophie said. She had positioned herself near the window, and had a far-away look, as if she were listening for a very faint sound in the distance.

Aunt Celia cast her a pitying smile. "Sophie dear, your cousin Hyacinth seems to have attracted two suitors without my help."

"Two suitors!" Sophie exclaimed.

"They are not suitors," Hyacinth protested.

"Of course, they are both entirely inappropriate," Aunt Celia said, ignoring both of them. "We must find her some more suitable young gentlemen." She turned to her daughter. "Sophie, bring me my writing things. I believe I will be able to arrange a few fortuitous meetings."

Hyacinth fumed, but held her peace. The tea came, and as they sipped it, Aunt Celia prattled about one young gentleman and another whose mamas she knew, and whose families were well-connected. She had not even met most of the young gentlemen themselves.

*

When Hyacinth at last retreated to her room, she had a headache. A small one. She wanted to climb into bed and stay there until morning. The thought of facing her aunt over dinner nearly turned her stomach, and the revelation that Mr. Smithson was not who he'd pretended to be twisted her mind into knots. He'd hinted that he didn't relish the thought of returning to his family, but he hadn't said that they were aristocrats. She'd thought that they might have been tradesmen, or even landed gentry. If his family were so powerful, as well as somehow vile to both Mr. Smithson... no, Sir Pently, and her own relations, then perhaps he'd needed to go to the far side of the world to escape them, but he'd *lied* to her, by omission, at least. He wasn't honest.

She flopped on the bed for a moment and let it all whirl around her. She must not sulk, she reminded herself. She would not allow her aunt's schemes to drive her into a full retreat. Besides, there was Sophie to consider. Sophie had seemed quite delighted with the parade of young men to be presented in the coming days, and it was so rare to see her brighten up.

Hyacinth sat up and began to compose herself. She looked around for something to read, but the upstairs maid had taken the book she'd borrowed back to the house's library, enforcing her aunt's absurd idea that reading could ruin a girl's looks, as if her looks were any good to her now. She glanced at the reflection of her tear-stained face, then threw a shawl over the mirror. Retrieving the book would mean going back downstairs. Perhaps she would write a letter to George. It would be good to see him again, perhaps before his school's new term began.

She sat, pen in hand, blank paper in front of her, for a long time. What could she say to George? He wouldn't be allowed to visit Aunt Celia's house, and she wouldn't be allowed to travel so far alone, or even with Maria, to visit him. She missed him. His letters weren't reassurance enough. She had gotten as far as, "My dear Brother," when she heard a light tap at the door, and

Maria slipped in.

"I have it," Maria whispered. She blushed. "Harold rode to pretend to take it back, but I convince him that you should have it." She produced the package from the folds of her skirt.

"Oh, thank you!" Hyacinth sprang up and hugged Maria. "Thank you. I don't know how you did it."

Maria shrugged, then put her finger to her lips.

"You're right, we should be quiet," Hyacinth said. "I wonder what it is."

"A book?" Maria suggested.

Hyacinth turned the package over in her hands. It certainly felt like a book. "But why?" she wondered aloud.

"Open it and see?" Maria said.

Hyacinth set it down on her writing desk. "I will," she said, "but I have another puzzle to work out, too. I would like to see George."

"Oh, that boy!" Maria sniffed and shook her head. "So would I. It is dull without him. Who knows what mischief he makes at that school?"

"Perhaps he could come to London for a visit before the Lent term begins, but Aunt Celia has made it clear to me that he would not be welcome in the house," Hyacinth said. "I have no idea where to begin."

"I..." Maria thought for a moment. "I will ask Harold."

"Yes," Hyacinth smiled, "if he is willing, and doesn't mind... I shouldn't encourage him to be disloyal."

"He will still do his work," Maria said. "It will be fine." With that, Maria went back to the stables, fairly skipping away to the servants' stair.

Hyacinth sighed. At least Maria was happy and courting, already. She felt the package in her hands, turned it over, and cracked the seal. Inside, she found a small volume, bound in worn green leather with a fading gilt *fleur de lis* pattern on the spine. She ran her hands gently over it.

A letter fell to the floor. She picked it up and read it quickly.

Miss Grey:

Pardon my slow reply. I have only just returned from the country. I trust you are in good health. I will be at Lincoln's Inn every day but Sunday, and I look forward to meeting you there at your earliest convenience.

In the meantime, you may wish to get better acquainted with your grandmother. Enclosed is a journal she kept in her later years, in which she might have communicated some of her wishes and intentions. I have not read it myself, as she wished it to be passed on to you alone, along with her properties.

Sincerely,

John Butler, Esq.

Hyacinth looked at the book again. It fit neatly in her hand, and was small enough to tuck into a reticule. She could take it with her anywhere. Perhaps she would.

The bell rang for dinner. Hyacinth hid the book in her desk, straightened her skirts, and went downstairs to dine.

࿔

That night, Hyacinth lit a candle by her bedside and began to read. Her grandmother's hand was clear and decisive, but she wrote in French, which Hyacinth did not know quite as well as her Spanish, Latin, and Greek. She read slowly, puzzling out some words via their Latin cousins.

I suppose that I could write in English, now that there is no one left to pry, no one but my own servants and tenants, who would never dare broach my sanctuary, but the French language is my old friend, and I would miss it if I abandoned it after so long together. I was so young, when I first arrived in Paris, and at first, I hated it. I do not know who will read this. I do not know if I have anyone left. Violet, my dear Violet, is gone, and her daughter is little more than a child, though older than I was when I considered myself a woman.

Ach, I had hoped for a quiet hour, but a carriage has arrived, one of the neighbors come calling, with no notion of who I am, or who I have been.

Hyacinth skipped to the next entry.

The roses are coming into bloom in the garden below. Bereford gave me yellow roses on the night we met, and a rose-covered cottage five long, trying years later. I always wondered when he would abandon me. I saved every penny I could pinch. Until... well, that was all long ago, now, and it was gentler than those early years in Paris.

I knew so little when I arrived that I wonder how I came so far. It was only chance, a chance I cursed at first. It is strange to think of it after so long. I must be growing old at last, or allowing myself to think like an old woman, which I never could do until last summer.

I loved Bereford at times, but I was always anxious to please, always at the ready, waiting for him. After he died, I mourned, and I let myself go. Madam had always warned me against letting myself go. I think she must be in the grave, too, if there is any justice in the world. She was not a young woman when she found me.

I am running all out of order. I should start at the beginning, as if this will be my memoir. I was born in H--shire. My father was a laborer on a large estate, and my mother was from the town. They had five more children, after I was born. Two died in infancy, and the last was sickly, so sickly that they took him to see a physician who demanded fees they could not dream of paying. Until I returned, I had always hoped that he lived, and wondered if there were more children, after I was sent away.

I was twelve years old and a woman by some people's reckoning, by my own estimate at the time, as well. Looking back, I can see that I was only a child. I heard hushed voices below when I was supposed to be sleeping. The next night, a man came, a merchant, who said that his wife needed a girl to help her.

They sent

I woke the next morning in the alley behind the apartment, my face swollen with bruises. I tried the door, but he had taken my key. I did find a small sack of coins tucked into my bodice. Perhaps he felt some remorse. I do not know.

I waited for three days, but he never returned to the apartment, and I gave up. I spoke only a little French. I did not know what I would do, how I would survive. I begged for employment at restaurants and cafes, and, at last, at the theater. Seeing my battered face, they turned me away, but I came back every day, asking only to sweep the floors and be given a place to rest and a bit of bread in return. That is where Madam found me.

I am tired, even thinking of it, of those years. Madam saw me at the theater. She tested me, tormented me, then she took me under her wing. When she discovered that my misadventures had left me without the usual diseases of my profession, she brought me into her house, and spent years preparing me to pass as a lady of breeding, to be auctioned off to the highest bidder.

Those were happy years, nearly six long, well-fed years in the best brothel in Paris, but I know that Madam got her money's worth for me in the end.

me away with him, believing that I would be a maid of all work in a merchant's house, but no sooner had we arrived in his house, in the town, than he announced that he was going to Paris to purchase porcelain for his shop. His wife ranted at him, and he laughed in her face, slapped her, and bundled me into a wagon in the dead of night.

He did not ill-use me at first. He might have wished to keep me on as a mistress, but he must have feared his wife. I traveled all the way to Paris in the back of that wagon and on a ship and in other wagons, following at his heels, playing the part of maid and mistress to him and crying all the while for my lost home. He said that he would be pleased with me, if only I would stop my sniveling. I only cried the more. I could not help myself. That is what I mean when I say that I was only a child, then.

The merchant, my first master, was decent sometimes, but he had fits of rage when he gambled and lost, or when he drank too much, as many men do. We had been three months in Paris when he went out one night, leaving me alone in the small apartment with the boxed porcelains and imitation jewelry he had bought for his Hereford shop.

He returned, purple in the face from drink and shouting...

Hyacinth shut the book and gathered her breath. Her grandmother's youth had been a horror. She could hardly face it, but she knew that Grandmother Miller had survived it, and come to prosper. She steeled herself to read on.

Hyacinth could not bear to read more, not yet. She closed her grandmother's diary and hid it again. She snuffed the candle and lay down to sleep, with the dark story of her grandmother's life turning in her mind. She would redeem that memory. She would. Somehow, she would redeem all that suffering.

❦

She woke in the morning determined to visit Mr. Butler at once, but Aunt Celia announced that they would go to ride in Hyde Park immediately after breakfast.

"But Aunt Celia," Hyacinth said, "I hardly ride at all."

"All the more reason," Aunt Celia said briskly. "You'll learn, and it will stand you in good stead. Besides, I've already ordered riding horses from the livery stable."

Hyacinth sighed. She would try again in the afternoon.

Hyacinth enjoyed the ride, despite herself. It was a rare, sunny morning, and the park was quite beautiful. Her aunt introduced her to one lady after another: mamas, she said, of suitable gentlemen, and in some cases their sisters. Their grey-haired sisters.

Long before they turned their horses back towards Bloomsbury, Hyacinth had lost track of who was who and whose son was a Sir Pently and whose brother was a knight, never mind their names. On the way back to Aunt Celia's house, she looked at the streets, long rows of brick buildings without an inch between them. It was all very different from Gibraltar. Here and there, she saw signs, indicating the names of the streets. Idly, possibly just because they were something to read, she started looking at them. And then she saw it, a small, unassuming sign on the side of a building.

"Lincoln's Inn Field," it announced. Hyacinth sucked in her breath. Over the heads of the crowd, she could just see the field.

"Are you all right, Hyacinth?" her aunt asked.

"Fine," Hyacinth said. She had fallen behind, and urged her borrowed mount forward. "I'm fine," she said as she came up next to her aunt, "it's just that I'm a little tired. Do we have much farther to ride, until we get back to the house?"

"Not at all," Aunt Celia said. "Less than a mile."

Hyacinth tried not to show how much that news cheered her. She wanted to look back, to see that the sign was still there.

"I'm glad," she said, instead. "It's a lovely park, but I'm not used to riding."

Aunt Celia frowned. "You will have to get used to it. I will have to give you lessons, I see. We will go again tomorrow, earlier, before the fashionable world arrives in force."

"Yes, Aunt Celia," Hyacinth said. "I'm sure that would be lovely, and I would like to learn to ride better."

She cast a last, darting look over her shoulder and began to pay closer attention to where they were going. Less than a mile. She could walk that, and back, in the time it took Aunt Celia to arrange her hair.

॰

But Aunt Celia foiled her. They rode past the Lincoln's Inn sign the next morning, Saturday. On Sunday, they walked to a fashionable church, and sat idly at home the rest of the day. Mr. Butler would not be there, so it would have done her no good to slip out then. Monday began with a ride and then there were visitors, calling one after another, chatting endlessly about the coming week's social engagements, who was in town, whose grandchild had been born, and of course whose dresses would be the talk of the season. Tuesday was nearly as bad, but there was no ride in the park, so that they could save their vigor for the soirée that evening.

"I think I'll go take a rest," Hyacinth said after breakfast.

"Nonsense," Aunt Celia said. "You can't be tired. I'll have the carriage brought around and we'll go to Mrs. Benoit's to see how your gowns are coming along. The Spencers are having a ball on Saturday."

Hyacinth just nodded. It had been almost five days, including Sunday, since she'd gotten the package, and she hadn't even had a chance to send a note to Mr. Butler. The notion that she couldn't escape for an hour irked and baffled her, and surely it would make no sense to a man who worked, who had actual business to attend to.

॰

In the late afternoon, Aunt Celia at last decreed that they could have a rest before supper.

Hyacinth hurried to her room and rang for Maria.

"I must escape," she said. "I only need an hour or so. Do you think you can keep Aunt Celia at bay?"

"But you cannot go alone!" Maria said. "The streets, they are

153

too dangerous."

"It is only a mile."

"To where, this Lincoln's Inn?"

Hyacinth nodded. Maria mused.

There was a knock at the door.

"Hyacinth?" Sophie ducked her head in. Seeing Maria there, she bit her lip.

"Yes, Sophie, what is it?"

Sophie hesitated.

"It's all right, Maria won't mind."

"I'll go... downstairs," Maria said.

Hyacinth beckoned for Sophie to come in, and Maria bustled out.

"It's just," Sophie said, glancing nervously towards the door. "It's just that with Mama resting, I thought maybe we could go to the lending library. We could go out through the mews."

Hyacinth closed her eyes to think, then looked directly at her young cousin, so hopeful.

"Maria says it's not safe to go alone," she said, "and probably even more so for you. I, at least, was used to the streets in Gibraltar."

"I know the way," Sophie said, hopefully.

"Perhaps we can go together," Hyacinth said, "and ask your mama's permission." It was bad enough to resort to sneaking out through the mews for herself, but if she did it alone she would only be an ungracious guest. She would not endanger Sophie, too. She let go of the notion of seeing the solicitor. She would just send a note along from the lending library.

"What errand would she countenance?" Hyacinth asked.

"She likes if I go buy ribbons," Sophie said.

"Then we will go buy ribbons," Hyacinth said. "Where are the ribbon shops, and where is this library?"

"It's just a few streets over," Sophie said, gesturing vaguely. "There are some shops near there, too."

"Do you think one of the other servants, or Maria, would come with us?"

Sophie considered. "Joseph the footman, maybe."

"Very well," Hyacinth said. Whatever guilt she felt at the subterfuge wouldn't stand in the way of a small venture on Sophie's behalf. "Let us get permission to go shopping."

❧

In the end, Maria and Joseph the footman chaperoned the two young ladies. Joseph was a pleasant enough looking young man, with blond hair and a vacant expression in his eyes. He was, Hyacinth had concluded, devoted to Sophie in a way that might have been alarming if he weren't so gentle and dull-witted. Maria seemed to like him well enough, and they talked at length about Harold the coachman as Hyacinth and Sophie walked ahead.

They were walking, Hyacinth observed, in the general direction of the Lincoln's Inn Field signpost.

"Here we are!" Sophie announced proudly. They stood in front of a tidy modern townhouse, only steps away from the Lincoln's Inn sign.

Hyacinth and Sophie entered the building and walked up the stairs to a cozy, well-lit room. A thin-haired gentleman sat behind an impeccably tidy desk, going over a ledger. He looked up as they entered.

"Miss Talbot," he said. "I think you've grown a foot since last summer."

Sophie blushed. "Not at all. Mama says I will be too tall."

"Nonsense," the man said genially. "And who is this?"

"Oh!" Sophie said. "This is my cousin Hyacinth. She's just recently in England. She loves to read, too."

Hyacinth nodded.

The man stood and extended his hand to shake hers. "Pleased to meet you, Miss Talbot's cousin!" he said, as Hyacinth shook his hand. "I'm Mr. Benchley, proprietor of this library. Would you care to become a member?"

Sophie realized that she'd been remiss in her introductions. "My cousin is Miss Grey," she interjected. "She's from Gibraltar.

She has Latin and Greek, as well as French and Spanish."

Hyacinth sighed.

"Do you?" the librarian asked.

"I do," Hyacinth admitted, "and I'm sure I would love to become a member of your library." Sophie had hurried over to a shelf of new novels. Hyacinth would have chosen something different to read, but she had other things to attend to.

"Sophie?" Hyacinth said.

Sophie looked up eagerly. "Isn't it wonderful?"

"Yes, it is, but I have a small errand near here. If I leave Joseph here with you, would that be all right? Maria and I will be able to return in half an hour, I think."

Sophie was so distracted by the wealth of stories in front of her that she was only barely paying attention.

"Yes, that's fine," she said.

"And Mr. Benchley," Hyacinth said, "I trust you will also make sure my cousin finds something suitable. Not too frivolous."

He smiled, and she felt assured that Sophie would be safe enough with the two benign gentlemen to guard her.

On the landing, she briskly told Joseph to keep an eye on Sophie – a superfluous instruction, since he was so transparently fond of her – and took Maria's hand.

Maria looked anxiously behind her.

"Will she be all right?" she asked.

"I'm sure she will," Hyacinth said, wishing she could say the same for herself. Aunt Celia would have her head if Joseph said anything about their multiple clandestine stops on the way to ribbon shopping. "We must hurry."

❧

Hyacinth was glad, for a change, of the crowds on the streets. Whenever she sighted someone who looked like they might possibly know her aunt, she ducked her head to the side. Fortunately, they reached Lincoln's Inn Fields without incident, and found the solicitors' offices.

A clerk answered her knock at the door.

"Miss Grey," she said. "Miss Hyacinth Grey, to see Mr. John Butler."

"Junior or senior?" asked the clerk.

"Senior, I believe."

"He's busy."

"He said I was to come any time," Hyacinth said.

"Did he? We'll see about that." The clerk waved them in. "I'll show you to the parlor," he said. Hyacinth and Maria followed him to a sunlit front parlor, where he left them without a word.

Moments later, a small, older gentleman with a trim white beard stepped in.

"Miss Grey," he smiled broadly. "I am so pleased that you have come at last."

"Thank you, Mr. Butler," Hyacinth said hesitantly. He had a very pleasant face, but quick eyes, too.

His face fell when he saw Maria. "Is this your only escort?" he said worriedly.

"Maria is my maid," Hyacinth said. "She's come with me from Gibraltar. My aunt, who I am staying with, is... was unable to come."

"Unable. I see." He nodded.

"I'm afraid we're in a bit of a hurry," Hyacinth said.

"That's all right. It's London. Most people are in a hurry." He opened the door again. "Come this way."

Mr. Butler led Hyacinth up the stairs, with Maria trailing behind. "You've been a long time getting here," he said as he opened his office door.

"Yes," Hyacinth said. "It's my aunt. She keeps us busy with social calls, and..." Hyacinth looked over her shoulder down the hall.

"Come in," Mr. Butler insisted, ushering her into the office. "Respectable ladies never did approve of your grandmother. But that is not my concern, or yours."

Hyacinth nodded. She wished that she didn't have to worry about her aunt's approval, either, but she did. She would have to see what waited for her here. Maybe then she would be able to declare her independence. It was a slightly terrifying prospect.

Mr. Butler's office reminded Hyacinth of her father's world – a more reassuring world than all her aunt's social calls. Here, with men bustling up and down corridors, shouting about dossiers, she felt that she could ask what the rules were, that no one would think ill of her for not knowing all those rules already. Even if her grandmother had been part of the demi-monde, her solicitor was not.

"Your grandmother," the solicitor said, "was very firm in her wish that you have exclusive control over your inheritance, and that includes keeping a tight lid on any details regarding the properties in question." He paused as he searched the shelves for a box of papers.

"I'd advise you not to disclose any information to anyone until you're firmly decided about how you will dispose of the property. Much of it would be protected by a trust, but if you do marry, nearly half will be under your husband's control. Your grandmother would have liked it otherwise, but we could not manage it."

"What half would that be?" Hyacinth asked .

"Principally the estate," the solicitor said.

"Estate?" Hyacinth asked. She'd understood that her grandmother had owned a cottage, not an estate.

Mr. Butler took the folio to a long table in the middle of the room. He stacked a few other papers together to clear space for it, then set it in front of Hyacinth.

"Here we are," he said. "You should sit down." He gestured to a stool near Hyacinth, which she shifted into position in front of the folio. Maria waited awkwardly by the door. "Your maid may wait in the hallway," Mr. Butler said. "There's a chair in the nook opposite."

Maria nodded and bowed out. Hyacinth could just see the edge of her skirts through the door, which stood ajar.

"I like to keep the door open," Mr. Butler said. "It's harder to press an ear to it." He pulled out a sheaf of documents.

"Now, if you'll sign here," he passed her a paper, "that is a declaration that you are the Miss Hyacinth Grey, daughter of Horatio and Violet Grey, nee Miller, born the seventeenth of April, 1784, in Portsmouth. Do you swear that to be true?"

"I do," Hyacinth said, "but how do you know that I am who I say I am?"

"You're the image of your mother," the solicitor said. "We all grieved at her passing. It seems like it was only yesterday that she was here, too."

"It seems a very long time ago, to me," Hyacinth said. It was so strange, that this stranger had known her mother well enough to remember her after so much time had passed.

Mr. Butler glanced at his watch. "I'll tell you the outline of things now, and you can make an appointment with the clerk to return. Tomorrow afternoon I have a bit of time."

"I don't know that I'll be able to get away," Hyacinth said apologetically.

Mr. Butler squinted at her. "Ah, yes. Your aunt. Who is she?"

"The dowager countess Talbot," Hyacinth said.

Mr. Butler frowned. "Can't say I know her. But I know her kind. I'm sure you'll find a way, if not tomorrow, another day. Also, the size of the fortune might change her opinion of its respectability. I suspect she thinks your grandmother left only a few tainted baubles."

"I don't know," Hyacinth said. "I doubt she'd allow anything to change her mind."

Mr. Butler sifted through the documents.

"Here is the deed to Lindley Hall, with a map of its properties," he said, handing her one sheaf of papers. "It includes three crofters' cottages, all still occupied, I believe."

Hyacinth looked at the map. The property encompassed at least forty acres, and was far more than a cottage.

"This is larger than I expected," she said.

"Yes, it's not the house her patron left her with, although this one is also near the Welsh border. I believe that Mrs. Miller was born somewhere in that part of the country, though she never spoke of it directly," the solicitor said. "Shall I write to the manager and let him know that you're in London?"

"Yes, do," Hyacinth said. "I would like to visit soon, if I can find a way."

The solicitor nodded. "Mrs. Miller was an astute investor, very astute. Here's a folio of stocks. Some of these should be cashed in, but others of the companies are still gaining in value."

Hyacinth looked at one piece of paper, then another. The sums named were considerable, not enough to finance a clipper ship, but close to it.

"In addition, there is cash money at Lyons' Bank, roughly twenty thousand. Here is the pass book."

He handed her a small leather-covered folio.

"Twenty thousand pounds?" Hyacinth asked.

"More than that, but I haven't checked the exact amount lately. You can go over there and ask for yourself." He stood up from his desk at the sound of the clock on the tower beginning to strike the quarter hour.

"Fifteen minutes until I need to be at the bar," he said. "Return tomorrow afternoon. Have the clerk enter it in my book."

"I don't know if I'll be able to get away," Hyacinth reminded him.

"Send me a note if you cannot come," he said. "I can call around to your Aunt's residence on Saturday, if you cannot come before then."

"Yes," Hyacinth said. "Come in the afternoon. I will be sure to be at home."

"Meanwhile, I advise you to pay a visit to Lyon's Bank."

"I will try to do that." Hyacinth looked at the sheaf of stock folios in her hand, staggered by the amount of money they represented. Those, with the twenty thousand in the bank and the estate, represented a sizable fortune. It was hers alone, and it was enough, more than enough, to start a school. In fact, she realized that she was quite out of her depth with it.

"Shall I leave these here?" she said, handing the stock

certificates to the solicitor.

"Yes, they'll be secure with me, as they have been." He slid them back in with the rest of the documents and ushered Hyacinth out of the room, locking the door behind them. Maria rose from her seat and fell into step behind as Mr. Butler led them back to the front door of Lincoln's Inn.

"One more thing," he said as he hurried down the stairs. "Here is the key to the deposit box at the bank. Go see the director, Mr. Lyons, when you arrive there. I'm sure he'll be able to recognize you as I did. You might want to see what's in there before we meet again."

Hyacinth scarcely had time to say goodbye before the door closed behind her and they were back out on the busy London streets.

❧

CHAPTER 10: GEORGIANA'S SOIRÉE

Hyacinth waited in the front parlor where Sophie was sulking, dejected at being left behind.

"At least you have something to read," Hyacinth said.

Sophie brightened. "Thanks to you! It was such an adventure." A puzzled look crossed her face. "Where did you go, though?"

Hyacinth glanced at the door and listened for any sound of her aunt's approach. She didn't want to lie, but maybe a half-truth would do.

"I was... I had to find out something about the other half of my family," she said.

"And did you?"

"I did, but I can't tell you about it, not yet."

Sophie's eyes went wide. "Mama is coming!"

Hyacinth hadn't heard anything. It was her turn to be puzzled.

"I heard her door," Sophie said. "It creaks just a little, like this." She leaned forward and made a soft, high-pitched sound which Hyacinth could barely hear. She looked very childish when she did it.

"I couldn't hear a thing," Hyacinth said, "but I believe you."

Sophie flounced her skirts and straightened her posture. "I will be so bored," she complained loudly.

"I don't know that the soirée will be very exciting, either," Hyacinth offered.

"Mama tells me that the Pentlys are never boring."

"I see," Hyacinth said, though she didn't really. Clearly, Aunt Celia hadn't obeyed her own rule about never mentioning the Pentlys.

"She often visits Georgiana, who is an old maid," Sophie confided.

"Is she?" Hyacinth asked. "She didn't seem much older than I am."

Sophie shook her head vehemently. "I don't know how old she is, only that she is considered to be on the shelf. And she is nearly as obsessed with fashion as Mama is. That's what they always talk about, Mama says."

Finally, Hyacinth heard the sound of Aunt Celia coming up the hall, skirts swishing. Sophie picked up her embroidery.

Aunt Celia entered and inspected Hyacinth. "I think that is quite a good color for you," she declared. Hyacinth's gown was made of soft, pale blue silk, which set off her eyes perfectly. "You will have a good complexion once another month here drives that Mediterranean sun off your face," she added.

Hyacinth wished there were a bit more sun in London to keep her complexion ruined.

"Your gown is exquisite as always, Aunt," she said, instead. Aunt Celia favored bright, intense colors. She wore a dress of lapis lazuli blue velvet with ornate gold trim. She looked nearly regal.

She acknowledged Hyacinth's compliment with a brief nod. "Well, we really must be going," she said. "It is good to be late, but not *too* late!"

❧

Aunt Celia spent the entire drive to Windcastle House enumerating her daughter's shortcomings and worrying about her entrance to society, still nearly five years away. Hyacinth could not agree with most of her aunt's judgments, but the carriage was dark and her aunt ignored her long silences. She ought to tell Aunt Celia about her inheritance. She ought to mention her plans to build a school, but not yet, and not on the way to a soirée.

"Well," her aunt said. "Which do you prefer?"

"Which what?" Hyacinth said.

Aunt Celia let out a deep, exasperated sigh. "Have you heard anything I just said?"

"I am sorry. I must have nodded off," Hyacinth said. It was better than admitting what she'd been thinking about. "It's very late."

"Nonsense. You will have to get used to fashionable hours. Now, which of the young gentlemen do you prefer?"

Hyacinth shook her head. "I don't know. I don't think I prefer any of them. I've only met Viscount Whitley and Sir Albert."

"I've told you about the others, though, and you might meet Lord Rawley here tonight," Aunt Celia said. "He has a fine estate in Yorkshire, they say."

"I have never been to Yorkshire and have no opinion of it," Hyacinth said.

Mercifully, the carriage turned, entering the circular drive in front of Windcastle House.

The house loomed over them, a Classical portico on a facade which stretched across one side of an elegant square. Ten or more of Aunt Celia's perfectly respectable house might have fit inside it. The wings looked as though they'd been tacked together from two houses from a century or more ago, either of which would have been an estimable residence in its own right. Hyacinth swallowed deeply. This was the home of the so-called Mr. Smithson's family, of Thomas's family. It was not the kind of house which could belong to a tradesman, no matter how successful. It was the kind of house which belonged to a family within a handsbreadth of the monarchy.

If the grandeur of their house was any indication of the

strength of their influence, it was a wonder he'd been able to escape them at all, even in India. He had been dishonest in not telling her who he really was, even on shipboard. He should have, even if he had attempted to run away from them, for whatever reason. Aunt Celia was probably right – the Pently men were not to be trusted.

"Come," Aunt Celia urged.

Hyacinth realized that she had frozen on the step of the carriage. She let the footman help her down and took a step toward the house.

"The house isn't in the latest style," Aunt Celia whispered, "but Georgiana has had a few rooms done up with furnishings from the continent and the effect is quite impressive."

"It is rather larger than I'd thought a house could be," Hyacinth said.

Aunt Celia tsked. "If you say that in company, you'll sound like a country mushroom." She took a deep breath and ushered Hyacinth in.

They were led through the entrance hall and to a room which gleamed with ornament. Glistening chandeliers, impossibly bright with candles, hung from a vaulted ceiling. It was like standing inside an enormous jewel, a ruby, flecked with gold.

"Lady Talbot and Miss Grey," the butler announced.

Hyacinth stepped forward, with Aunt Celia at her elbow. The room glistened, but so did the figures in silk and damask and jewels milling beneath the chandeliers. There were dozens of them, not what Hyacinth would have considered a small party, at all. A dense group of younger people clustered at the far end of the room, admiring something.

"Ah, look!" Aunt Celia said. "There's Viscount Whitley and his mama." She steered Hyacinth to one side and exchanged greetings with her friend. Hyacinth merely smiled in response, hoping to escape. She had met Viscount Whitley while riding in the park, and had not heard him say anything beyond the most inane pleasantries. His gaze had lingered on her bosom, and whenever the older ladies looked away, he leered. He might have been considered handsome, except that his face was spotty and he slouched.

"Why don't you two take a turn around the room?" Aunt Celia suggested.

Hyacinth smiled weakly and Aunt Celia took that for assent. Viscount Whitley's clammy hand rested on her arm. She gritted her teeth.

"Shall we walk on the balcony?" he suggested, almost immediately.

Hyacinth took a deep breath. "No," she said, "I think I'd rather see what everyone is looking at, over there." She walked towards the group of young people, forcing Viscount Whitley to follow her. He was annoyed, but at least they weren't out on the balcony. She looked over her shoulder. Aunt Celia was nowhere to be seen.

A small pianoforte stood at the center of the group.

"Marvelous inlay," one of the young gentlemen said.

Hyacinth agreed – the inlaid rosewood and ivory made a floral pattern, which was really quite beautiful.

"But how does it sound?" one of the young ladies said.

"Do you play, Miss Grey?" Viscount Whitley asked.

"Not well," Hyacinth said.

"I am sure you are only being modest," Viscount Whitley said. "Why don't you take a turn?" He tried to nudge her onto the bench, but she managed to jump out of the way.

"No, I really don't play well," Hyacinth said. She didn't want to thrust herself into the center of attention like that. The group around the pianoforte turned their eyes on her, as if gauging the interloper's weaknesses. "Besides--"

"We're waiting for Georgiana," one of the young ladies cut her off. "It's her new instrument. She's to be the first to play it. Really." She glared at Hyacinth.

"What have we here, Whitley?"

Hyacinth turned to see a gentleman with a canary waistcoat and a florid complexion leaning heavily on the piano. There was something vaguely familiar about him.

Whitley leered again.

"Miss Grey, may I present The Honorable Nathan Pently."

Hyacinth curtsied. He didn't look honorable.

"Someone go find Georgiana," demanded a pale girl, with indifferent brown eyes. "I want a turn to play."

Nathan Pently grunted and wandered off, presumably in search of Georgiana.

"I'm sure you'll get to play soon," Hyacinth said to her.

The girl looked down her long nose at Hyacinth. "I don't mind. We have a better pianoforte at home, anyway." She turned to inspect the collection of sheet music.

"Perhaps you can sing, later," Viscount Whitley said to Hyacinth, leaning in too close again.

"I don't care to," she said, stepping back. "No one else is singing, are they?"

"But they will, later," he answered. "You may be sure of it."

Hyacinth was saved from responding by a round of applause which rippled through the room as Georgiana approached the pianoforte. She swept the sheet music aside.

"What will you be playing?" Viscount Whitley asked her.

Georgiana ignored him and set her fingers on the keys. The viscount stepped back and dusted off his waistcoat. Hyacinth shifted away from him. Perhaps she could find a seat along the edges of the room, with the older ladies. Aunt Celia was nowhere to be seen.

As Georgiana struck the first notes, Hyacinth looked up and saw Thomas just entering the room. Even from the far side of the party, she could sense that he didn't share in the festive mood. He wore the same black suit he'd worn at the funeral the week before. His jaw was clenched into a frown, and he looked distracted. He wasn't enjoying himself, but then, neither was she.

Then the music began, an ascending ripple of notes, light, then a thunder of bass underneath, creeping up ominously. Hyacinth was transfixed. She wondered, momentarily, if Thomas had seen her, but the fluid, precise movements of Georgiana's fingers over the keys captivated her attention entirely, and the music swept her away.

She had not seen him, Thomas thought. That was probably for the best. Hyacinth was standing too close to the piano to pay attention to anything else. Even from the far side of the room, Thomas could feel the force of Georgiana's musical mastery. He had forgotten about that, in India. There were many things he hadn't thought about in all that time, the finer points of life in London, and the fact that not all of his relations were boors.

No, they were not boors, not generally. They were men of influence, and most people conferred respect on them unthinkingly, overlooking their abuses of power, of which there were plenty, and more in every generation, as far as he could tell. He simply wanted no part of it, but here he was.

Georgiana had quizzed and ribbed him over breakfast, day after day, to ensure that his long absence and dabblings in trade had left his breeding and comportment intact. She was provisionally satisfied that he would not make a fool of himself and the family, but he couldn't help but look at the soirée as a field of battle, or at least a test. A pair of matrons on the far side of the room eyed him from behind their fans. He retreated.

He made it through the doorway as Georgiana began the last movement of the piece, but he had to stop in his tracks to avoid stepping on a delicately slippered foot. He stood toe-to-toe with a rouge-cheeked woman in a vibrant blue gown.

"Pardon me," she said, fanning her décolletage.

She was familiar somehow, but Thomas couldn't place her right away. She drew back a step and looked up at him.

"Ah, Sir Pently, isn't it?" she said.

"It is, Ma'am. And who would you be?" He didn't like having to ask, but he lacked the presence of mind to beat around the bush. The miasma of his circling family made it difficult to think clearly.

The lady sucked in her breath. "Well. From any less handsome man, I would take that as an insult. I must take care to make sure you remember me this time. We met on Thursday…"

The pieces clicked into place at once. "At Admiral Nelson's funeral. My apologies, Lady Talbot."

"Not at all. I can see that you are quite out of practice. Your cousin's soirées may not be large, but they are social events of a very high standard."

"Everything Georgiana does is to the highest standard," Thomas said. Hyacinth's aunt was standing so close to him that the thought of someone coming upon them made him uneasy. Besides, he would far rather have been talking to Hyacinth. "I believe I will go watch her play the last chords," Thomas said.

"So will I, then," Lady Talbot said. She stepped forward in such a way that a gentleman would reflexively take her arm, but Thomas sidestepped. He was still standing there, not taking her hand, as the final chords crashed out of the piano.

"Ah," Thomas said. "I have missed it. And now I must go on with my errand."

He turned on his heel, escaping before Lady Talbot could entrap him again.

❧

Hyacinth watched Georgiana's fingers fly over the keys, coaxing out a music that made her forget everything else, at least for the moment. At the end of the piece, she joined the applause and looked around the room. Thomas was gone from his place by the door, and she couldn't see him anywhere else, either. Viscount Whitley was at her side again, asking if she wanted a glass of orgeat.

"Orgeat?" Hyacinth echoed. "Yes, I think I would, thank you."

"I'll be back shortly," he said, his eyes lingering on her bosom.

Her gown was cut too low, but then they all were. Aunt Celia insisted that such necklines were the height of fashion: their hostess's gown covered no more than hers did, and several of the youngest ladies were tugging their necklines down surreptitiously.

One of the young ladies took a turn playing a light air. As she played, Lady Georgiana made her way across the party, greeting her guests. By the end of the piece, only the small cluster gathered around the piano were pretending to listen.

Next, another girl announced that she wished to play "The Golden Vanity," and cast about for a singer. Of all the young people, only Hyacinth admitted to knowing all the verses through, so she was pushed forward. Singing offered Hyacinth a ready escape from Viscount Whitley's conversation, and it began well enough. Very few of the guests paid much attention. Thomas was no where to be seen, and Aunt Celia was probably in the card room.

The first verse passed without incident, except that the din of conversation seemed to recede a little. She supposed it would seem that way, whether it had or not, and she carried on into the second verse. Then she looked up, which was a mistake. Thomas had arrived.

❧

Thomas looked down at the party. He had always liked this spot when he was a boy, but he felt a bit ill-at-ease now. It was not the sort of place that a grown man should frequent. Hyacinth's aunt had gone into the card room, but Hyacinth herself still stood by the piano. The weedy gentleman who'd been circling her slithered off towards the drink table. The aunt's chaperonage was deplorably sloppy. He wouldn't have let that go, if he'd been her commanding officer in India. But of course, he wasn't. If anything, he was on the opposing force, though looking at the young gentlemen below, he didn't think he wanted to be on that side, either.

Thomas was lying on his belly in the upstairs corridor, looking down through a hidden spyhole in the floor, which was usually covered by a carpet. It had provided hours of entertainment for the Pently children, each generation certain that their parents had never found this secret place. Thomas heard footsteps coming up the servants' stair. He got up and brushed himself off. An upstairs maid hurried by, her gaze locked forward. The servants probably knew about the spyhole, too, Thomas realized. It was past time to go downstairs and face the music.

By the time he made his entrance, yet another player had begun to pick out chords. The player lacked Georgiana's confidence, but then, most people did. The hands hesitated over the keys, but then she settled in a bit, running through the first bars of "The Golden Vanity," a dire, depressing song.

As he stepped into the room, the singer let her first note out. It was Hyacinth. He half wished he'd stayed at his spyhole. He would have been able to see better from there without worrying about who he would have to talk to next. Her voice was light and clear, not overly schooled, but pleasant. Thomas sat down on an empty chair, behind a large vase. He would not be able to see her from there, but at least he could listen.

Conversations spilled out of the card room, though, and he could barely hear Hyacinth's singing over all the competing noise. It was no good, all this cowering in corners. He should stand up. As he did so, their gazes locked for a split heartbeat. Hyacinth's voice faltered. He smiled at her, as if he'd been standing there in the open all along. She steadied herself and continued on into the third verse, her voice growing more emphatic towards the end.

"Pretty little chit, isn't she, Tom?"

Thomas turned around to find Nathan standing just behind him, holding a decanter of brandy. The hubbub of conversation threatened to drown out Hyacinth's voice, not to mention the sudden rush of blood to Thomas's ears. Hyacinth came to the end of the verse and stepped back from the piano. Her accompanist launched into a final, excessively flourished round of the tune.

"Do you mean to drink that all yourself?"

"Not at all," Nathan said. "I was only bringing it over to a the lady in the card room." He nodded towards the door. He hailed a passing servant for a glass, and poured out a few fingers for Thomas.

Thomas drank, hoping it might ease his nerves. Nate had made a wreckage of himself with drink. In India, he hadn't had the time or inclination to drink to excess, and the liquor was of dubious quality most of the time. Now, he was glad of it.

"Next, I'll see if that singer fancies a stroll in the garden," Nathan said.

Thomas straightened up to his full height. "You most certainly will not."

Nathan laughed. "And why wouldn't I? She's quite pretty, and not a connection to speak of."

Thomas bristled. "I believe the dowager Countess Talbot is her aunt."

Nathan snorted. "That is hardly a connection to speak of." He chuckled at his own wit.

Thomas couldn't argue against that point, from the little he'd seen of Hyacinth's aunt.

"Miss Grey is an acquaintance of mine," he said at last. "I have found her to be more honorable than most gentlemen here, and if you raise so much as an eyebrow against her virtue…" Thomas stepped in close to his brother and raised a hand to seize him by the cravat.

The last chords crashed down. People around them had turned to watch the two brothers. Thomas gave his brother a hearty pat on the shoulder and relaxed his posture. The onlookers quickly lost interest.

"Have an eye for her yourself, do you then?" Nathan hissed.

"I'm not in the business of despoiling young ladies," Thomas said. He took the decanter from Nathan and filled his own glass again. "I believe I will go pay my respects to Miss Grey now," he said.

"Happy despoiling," Nathan whispered, and slunk off to the card room.

❧

Thank goodness that was over, Hyacinth thought as she stepped back from the piano. Across the room, Thomas was engaged in what appeared to be a heated conversation with another gentleman. He wore a canary yellow waistcoat, quite distinctive, though it did his complexion no favors. Ah. It was the Nathan Pently she'd been introduced to earlier. They were definitely arguing, and the family resemblance was unmistakable.

The young lady at the pianoforte sounded her final chords, and the audience gathered around the instrument erupted into applause, while most of the rest of the room went on ignoring them. Hyacinth knew she was blushing now, but it didn't matter. She'd sung and played the pianoforte at larger gatherings, but she sensed that the audience at Georgiana Pently's soirée was a good deal more critical than any gathering at Gibraltar.

"Splendid!" Viscount Whitley grinned.

Hyacinth shook her head modestly. She hoped he would find another young lady to talk to, and soon.

"Would you like to take a turn on the patio?" he asked instead.

Hyacinth wanted to shout: "No!" Instead, she begged off on account of the climate. "I am not used to these winters," she said. "The damp, yes, but not the cold."

"I'll fetch your wrap, if you like," he said. He was awfully persistent.

"Would you mind fetching me another glass of orgeat instead?" Hyacinth asked. "I am parched from the singing."

Viscount Whitley agreed reluctantly. As he walked away from the piano, Hyacinth spied an empty seat near a window. She set off towards it.

An older lady sat on an armchair halfway along the wall. She nodded to Hyacinth as she passed. "A fine performance, Miss," she said. She wore her hair in an old-fashioned style, powdered. Her eyes had the same pale blue color as Thomas's.

"Why, thank you," Hyacinth said.

"I don't believe we've been introduced," said the older lady.

"I am Hyacinth Grey," she said. When the woman looked at her questioningly she added: "Lady Celia Talbot is my aunt."

"Ah. *Those* Greys." The lady seemed to be none too happy about the discovery. "I am Lady Penelope Thornton. The Duke is my elder brother."

"I am pleased to make your acquaintance," Hyacinth said, not altogether truthfully. Lady Penelope Thornton had wrinkled her nose quite distinctly when she'd said, "*Those* Greys."

There was an unoccupied hassock beside Lady Thornton. Out of the corner of her eye, Hyacinth saw the viscount weaving back across the party with her glass of orgeat.

"May I sit here?" Hyacinth asked. It would be a far better place to discourage the young viscount than the semi-secluded window seat she'd been aiming for. Lady Thornton's open distaste for her family wasn't exactly inviting, but perhaps she could come closer to finding out what the matter was that lay between her family and Thomas's.

"Sit if you like," Lady Thornton said, fairly grumbling. She cast an eye at Viscount Whitley, who was standing by the punch bowl, scanning the room for Hyacinth. "Are you giving that young man the run-around?"

"I'd rather not encourage him."

"Do you lack ambition, girl, or have you set your sights higher?"

"The former, I think," Hyacinth said. "I've only just arrived in London, and I feel no need to marry in haste, if at all."

Lady Thornton harrumphed. "Many young girls say that, but their mamas generally set them straight soon enough."

"I don't know about that," Hyacinth said. "My mother is long since departed, so I have only my aunt to worry over that."

"How unfortunate," Lady Thornton said. "Your mother's death, I mean, as well as your aunt's guidance."

Hyacinth stiffened.

Lady Thornton shook her head and a light dusting of powder escaped from her wig onto the cushion behind her. "I did not mean to distress you," she said. "It is my habit to say things which others might not."

"Is it?" Hyacinth asked.

Lady Thornton gave Hyacinth a second appraising look, then waved her off without answering. She reached for her cane and began to stand up.

"Lady Thornton, have you been long acquainted with my family?" Hyacinth asked.

The older lady sat back down, and her lips twitched into a suggestion of a smile as she peered at Hyacinth. "Personally, no," she said, "but I believe there was some question of honor raised a few decades ago. It was soon put to rest, but not entirely forgotten."

"Whose honor was in question, then?" Hyacinth pressed.

Lady Thornton fluttered her hands. "Oh, nearly everyone's. It was quite a messy affair. There were accusations and threats of blackmail on both sides, but it was a long time ago, possibly before you were born. It might be more appropriate if you were to ask your aunt about it, don't you think? Except that might be cutting too close to the bone. Whatever you hear, it wasn't from me."

"You've told me nothing at all," Hyacinth said.

Viscount Whitley had finally arrived with Hyacinth's glass of orgeat. He approached warily.

"Good evening, Lady Thornton, Miss Grey," he said.

"Ah, you've brought me some orgeat!" Lady Thornton said. "What a considerate young man."

The young viscount's face flushed and he glanced apologetically at Hyacinth. "I'm delighted to be of service, Lady Thornton," he said, handing her the glass. "Would you like one too, Miss Grey?"

"Why yes," Hyacinth said, "I certainly would."

"Then I will fetch it." With that, he was off again, weaving across the crowded room as another of the young ladies sat down at the pianoforte.

"You'll be better off to steer clear of that one, I think," Lady

Thornton advised.

"My aunt seems to think him quite appropriate," Hyacinth said, without enthusiasm.

"Your aunt's judgment in matters of fashion is impeccable," Lady Thornton replied. "In the appraisal of gentlemen's characters, it is less well esteemed."

"I see," Hyacinth said.

"Ah," Lady Thornton said, "here comes my long lost nephew. I wonder if he's gone as savage as they say."

Hyacinth turned to look. Thomas was halfway across the room, trying to break away from a conversation with a young gentleman and looking really quite out of his element. His eyes met hers for a fraction of a heartbeat then he turned his half smile into a broad grin as he nodded to Lady Thornton. He gestured to her and the young gentleman he was speaking to clapped him on the back and hurried away.

"Aunt Penelope!" Thomas said. "Georgiana told me you would be here. You don't look a day older."

"Don't try to flatter me, nephew," Lady Thornton said. "You do look older, so I'm sure I must, too. The effect is better on you."

"I thank you, but really, you do look to be in good health."

"As do you," Lady Thornton said, "unlike some of my other nephews. Dead. Imagine that. And a drunk."

Thomas shook his head and pulled a footstool closer. He sat down at his aunt's feet, as if he were still a boy.

"I see that you've met my shipmate," he said, indicating Hyacinth.

"Shipmate?" Lady Thornton turned to Hyacinth. "You didn't tell me that you were already acquainted with my favorite nephew."

"We'd only just begun talking," Hyacinth said, "and how was I to know he was your nephew?"

Lady Thornton shook her head. "You must begin to take note of these things, Miss Grey. It will help you immensely."

"Am I still your favorite, then?" Thomas interjected. "I would have thought I'd be supplanted by now."

Lady Thornton raised her glass. "Richard was loved by all. He didn't need to be my favorite. Gregory is dead. Your surviving brother is unlikely to supplant you."

"There is that," Thomas said, looking towards the doors to the balcony.

Hyacinth followed his gaze. The man with the canary yellow waistcoat was speaking to a young lady, who seemed eager to return to the party. As they watched, an older woman, plainly dressed, rushed to join them and stared daggers at Nathan, who backed away to the balcony alone.

"Here comes your shipmate's suitor," Lady Thornton announced. While Hyacinth had been preoccupied with the little scene, she had taken it all in at a glance and gone back to surveying the rest of the room.

Viscount Whitley approached, holding two glasses of orgeat. He handed one to Hyacinth with a flourish.

"Your orgeat, Miss Grey."

"Thank you," she replied.

"I thought I might join you," Viscount Whitley said, taking a sip from the second glass, "but it seems that there are no more footstools near at hand." He looked at Thomas with a frown.

"Indeed, they do all seem to be taken," Lady Thornton said briskly. "Perhaps you should go encourage Georgiana to have another turn at the pianoforte. It sounds so crass when the other young ladies play."

Viscount Whitley withdrew, flustered.

Hyacinth looked over her shoulder. Her aunt should have been nearby, or at least within sight, but she was nowhere to be seen.

"I should go find my aunt," she said, "and leave you to your reunion."

Thomas opened his mouth to speak, but his aunt held up her hand. "Not at all. If I know Lady Talbot, she is in the card room, and would not like to be interrupted. Do stay."

Hyacinth cast another glance at the card room's doors, but

kept her seat, as ordered.

"From what port did you journey together?" Lady Thornton asked her.

"From Gibraltar," she said. "I have lived there for many years, ever since my mother…"

"Ah, your mother!" Lady Thornton exclaimed. "Now I remember. *That* scandal nearly eclipsed the other one, for a season, at least. It's a pity that your mother wasn't able to go out in society. Had your father been a little more influential, it might have happened in time… but he wasn't, and so that's done. Is he still among the living?"

"My father?" Hyacinth said, taken aback by Lady Thornton's directness. "He is in good health, or was when I left Gibraltar, and hasn't written anything to the contrary since."

"I formed the impression that all the captains in the Mediterranean fleet bow and scrape to him," Thomas said. "He holds the keys to the Navy's stores on Gibraltar."

Lady Thornton looked at her nephew. "I suppose I don't care much what Captain Grey does with his time, as long as he's out of our hair. What's been occupying you, boy?" she asked. "You're starting to take on the look of a man."

Thomas didn't seem to mind being called a boy, at least not by his elderly aunt.

"I suppose you could say that India has been occupying me," he said with a shrug, "and since I returned, I've had some visits to the tailor and a nagging sense of obligation to distract me."

"Ah, yes, you do have obligations now," Lady Thornton said.

"Nate tells me that Father is at the castle with His Grace," Thomas said.

"So I hear. They don't tell me anything," she said.

Thomas laughed. "But I'm sure you know more than they do, anyway."

Lady Thornton let out a sigh. "It's a pity Georgiana wasn't a boy, but you'll do, I suppose."

"Tho… Sir Pently will do for what?" Hyacinth interjected.

"My dear," Lady Thornton said, "didn't you know? I told

you: you must start paying attention to these things! Thomas is second in line to the duchy of Windcastle, after his aged uncle and his almost-as aged father pass on. It's all over town."

Hyacinth calculated. She thought of the house, what she saw around her, what she'd seen on approach. This was the family obligation that had brought Thomas, Mr. Smithson, back to England? No matter how despicable his relations were, or at least some of his male relations were, it was a great deal to leave behind, in favor of malarial jungles. She turned to him.

"Did you know when we were on the *Whistler*?" she asked.

Thomas shifted his weight around on the stool. "I rather hoped it wasn't true," he said, "and besides, the duke is still very much alive—"

"I wouldn't say, 'very much,'" his aunt interjected.

"As is my father—"

"Again, he is younger than me, but..."

"And I am told that my cousin left a widow, only a few months ago."

"There is that," Lady Thornton said, "but really, Gregory was hardly the picture of health, and..."

"I still hold hope," Thomas said.

"But there is still your father's estate and title, and unless your younger brother murders you for the contents of the wine cellar, they are yours."

Hyacinth guessed that his father's estate, while maybe not quite a duchy, eclipsed anything she would have imagined. She looked at Thomas and shook her head. "Why did you insist on going by Mr. Smithson, though?"

"Mr. Smithson?" Lady Thornton laughed.

"I mentioned my family name once in Gibraltar, to your father, and thought better of it after that."

"Oh, dear," Lady Thornton said. "I should be going."

"No." Hyacinth rose to her feet. "It is I who should be going. Good bye, again, *Sir Pently*."

❧

She sailed away across the room. She looked exquisite in her pale blue gown, and he wasn't the only one to have noticed it. Of course, she had been beautiful aboard the *Whistler*, too, even in her schoolmarmish clothes, it had just taken him a little longer to realize it. In her very fashionable, rather thin gown, every half-blind fool of a gentleman in the room was angling to take her out for a stroll in the gardens, especially as her chaperone was nowhere to be seen.

"I should—" Thomas began.

Aunt Penelope laid a hand on his arm. "She has enough sense to cross the room alone without being ruined," she said. "Besides, she's going to the card room. Really, I don't think much of that Lady Talbot."

"Nor do I," Thomas said.

"Let them be," Aunt Penelope said, "and tell me all about India."

ॐ

CHAPTER 11: A RIDE IN THE PARK

Thomas sighted Hyacinth once more that evening. She appeared to be tugging her aunt towards the front door. He couldn't break away from the string of re-introductions and inane conversations to find her, and when he did glimpse her, her back was turned. What would he have said to her, in any case? He took a turn at the piano to escape the maze of mostly-forgotten names and titles for a short while. He played a Bach cantata, which he'd once known well, and fumbled half the notes. The entire gathering applauded anyway, at the novelty of a future duke who would play the pianoforte. It gave them even more to talk about, beyond his darkened skin or his general unsuitability for the title.

The next morning, he had the breakfast table to himself. He settled in for a quiet cup of coffee, gazing at the spread of kippers and bacon on the sideboard. He had not slept well, and his appetite wasn't as good as usual. He wished he'd been more forthcoming about his background aboard the *Whistler*, at least with Miss Grey. He did not want to lose her friendship over his reluctance to take his place in England. He felt the aristocratic world closing its clutches around him. That world would not approve of their acquaintance. Even if she had been at the soirée, she was on its outskirts, while he was being pulled relentlessly towards the center. Aunt Penelope might find Miss Grey amusing, but would quickly change her tune if he were to express any serious attachment to Hyacinth. He sipped his coffee with his eyes closed, trying to clear his head.

"Good morning, I said."

Thomas looked up to find that Georgiana had entered. She wore a brown riding dress and smelled of horses and leather.

"Woolgathering, are you?"

Thomas shrugged. "I suppose so. It's a bit daunting, all this talk of succession."

"Hmm," Georgiana frowned. "As if it's all settled."

"Isn't it?"

Georgiana went to fill her plate. "I'm famished," she said. She sat down across from him and began to wolf down some of the previous night's roast, laid out cold for breakfast.

"Would there be some doubt?" Thomas said.

"About the succession?" Georgiana asked, with feigned lightness. "How would I know?"

Thomas rolled his eyes. "You know everything, nearly as much as Aunt Penelope."

"I doubt that," Georgiana said, "but for once, for the first time in history, you and our esteemed fathers are in agreement. Not one of you is happy with this situation."

"I quite enjoyed being Mr. Smithson, and being judged chiefly on my own merits," Thomas said.

"That has nothing to do with it. You are all displeased, and I am sure that somehow the fates will contrive to bow to your wishes."

"I don't think the fates are so malleable," Thomas said.

Georgiana shrugged again. If she knew something that he did not, she wasn't telling. "So why didn't you stay in India, again?" she pried.

"It was complicated," Thomas said.

He needed to change the subject.

"I have a small difficulty," he said.

Georgiana rolled her eyes. "And you think I can help? Has

one of these young misses caught your eye already?"

"Not precisely," Thomas said. "It's more that I have an apology to make, and the young lady in question might refuse to see me."

"Really?" She raised her eyebrows and smiled broadly. "No one in London would refuse to see you, our future duke."

"I do not think that my title will help, in this instance."

Georgiana's hand paused, leaving a fork full of herring hovering an inch from her lips as she spoke. "Is it that Miss Grey? The one who sang that abominable sea chantey?"

Thomas nodded. "It *is* an abominable song, but I don't think it reflects on the singer. I rather like her."

Georgiana leaned back, chewing pensively. "That won't do, you know."

"I believe she has declared herself to be uninterested in matrimony," Thomas said, "if that is what you are thinking of."

"Young ladies sometimes say that," Georgiana said. "I've been known to say it myself."

Interesting. That suggested that the famously independent Georgiana was not as opposed to marriage as she'd been at sixteen. He wondered, briefly, if she had anyone in mind, but that was a matter for a different day. He had to apologize to Miss Grey first.

"Matrimonial intentions aside, I need to apologize to her," Thomas said.

Georgiana snorted. "That would be a change."

"I have been known to apologize," Thomas said. "Occasionally."

"It is not a behavior the Pentlys are known for," Georgiana said. "We tend to prefer swords at dawn, haven't you heard?"

Thomas rolled his eyes. "Never mind. There's a very small chance she would open my letter and read it. I will have to try that." He rose to go.

Georgiana waved him back into his seat. "No, no," she said. "I will see what I think of this Miss Grey. Then I will decide whether or not you are a fool for courting her good opinion.

Give me three days. If she passes muster, you may dance with her at the ball on Saturday."

Yes, Thomas thought. Georgiana *was* getting ready to step into Aunt Penelope's shoes.

☙

"You will never be a success if you insist on leaving early," Aunt Celia said over breakfast. Sophie had breakfasted earlier, and the servants had withdrawn, so they were alone.

"I will never be a success if I do not have a chaperone, either," Hyacinth pointed out.

"Ah, but then you wouldn't have had your little *tête-à-tête* with the future Duke, then, would you."

"He says that he wishes he won't be the duke," Hyacinth said. Aunt Celia hadn't seen her talking to Thomas, because she'd been in the card room the entire time, but evidently someone had told her.

"Nonsense. Everyone else is sure," Aunt Celia said. "They say that he intends to make you his mistress."

Hyacinth pushed her half-finished breakfast away. "That is patently ridiculous," she said, standing up. "I have no intention of being anyone's mistress."

"Well, my dear," Aunt Celia said, "no young lady *intends* to be anyone's mistress, but you should be on your guard. I do intend to find a respectable marriage for you."

"And what constitutes a respectable marriage?" Hyacinth fumed. "Some young gentleman who spends the entire evening--"

Aunt Celia held up a hand. "A man of appropriate rank. Do not reach above your station. It can only lead to disaster."

Hyacinth stood, one hand on the back of her chair, dumbfounded. If she denied that she'd had any courtship with Thomas, Aunt Celia would only laugh, even though it was really only sensible, and true insofar as her time in London went. The *Whistler* was behind them now, even if it had been a happier time. If she claimed that she was, somehow, setting Thomas in her sights, like an overreaching gunner, then Aunt Celia would gloat, and tighten her grip, and push her into the company of Viscount Whitley and an arsenal of other dull-witted gentlemen, their mamas lining up outside the door to inspect her like a bargain heifer.

"I am not 'reaching' in any sense," Hyacinth finally said. "I was merely having a conversation with an older lady when Thomas came along."

"Thomas, is it?" Aunt Celia tittered. "Oh, I'm afraid they are right, dear. We must get you married as soon as possible."

Hyacinth blushed deeply. She had slipped. Could she recover by calling him Sir Pently? She doubted it. Since there was nothing more to be said, or at least nothing she could think of, she retreated. She was about to walk out of the room when she remembered something. She turned back to face her aunt.

"Lady Thornton said you might know something about a scandal, yourself," Hyacinth said. "Do tell me about it someday."

She did not wait to see the anger rise in her aunt's eyes, but she heard a cup smash to the floor as she closed the door behind her.

❧

That afternoon, Hyacinth and Sophie were working on their embroidery in the front parlor when a gleaming black carriage with gold leaf trim pulled up to their door. Aunt Celia had just called for her own carriage, but this was someone else. Her usual round of visits would have to wait.

"Who is it?" she called down the stairs.

"The carriage has the Windcastle coat of arms," the butler informed her.

Sophie dropped her needle and ran to the window. "Who do you think it is, Hyacinth?"

Hyacinth's needle hovered above her canvas.

"I don't know," she said. "Perhaps it's Lady Georgiana Pently?" She certainly hoped it wasn't Thomas. Or, rather, she would have liked if it had been Mr. Smithson, but since he was actually Sir Pently, and not the man she'd thought he was, she didn't want to see him at all. He was an impostor, even if his deception lay in lowering himself, rather than taking on airs.

Sophie leaned up to the window. "Oh, I hope it is! I've heard so much about her! Mother says she's quite elegant."

Hyacinth looked away.

"Yes! Oh yes, there she is!" Sophie said. "She is elegant. And taller than Mama, too."

Hyacinth carefully pulled her needle through the canvas.

"Are Lady Talbot and Miss Grey at home?" Georgiana asked.

"I will enquire," the butler said.

A moment later, they heard Aunt Celia's step in the corridor above, then the swish of her skirts as she came downstairs.

"Lady Talbot!" Georgiana gushed. "Such a pleasure to see you."

"Do step in to the parlor," Aunt Celia invited. "I will send for tea."

When Georgiana walked in, Hyacinth and Sophie rose to greet her, and Aunt Celia introduced her daughter to Georgiana.

Sophie blushed and curtsied. "I am glad to meet you, Lady Pently. I've heard so much about you!"

Aunt Celia's mouth twitched as she swallowed an admonition. Sophie's bobbing up and down did look rather gauche, even to Hyacinth's less critical eye.

The ladies drew their chairs into a circle and sat. Georgiana and Aunt Celia launched into an animated discussion of the previous night's gowns, and who was wearing the latest fabrics from France. Hyacinth studied her tea leaves. The conversation seemed perfectly inane. Her thoughts drifted back to her grandmother's diary, and how good it would be to escape Aunt Celia's petty world, to do something, to teach.

"About a ride in the park?" Georgiana said to her. "You do ride, don't you?"

Hyacinth startled up. "I'm sorry, I wasn't listening."

Aunt Celia glared at her.

"I regularly go riding in the mornings, and have agreed to help chaperone some of my younger cousins," Georgiana said to Hyacinth. "Would you care to join us tomorrow?"

Sophie leaned forward eagerly. "May I, Mama?"

"And of course, you may come, too," Georgiana said to her, one corner of her mouth twitching in amusement.

Sophie's cheeks turned a deeper shade of pink.

"Well, I have a fitting first thing, and I will not go to the atelier on horseback," Aunt Celia said. "I don't know that I can provide a suitable chaperone for Sophie and Miss Grey."

"My old governess will be along, as well," Georgiana said. "She frequently chaperones my Aunt Penelope's grandchildren, and I'm practically a suitable chaperone myself, these days."

Aunt Celia nodded mutely, as if unsure whether Georgiana was looking for confirmation of her respectability, or reassurance that she was still too young to be considered a chaperone.

"I've only just begun to learn to ride," Hyacinth apologized. "We did not keep horses in Gibraltar. Father said there was no need."

Aunt Celia cleared her throat. "Sophie's pony has just come down from the country, and I'm sure she could do with the exercise." She smiled on her daughter with a sort of tense benevolence. Georgiana caught Hyacinth's eye and winked.

"So, shall we?" Georgiana asked Hyacinth. "We will collect you before breakfast."

Hyacinth smiled. "Yes," she said. "An early ride in the park sounds delightful. I quite look forward to it."

Aunt Celia frowned, as if she were holding back a sharp remark, but then smiled graciously to her visitor, and stood to see her out.

෨

The sun must have risen, somewhere behind the dark clouds over Hyde Park, but it did nothing to warm the air. Georgiana rode a milk-white Arabian gelding. She wore a dark green scarf with intricate embroidery on it draped around her neck. It reminded Hyacinth of the shawl Thomas had given her, still wrapped in its brown paper at the back of her wardrobe. She could hardly wear it out, she thought. She wouldn't have thought that it would suit the *ton*'s fashion sense, but if Georgiana was wearing one, then others would follow. Hyacinth still had half a mind to send hers back to Mr. Smithson. Thomas. Sir Pently.

Hyacinth's mount was an indifferently-groomed livery stable nag, better looking than the pony she'd ridden the past two mornings, with Aunt Celia, but more temperamental. She struggled to keep pace with Georgiana and her steed while Sophie and the younger Pently cousins raced ahead on their ponies, laughing despite the cold. The youngest was a boy of about six or seven, and the oldest was a girl about Sophie's age. The governess rode within arm's reach of the youngest – as much as she could manage – while the older girls trotted ahead, carrying on some sort of guarded conversation. Sophie seemed happy. The poor girl was lonely. She didn't take to solitude well.

Georgiana seemed to be looking more at the tree line and the far reaches of the park than at her cousins, who really did seem to be adequately overseen by their governess.

"I think we shall have snow," Georgiana said idly.

"Do you?" Hyacinth answered. "I haven't seen snow since we've been in London."

"It's one of the best things about being here in winter," Georgiana said, wrinkling her nose. "It covers up the dirt and muck for a few hours. It's really quite lovely."

Hyacinth eyed the clouds. They did not seem inclined to produce anything lovely, just more dreariness.

"Then again, it could just be sleet," Georgiana sighed.

There was a long silence. Hyacinth felt that she ought to say something.

"Thank you for inviting us out," she said. "Sophie hardly ever gets to see other girls her age."

"So I heard. And you are new in town. It isn't my habit to

bring young ladies into Society, but I thought you might be interesting."

"Interesting?" Hyacinth said.

"You're well-favored, and Thomas tells me that you have Greek and Latin, and better grasp of mathematics than most factors," Georgiana said. "Is that so?"

Hyacinth shrugged. "I do have Greek and Latin, as well as Spanish and a little French, but I don't expect any of that to do me much good here in London, from what I've seen so far. Except possibly for the maths, if I need to cross-examine accounts."

Georgiana rode on in silence for a few paces. "Whose accounts?"

"My own," Hyacinth said.

"Your aunt tells me that you haven't a penny to your name."

Hyacinth tugged hard on the reins, not that she'd meant to. It sent her nag shuffling sideways. The horse jerked its head forward and it took all of Hyacinth's attention to bring the beast back into line. She returned to her place beside Georgiana, who had stopped to wait for her.

"Is that not correct?" Georgiana said.

"It is not," Hyacinth answered, "but she would rather I not claim my inheritance, since she says that it is tainted with scandal."

Georgiana considered that for a moment. "Was it acquired through trade? Your aunt seems woefully old-fashioned sometimes. Trade is growing almost... if not respectable, then at least more influential, even in our circles."

"Not the flesh trade," Hyacinth said.

Georgiana gasped, and momentarily dropped her reins. Her mount stayed on course. Georgiana regained her composure quickly, too.

"How?" she whispered.

"I really shouldn't be saying this," Hyacinth said.

"I won't tell," Georgiana said. "I am not... I have no need to stir up other people's scandals. My life is not that boring." Her full attention was trained on Hyacinth, who felt just a little uncomfortable with the scrutiny, so different from her aunt's, curious, more than critical. Or so she wanted to think.

Hyacinth frowned. "Aunt Celia's life seems to be. Boring, that is. But that's beside the point." She had no one to talk to, not really, and though Mr. Butler seemed friendly enough he was a man, and a stranger, and really only a sort of business associate. She wanted to trust Georgiana. After all, if she were to start a school, it would be good to have benefactors and supporters.

"My grandmother, my mother's mother, was a famous courtesan. Her early life... well, it was simply unspeakable. Later, she became the paramour of a man she calls Bereford."

"That must be the current earl's father, or grandfather," Georgiana mused.

"I know nothing about him, not really," Hyacinth said, "only that he left my grandmother with a cottage. Through investments or selling jewels or possibly gambling, she ended her life with an estate and five tenant farmers."

"Where is this estate?" Georgiana asked.

"In H—shire. I don't know anything more about it."

"It's not a bad dowry. I don't see why Lady Talbot is so set against it."

"She doesn't know about the estate, only that my grandmother..."

"Was the exact opposite of everything she has striven to be," Georgiana said.

Hyacinth nodded. "Apart from her devotion to fashion," she said. "I only saw my grandmother once, when I was about the age that Sophie is now, but she was stunning. She eclipsed Aunt Celia, who drove her away the moment she stepped in the door. I think she would have set out armed guards to drive her off, if she'd known she was coming."

Georgiana snorted. "I can't say I'm surprised. Celia dislikes competition."

Hyacinth sighed. The clouds above them seemed to be growing darker. "What would you do?" she asked Georgiana.

"I suppose I would see to my estate, first," Georgiana said.

"I wouldn't know where to begin. I don't even know how to get there, let alone how to manage an estate," Hyacinth said. "Aunt Celia is determined to keep me under her watch—"

"Except when there are eligible louts in the room," Georgiana interrupted.

"Yes. I've only barely managed to escape getting mauled by that Viscount Whitley, and getting out to see my solicitor required scheming and subterfuge. I have no idea how I will get to the bank."

"A visit to the bank can be arranged," Georgiana said.

They had reached the end of the park. Sophie, with the Pently children and their governess, waited by the gates. A few snow flakes drifted down through the air, only to melt the moment they touched the muddy ground.

"We will go shopping tomorrow," Georgiana told Hyacinth, loudly. "I'm sure your aunt will approve," she added, a bit more quietly.

Hyacinth was not entirely convinced. "She might approve, or not," she whispered, "but she won't snub you; I'm sure of that."

Georgiana laughed. "No, she won't. It's a pity…" she trailed off, shaking her head, and turned away from the younger people. "It's not my business, but I don't mind helping you," she whispered. "I think it will be rather better for you to have your own income, as Thomas has his."

"Thomas? What does he have to do with any of this?" Hyacinth said.

"You see," Georgiana said, "you've had your secrets, too, and he, as Mr. Smithson, became quite the nabob. Even if he doesn't become a duke…"

"Do you think he won't?" Hyacinth asked.

"Come on, Aunt Georgie!" one of the boys called.

"Coming!" Georgiana called back. She pursed her lips. "I don't know," she said to Hyacinth, "but there's a chance he'll be only Sir Pently of Lawton, and that estate is… not so much of a burden. So you might have your Mr. Smithson nearly back."

With that, she rode up to the others and entered their midst.

Hyacinth gaped. Did Georgiana *want* her to court Thomas? She pulled her horse into line behind the others as they left the park, trying not to fall too far behind. She liked Georgiana, not only because she played the pianoforte better than anyone she'd ever heard before, or that she was still independent and unmarried. She seemed intelligent, too, and for all her talk of fashion with Aunt Celia, she seemed to be not entirely a creature of appearances.

As they approached Aunt Celia's house, the snow began to stick to the rooftops and railings, a lacy dusting of white. It was really quite wonderful in its cold, delicate way, so much so that Hyacinth nearly forgot her cold fingers.

Georgiana dropped back to ride beside her for a few paces as they approached the house.

"You ought to forgive him, I think," she said. "He only wanted to escape, even more than you want to escape your aunt now. I can't blame him for trying to shirk his duties. No one ever expected he would be heir."

Hyacinth looked away. "He wasn't being honest. I like honesty."

"He was only trying to be himself. It's hard to do with the whole clan breathing down your back."

"I wouldn't know. I don't have a clan," Hyacinth said.

"Then we will find you one," Georgiana decided. "And go shopping for bonnets tomorrow afternoon!" She clicked to her magnificent gelding and trotted away.

ॐ

Georgiana's response to his plight had not been encouraging, Thomas thought. Three days seemed like an eternity. She'd quizzed him about Hyacinth's character and situation. When he revealed that he knew next to nothing about her connections, her intentions, and her family, she brushed him away. He could not be serious, she said, and still know so little about the lady whose regard he seemed to care for so much. He would forget her, she declared. First, though, he had it on good authority that she'd visited Lady Talbot, and, by consequence, Hyacinth.

He decided to write to her anyway.

❧

Hyacinth watched Georgiana go with mixed feelings. There was something frivolous, even dismissive, about the way she'd decided to take on Hyacinth's clandestine mission, sweeping her out from under Aunt Celia's nose.

"Come on inside, Hyacinth," Sophie called. "I could eat two breakfasts!"

The boy from the livery stable was stomping his feet to keep them warm, waiting to take her intractable mount. She turned away from the retreating Pently party and dismounted.

"Mama has already gone out," Sophie reported as she entered the house, "and there's post for you! Two pieces of post. From gentlemen, I think."

Sophie handed her the post, and Hyacinth nearly laughed. One of them was a thin letter from George. "That one is not from a gentleman," she said, "only from... a boy." She wished she could tell Sophie about George.

"A boy?" Sophie asked.

"He is nine years old, and I tutored him in Gibraltar," Hyacinth said, hoping that would be enough to satisfy Sophie's curiosity. Then she looked at the second letter, closed with an intricate seal. It was from Thomas.

"You mean you worked as a governess?" Sophie asked.

"Well, not exactly, but close enough," Hyacinth said. Aunt Celia's butler helped her with her coat and led the two young ladies to breakfast.

"Is he very clever?" Sophie asked.

"Who?" Hyacinth said.

"The boy you tutored in Gibraltar, of course!"

"Clever enough," Hyacinth said.

"Do you think I'm clever?"

"What a vain question!" Hyacinth laughed. "I do think you're clever, but without education..." She couldn't go on. Aunt Celia would have her head. "Oh, never mind. Let's eat."

"But..." Sophie began.

"But it is a matter for your mother to decide," she sighed. Unfortunately, in Sophie's case. That was enough to hold off further conversation on that topic, and Sophie turned to talking about the Pently cousins' ponies, and their stern-looking governess. Hyacinth's letters were forgotten.

After breakfast, Hyacinth retreated to her room and rang for Maria. She waited. Maria usually came quickly, but now Hyacinth found herself pacing and fretting, wondering what was keeping her maid away. She looked at the two letters in her hand. She wanted to share George's note with Maria, but not the other one. She hid Thomas's letter under her pillow and paced some more. She kept going back to the pillow, then dragging herself away, walking back again, until finally she drew out the letter.

She studied the seal's curls and flourishes, tracing them with her finger. She ought to send it back. After all, he could ask his cousin how she fared, if he wanted to know. He must know that she and Georgiana had been riding together that morning. She didn't want to send it back, though. It had swum through the post and arrived with George's letter, and if it weren't for Mr. Smithson, she would not have George's letter at all. She wished they were all back on the *Whistler*.

Hyacinth went to the door, listened, and when she heard no footsteps approaching, opened the letter.

My dear Miss Grey,

It seems that I have miss-stepped, again, and again I beg your pardon. I understand that my cousin has come to visit you. Georgiana is not at all like most of my other relations. If they were all like my Aunt Penelope and Georgiana, I might have stayed in England, and never known the heartache of India.

As you have heard, I now stand in line to inherit my uncle's title, provided he does not sire an heir in his dotage, but as vile as he can be, I doubt he would sink to murdering his aged duchess in order to get a younger one, still able to bear an heir.

When I neglected to tell you all of this, I was still Mr. Smithson, the person I have been for all of my life as a man, a person of no family connections, just another youth gone East to find his fortune. I had been free for ten years, and was not ready to relinquish that freedom any sooner than I needed to. That included taking back my family name. If I deceived you by omission, it was a matter of wanting to believe in myself as I have been, not as I might become, in the situation awaiting me here in England.

Will you pardon me, and may we begin again?

Yours Sincerely,

Thomas Smithson Pently

Hyacinth jumped as a knock sounded on the door.

"Come in," she said reflexively. She still had the letter in her hand, and hurriedly tucked it into the desk drawer, crumpling it a little. She felt sorry for him. Almost. It was hard to feel sorry for a man who had won so much wealth in trade, and had also won it by birth. Besides, if she could tolerate Aunt Celia, then surely he could muster the courage to face his own father. However, Hyacinth didn't know what Thomas's father was like, and if he thought his uncle nearly capable of murder, then perhaps there was something to justify his running away and wanting to escape them until their noose settled on his own neck – not that being a duke was a death sentence.

Hyacinth composed herself as Maria entered. When she looked up, Maria had bent over to remove a piece of straw from the heel of her boot. Her cheeks were flushed, as if she'd run all the way up from the back of the garden. Possibly, even, from the stables.

Hyacinth reached back into the desk, looking for George's letter.

"What took you so long?" she asked Maria, to cover her own embarrassment.

"I am sorry," Maria said.

"Never mind," Hyacinth said. "I just wanted to show you that we have a letter from George. If only I can find it now!" She rustled through the pages. Thomas's letter kept finding its way to the top, and she shoved it back again and again. Maria was still busy checking her boots for stray bits of straw. Hyacinth finally found George's note, which she must have knocked to the back of the drawer in her haste to hide the other letter.

"Here it is!" she announced. "Let's sit."

They drew their chairs up to the cold grate, and Maria took the tinder to light the fire.

Dear Sister,

Mrs. Portnoy says I should take the early coach for London on Saturday, and I will arrive by midday. I will walk to Bloomsbury if you send directions.

Yours,

George

"Directions!" Hyacinth said. "Can he know how large London is?"

Maria shook her head. "No, of course not. He cannot walk alone. I will ask Harold where the Portsmouth coaches arrive. He will know, I think?"

"Yes, do," Hyacinth said. "We will go to meet him."

Maria looked at her. "Do you think you can get away?"

"No. Probably I won't be able to escape the house, or whatever expedition Aunt Celia has planned," Hyacinth sighed. "Where will he stay?"

"Don't worry," said Maria. "I will arrange it." She winked, and Hyacinth thought that she blushed again. Yes, Maria and her new beau would arrange it. Maria and the coachman. No one could object to that match, not on grounds of rank. Hyacinth sighed. She was going to have to deceive her aunt yet again, first by going "shopping for bonnets" with Georgiana, then some other subterfuge to meet her own brother. London was thick with deception.

&

CHAPTER 12: FAMILY MATTERS

Maria reported that Georgiana had told Lady Talbot that her niece had expressed a wish to surprise her with a gift. She'd offered to help Hyacinth find something that would meet Lady Talbot's exacting standards. She arrived in the Pentlys' town coach to collect Hyacinth and Maria for a tour of some of the most fashionable shops, or so she said.

"But what will I buy her?" Hyacinth asked, as they pulled away from Aunt Celia's house.

Georgiana laughed. "This." She produced a striped hat box from underneath the blankets and handed it to Hyacinth.

Hyacinth peeked inside. It was a gaudy confection of yellow fabric flowers on a dark blue velvet ribbon. The hat itself was hardly noticeable beneath its decorations.

"You wanted to buy something in primrose blue," Georgiana told Hyacinth, "but I informed you that Lady Talbot doesn't like pale colours."

"On herself," Hyacinth said. "I had noticed that."

"You may not have to concoct much of a story at all, then," Georgiana said, "but at least give me credit for approving of your choice."

Hyacinth picked the hat out of its box. The work was very fine. She would not have chosen it for herself, but she could see that it would suit Aunt Celia very well.

"Was it very expensive?" Hyacinth asked, after a while. She knew that Georgiana was wealthy enough to pay for the hat, but didn't want to be a charity case.

"I suppose it might have been," Georgiana said, "but I didn't buy it. It was a gift from an admirer of mine. It doesn't suit me, and if he sees it on Lady Talbot, he will know what I think of his gifts."

Hyacinth nodded. "So this suits your purposes, too."

"It does," Georgiana said.

Maria sat quietly in the corner of the carriage. She kept her eyes on the street outside, but Hyacinth knew she'd been listening.

"Does your maid speak English?" Georgiana asked.

"Yes. Maria speaks English and Spanish well, and a little French, too."

Georgiana assessed Maria. "How do you find London?" she asked.

Maria blushed. Hyacinth was fairly sure that Aunt Celia had not addressed her directly since they'd arrived at her house. "It is colder than I am used to, but I like it, the... how do you say it, bustle? I think I would like to stay here."

Hyacinth had imagined Maria following her to the country, to her grandmother's estate, wherever it was, but if this romance with Aunt Celia's coachman continued, if Maria were to marry—

Georgiana's voice interrupted her thoughts. "What was the name of your bank?"

"Lyon's," Hyacinth said. "I don't know where it is."

"Ah, but I'm sure our coachman does," Georgiana said. She tapped on the roof of the coach and put her head out to tell the driver where they were going. The man responded with a "Yes, m'lady." The horses snorted and protested as they turned in the street, the coach heaving a little as they reversed direction.

"Now," Georgiana said, once they had settled into their new route, "what do you propose to do with this fortune of yours?"

Georgiana was a duke's daughter, fabulously wealthy, well-spoken, and an accomplished musician. That was all she knew of her new ally. She was independent, or so it seemed, and for some reason she had taken up Hyacinth's cause, whether out of boredom or because Thomas had piqued her interest in his shipboard friend.

"I have been thinking of starting a school," Hyacinth said. "For girls. Girls like my grandmother was, thrown out on their own resources, when they have none. I don't know what else I can offer, but I know that I can teach, and if a few could become governesses, or even housekeepers, rather than dying in the stews... well, maybe that would honour my grandmother's memory."

Georgiana thought a moment before replying. "But your grandmother did quite well in the stews, it seems."

"Only by the barest of chances. It was not, I think, the life she would have chosen, if she'd been given a choice."

"And you," Georgiana said, "would you be happy to spend your life as a maiden schoolmarm?"

"Why not?" Hyacinth said. She felt sure, now, that Georgiana would report back to Thomas. "And what of you? Are you happy to spend your life as a maiden fashion icon?"

At that, Georgiana laughed. "There are worse fates. There are certainly worse fates."

❧

Georgiana offered to lend her support to Hyacinth's proposed school, but Hyacinth wanted to go into the bank without her.

"Are you quite sure?" Georgiana asked.

"I think so. I must know for myself what I have in hand. I must sit with it alone, to think."

"Very well then, I will go bonnet shopping by myself. It would be strange to come back with only one, don't you think?"

Hyacinth shrugged. "I trust your judgment in that."

Maria had been silent in the coach, but as soon as they were away from Georgiana, she spoke.

"*Do* you trust her?" she asked.

"I don't know, entirely," Hyacinth mused, "but I like her, and I need to escape Aunt Celia's clutches somehow. At least she can't want any of my money, because she has so much of her own. Why not trust her?"

Maria pursed her lips. "It is only that she seems... frivolous."

"I am starting to think she only wants people to believe that," Hyacinth said. The bank doors loomed before them. "But enough of Lady Georgiana. Let's go in."

Maria toyed with her rosary – something she only did when quite nervous. Hyacinth tried not to let her own nerves get the best of her. A guard opened the door for them without question, his eyes on the gleaming coach they'd arrived in.

Hyacinth looked back at the coach and waved to Georgiana, who smiled and waved as the coachman snapped the reins and they drove off. A momentary look of worry crossed the guard's face.

"They will return for us in half an hour," Hyacinth said. "I am here to see Mr. Lyons."

"He's going home shortly," the guard said. "He keeps early hours, you know, but..." His eyes followed the coach as it turned the corner, with the two liveried footmen hanging onto its sides. "Who shall I tell him is here?" he asked.

"Miss Grey, regarding Mrs. Miller's accounts." Hyacinth said.

If the guard had any prejudice against the infamous Mrs. Miller, or even knew who she was, it didn't show on his face. He stepped away, and another guard replaced him while Maria and Hyacinth waited just inside the door. Moments later, the guard returned with a harried expression.

"Please, Miss Grey, follow me. Mr. Lyons will see you now."

They followed a carpeted corridor to stairs which led up to another, more richly carpeted corridor. At its end, an oak door stood open, brass hinges gleaming. Hyacinth stepped through the door into a high-ceilinged office overlooking the street. Iron bars guarded the windows, and a dozen gilt-framed portraits adorned the inner walls.

Mr. Lyons stood as Hyacinth entered. He was about the same age as Mr. Butler, but more portly. He wore a velvet waistcoat and tipped his pipe into a tray.

"Miss Grey," he said, coming out from behind his desk. "You are the image of your grandmother."

"Of my grandmother?" Hyacinth said. "I am pleased to make your acquaintance, but I confess I am surprised how well both you, and the solicitor, seem to remember my mother and grandmother. They cannot have been my own age for many years."

"Ah, her image is a pleasure to hold in the mind, Miss Grey," the banker answered. "She was a beautiful woman, as I'm sure you've heard. But, as it happens, I have an *aide memoire*." He gestured towards the wall.

Hyacinth turned to see a large portrait hanging on the wall behind her. It was like looking into a very flattering mirror. The woman in the painting wore an old-fashioned dress, and her hair was held in a high, powdered wig in the style of the last century, but the banker was right: she looked very much like Hyacinth... except that she had been a famous beauty, and Hyacinth had always considered herself rather ordinary looking.

"It is good that you take after her," he said. "Your father's family may be fine people, but you could hardly do better than to resemble your grandmother."

Hyacinth thought she ought to feel uncomfortable at being compared to an infamous courtesan, but the banker's praise seemed so wholehearted that it would be petty to take offense – especially because this was her own grandmother, too, as well as a courtesan.

"She was a great lady, no matter what others might say of her," he continued. "I have her portrait here not only because she was a beautiful woman, but also because she was one of the first and strongest backers of my enterprise here. Without her, I don't think I would have this bank today. Perhaps some lesser place of business, but not at this address, and not with the other clients I have now. She did a great deal for me, your grandmother did."

"I know very little about her," Hyacinth apologized, "having grown up away from England."

"Well, Miss Grey, it's a shame you didn't know her better in life, but there's no denying that you're her heir, and so it's time you learned what you can. Are you of age yet?"

"I am twenty-two," Hyacinth answered.

"That will do, according to the terms of the will," he said. "You'll have to learn to manage your own affairs, but if you take after your grandmother at all..." He trailed off, looking at the portrait.

"I managed my father's household in Gibraltar," Hyacinth offered. "I understand that my grandmother left me rather more than I'm accustomed to, but I have a little experience."

The banker nodded. "Good. I hope that you do well. In the meantime, let us bring you her deposit boxes, and I'll send for the account books."

A few minutes later, Hyacinth and Maria sat in a private room near Mr. Lyons' office with two large boxes perched on the table before them.

"Your grandmother must have been very rich," Maria said.

Hyacinth nodded, wondering which box to look into first. "I wish I'd known her," she said. She chose one box and fitted the key into its lock.

The musty smell of old paper and leather wafted out. Inside, Hyacinth found a stack of two dozen leather-bound journals, much like the one Mr. Butler had sent her, along with a packet of letters. She picked up the journals, one by one. She could not read them all, not all at once. Her grandmother's final journal had been full of peaceful reflections on her life as the owner of an estate, plus a few complaints about old age, but Hyacinth did not relish the thought of reading a closer account of her years as a kept woman, let alone as a denizen of the demi-monde.

The weight of all her grandmother's experience, or what was left of it, seemed to be contained in those volumes.

"I'll take them with me," she decided. "Let's look into the

other box."

The second box was heavier, so much so that Hyacinth could not move it on her own. Maria helped her shift it closer to the window, where the light was better. The box was full to the brim of small packets wrapped in leather and silk and velvet. Hyacinth chose one and untied its string, pulling out a long string of freshwater pearls with golden clasp, figured like an oyster shell.

Maria's eyes went wide.

Hyacinth picked up another packet. It held a silver necklace with a piece of red coral, heavy and strange, yet compellingly shaped. She untied a third packet, then a fourth and fifth, finding earrings, baubles, a thin bracelet of diamonds. Each piece was beautiful, and most looked as if they had been very expensive indeed.

"I can't imagine," Hyacinth said, "how she wore all these, never mind how she acquired them."

Maria frowned. "Maybe it is better not to think about that too much," she said.

Hyacinth shook her head. "I must think about it. I cannot ignore it. Oh, how I wish I had known her!"

She pushed back the jewelry, all those pieces that her grandmother had paid for with her favors, or so she presumed. She didn't feel quite right, possessing all of it. Her father and mother had taken her away to the Mediterranean so that she would grow up untainted by the scandals which had brought her all of this, and yet they would buy her independence, and maybe, just maybe, she could bring that to other young women. Maybe.

"We should go," Hyacinth decided. "Let's wrap these up." She reached for the bracelet on its pouch of leather. Then she spotted one more intriguing packet in the box, tucked into a bottom corner. She reached for it.

"I want to open just one more," she said.

The wrapping was a multi-coloured, textured silk, quite different from the dark velvets and soft leathers covering the other pieces. Hyacinth untied its complicated knot, no practical dockyard knot, but a weaving of silken cord, almost an ornament in itself.

The necklace slithered out onto the table top, a coil of warm gold chain, round like a snake. Dangling from it was a piece of sapphire, set again in gold, with a color as blue as the Mediterranean on a sunny day.

"*Que bella*!" Maria exclaimed.

"It is beautiful," Hyacinth echoed in a whisper. It would also go perfectly with the ball gown that her aunt was having made for her. "I think I will take this with me, too," she decided. She retied the knot, trying to reproduce what she'd just unraveled, and slipped the necklace into her reticule. Maria bundled the journals together and wrapped them in cloth.

"I suppose we'll have to tell Aunt Celia we stopped at a book shop, too," Hyacinth said. "She won't like it, and I don't like this sneaking around behind her back, but what can I do?"she said, thinking out loud.

"You must claim your inheritance," Maria said firmly. "You can't go on living with your aunt. You've been sad there, more sad than I have been. I cannot blame it all on the weather."

Hyacinth sighed. "But you are happy enough there, I think. I feel ungrateful, ungracious towards her."

"So do most of her staff, even though she treats them well enough," Maria confided.

"Would you come with me, if I left?" Hyacinth asked.

"Of course I would! I would always come with you."

"Even though..."

Maria waved her concern away. "Harold can come to me, if he likes." She smiled. "And so can your gentleman."

Hyacinth laughed. "I don't have a gentleman."

"I think you do."

Hyacinth shook her head. "Let's go. Lady Pently will be waiting." Thomas was her friend, perhaps, but with her grandmother's story in her hands, she felt she could not have the makings of a duchess. She would not be his lover, either. No, she did not have a "gentleman," no matter what everyone else thought, or what she, herself, might dream in an unguarded moment. She had seen Thomas's world, and she was not a part of it. She would be a schoolmarm with a few choice jewels hidden away at a bank, and that was that.

❧

Thomas's cousins streamed into the breakfast room, rosy-cheeked and alive, snowflakes trailing them. It was enough to make him want a horse. After breakfast, he left Windcastle house to tour all of the horse markets in the vicinity, with one of the grooms. He found nothing which quite pleased him, but the next morning the groom suggested they visit the house of a man he knew of, who had recently found himself in debt and had fine stables.

"Why didn't we come here yesterday?" Thomas asked, looking down the row of well-kept stalls, housing some of the finest horses he'd seen in years.

"Begging your pardon, Sir, but I thought if you were happy with what you found yesterday, there'd be no need to tell you about this lot."

Thomas thought of grumbling, but then the swish of a tail caught his eye. That tail belonged to a fine black horse, taller than most, but with a racehorse's build. He stomped in his stall. He had a white star on his forehead, and white socks, and looked like he was thinking of breaking down the stable doors.

"That one," Thomas declared. "I think that one will do."

The next morning, Thomas joined Georgiana and the younger Pentlys for their ride, well-mounted, but with much lighter pockets.

"You're sure to impress Miss Grey with that prime bit," Georgiana teased. She approved of the horse, though. How could anyone not? He was worth enough to settle half his former master's considerable debts, and looked every inch of it.

"Miss Grey?" Thomas said. "Do you think we'll see her?"

"It's possible, but don't worry, your stallion there will terrify her livery-stable screw into bolting across the green. You'll be spared conversation."

Thomas sighed. "Not what I'd had in mind."

"I see," Georgiana said. "Of course, then you can swoop in and rescue her when the nag bolts. What's this boy's name?"

Thomas patted the sleek black neck of his horse. "They called him Polaris. I think I'll keep it. Wouldn't want to confuse him."

"It suits," Georgiana said.

"Yes," Thomas agreed. "And now, I think I'll give him his head. See what he can do."

Polaris didn't need to be asked twice. He shook out his mane and thundered across the park. Thomas reveled at the wind in his hair, the feeling of freedom, and the sheer speed of it. They reached the far end of the park in only a few minutes, and he doubled back to rejoin his cousins, thundering across the grass, faster than he'd ridden in a very long time, if ever. Polaris slowed reluctantly.

"You'll have to take up racing," Georgiana said as he returned.

"I think I might," Thomas answered. "Break my neck, if I'm lucky."

Out of the corner of his eye, Thomas spotted a garish yellow flare on some unfortunate lady's head.

"Ah. I see my gift has found its roost at last," Georgiana said, raising a hand to greet the trio of ladies just entering the park. "You must not tell Lady Talbot where it came from."

"It? You mean that yellow thing?" Thomas said. "It's nearly as bad as Nate's waistcoat."

"It is," Georgiana said, "but I couldn't throw it away. The workmanship is very fine, very fine indeed. As it is on Nate's waistcoat. You should know that your Miss Grey is supposed to have bought it for her aunt."

"I see," Thomas said.

The ladies rode towards them, Hyacinth behind her aunt while her young cousin, a girl who could not be more than twelve, waved frantically to the Pently children.

"Please, Mama," the girl said. "May I ride with them?"

Lady Talbot frowned. "You may, but stay in sight," she said.

Georgiana greeted them. "And you must ride with us, Lady Talbot, Miss Grey."

Thomas tipped his hat to the ladies.

"I simply must tell you all about some of the atrocities we saw in the bonnet shops yesterday," Georgiana said, drawing up alongside Lady Talbot.

Lady Talbot smiled thinly. "I'm sure, but I'm glad you were there to guide Hyacinth. She knows nothing about style, but perhaps she's beginning to learn." She patted her new hat affectionately. It was disgusting, Thomas thought.

He backed away, and so did Hyacinth. How could she endure her aunt?

"And how are you this morning?" he asked her.

"Well enough," Hyacinth said, pulling her horse's head up from the grass. The nag was no better than Georgiana had implied she would be.

"I should lend you a mount from my family's stables," Thomas said, looking at the unfortunate bit of horseflesh.

"You certainly should not," Hyacinth said. "I wouldn't know what to do with a better horse."

Polaris shied away, as if agreeing with Hyacinth's assessment.

"You won't learn anything but frustration on that one, though," Thomas said.

Hyacinth frowned. The horse was trying to graze again, and wandered off the path.

Lady Talbot looked back at them. "Do catch up!" she scolded.

"I'm coming," Hyacinth said. The horse had other ideas. It wandered towards the woods. Sighting something in the trees, it picked up its tired hooves and trotted away from the others.

"Really, Celia, you must get your niece a better mount," Thomas heard Georgiana say. "The nag does nothing for her looks, and that stunning cloak you must have chosen for her would look so much finer if your niece were better horsed."

"It seems a waste, for someone who can barely tell one rein from the other, but you may be right." Lady Talbot looked disapprovingly after her niece. "Still," she said, "the girl's posture is not bad, and at least my Sophie knows how to control her pony."

Thomas spurred Polaris after Hyacinth, if only to get away from Georgiana and Lady Talbot. He suspected that Georgiana was playing a deeper game, but he found her friend too much to bear.

Hyacinth's ill-bred beast had stopped to graze on some tired tufts of grass at the edge of the trees. He reached down from Polaris's back and took her reins.

"Shall we rejoin the others?" he asked.

Down on the green, Lady Talbot and Georgiana were riding towards the young people. Lady Talbot glanced back at Hyacinth, caught halfway to frowning.

"Not yet," Hyacinth said, turning away from them. "I received your letter the other morning, but I wasn't sure how to reply." She looked up at him. "I'm sorry. I think I do understand, at least a little."

"Thank you," Thomas said. "I am not truly comfortable with my situation here yet. I still nurse hopes that, one way or another, I'll be able to live out my life as a free man."

"It seems unlikely," Hyacinth said, "and it is just as well that we never had any formal courtship."

Thomas shook his head. "Or much informal, at least not..."

"Not publicly, and nothing that can't be ignored, where others are concerned."

He thought he heard a note of regret in her voice, but he couldn't be sure.

"You know, I think I would still rather marry you than any of the young ladies I have met here," he said.

"That is beside the point," Hyacinth said, looking away. "It is impossible. You are to be a duke, and I am a courtesan's heiress, which is a dubious distinction, at best." She tried to take the reins back from him.

"A courtesan's heiress?" Thomas echoed. "How?" Hyacinth was so prim and proper in her appearances, it seemed absurd to think of her having any association with courtesans at all, even long-ago courtesans.

"My grandmother. I thought Georgiana would have told you." She tugged on the reins again, but he held tight.

"No, Georgiana has told me nothing, but she's not shooing you away from me, so she must approve."

"Approve?" Hyacinth snorted. "I don't know what she thinks, but she did say that she would help me start the kind of school I had in mind."

"What kind of school?" Thomas asked. He wanted to ask about the courtesan, but that was more awkward. Courtesans weren't known for leaving their heirs much of anything, as a rule. He made a show of leading Hyacinth's horse away from the trees. Polaris stomped impatiently, wanting to run again, but he held firm, and the horse listened.

Hyacinth explained her scheme to squander her inheritance by teaching friendless and downtrodden girls everything from mathematics to Ovid, along with more practical subjects. She told him that she had an estate, somewhere near the Welsh border, and that there was enough money to begin a school there, if the place suited. With Georgiana's backing, especially if it became a fashionable cause, she could probably do well. Certainly, England had an abundance of girls who were, as Hyacinth said, alone and needing friends.

"I don't know of any schools like that," Thomas said. "It sounds like the sort of thing that a religious order might take up as a missionary effort."

Hyacinth frowned at that. "It does," she agreed, "but I do think that education could improve these girls' prospects, or give them hope of a less... a less beastly life."

"Beastly?" Thomas said. "It can't be all bad, if your grandmother prospered enough to will you an estate."

"No," she said. "I've read her journals, or some of them, anyway. I only got them yesterday, except for the last one, which was mostly peaceful. She came so close to death, so many times. It's a miracle that she even lived through all of that." Hyacinth wiped a tear from her eye. "Come on. I think I should rejoin the others."

He wanted to say something, but what was there to say? He let her have the reins. She kicked her reluctant mount back to the group of young people, gathered on the path under a cloud of Lady Talbot's disdain. Hyacinth seemed to wish that she'd known her grandmother, which was only natural, but difficult, if your grandmother were so notoriously a courtesan. It was too bad that her family were so awkward, Thomas thought. Then he recognized the thought for what it was: pure aristocratic snobbery. Her grandmother had survived and prospered. Her aunt appeared to represent everything he despised about London society, but Hyacinth wasn't her aunt, any more than he was his uncle, and by Jove, she was fascinating.

Georgiana winked at him as he returned.

"Be quiet," he grumbled.

She rolled her eyes. "Go on with your ride then," she said. "We'll see you back at the house."

Thomas let Polaris gallop again, but once out of the park he slowed to a walk and drifted home by a circuitous route, not ready to face his gaggle of half-grown cousins over kippers and coffee. He was so preoccupied that he almost collided with the carriage in front of him as it turned into Windcastle house. Only Polaris saved him, swerving and carrying him into the courtyard alongside it. The carriage bore the duke's coat of arms. Thomas drew back sharply on the reins.

"Sorry there, boy," he said to the horse, who was tossing his head at the affront of the near-collision, and his rider's inattentiveness.

Thomas did not feel at all ready to face the duke. Or his father, for that matter. He had no time to collect his thoughts, let alone flee into the house, before the footman opened the carriage door.

At the first glimpse of a delicately slippered foot, he tensed.

The lady turned back to speak to someone else in the carriage. The voice was familiar, but for a moment he couldn't place it. Even her traveling dress rustled with bits of silk. Thomas dismounted from Polaris and handed the reins to a groom. The woman turned around.

"Mother?" he said.

The half-smile on her lips faded. "Am I?" Heloise, Baroness of Lawton, looked him over slowly. "I could have sworn that none of my boys were ever so brown."

"India will do that to a man," Thomas said after a pause, straining to maintain a sociable smile. His mother looked well for a woman with grown sons, though crow's feet were settling around her shrewd eyes. She had inherited the title, and although Lawton was hers by inheritance, her husband had ruled it from the moment he married her, if Thomas recalled correctly.

"I see the subcontinent has not ruined you utterly," she said, affecting a jaded tone, though her eyes brightened, as if she were holding back a smile. "But you must excuse me, Tommy." She turned back to the carriage to help someone else down.

A young lady emerged, clutching his mother's arm with a pale, thin hand. She had a smooth face which was almost heart-shaped, and her eyes were a bright, tear-stained blue. Although her hands were thin, her waist was not. Her belly bulged beneath her traveling coat.

"Thomas," his mother said. "May I present Lady Caroline."

Thomas bowed to her. "I am pleased to make your acquaintance," he said.

"Hmm," his mother said. Lady Caroline opened her mouth to speak, but no sound came out. She looked at Thomas as if he were a viper preparing to strike. Thomas backed away.

"Lady Caroline is Marquess Gravely's widow," his mother informed him. "Poor Gregory."

"Gregory?" Thomas said. His heart lightened. "How wonderful." He smiled more broadly than he had in months, maybe even a year. "I am delighted. Simply delighted to meet you. And I hope, along with everyone else here, that you bear a son, a good, healthy son."

Lady Caroline's impossibly smooth brow wrinkled with puzzlement. "Truly?" she said.

"Yes, truly," Thomas said.

His mother cleared her throat. "Thomas," she chided. "You must not keep us standing here in the cold. Our journey has been wearying, and we are not quite collected yet."

The footmen had taken their trunks down, and were awaiting instruction.

"I will meet you in my parlor in an hour's time," she said to Thomas. With that decree, she took Lady Caroline's hand and walked into the house, not looking back once to see the son she had cut off a decade before.

≈

Thomas paced up and down the library carpet, reading the book's spines through the glass doors on their shelves. He had never liked waiting, but maybe it was good to have a little time to prepare himself. He wondered if she would have spoken to him, even after so long, if Richard had lived. He didn't think so.

He had not expected to see his mother, so much so that he'd missed Georgiana's broad hints that someone, if not his father, would soon be arriving from the country. Looking back, he realized that she'd as much as told him that his mother, the Baroness of Lawton, would be coming. There was a real, honest hope that poor, sickly Gregory had managed to sire an heir. Thomas hoped that his pale young bride might win out, and bring the next Duke of Windcastle into the world. But first, he must face his mother.

He thought back to the last time they had spoken, all those years ago.

Thomas had been home from his second term at Cambridge. On a ride into the woodlands, he happened upon his father and a village girl, only slightly older than himself. He should perhaps have turned away, but he didn't think to leave until it was too late.

"You cannot do this to us!" the girl said.

His father had laughed, the old humorless laugh that he'd always had when he was about to punish one of his children for a minor infraction.

"There, you are wrong, my dear," said the Sir Pently. "I can do whatever I like."

The girl said nothing to that, only walked away... straight towards where Thomas sat, half-concealed, on his horse. Her eyes startled for a moment when she saw him. They were red from crying, and they were cold, calculating, just like his father's. He had ruined her. That must have been what was going on.

"Help me," she pleaded.

Thomas was reaching down to help her up onto his horse when he looked up to see a gun pointed at them.

"Who goes there?" demanded the Sir Pently.

Thomas spurred his horse forward.

"What are you doing here?" he demanded, clearly annoyed. He lowered his gun, though.

"I was out for a ride," Thomas said. "I did not intend to intrude upon your tryst."

"It was no tryst," his father said coldly.

"I do not believe you," Thomas had said. He turned to aid the girl, but she had already disappeared into the underbrush.

"Stop!" his father ordered.

Thomas, despite himself, reined in his mount and turned at his father's command.

"You will say nothing of this. Is that understood?"

"Why would I say anything?" Thomas said. "You despoil the village girls and expect them to fend for themselves afterwards?"

"I do no such thing," said the Sir Pently.

"But you do. It is despicable. I am ashamed to be your son," Thomas had said. Looking back at that memory, he wondered where he'd found such moral fervor, but then he realized that it wasn't that, at all, or at least not entirely. His father had never been there, at the estate with his children, or if he was, it was only to make an ill-tempered appearance at the supper table. He felt... jealousy, perhaps, that his father's unwelcome attentions were elsewhere, and not with them: himself, Richard, and even Nate.

Back at the house that long-ago day, Thomas decided to pack his trunks and go back to Cambridge. His valet dallied. If he had been able to leave immediately, that might have been all, but a storm blew in, making the roads too muddy and dark for travel.

He'd been summoned to his father's study. The whole scene was repeated, more or less, except that the village girl was not there, and his mother was. They told Thomas that he had misinterpreted the scene. Thomas had not believed them. His father had ordered him off the estate, and Thomas had gone, gladly, as far as the seas could carry him, all the way to India.

As he waited for his mother to call him in again, he tried to remember what their excuse had been for his father's dalliances. If he remembered correctly, they had offered none.

Jones appeared at the door. "The Baroness Lawton will see you now," he said.

Thomas nodded and stalked to the door.

"There's no need to worry, Sir," the butler said. "I'm sure the maharajas were much more fearsome."

Thomas shook his head. "There, you're wrong. Though they wore more jewels, as a rule."

"Did they, Sir?" the butler asked.

Thomas forced himself to relax as he entered his mother's sitting room. A fire burned in the grate. The room had been redecorated since Thomas had seen it last, with a burgundy brocade on the walls. His mother stood with her back to the door, looking out the window into the blustery day. Clouds blew across the sky, echoing the day when Thomas had left so many years before.

"Leave us, Jones," she said.

The door clicked shut.

His mother remained silent for a moment before finally turning to look at him.

"I take it that Father is well?" Thomas said.

His mother shook her head. "Not what one would call well. Rather sickly, in fact, and no more bearable for his infirmity. Your uncle, on the other hand, seems to have sprung back from last winter's influenza, but he is not young. You must be on hand. Babies are frail, and some of them are girls."

"I am in no way prepared."

"You will have to be," she said.

"Is that all?" Thomas asked.

His mother looked him over in silence. "Yes," she said. "I think you will do after all."

Thomas grimaced. He turned to go. His hand was on the doorknob when his mother spoke again.

"You were wrong about that girl," she said. "Your father was in no way dallying with her. She was his daughter. She had been tolerably well looked after."

Thomas hesitated. Yes. The pieces could fit together that way, too. It was a wonder he hadn't considered the possibility before. He gritted his teeth. The revelation made him feel keenly how very young he had been at the time.

"You thought that he had ruined her," his mother continued, "but he had not. He never dallied with a girl who had not been thoroughly ruined before he met her. With the possible exception of myself."

Thomas's ears pulsed. She had no reason to lie about this, though he would have preferred not knowing, and certainly not hearing it from his mother's own lips. His father had taken everything he could from her. Thomas was not a child any more, though, not even in his mother's estimation. He preferred the story he'd held on to through all his years of exile, but the truth changed nothing. His father was still no one to be admired, emulated, or bowed down to.

"I am sorry," he said to his mother. "So sorry."

❧

CHAPTER 13: THE BALL

Hyacinth's gown was fitted, tried on, and re-fitted again. She had thought it perfect the first time, but Aunt Celia demanded adjustments: a tuck here, an extra bit of lace on the sleeves, less at the hem. The house buzzed with preparations all day Friday, the day before the ball.

"We must rest tomorrow," Aunt Celia said.

Hyacinth would rather have gone riding in the park again, even with the recalcitrant horse she'd had the day before, if only to escape her aunt's realm, the house with its well-kept front rooms, its respectable address. A ride in the park would also offer a small chance of seeing Thomas again, but even without that thought she would have longed to escape.

Lady Talbot was resting in her bedroom, in preparation for the exertions of the night ahead, so Hyacinth and Sophie were alone at breakfast.

"Does your mother ever entertain here?" Hyacinth asked Sophie.

Sophie glanced sidelong towards the servants' door.

"No," she whispered. "She says she won't do it if she can't do it in the finest style, and for that she would need a French chef."

"Couldn't she get one?" Hyacinth asked.

Sophie shook her head. "Cook has been with us since she was a girl. Mother could never stand to let her go. We wouldn't know what to do without her."

Hyacinth nodded. She had assumed that the servants in Aunt Celia's house came and went. She'd overheard more than one quarrel among the staff since she'd arrived. But perhaps her aunt appreciated their loyalty, and recognized that she might not find others who were so able to endure her moods.

Hyacinth was still musing on this when the butler appeared a few minutes later.

"Miss Grey?" he said. "There's a man here to see you. He is waiting in the hall."

"A man to see me?" Hyacinth said. Then she remembered. "Oh! Is it… is it Mr. Butler?"

The butler nodded.

"Show him in to the library, if you could," Hyacinth said. "I will be with him directly."

"I don't know if Lady Talbot would approve, Miss."

"In that case," said Hyacinth, "we will converse on the doorstep." She would not allow her aunt's scruples to interfere with her meeting with the solicitor. She would not.

The butler sucked in his breath theatrically. "Well then, Miss, I will show him to the library."

Sophie leaped up the moment he was gone. "Who is it, Hy?" she demanded, clutching Hyacinth's arm. "Is he another suitor?"

Hyacinth laughed. "Hardly," she said. "He is my grandmother's solicitor and man of affairs. He is here to discuss details of my inheritance with me."

"Oh!" Sophie said. "The inheritance mama didn't want you to collect?" she whispered.

"The very one," Hyacinth said.

"Is it a terribly big fortune?" Sophie asked breathlessly.

Hyacinth shook off her younger cousin. "You *have* been reading too many romantic novels, haven't you?" she said. "I really must go, now."

Sophie released her reluctantly. "Mother will know. She'll be down in a flash."

"She's not down yet, though, is she?" Hyacinth said. "I'll be in the library."

ﾗ

When Hyacinth arrived at the library, Mr. Butler had already spread out an array of documents on the rarely-used desk, under the butler's watchful eye.

"Miss Grey," he greeted her with a smile. "So good to see you again."

Hyacinth returned his greetings, but the array of documents distracted her. There were two piles of what appeared to be stock certificates, some deeds to land, and a bundle of letters, along with an appraiser's list of the contents of the house.

"There is really quite a lot, isn't there?" she said.

The solicitor considered. "I don't think you will find it overwhelming, once you get acquainted with it all. Where shall we begin?"

Hyacinth chose to start with the estate. Its income had amounted to about three thousand per annum in the last few years – not a princely sum, but more than her father's income, which was respectable enough for a Navy man. The solicitor expressed the opinion that the orchards on the estate might become even more profitable with careful management. She inspected some of the maps he'd brought with him, and asked how long it would take to travel there.

"About four or five days, in good weather, maybe a bit less in summer," the solicitor said. He glanced at his watch. "Shall we move on to the stocks, now?"

They were about half way through the next set of documents when Lady Talbot burst in.

"What is this?" she demanded.

Mr. Butler stepped back while Hyacinth turned to face her aunt.

"This," she said, "is a long-delayed meeting with my

grandmother's man of affairs."

"Behind my back?"

"You would not allow me to do it in front of your face, so yes, I had to arrange things on my own."

"I will not countenance it!"

"I didn't imagine that you would. I will take myself off directly and find lodgings," Hyacinth said.

"You will do no such thing!"

Mr. Butler cleared his throat. Both women ignored him.

"That would be most unwise," Aunt Celia said. "Think of the scandal it would cause! Think of my reputation!"

"You have looked after your own reputation well enough to this point," Hyacinth said. "I think you could recover well enough." She made a move to begin gathering up the maps and folios of stocks, but the solicitor shook his head and waved her away. Her aunt clutched the back of a chair with one white-knuckled hand. She had gone quite purple in the face. She gulped, took a deep breath, and spoke again.

"I have my reputation thanks only to my elders' careful council, and a few heavy-handed maneuverings when I was a young lady. You are still young, and if you were a year or two younger, and paid more attention to your attire, you'd be hailed as a diamond of the first water. You clearly have no idea what trouble could come your way. I will not allow you to make such a serious mistake."

A diamond of the first water? Surely she exaggerated. Hyacinth wondered again what her aunt's ancient indiscretion had been, but for the moment she was more concerned with her own fate.

"A serious mistake?" Hyacinth said. "How, pray tell, is taking charge of my inheritance, becoming knowledgeable about my property, a serious mistake?"

Aunt Celia fanned herself. "Surely you cannot be so naive as all that?" she demanded. "Everyone, and I mean everyone, will know where it came from. No other lady will be able to converse with you for fear of her own reputation... No, it really does not bear thinking about." She paused for breath, then addressed Mr. Butler.

"Take yourself off, man," she said. "You are not welcome in this house."

He acknowledged her command with a slow nod of the head, but did not speak to her.

"Miss Grey," he said. "Would you have me retain these for safekeeping?"

"Yes," Hyacinth said. "I will inform you when I have obtained my own lodgings and we can meet again."

The solicitor shook his head. "I believe that in this, your relative..." he gestured towards Lady Talbot, "has the right of it. It would be most unusual for a young lady to take her own lodgings, and I believe that even the sainted Mrs. Miller would have counseled you against it."

"Sainted!" Aunt Celia clutched a chair for balance, horrified at the thought.

"I will take that into consideration," Hyacinth said noncommittally. She could not tolerate her aunt's interference any longer. She was determined to take herself off, and soon.

Mr. Butler swept the papers into his case, bowed, and departed.

The door closed behind him. Aunt Celia leaned against it and took a deep breath to steady herself.

"I forbid you to go out," she said. "You will stay in this house until you see sense."

Hyacinth's heart raced. She would not be kept prisoner. "Oh, will I?" she said, trying not to shake. "What about the ball? That is tonight, isn't it? People are expecting to see me there."

"I will tell them that you are indisposed."

"That would be a terrible waste of a ball gown."

Hyacinth pushed past her aunt and into the hallway. She barely noticed the flash of Sophie's dress as she slid into her hiding place behind the stair. She went straight to her own room and closed the door. Blood pounded in her ears. Her hands shook. She clutched her skirts, trying to still them. The dress

Aunt Celia had had made for her. She wanted to tear it off, but what else was there? Her dresses from Gibraltar were too thin, and besides, they looked shabby to her now, only a half-dozen weeks after her arrival into Aunt Celia's realm in the darkest month of the year. Her fine gown of a morning dress burned into her as if it were her aunt's eyes, constraining her to habits that were not her own.

She took a deep breath and sat down at her desk. She had enough money to travel, she thought, and she could have the solicitor arrange for more to be sent to her. She must go. She would go. Maybe even before the ball.

She opened the drawer and set out paper to write on. She found her pen, the blotter, and a bottle of ink. It was almost dry. How much money would she need to rent lodgings, or, better yet, escape to her grandmother's estate? Her plans for a school would have to wait. Yes, she would go.

A knock at the door startled her. Hyacinth put her head in her hands, despairing of the lack of ink, the small writing desk, the frustration.

"Go away!" she said.

"Miss?" It was Maria. Maria. Hyacinth sprang up to let her in.

"Come in!" she urged. "I'm sorry, I thought you were my aunt, and I can't... I just can't bear to see her."

Maria looked over her shoulder down the hall and slipped into the room. "She is in her room," she said. "With a headache."

Hyacinth nodded. "Maria, can you bring me ink?"

"Yes, but... the coach from Portsmouth will arrive soon."

"The coach from Portsmouth?" Hyacinth echoed. "Oh! George!" She laughed at herself. "I nearly forgot. I'm sorry Maria, I've been very angry. We really must go."

"Now?" Maria said.

Hyacinth nodded. "As soon as possible. I am going to give you a short letter to deliver to Mr. Butler at Lincoln's Inn. Take it on your way to the coaching inn. You are to ask him for a bit of money, for the fare for both of us to travel to H-shire in the morning. Buy tickets when you collect George. But first, bring me ink."

Maria nodded.

"Good," Hyacinth said. She straightened the paper on the too-small surface of the writing desk and used the last ink from the old bottle to write to Mr. Butler.

❧

She would write to Aunt Celia, and leave the letter on her desk. Father could be reached through the Navy's offices, so she wrote to him there. She was considering whether or not to write to Sophie, or Thomas, when there was a knock at the door. Surely Maria wasn't back already?

"Hyacinth?"

It was Sophie. Hyacinth sighed and tucked her letters away, then went to open the door.

"Come in," she said. "I was just... getting ready for the ball."

"No you weren't," Sophie said. "You were writing. Who were you writing to?"

"Well, I was thinking of writing to you," Hyacinth said.

"Why?" Sophie plunked herself down in a chair, letting her skirts bunch up into wrinkles.

Hyacinth walked to the window and looked out at the grey, cold day. She thought she saw a break in the clouds, but it darkened a moment later.

"I'm leaving," she said at last.

"Leaving? But I'm sure mama didn't mean..."

"No," Hyacinth said. "She would let me stay, even if we disagree, but neither of us are happy about it. I can't stay here."

"Is it about your inheritance?"

Hyacinth nodded. "I have my own house, in the country. I've never seen it. I'll go there, I think."

"But we could take you there!" Sophie said. "Don't leave me. It's so boring with just Mama."

Hyacinth sighed. "I'm sorry. I don't think your mother would want to have anything to do with the place, and you must stay with her. She's … oh, I don't know. She's your mother." She looked at Sophie, caught between pity and envy. She had a mother, which Hyacinth hadn't had since she was even younger than Sophie, but such a difficult mother. Aunt Celia did mean well, though. She did. She was just impossible in her ideas of respectability, in her contradictory flirting and obsession with fashion.

"I have to go," Hyacinth said. "By myself. I mean, I'll take Maria, but you must let us go. Don't let your mother know until I've left. I've written to her. I'll leave the letter here."

Sophie pouted. "But I'll miss you."

"And I'll miss you, too." She looked around the room. She would have to instruct Maria to pack her things.

"Will you keep my books for me?" Hyacinth asked.

Sophie brightened. "Oh, could I?"

"You must. They'll be too heavy for Maria to carry, and I'm sure there will be some at my grandmother's house, my house. In any case, I'll be buying more. For the school."

"What school?"

Hyacinth cringed. She wished she hadn't said that, but her guard, her sense of discretion, had been worn to the breaking point. "I'm thinking of starting a school," she said. "For girls. Girls about your age. To train to be governesses and such, housekeepers, maybe."

"Oh, I'd love to go to your school."

"But Aunt Celia would never permit it. She'd worry about you too much. I think you're very precious to her."

Sophie squirmed in her chair. "May I take your books to my room now?" she asked.

"No!" Hyacinth exclaimed. "My goodness. I'm not gone yet. You may come get them at breakfast time tomorrow. I'll leave them in a bundle on that chair for you."

"Thank you," Sophie said. "I'll make do with them until we come visit you."

"All right," Hyacinth said. "Now you really must go. I have another letter to write and I have to decide what to bring with me." She led Sophie to the door and ushered her out.

Back inside, Hyacinth frowned and bundled the books. She certainly *hoped* that her grandmother had a library, and that somehow Sophie could persuade Aunt Celia to at least find her a governess, or maybe a day school in London. She would ask Georgiana to help. She sat down to write her a short letter, and just as she was folding it to send, there was another knock at the door.

Maria slipped in, with George at her heels. He was the same, only ever so slightly taller. The school seemed to have improved his posture. He crossed the room in two long strides and embraced his sister.

"How are you, Hy?" he said.

"I'm well. And you?"

"Oh, grand. You were right. School's not so bad, but this weather is beastly, isn't it?"

"It is." Hyacinth squeezed him close, then pushed away.

"I'm sorry about all this sneaking around," she said.

"I don't mind at all! Evil step-aunt."

"She's not evil," Hyacinth said – too quickly.

Maria rolled her eyes.

"She's just insufferable. That's different." Hyacinth looked at George. He was definitely a little taller, it wasn't only that his posture had improved. He didn't look in the least bit sickly.

"I'm so glad you could come," Hyacinth said, "but it isn't going to be much of a visit, I'm afraid."

Maria nodded. "And Mrs. Murphy, that's the housekeeper, she'll wonder what Harold's nephew is doing in the house."

George grinned. "Yes. I'm to pose as the coachman's nephew," he said. "Isn't that grand?"

Hyacinth sucked in her breath and exhaled slowly. "I suppose it's as a good a tale as any, but I only wish we didn't have to tell tales to visit. Don't worry, though. Next time we'll be at my own house and we won't have to pretend. Now. Tell me all about school, and the journey here."

᪥

Maria spirited George away to the servants' quarters at supper time. In the dining room, Sophie sat demurely – or at least not visibly sulking – near her mother. She looked up when Hyacinth entered, and Hyacinth answered with the barest of nods. Aunt Celia refused to look at her. Hyacinth sat. The footman served her. No one spoke. Forks clinked on plates. She could hear the crinkle of linen as glasses were set down, or lifted up. Her heart beat quite loudly, but the sound of the footman shuffling his feet was also quite prominent. In the dim background, rain fell on the streets outside. Sophie cleared her throat and eyed her mother.

"You may go," Aunt Celia said, breaking the silence at last.

"I intend to," Hyacinth said.

Sophie scurried out. The moment the door closed behind her, Aunt Celia rose, too.

"You will go to the ball, I mean," Aunt Celia said to Hyacinth, without actually looking at her. "The carriage will come around in one hour. I will send you my maid. I'm sure that Spanish girl doesn't know a thing about coiffure."

Hyacinth opened her mouth to speak, but Aunt Celia held her hand up to stop her.

"One hour. At the door. You needn't thank me."

The door swung shut behind her. Hyacinth looked down at her plate. The food was nearly untouched, but now that Aunt Celia had left the room, she realized that she was quite hungry. With the footman standing uneasily at the kitchen door, she wolfed down her cold lamb and a bit of bread, then set off to prepare for what would probably be her only London ball.

Upstairs, Aunt Celia's maid waited with her ball gown. Maria stood beside her, looking skeptical, and helped Hyacinth out of her afternoon dress, which was plain but flattering. In contrast, the ball gown was a confection: pale blue silk, trimmed with sapphire velvet and a hint of gold. Stepping into it, she was transformed. As she sat before the mirror, the maid swirled her hair into an artful coiffure, kept in place with a borrowed comb. The lamplight caught in the thread of gold. Hyacinth glimpsed herself in the mirror, still trying to steady her breath and her racing heartbeat against her anger, her apprehension.

The lady in the mirror before her looked a bit like a fairytale princess, certainly not a schoolmarm. A diamond of the first water? Was that what Aunt Celia had said? The mirror suggested that she might have been right, ridiculous as it was. And Hyacinth had a ball to attend.

She decided that she would enjoy it.

❧

Thomas dressed according to the recommendations of his new valet, the younger son of a wool merchant. Jones approved of his eye for details, and Thomas liked him: he was sensible, moderately well-read for someone of his class, and seemed to be patient and even-tempered.

A little after eight o'clock, they gathered to wait for the coach. Thomas's mother nodded to her sons as they entered, but was deep in conversation with Georgiana.

"Do any of the young ladies suit?" she asked.

"For Thomas?" Georgiana said. "I'm sure I don't know. There's a Miss Bennett who is a favorite this year, but only for her looks. They say that she has outstripped her allowance on her wardrobe already."

"If a young lady is going to spend her money, she could do worse, I suppose," his mother said.

Georgiana's silence did not imply that she agreed.

"And then there's Miss Grey. Thomas went riding in the park with her."

"Did you?" his mother said, turning to him as if she suddenly cared for his opinion. "Who is this Miss Grey? Has she a respectable fortune?"

"I don't see what her fortune has to do with it," Thomas said. "Nate's the one with gaming debts." Nathan had shuffled into the room and slumped in a chair, apparently still suffering from the previous night's excess.

"If there weren't ladies present," he grumbled, "I'd ask you to step outside."

"You wouldn't," Thomas said.

"...Lady Talbot's niece," Georgiana was saying.

His mother fairly hissed. "No. Not those Greys. That is too bad. Thomas, you must see that that will never do, never."

"And why not?" Thomas said.

"First, there is the question of her fortune. I cannot believe it would be sufficient."

"Sufficient to what?"

"Well, it's not *desperate*, you understand, but the Lawton hasn't been terribly profitable in the past few years, and I'd like to see it brought back to itself before I die."

"I am hardly a pauper, myself," Thomas said, "and you don't look like you're about to fall into the grave."

"I should hope not," his mother said.

If the estate were in jeopardy because of mismanaged funds, that was a problem he could sort out on his own. The idea that he would have to marry for money was ridiculous.

"I had accounted the rumors of your recently acquired wealth as mere gossip," his mother sniffed.

"Does it displease you, then?" he asked.

She coughed. "It is demeaning for someone of your standing to engage in trade."

"I did not find it to be demeaning. Quite the contrary," Thomas said.

"So what's the trouble with 'those Greys'?" Nathan butted in.

"To begin with, that woman, Lady Talbot, is a viper," their mother said, as if relieved to have something other than Thomas's dubiously-earned fortune to think about. Here, Thomas thought, she was on more familiar territory. "The family are completely without a sense of propriety. I shudder to think of any child of mine tolerating their company."

Mr. Jones appeared at the door.

"Your carriage is coming around, my lady," he said.

"Thank you, Jones," Thomas's mother replied.

Georgiana strode from the room. In the hallway, a handsome footman appeared with her coat. Thomas hurried after her.

"What *is* the story?" he asked her.

Georgiana shrugged. "It's some story about Lady Talbot and my father. It was a very long time ago. I don't think she was out of the schoolroom."

"And what, exactly, occurred?" Thomas asked.

"I don't know, but I believe that one of Lady Talbot's brothers challenged father to a duel."

"I see," Thomas said. The challenger must have been Captain Grey. It might not have taken much to raise his hackles, or prejudice him permanently against the Pently clan.

"We had better go," Georgiana said, "or we'll be more than fashionably late."

The men rode in silence most of the way, while Georgiana informed his mother of various pieces of London gossip. They continued to chatter as the footmen opened the carriage door and they walked into the opulent town house. Inside, they scarcely looked around except to greet their hostess. Out of the corners of his eyes, Thomas glimpsed several young ladies and their mamas, eying him. He feigned interest in Georgiana's story about one of the young Pently's ponies and ignored his brother, who shortly disappeared into the card room. Thomas's mother eyed a row of young ladies in pale gowns.

"Do you like none of them?" she asked.

"I suppose they are all fine girls," Thomas said, "but no, I would not choose any of them to be my bride."

"You'll have to, you know," she said. "Unless you think that Nate is suited to manage even a little place like Lawton. I've become accustomed to life in Town, and no one ever expected me to manage the estate."

"But you know it as well as anyone, don't you?" Thomas said.

She waved him away, as if he were a fly buzzing in her ear. "You wouldn't want to charge Nate with siring an heir for

Lawton, let alone the duchy, in case Lady Caroline is only carrying a girl, after all."

Thomas stopped listening. Across the room, Hyacinth emerged from a crowd of admirers. Their eyes met. Then he noticed the bauble on her chest. And what a bauble it was. He intended to claim his dance at once.

❧

Hyacinth rode to the ball with one hand clutched around her reticule. She hadn't put on her grandmother's necklace, not yet, but she carried it with her. She wasn't even sure if she would wear it. What if someone recognized it, and associated it with her grandmother? But how could they? The very proper ladies of the *ton* would hardly admit to having known a courtesan, even if they'd crossed her path. If they had, Hyacinth considered, there was a very small, though unlikely, chance they might have considered her grandmother a friend. That would be worth the risk, that very small chance that she might find another friend. Besides, while Aunt Celia would berate her in private, she would not want to create a scene with half of society in earshot. Aunt Celia would know that she was not bowing to her will, and would be less surprised when she woke to find her gone the next morning.

The carriage drew up to the steps and Hyacinth stepped down into a narrow street crowded with carriages and matched teams of horses, each finer than the last. Candlelight blazed from the windows, and they entered into a hall so richly furnished that Hyacinth thought she might have stepped into a giantess's box of jewels. Her grandmother's necklace would be entirely appropriate to the surroundings. She handed her cloak to a waiting servant and stepped into a fairytale of laughter and light. A small orchestra was tuning their instruments at the far end of the room, the thin sound the plucked and bowed strings just audible against the noise of conversation. It filled the air with anticipation.

"Excuse me a moment," Hyacinth said to her aunt. She

ducked into a neighboring room before Aunt Celia could follow her, and set her reticule down on a side table. She pretended to be looking at a painting, a bucolic landscape, while she surreptitiously fastened the clasp at her neck. With a quick glance back over her shoulder, she returned to the ballroom.

Aunt Celia had abandoned her again. She was halfway across the room, greeting a pair of acquaintances – a very handsome gentleman and a lady. The lady, presumably the man's wife, eyed Aunt Celia with distaste. Hyacinth returned to her aunt's side.

Aunt Celia glanced at her, as if to brush her off like a fly, but froze for a moment before returning her attention to the gentleman she'd been talking to. She'd seen the necklace, and how could she not? As dazzling as the room was, it did not at all detract from the dazzling glow of the stone at her chest.

"May I present my niece, Miss Grey," she managed to say.

Hyacinth curtsied.

"We really must be going," the lady said. "Lord Darling has promised me the first dance." She tugged on her husband's sleeve, and he left, not altogether reluctantly.

"What is that *thing*?" Aunt Celia hissed.

"It belonged to my grandmother," Hyacinth said. "And now, if you please, this is my first ball, and I would like to dance. I believe that, as my chaperone, you should see that I am introduced to a suitable partner."

Aunt Celia grumbled, but led her straight to a rather dapper-looking young man who was probably a little too young to be seriously in search of a bride. Hyacinth barely heard his name, caring only that he was pleasant and courteous, a tolerable dancer, and, unlike Viscount Whitley, seemed more interested in dancing than in peeling her gown away. He led her out to their place in the line, and the orchestra fell into a country dance, one well-enough known that Hyacinth had danced it even in Gibraltar. She turned and stepped to the rhythm, and really, yes, she was enjoying herself.

After the set, her partner gamely led her back to Aunt Celia's side, thanking her graciously. As she smiled a farewell, her cheer faded. People *were* looking at her necklace. Although there were many fine and ornate jewels on various bosoms and hands around the room, hers was, undoubtedly, among the largest. If not *the* largest. Aunt Celia looked annoyed.

"I hoped you would dance another set with that one."

"I might," Hyacinth said.

"People are staring at you."

Hyacinth shrugged.

Underneath one of the doors out to the balcony, a cluster of women, including Lady Spencer, had gathered around two tall, blond gentlemen.

"There's your beau," Aunt Celia said. "I told you that you were setting your sights too high."

Thomas peered over the ladies' heads and smiled at her. Hyacinth smiled back. Thomas extracted himself from the conversation and began to make his way towards her. Aunt Celia shook her head and walked away.

"I am delighted that you've arrived," Thomas said. "I saw you dancing – I'm sorry I was too late to claim your first set, but may I have the next, before my mother insists that I dance with someone other then you?"

"I suppose... well... yes, yes I would like to dance."

There was something about Thomas's eyes that discomfited her, something new. Hopeful.

"I'm surprised that your card isn't full," Hyacinth said.

Thomas shrugged. "I believe the mamas are drawing lots to decide who will be allowed to pounce on me next."

"Really?" Hyacinth laughed nervously. "My aunt informed me, yet again, that I was setting my sights too high." She looked up into his eyes, and wished that they were somewhere where they could talk freely. "I should tell you…" she started, but then she looked over her shoulder to see a lady, a little older than her aunt, glaring down at her.

"Is this Miss Grey, then?" she said.

"I am," said Hyacinth.

"Allow me," Thomas said, "to present my mother, the Baroness Lawton."

Hyacinth curtsied. Thomas's mother might find her wanting, might dislike her entirely, but it didn't matter. She would be leaving their glittering London world on a morning stagecoach, and tonight, she would dance with Thomas. And say goodbye.

"I am pleased to make your acquaintance," Hyacinth said cheerfully. Even Lady Lawton seemed to take a little too long looking at her necklace.

"Shall we take our places?" Thomas proposed.

"Yes, let's." Hyacinth took his arm and felt a thrill shiver up her spine. As the musicians took their places and the lights dazzled above, for a moment, she could pretend to herself that they really were courting.

"You look... stunning," Thomas said, as they settled in across from each other.

Hyacinth blushed. The dance began. The steps led them apart and back together before they stood close for a moment.

"What is that necklace?" Thomas asked.

"It was my grandmother's," Hyacinth answered. The dance pulled them apart.

"It is a very fine piece. Very fine." Thomas said when they passed again.

Hyacinth took in the music, the elegance of the narrow tables along the walls, the society matrons on their chairs, watching, ruling from their perches, in their fine jewels and elaborately coiffed hair. Not that the dancers were any less fine. Hyacinth admired the dancing slippers, the swirl of gowns and coat tails, the studied movements. And here and there, in a turn, she touched Thomas's hand. She wished it might last forever.

But soon, too soon, the set drew to a close. She curtsied with the other ladies, and turned to go.

Thomas took her arm and led her to the side of the room. "Perhaps we might take a moment to stroll on the balcony," he said.

Hyacinth felt a moment of alarm. "I can't... I mean, don't you have to find your partner for the next dance?"

"We have some few minutes."

Aunt Celia, of course, was nowhere to be seen. A relatively shabbily dressed gentleman was making his way towards them. "Who is that?" Hyacinth asked.

Thomas stilled for a moment, studying him. "I don't know what he'd be doing here. I'll have to speak to him later. Come." He hurried her out the doors.

The balcony looked out over a park, dark in the night. Far away, scattered glints of lamplight shone through the trees. They were not alone on the balcony, but at least it was a little less crowded, and cooler. The breeze whisked the perspiration from Hyacinth's brow

"Thank you for the dance," she said.

"No, I thank you," Thomas said. A lady of middle years passed and nodded to Thomas, her eyes lingering disapprovingly on Hyacinth, or maybe it was just a look of disappointment.

"I would speak to you about... about my situation," Thomas said.

"Can anything have changed?" Hyacinth said. "I am practically a commoner; you are to be a duke."

"Perhaps not," he said. "My cousin left a widow. She... she will bear a child in the coming months. If it is a boy, and if he thrives, he will be my uncle's heir, and I wish him well."

Hyacinth considered. The baby could as easily be a girl. She shook her head. "Send word, then, after her confinement."

"I will see you, though. If I can, I would... I would like to renew my suit."

"You must see that we cannot," Hyacinth insisted. "In any case, I will be working to establish that school I told you about. I think that Georgiana will help."

"I am sure she will."

Inside, the musicians picked up their instruments, and the dancers took their places on the floor.

"We should go back in," Hyacinth said. The balcony had

emptied. For a moment, as the music began, they were alone.

"I think of you all the time," Thomas said. "I have no interest in any of the young ladies my mother would have me marry."

Hyacinth had to leave. She turned away. She could not stay for this hope of a promise, this hope that in a few month's time, her old shipboard friend would come calling again. She stepped into the hall and found Aunt Celia, to escort her to her partner for the next set.

à

Thomas leaned against the balcony wall and took a deep breath of cool air. In the park, bare branches scraped quietly against each other. He could hear the sound of horses and carriage wheels from the streets on the other side of the house. Still, the music played, and some young lady was to partner him in the dance. He must go find her.

He entered the hall only to find himself face to face with his mother.

"You are not to court that girl," she said. "No matter if she wears jewels that rival the queen's."

"It is a fine piece," Thomas said, "but I was just catching a breath of air."

His mother rolled her eyes.

"I believe I have a partner for this set. I hope you can help me find her?"

She cleared her throat. "Miss Bennett is very much in demand, as I'm sure your cousin told you. She found another partner when you did not appear. You must sit this one out." Thomas's mother looked over his shoulder. "And I have promised to keep Lady Gavin company while her daughter dances. Be a good lad and fetch us a bottle of port."

Thomas bowed. "As you wish, Mama."

Skirting around the edges of the room, avoiding conversation, Thomas tried to keep his eyes away from the dance floor, but despite his efforts, he saw her out of the corner of his eye, and even heard her laugh once. He was so intent on not looking in her direction that he didn't notice when the somewhat rough merchant he knew, the very one who Hyacinth had noticed earlier, stepped into his path.

"Mr. Smithson!" the man said, rather too loudly. People turned to look. Thomas raised his eyebrows at them, and for the most part they looked away.

"I don't really go by that name here, Churchill. Not these days. I should have told you as much when we met at the club."

"Oh, pardon me," Mr. Churchill said. He scratched his chin and dusted off his waistcoat, which was made of a rather good Indian cotton. He still wore his clothes from the subcontinent, and they did not quite suit the ballroom.

"I confess, I'm surprised to see you here."

"Ah, well, our hosts have seen fit to invite me, a mere tradesman, to their affair," Mr. Churchill said. "I am quite pleased."

Thomas smiled blandly. Yes, Mr. Churchill ought to be pleased. If there were investors to be found in London, the Spencer ballroom was not a bad place to be seen. Despite himself, he looked out towards the dancers. Hyacinth's partner was a Sir Pently of some sort, one who was a good dancer and charming enough, though Thomas suspected he had more interest in the other gentlemen's tight breeches than in Hyacinth's creamy décolletage.

"Who is that chit?" Mr. Churchill asked.

"What *young lady* do you mean?"

"The one who is wearing the Star of Kanchen." He was staring right at Hyacinth. There was no mistaking it. "You know the Company lost their treaty with the King of Sikkim over that bauble," Mr. Churchill went on. "I'm quite sure that's it. I've heard so many descriptions, and that chain, it's very Sikkimese. It has to be the one. The King demanded that the company return it. They promised it, and they never delivered. I suspect they couldn't find it. But there it is. What a stroke of luck."

Thomas looked down at the man. He spoke softly. He was absolutely earnest. He had locked his gaze onto the jewel resting on Hyacinth's perfect bosom, completely indifferent to the lady who wore it.

≈

CHAPTER 14: A JOURNEY

Iₜ's morning."

Hyacinth had scarcely closed her eyes. Music and ballroom lights echoed in her mind, and her feet ached from dancing.

"We must go, and go soon," Maria said.

Hyacinth opened her eyes. Outside, the night was pitch black.

"But it's dark out," Hyacinth protested.

"The coach leaves in an hour and a half. It will be just getting light then."

Hyacinth gritted her teeth and pushed herself out of bed. The house was silent. In the night, Maria had finished packing her bags. Her traveling clothes were laid out, lying dully beside the still-luminescent ball gown. George sat by the fire, poking at a few dying embers.

"Will you come with us?" Hyacinth asked him, turning away from the gown.

George shrugged.

"Of course he won't. He'll get the coach to Portsmouth."

"I could come with you if you want," he offered.

"No, stay at school. You can come to us at the next holidays. I'll write," Hyacinth said. She swung her feet out of bed and went behind a screen to dress as Maria tidied her bed.

"What was the ball like?" George asked.

Hyacinth felt like she'd left half of herself in that dream, that few hours' dream of dancing, music, and the ladies and gentlemen in their finery.

"Wonderful," she said. Of course, there was one gentleman in particular that she hadn't quite managed to say goodbye to.

In minutes, she was following George and Maria down the servant's stair. It was a narrow, dark place, one totally unfamiliar to her, despite her weeks in the house. She thought that maybe, if she'd grown up in this place, she might know it from childhood explorations, on slow, rainy days. George seemed quite thrilled with the adventure.

Harold waited for them at the back of the garden.

"Can't have a young miss out this time of the night with only another young miss and a boy," he said, joining them as they threaded their way through the mews.

"Thank you," Hyacinth said. "If there's any trouble..."

Harold waved her concerns away. "There won't be none," he said decisively. "Come on, then."

He had not harnessed the horses – it would have been too much of an affront to Aunt Celia, and besides, Hyacinth didn't want to draw attention to herself when she arrived at the coaching inn. She had dressed simply, too, in hopes of simply blending into the background as she traveled. She'd seen all manner of travelers in her life on Gibraltar, and it was always the ostentatious ones who complained of being robbed, everywhere they went.

She wished, again, that she'd said goodbye to Thomas.

"What will you tell your fellow passengers on the coach?" George said.

"What will I tell them?" Hyacinth said. "Why, nothing at all. Why should I?"

Harold shook his head. "You'd want to be friendly like."

"On the way up from Portsmouth they were all talking to

each other," George said. "One was a milliner, another one on

the way to meet his grandson for the first time. There was even a nun."

Hyacinth considered. "I suppose I'll just say I'm a governess."

George was about to speak when Harold held up his hand for silence. They stopped to listen. Harold peered back along the street.

"I thought I heard someone back there, following us, like," he said. "Might've been nothing." He motioned for them to move on. "It's safer than it was, like," he said, "but you can't be too careful. Footpads and all."

Maria thanked him, but for the rest of the walk, Hyacinth was constantly looking back over her shoulder, thinking, from time to time, that she'd glimpsed a shadow of a man, ducking into alleyways behind them.

☙

As they approached the coaching inn, the empty streets began to fill – a shutter opening here, a laborer on his way to work there, a maid of all work with a shopping basket, hurrying towards the market. Still, the shadows seemed to hide furtive movements.

"I think I prefer London in the daylight, at least the streets," Hyacinth confided to Maria.

"No sense turning back now; we're nearly there," Harold said.

George ran ahead.

"I'm sure your aunt won't object if you want to go back," Maria said, sensing Hyacinth's unease.

"No," Hyacinth declared. "We must keep on. I'll never see this estate if I don't go now. I won't lose my nerve."

"That's the way," Harold said. "You just keep to yourselves on the journey, and you'll be fine."

"But you and George were just saying to be friendly," Hyacinth pointed out.

"Oh, friendly is one thing," Harold said, "but don't let on too much. You never know what scoundrels you might meet on the road."

"That is not very calming," Maria said.

"We'll manage. Won't we?" Hyacinth said.

George had reached the gates of the inn yard. He ducked in for a moment then reappeared and ran back toward them. "They're selling mincemeat pies already," he reported, "and tea and coffee. Both!"

"Very well," Hyacinth said. "We'll breakfast before we go our separate ways."

At the inn yard gate, Harold stopped. "I'd best be getting back," he said. "The horses will want their feed and water." Maria ran to grasp his hand.

"All right, George," Hyacinth said. "Where was it that you saw those pies?"

He pointed to a window half-obscured by the waiting crowds. A few urchins sat near the little shop, their cheeks hollow, noses upturned as if smelling the victuals could satisfy their hunger in some small way.

"Could we buy pies for them?" Hyacinth whispered to George.

He shook his head. "If you did, it would be telling everyone in sight you've got more money than sense. That's what Mrs. Portnoy warned me, before I came here. She said these London folks are hard, even when they're only young."

Hyacinth frowned. She wouldn't be able to feed them all, in any case, and if she only bought one or two to give away, it wouldn't help the others. She wouldn't know how to choose. But with the school, yes, with the school she would be able to help at least a few.

She glanced back at Maria and Harold. They were pulling apart, but their hands were still clasped. She envied their openness. Behind them, a man with a slouching cap and a rather unusual cotton coat entered the inn yard. He looked around, then leaned against the wall, watching.

George plucked at her sleeve. "What are you looking at?"

"Nothing," Hyacinth said. "It's only that there are so many people here. It's just so vast, and I'm only really used to Gibraltar. That was a town, and a port, too, but here..."

"Chin up!" George said, teasing. "You'll show that stuffy aunt of ours what's what!"

Maria rejoined them, and they ate their pies at the edge of the inn yard until the Portsmouth coach boarded.

"Take care of yourself, George," Hyacinth said, "and write to me at Lindley Hall. I'll write you the very day we arrive, to let you know all about it."

She hugged him, but he stiffened and pushed her away, squaring his coat on his shoulders as he boarded the coach. Another bell rang.

"That is our coach," Maria said.

They ran across the inn yard, presented their tickets and their baggage, and were stuffed into the vehicle moments before the driver cracked his whip, sending the horses into a trot, rattling them over the streets of London.

There had not even been time to look around the conveyance before they started. Hyacinth was seated next to an elderly man with white stubble on his chin and a bulbous nose. He grunted as she tried to slide a little further down the seat, so that Maria could fit on.

"There's no room," he grumbled. "They sell too many tickets, they do."

"Well, we've paid for seats as well as the rest of you have. I'm sure we can all fit," Hyacinth said. She might have been more polite, but she was tired. The night of dancing, the long walk to the coaching inn, and the worry of setting out on her own had whittled away at her poise.

"Let the lady have 'er seat," said a red-cheeked woman on the opposite bench, the one facing forwards.

"Ye can sit in my lap, if you like," joked a rough-looking man. Fortunately, he was at the far corner of the carriage.

All of the women in the carriage shifted away from him, at

which he chuckled and spread himself out over a wider stretch of the seat. "Shy, are you?" he said.

Maria grasped Hyacinth's hand. "Don't worry," she whispered.

Hyacinth sunk her head onto Maria's shoulder. She could see glimpses of London as they rolled through the streets, but she was too tired to pay much attention. Eventually, she fell into a fitful dose, rattling along with the coach's motion, glad, in her half-slumber, that she didn't have to converse with her fellow travelers.

At midday, the coach halted for food and a change of horses. Hyacinth and Maria followed the other passengers into the inn, where they found seats in a low, dark dining room. A barmaid counted them as they arrived and ladled soup into bowls for each. It smelled of turnips and mutton. There was also bread and butter. Hyacinth waved away the offered ale and asked for tea for herself and Maria.

They were just finishing their meal when a lone traveler arrived at the door. He squinted into the darkness, as if deciding whether or not to enter.

"We've cabbage and roast coming in a short while," the barmaid told him.

"No, thank you," he said. "I find I must be on my way."

"We'd best be on our way, too," said the red-cheeked woman from their coach. "Come on, girls. I'd like to be at the next inn by nightfall."

"So would I," Hyacinth agreed.

"And I, too," said the man who'd so rudely asked her to sit on his lap. "There's highwaymen about, and those lot don't honor the Sabbath."

"Nor do any of us, traveling like this," the oldest of the male passengers said. "It's ungodly, I say."

Maria felt the beads of her rosary, and pulled Hyacinth aside. They made their way to the inn's shabby outhouses together, looking out over a byre.

"I don't like this talk of highwaymen," Maria said.

"Nor do I," Hyacinth agreed. In the privy, alone, she looked through her reticule and tucked a few notes into her boots, and moved the coins to her skirt pockets. She left the necklace where it was, though – even at the Spencer's ball it had attracted too much attention. To wear it here, it would be an invitation to be robbed blind, or kidnapped, or worse. She affected nonchalance as she and Maria climbed back into the coach.

❧

Thomas arrived late to breakfast. Georgiana was scraping her plate while his mother sipped coffee quietly at the far side of the table. Thomas filled his plate and sat. The silence pressed down on him.

"Good morning, Mother," he said. "Did you enjoy the ball?"

She sniffed. "I would have enjoyed it more if you'd danced with more suitable prospects."

Thomas wished he hadn't asked.

Georgiana pushed her plate away. "I thought he did rather well. He only sat out one dance, and apart from Miss Grey, you approved of his choices, didn't you?"

"I suppose," Thomas's mother conceded.

Mr. Jones entered, holding a letter. "For you, my lady," he said to Georgiana.

"But it's Sunday," Thomas's mother protested. "There's no post on Sundays."

"A boy delivered it last night, late," the butler said.

"Perhaps you have another admirer?"

"I don't think so." Georgiana took it and cracked the seal. She glanced through the contents and looked up at Thomas. "It seems your bird has flown," she said.

Thomas set down his fork. "What *bird*?" he asked.

Georgiana just looked at him.

He stood up and crossed over to her chair.

"Shall I read it?" Georgiana said, keeping it just out of his sight.

"Yes, do," Thomas said.

"And do sit down," his mother said. "You seem to have lost some polish, after all."

Thomas went back to his place. Georgiana cleared her throat.

"'My friend,' she writes, 'by the time you read this, I will be on my way to my new home, Lindley Hall.'"

"Lindley Hall?" Thomas's mother interrupted. "That's only ten miles from Lawton. What on earth is she doing there?"

"I believe she's inherited it," Georgiana said. "From grandmother."

"Oh dear." Thomas's mother wiped her mouth with her napkin. "I was told that a widow had it. She kept to herself mostly. As you would if..."

"If you were a notorious courtesan," Thomas remarked, affecting boredom.

Just then, Lady Caroline entered, her belly swelling under her skirts.

"Dear, go and rest!" Thomas's mother ordered, practically shooing her away.

"I'm sorry if I've interrupted," Lady Caroline apologized, "but I find I'm hungry again."

"You may continue reading later," Thomas's mother told Georgiana.

"I may continue reading now," Georgiana said, casting a conspiratorial glance at Caroline. She went on: "'I am quite anxious to get to know the place my grandmother left for me, and would value your advice on matters of the estate, as well as how to go about finding staff for the school, should the place prove suitable. I look forward to corresponding further, even though I must regretfully leave London sooner than I originally planned.'" Georgiana took a deep breath. "And she signed it; with no word to you, Cousin."

Lady Caroline stood beside her chair while the footman hovered at her shoulder.

Thomas's mother frowned. "Well, I should think the lady wouldn't be so brazen as to mention her *ambitions*," she said, eying her son disapprovingly, "or that you would be so foolish as to be taken in by her coy scheming."

Thomas pushed his chair away. "She is not scheming. I believe all this business of the duchy quite turns her stomach. As it does mine. Good day."

He stormed out, only noticing that Lady Caroline looked at him with what could only be called benevolence. Jones opened the door to speed his departure.

⋙

As they rolled on through the afternoon, the sun broke through the clouds. Hyacinth, having dozed through the morning, was no longer sleepy, though her feet still ached. The interior of the coach grew stuffy. They crossed rolling farmland, brown and barren with winter, then wound into low, wooded hills. Hyacinth gazed out the windows at the unfamiliar sights. She'd lived all her life in towns and had scarcely seen any woodlands, apart from that one summer on the Earl Talbot's carefully groomed estate. The tangle of trees and underbrush fascinated her. A squirrel ran up a branch, and a robin peered at them from its bough.

"Close the curtains, will you?" grumbled the old man.

Hyacinth sighed. She found it sad that her fellow passenger had no interest in the wilderness, but she closed the curtain, not wanting to argue. The coach grew even stuffier. She tried to close her eyes, but with the sunlight peeking through the windows, she couldn't rest. Finally, noticing that the man beside her had begun to doze, she peeked out of the curtains again...

Only to see a man on a horse staring at her from the underbrush.

She screeched.

Outside, a pistol cracked. The coach driver yelled, urging the horses on, but on the upward slope the single rider on his horse caught up with them easily.

"Is it a highwayman?" Maria said.

"'Course it is, stupid girl!" the red-cheeked woman tucked her bag further under her skirts, while the other passengers fussed with buckles and purses. The rough-looking man pulled out a wicked knife, longer than an honest man would want. The old man woke and muttered a curse. Maria pushed the rosary beads through her fingers, praying audibly.

The coach halted.

"Stand and deliver," the highwayman said.

"There's only one of you," said the driver, "and more of us."

From inside, they could hear him fumbling with the catch on the box by his seat. The highwayman fired again. The sound of fumbling stopped, and for a moment, all was silent.

"Very well," the driver said, "have it your way."

The horses shifted in their traces, glad of a rest. The highwayman whistled. A thin young man, bearing a musket of his own, took aim at the driver while the highwayman himself opened the door and trained his pistol on the passengers. He stared at Hyacinth directly for a moment, then quickly looked away.

"Hands where I can see them," he snarled. He trained his gun on the passenger opposite Hyacinth and Maria.

"Where's your purse, man?" he said. "Empty it in here, and no one gets a bullet."

The passenger fumbled at his belt and tossed a few coins into the highwayman's sack. He repeated that with the next passenger, and so on down the bench, checking to see that each one's purse or pocket was truly empty. When he came to the last passenger on the bench, the rough man with the long knife, he realized that he could not reach him by simply leaning in through the door, as he was doing. He skipped across the aisle instead. Perhaps he thought the rough-looking man was too poor to trouble with?

There was something odd about the highwayman, Hyacinth thought, as she followed along, placing her hands on her head. He was looking at her in particular from behind his mask. His ungloved hands were smooth, with fresh blisters on his trigger finger. They shook a little.

He didn't even look at the larger bags. In fact, Hyacinth

noticed, he didn't pay much attention to what was falling out of the various purses and reticules until he came to her. Then, as the elaborate silk package slid away into the musty darkness of his sack, Hyacinth thought his eyes smiled.

The highwayman didn't demand Maria's purse, either, as if he knew that she was a maid. He ducked back out of the coach and latched the door behind him, locking the passengers in. He whistled to his young helper and swung up onto his horse. Hyacinth squinted out through the crack in the window. It seemed as if they were riding away in the general direction of the last town they'd passed through – along the road to London. The city would swallow them whole, no doubt, and they'd escape with their loot. Chief of which was her grandmother's necklace.

Maria squeezed her hand. "I'm so sorry."

Hyacinth realized that she was crying.

"There, there, dearie," said the red-cheeked woman. "You'll be all right. It's only a bit of blunt."

Hyacinth shook her head. "It was my grandmother's necklace," she said.

"Sentimental," scoffed the old man beside her. "Your grandmother'd be right glad you got past a highwayman with your virtue."

Hyacinth nodded. There was something remarkable about that necklace, beyond the obvious value of its gems. She didn't know what it was, but there was something in the way people had looked at it in that ballroom which made her wonder even more. At least she was alive, and well, and on her way to her new home, so that was something to be grateful for. She spared herself a sniffle and dried her eyes. Above them, outside, the coach driver regained his pistol and reloaded. He fired after the robbers, but they were too far by then, and the shot was lost among the trees.

He climbed down from his seat and released the passengers.

"Is everyone all right in there?"

Hyacinth felt like crying.

"He only took a few bits and coins off me," said one passenger.

"Didn't come near me," boasted the rough-looking man, "but he did take a necklace off that young miss," he pointed to Hyacinth. "She's sniveling."

"Shush, you!" said the red-cheeked woman.

"Very well then," the driver said. "Off we go!"

᳕

At the next town, they reported the incident to the local magistrate.

"And what was taken, Miss?" the magistrate asked her.

"A necklace," Hyacinth said, "and a few coins."

"Just that? No notes?"

"No," Hyacinth said. "We'd been warned that there might be highwaymen about, so I'd tucked those into my boots."

"Well done," said the magistrate. "And the value of the necklace?"

Hyacinth hesitated. "I don't know. Priceless, maybe. It had a very large sapphire, on a gold chain."

"Probably paste," the magistrate mumbled. "Shall we say ten pound, then?"

"More, I should think," Hyacinth said.

"Twenty it is, then, and a few pence in coin," he totaled the sum of his estimate in a column next to her name and called the next passenger forward.

Hyacinth walked back to the coach, and though they came to their night's resting place well after sundown, the rest of the day passed without incident. They rode with that coach for one more day, then turned off to another road the following morning, creaking towards Lindley Hall on the local mail coach.

᳕

Thomas filled his days with activities his family approved of, for the most part. He rode Polaris in the park, visited Nathan's club – now his own club, too – and allowed his mother and cousin to introduce him to a number of eligible young ladies. He also continued to unpack his trunks from India, visited his bank, and in general considered his options for continuing in trade, at least in some small way. Lawton, while not immense, would require his presence several months of the year, and even if his father lived another twenty years, it would behoove him to see that it was well looked-after in the meantime, since his mother had warned him that all was not well.

On Wednesday morning, his mother greeted him cheerily.

"We're to visit that Miss Bennett again," she said, "and a few more acquaintances of mine, some of whom have rather beautiful daughters. Won't you join us?"

Thomas's stomach sank. "You know, I think I really ought to go visit Father," he said. "See how bad things are at Lawton."

His mother frowned, her powdered face crinkling a little around the lips. "I don't know that he'll be back at Lawton yet."

"I can go on to Windcastle, if needed," Thomas said.

"You're not going today, are you?" Lady Caroline burst in. Now that she'd recovered from her long journey to London, she was beginning to look nearly vigorous. In only a few days, her pale face had rounded out and acquired a healthy blush, and her belly swelled visibly.

Thomas considered. "No, I'll need to see to a few things here and there. Tomorrow or the next day, I should think, but I won't have the time to go visiting with you, Mother."

She nodded. "You certainly should go see the estate," she said. "The coach is in fine condition, and you'll want our best conveyance on that dreadful road."

The thought of being confined to a coach for five or six days turned Thomas's stomach. It would be worse than the *Whistler*. Besides, it would leave Polaris in the ignoble position of being trailed behind the pulling team. He had no intention of leaving his new horse in London.

"Don't bother," Thomas said. "I'll ride Polaris."

"*Ride?*" Lady Caroline gasped. "All the way to Lawton?"

His mother merely frowned.

"Why not?" Thomas said. "I'll travel faster. I'm as good a shot as any, and I don't need to carry anything that would interest a highwayman. Besides, I'll see more of the country that way. I've been a long time away."

His mother inhaled deeply. "If you insist," she said, "but at least bring a groom or two, and your valet, if he can ride." His mother did not entirely share Jones's good opinion of the valet. She thought him flighty.

"I will consider your advice," he said evenly. "And now, I must go settle a few matters and have my valet pack my bags."

Thomas left them there with their meal. His mother wouldn't be able to insist on the coach, especially when she might well want it herself, and Lady Caroline would need it far more than he would. He called for his coat and walked over to the club to read the morning papers.

Fog blanketed the streets of London that morning. Thomas looked in vain for a ray of sunlight. Despite the cold, the gutters stank. Yes, a good ride through the open countryside would clear his head. His valet could follow later. Much as he had hated the solitude of travel, he had grown used to it and the clarity it lent his thoughts. He needed that clarity now, needed to shake his misplaced affection for Miss Grey from his mind, if she did not so much as write to say farewell... but then, in her position, he could see why she wouldn't. It would lend credence to rumors spread by gossip-mongers like her aunt. He had even been congratulated on finding such a pretty new mistress. Would that it were so!

"Why the long face, Smithson?"

Thomas looked up to find that he was on the doorstep of his club. Mr. Churchill was on his way out, and looking positively gleeful.

"That would be Sir Pently, now that we're in London," Thomas grumbled.

"Prickly, aren't we?" Churchill gave him a friendly punch to the shoulder.

"And you're acting like a child."

Churchill rolled his eyes.

"Pardon me," Thomas said, "I have business to attend to."

"Very well then, have it your way," Churchill said. "I'm off to India again. Could still use a man like you in the home office, if the aristocracy can't keep you busy enough."

Thomas drew away. The man embodied everything about trade which his mother despised. Even at the ball, he'd been measuring the price of everything in sight, and couldn't hide his bald-faced desire to bring investors into his enterprise. He may even have found some. Thomas was not one of them.

"No, thank you," Thomas said. "I find my family obligations quite enough to occupy my time. Good day."

Churchill tipped his hat with a sneer, and then fairly bounced away down the lane.

❧

"I will be glad to reach our new home," Hyacinth said, on the last morning of their travels. They'd been in coaches and inns for four long days, each bumpier than the last, but after that first day, the company had been more genial, and there had been no more highwaymen. Something about the attack continued to prey on her mind. She had thought of confiding in Maria, but Maria was nervous enough already.

"Home?" Maria said. She looked rueful.

"Are you missing Gibraltar?" Hyacinth asked.

"I do miss the sun," Maria said, "but no, it is only London that I'm thinking of."

"Don't worry, I'm sure we'll find some way for you to see Harold again, before too long."

"And you, your gentleman?"

Hyacinth shook her head and looked out the window. All morning, the landscape had been hilly and half wild, but here, it flattened into a broad valley of well-tended farmland. The coach jolted to an abrupt halt.

"Lindley Hall!" the coachman announced.

Maria and Hyacinth jumped up. Hyacinth leaned out at the

doorway.

"Already?" she asked. "They said it was near the village of Grantley."

The coachman pointed. "Grantley's just ahead there," he said. Hyacinth had to get down from the coach to see the cluster of cottages nestled by the turn of a broad stream on the valley floor. Here, they overlooked it all, through gaps in the trees. "I can take you there, if you like," the coachman offered, "but the hall's only a half-mile from here, down hill all the way." He indicated a narrow but well-kept drive, just on the opposite side of the road. From where they'd stopped, the road ran steeply down toward the village. It would be a mile or so to walk back, up hill all the way, with their bags.

"No, that's fine," Hyacinth said. "We can walk from here. We'll see the village later." She beckoned for Maria to follow. They retrieved their baggage and the coach rolled away down the road. A man leading a donkey approached from the direction of the village and tipped his hat to the driver, who paused for a brief conversation which involved many broad gestures. The coachman waved back towards Hyacinth, and the man with the donkey nodded. As the coach moved on, he greeted Hyacinth.

"The man says you've come to see Lindley," he shouted to them from a hundred yards down the road. "I can help you with your bags – just going that way, myself."

"Thank you," Hyacinth shouted back.

Maria took a deep breath, and they waited for the man and his donkey. A few small birds flitted through the trees, and though the day was cloudy, it was not overly cold.

"Good day to you, ladies," the man said as he drew closer. He wore a tweed cap and rough-spun trousers. "My name's Matt," he said. "I'm a gardener down at the hall."

"We're pleased to meet you," Hyacinth said. "This is Maria, and I'm... I'm Miss Grey."

"Miss Grey, is it?" Matt looked puzzled. "I've heard that name somewhere, but I suppose it's a common name, Grey."

Hyacinth nodded.

"Now, wait!" Matt struck his head. "You're not *our* Miss Grey, are you?"

She blushed. "Well, I... I'm Mrs. Miller's heir, if that's what you mean."

"By Golly," Matt said. "And to think I'm the first here to meet you." He stuck out his hand for Hyacinth to shake, and then shook Maria's hand, too. "Come on to the hall then! No time to waste. We've all been waiting to meet you!"

Maria helped secure their larger bag on the donkey's back, and together they followed the drive through a small bit of woodland. It gave way to an orchard, on a south-facing slope.

"Them's apples," Matt said, "and cherries that way. We make a bit of cider, but they're mostly for pies."

Hyacinth was charmed. "I never thought I'd have an orchard," she said.

"Don't worry, we'll take care of it for you. You'll see it blooming soon enough, April or so, just a few months away."

"It's beautiful even now," Hyacinth said. Then they turned a corner and she saw the hall. It sat beside a lake, a well-kept manor house which must have been a hundred years old, or more. It had a newer wing, and at a glance, she guessed it would be large enough to accommodate at least twenty girls, and a few tutors. It would be a beautiful school, if she could manage it. Looking at Matt, the gardener, proudly leading his donkey down the lane, she realized that the people who were already here should have some say in the matter, too. She would consult them all.

"It's quite large," Hyacinth said. "I'd seen maps, but seeing it in person is quite another matter."

"It is a fine old house," Matt said.

"And how many are living here? Mr. Butler, the solicitor, mentioned a manager, but I know nothing of the rest of the staff."

Matt whistled. A moment later, a young boy emerged from the stables beside the house and started up to meet them. "You'll see yourself. There's myself and three other gardeners. Joe, there, is the stable boy," he said, pointing at the boy who was running up towards them. "There's the cook and three maids inside. We kept them on, on account of not having any reason not to, as Mrs. Miller provided for us all. Then of course there's Mr. and Mrs. Owen, who manage the place. It was Mr. Owen who said we might see you soon."

The boy arrived, panting.

"Joe," Matt said, "here's our own Miss Grey, and a Miss Maria with her."

"Pleased to meet you," Joe mumbled.

"Now run along and tell the others. We ought to line up to meet her, like they do at Lawton."

Hyacinth froze for a moment. "Lawton? As in the Sir Pently of Lawton?"

"There's a Lord Algernon Pently there, there is, and a baroness, too, though she's away in London."

"Oh. Dear. We'll be neighbors," Hyacinth said.

The gardener, preoccupied with his donkey, did not notice anything amiss.

"We all have neighbors," he said, "and some are good, and some are not so good, but we tolerate each other well enough most days." He stroked the donkey's neck. "And now you ladies had best go inside, and see the place. Mr. and Mrs. Owen will be along in a trice, I'm sure."

❧

CHAPTER 15: HOME

The sun woke her, peeking straight in through the curtains of her new bedroom, which looked out over the lower slope of the orchard. It would be her very own. Her grandmother's bedroom, the largest in the house, faced the lake, but she'd chosen this one for herself, with its yellow and pink drapes and its view of the trees. She and Maria had spent most of the day before in a whirlwind of introductions, meeting the people who lived and worked on the estate. The small staff seemed happy and quite informal in their distinctions of rank. She wondered what it would be like as a school and tried to imagine how two dozen or more girls and young women might find a place here. Already, it felt like home to her, but she did not want to be lonely here.

She would miss the lights of London and her shipboard companion. He might have a house just across the valley, but he would probably spend most of his time in London. He would be a world away, wherever he was. In a few years, they might be able to meet in the village and say hello without thinking too much of what might have been. She would have her school, and he would have his family, and it would all be well enough, she tried to tell herself.

Out in the orchard, one of the gardeners was walking amongst the trees, inspecting them. Below stairs, she could make out a few rattles from the kitchen. Rubbing the sleep from her eyes, she made her way to the writing desk, already supplied with paper and ink, thanks to Mrs. Owen. She wrote first to her father, to let him know that she had moved to her grandmother's old estate. Next, she wrote to George, omitting all details about the highwayman, except to say, "We even saw a highwayman outside London!" She penned a terse note to Aunt Celia, assuring her that she had arrived safely, and asking that her trunk be sent along after her.

Looking out the window, she saw the gardener making his way back towards the house for the servants' breakfast. She ought to go down, herself, but she wanted to let Thomas know that she'd arrived, too. She couldn't write to him. She wouldn't. She wrote to Georgiana, instead. *"My dear friend,"* she wrote:

"I arrived yesterday at Lindley Hall. I was surprised to learn that it is only a short distance from Lawton. Lindley is charming. There is a lovely orchard, and as far as I can tell it is in good repair and quite large enough for a small school, perhaps some twenty students, if they are two to a room. It would be a modest establishment, in any case. I plan to speak with some of the staff about the possibility later today.

Our journey was not without incident. Though most of it passed calmly enough, we met with a highwayman on our first day of travel, not too far from London. He made off with the contents of all our purses, which included my grandmother's necklace, the one I wore to the Spencers' ball last Saturday. I had wanted to bring it with me, which was foolish, I suppose. I feel that I ought not to have lost it, and worse, that the thief might have followed me from London – how or why, I do not know.

Do you think it would be possible to hire a Bow Street runner

*to see if it makes an appearance in a jeweler's shop? I don't mean
to impose, but I don't know who else to ask.*

Sincerely,

Miss Hyacinth Grey"

There, Hyacinth thought. That would do. She was still
distressed about the loss of the necklace – it had such weight,
such magnificence, that it must be worth something, but looking
out at her new home, it seemed a world away. Perhaps that was
why her grandmother had chosen to live so far from London, in
the end. Here, Hyacinth felt, she could build her own life, and
she was going to set out to do just that.

❧

Thomas mounted Polaris on a fine morning a few days after
the ball. He had a change of clothes in his saddlebags, a good
pistol at his side, and a warm, rugged greatcoat. Although it was
a fine coat, it was not too fine, and simple enough to let people
assume he was in some nobleman's employ, and not the owner
of the horse, himself. The coattails settled across Polaris's
haunches as they rode out of London.

He did his best to travel quietly, but Polaris attracted
attention on the road, just as Hyacinth's grandiose gem had
drawn stares and comments at the ball. Thomas acknowledged
them all, and did his best to deflect attention away from himself
where he could. He rode from first light to dusk, resting where
Polaris needed to pause, and settling in at whatever inn was
nearest at nightfall. He ate in taverns, listening to the now-
unfamiliar accents of his home country, musing.

In some ways, it was reassuring to be home. Here, despite his
fine horse, he could sit in the corner of a crowded taproom and
fade into the walls, into the crowds, in a way that had been
impossible in India. Though he'd prospered and even been a bit
happy in his time there, he'd never had this feeling of being
loosely akin to the people around him, whether they were

commoners or aristocrats. Here at last, he needed no translators; there were no wholly unfamiliar languages to make sense of; and besides, he looked like everyone else. In London, muffled in his family's pomp, he hadn't had time to see it, but now that he rode alone, he did. He hadn't known he was missing this, all those years.

On the fourth day, in the late afternoon, he reached the edge of the valley. Lindley Hall sat just down the road, if he remembered correctly. The little village of Grantley nestled by a bend in the stream, looking very much as he had last seen it ten years ago, if a little shabbier here and there. Just over the far ridge, and about two miles more along the road, was his father's house, or rather, his mother's house, though she seemed to have abandoned it. If he pressed on, he might reach it by sundown. Polaris shook out his mane.

"All right, boy," Thomas said. "On we go. It'll be a warm stables for you tonight, or my name's not Tommy."

The horse seemed to roll his eyes.

"Well, Tommy or Thomas Sir Pently future Sir Pently of Lawton and heir presumptive to Windcastle."

Polaris nodded, and trotted on down into the valley. At the village, Thomas and Polaris slowed to a walk. Here, as elsewhere, people noticed Polaris as a rare specimen of equine perfection. A few men, standing outside the village inn, hailed him.

"That's a fine horse you've got there, Sir," one of them said.

Thomas nodded. "Thank you," he said, "I'm just..." He hesitated. He'd been telling lies along the way, saying that he was only delivering the horse, but here, he was too close to home for that. The smell of a hot roast over a fire wafted out on the late afternoon air, and the ale in the men's tankards looked strong and as good as any he'd had in the past few days.

"I'm just traveling over to Lawton tonight," he said. "Is there a swift lad here who could carry a message ahead for me?"

"Sure there is," one of the men said. "I'll go fetch my Jimmy."

Thomas thanked him, then dismounted and led his horse

around to the stables. While he saw that Polaris was supplied with fresh water and a bucket of grain, as well as a rack of clean-smelling hay, a pock-marked boy of about sixteen appeared.

"My dad said you wanted a message delivered up to Lawton," he said.

"I do, but I haven't had time to write it down," Thomas said.

"Don't worry," the boy said, tapping his head. "I can keep it all in here."

"I'd rather..." Thomas would rather write a note, and remain anonymous just a little while longer, but if he kept the message simple, it would do. "No, I suppose you *can* keep the message in your head, can't you?"

"I can," Jimmy said, proudly. "And I'll only deliver it to Mr. Fowles himself."

"Fowles!" Thomas said. "Is he still with us?"

Jimmy looked confused.

"To be sure," he said. "He's only thirty. Took over from his father five years ago."

Timothy Fowles had been Richard's age. They'd all played together as boys. When Thomas had last seen him, he'd been on holiday from his college. It was not surprising that he'd taken his father's post as butler, even at that young age.

"And what's your message then, Sir?" Jimmy asked. "I've got to be back by full dark, or not too long after, or my mother'll worry."

"Very well, tell Tim this: Tommy... no, Thomas will arrive later tonight, prepare a bedroom and the best stall in the stables for his new horse."

The boy repeated the message. "Is that your name?" he asked. "Thomas?"

"It is, now get along." Thomas handed him a shilling.

"That's too much!" the boy protested.

"Take it," Thomas said. "Tell them I'll be along soon."

☙

Thomas carved his meat at the common board in the village

inn, surrounded by people he'd seen often, as a child. He was a stranger here now, but he wouldn't be for long. He felt the villagers eying him, heard the murmur of their speculative whispers. Finally, as he was sopping up the juices with a piece of crusty bread, the man who'd first spoken to him outside took the stool across from him at the table.

"My boy, Jimmy, said your name was Thomas," he began. "It seems to us," he said, with a nod to the group he'd just left, "that the Sir Pently's second son was named Thomas, and you have a bit, just a bit, of the look of that family."

Thomas shrugged. "I hope I've gotten the better part of it, not the worst."

The man chuckled. "I'm Griggs, the miller. It's up to you if you want to introduce yourself. We heard the second son got lost at sea on his way to India, but seems it was only a bit of a rumor."

"When was that?" Thomas raised his brow.

"Ah, now you look more like the family," Griggs said. "It was years ago, not long after we last saw the boy. Would that be you?"

Thomas took a deep breath. "It would."

Griggs slapped his thigh in satisfaction. "Ha! Then let me be the first to say, welcome home." He laughed, and waved to his friends. "You owe me a pint!"

The other men came to Griggs, hovering behind him for a moment before pulling up their own stools. A thin one, a farmer by the look of him, set his hand on Griggs's shoulder. "Don't mind Griggs if he's been impertinent, please," he said, a little nervously. "He's had a few pints already."

"No, no, I don't mind," Thomas said hurriedly. "Truth is, I've been traveling alone all the way from London, and I could do with a bit of friendly company. Besides, I wouldn't mind knowing what's been happening in the neighborhood while I've been away."

"Ho!" Griggs said. "Mary there! Bring us more ale. We'll be here all night!"

"I don't know that I have all night," Thomas said. "I mean to reach Lawton this evening."

Mary, a barmaid with more gray in her hair than brown, wove her way across the taproom with a half-dozen tankards of ale. She looked at Thomas, then questioningly at Griggs.

"I'll buy his lordship a pint!" Griggs said.

Thomas held up a hand. "Now, I'm only an heir, not 'his lordship' yet."

The barmaid startled. "Sir Thomas?" she said. "Blimey. Well I'll just add it to his lordship's tab, then."

"I'll pay now," Thomas said, reaching into a concealed pocket in his breeches. "I can't start back with debts, now, can I?"

The barmaid, Mary, set the tankards down on the table and took Thomas's offered coin. She bit it to see that it was real, then tucked it into her bosom. "We do appreciate that," she said, assessing Thomas guardedly. "We do."

Thomas nodded slowly. It might be that "his lordship" hadn't been paying his bills, even in this nearby establishment. If so, it didn't bode well for the estate. He took a deep drink from his tankard. It was good ale: dark, strong, and sweet with barley. He set the tankard down on the table and looked at the men across from him. Griggs, the miller, was heavyset and had cheeks like a fat baby, except for the scraggly beard growing out of them. The farmer beside him was thin, just shy of frail-looking. There were three others, who looked as though they might be brothers, or at least cousins. One had the rough, blackened hands of a smith, another wore a yellowed apron – a baker, and the third smelled faintly of pigsty, even over the sweat, smoke and ale of the tavern.

"So tell me," Thomas said, "what news?"

❧

Thomas left the tavern as the sunset faded from the sky. The waxing gibbous moon had risen, and the clouds had cleared, so he and Polaris could see the road well enough. They had just reached the ridge when the boy, Jimmy, came into sight. He ran with a steady lope, back towards the village, but slowed at the sight of Polaris.

"Are you Sir Thomas, then?" he said, as he came abreast of the horse.

Thomas pulled almost imperceptibly on the reins and Polaris stopped. He really was a beauty of a horse, he thought, for about the thousandth time that day.

"I am," Thomas said.

"So why didn't you say so?" the boy asked. "And why are you riding alone?"

Thomas laughed. "Your elders down there in the village might say those were impertinent questions. They seem quite on guard against impertinence, there in the tavern."

"I'm sorry," Jimmy flinched.

"Don't be. It's only natural to be curious," Thomas said. He didn't like much of what he'd heard, but it was only half-tales, most of the time. Indeed, the cheeriest news had been that the new mistress of Lindley Hall had taken up residence, and that she was a great favorite of the people there already, despite having only arrived three days before.

"I'll be going, then?" Jimmy said.

"But I haven't answered your questions," Thomas said. "I didn't say that I was Sir Thomas because I've been traveling alone, and I didn't want to mark myself as the kind of man a robber might profit from. I'd rather people take me for my horse's groom, so that I *can* ride alone, and see a bit more of the country. It's been a rather enlightening journey, and I've enjoyed it."

Jimmy nodded. "I'd love to travel," he said.

"But your parents would worry," Thomas said. "And now, I'm off to meet my father again. Safe journeys to you, Jimmy."

"Thank you, Sir," Jimmy said. "Good night to you, Sir Thomas." He saluted, then ran away home.

Polaris continued on at a walk. The road was in indifferent repair, nearly good enough for an occasional coach or carriage, much better suited to farm carts. Lawton was in a remote corner of the country, but it had decent cropland and excellent pasturage. His great-grandfather on his mother's side had prospered, and the estate had supported several generations well, until now. When his grandfather's only son had died in a hunting accident, his granddaughter Heloise, Thomas's mother, had become heir to the title.

The Lawton line of men seemed to be plagued by hunting accidents, Thomas reflected. For now, he had no desire to continue that part of the family tradition, any more than he wished to continue his father's habits of neglect and waste. It felt, for the moment, like a new adventure, a rather challenging business enterprise, and a chance to redeem his mother's inheritance, if he could. He would never be Richard, of course, never be the blessed and beloved firstborn son, but he would do his best.

With that thought in mind, he rode up to the door. A curtain moved in an upper window. In the still of the winter night, he heard a bell ring from somewhere deep inside the house. He dismounted. No groom appeared to take Polaris's reins. That in itself was worrying, and even in the moonlight, he could see thin cracks in the house's stonework, flaws which should have been repaired. Ivy twined over some of the windows. Finally, a lamp flared to life in the hall and the door opened.

"Sir Thomas? Welcome home, Sir."

Thomas squinted into the light. "Tim?" he said.

"The same, though I usually go by Fowles these days." The butler stepped outside, carrying a lantern. "I am sorry we are not all here to greet you," he said.

"Indeed," Thomas said. "The house seems a bit dark."

Tim, his brother's old friend, nodded. "It's a pity."

"Mother said that things were bad here, but..."

"The staff mostly left here after she left for London. They were more loyal to her than the old man. There'd been no wages paid for two years, and after Christmas, I think we all just gave up hope." Tim reached for Polaris's reins and led the horse around to the stables with Thomas following. "One of the men still comes now and again to see to the stables, and it's a quiet time of year in the gardens, in any case."

"I had no idea," Thomas said.

Tim shrugged. "I stayed on for want of anyplace to go. Besides, someone's got to look after the old man. Betsy's still in the kitchen, no family, either, and Nestor's still the manager – I think your mother pays him wages out of her pin money."

Thomas calculated, wondering what sum was owed to all the servants. "I'll speak to him tomorrow."

"You'd better speak to your father first, Sir Thomas, if you don't mind, Sir." Tim swallowed. "I think he may not have much time left."

"What is it?" Thomas asked. "The clap, or—"

Tim shooed the notion away. "No, it's consumption. And a bit of gout. He scarcely leaves his bed."

Thomas frowned. "So the only thing that could keep him home was sickness."

Tim didn't comment. He opened the stable doors and led Polaris to a reasonably clean stall. There were only a few odd farm horses here, now that the carriage horses had gone to London, and a couple of cows had been moved into the barn, too, looking a bit above their station in the horse stalls.

In silence, Thomas and the young butler settled Polaris in for the night. Tim found a little bit of grain in a hidden corner, away from the main stores, and they pumped water into a bucket from the well in the yard.

"I'll see to him myself in the morning, Tim," Thomas said. "I suppose I should get used to calling you Fowles."

"It's up to you, Sir," Fowles said. "I don't think I should call you Tommy anymore."

"I wouldn't mind too much, but..." Thomas looked up towards the dark windows, grudging, neglected eyes. They'd stopped in the stable yard. "We'd better go in."

"Certainly, Sir Thomas," Tim said.

"Then let's go."

Fowles led him back around to the front of the house,

warning him of an uneven paver in the path, just before he might have tripped. He pointed out a few things that were still in good repair; the terraced rose garden, the ha-ha, the upper pastures. "And the roof's not bad," he said.

"Well, that's good," Thomas agreed.

Entering the front hall, Thomas could smell a hint of mustiness. "You say the servants only left after Mother came to town."

"Well, after she went to collect Lady Caroline. You've heard about her... condition?" Tim asked.

"I have," Thomas said. Tim, Fowles, waited. "She looks well. I hope that the child is a boy, for my own sake as much as for my cousin's memory."

Fowles nodded. "It would be a fine thing, to be duke of Windcastle, but this place..." he waved his hand. The furnishings were draped, the banisters dusty, even though the servants had been gone less than a fortnight.

"Yes," Thomas said. "I think I should go see Father now."

The younger Fowles led the way up the grand staircase to the master suite. A faint moan greeted them as they opened the door.

A grumble rustled the bed. "Go away." In the lamplight, the pale, thin figure barely ruffled the counterpane, propped up on a pile of pillows. He coughed, shaking and rattling.

"Go away," he repeated.

Thomas approached the bed. If it weren't for the hostility in the voice, he wouldn't have believed that this frail being, scarcely tied to life at all, could be his father. The old man's eyes were closed, and he frowned. Thomas reached for his hand. He jerked at the unexpected touch, and opened his eyes.

"Who are you, some new quack sent up from London?" He coughed again. "Insufferable woman."

"Would that be my mother you're referring to?" Thomas said.

The man on the bed straightened and looked at him, opening his eyes for the first time since they'd entered.

Fowles cleared his throat. "I thought it best to leave it, in case it wasn't you, after all."

Thomas frowned.

"What am I, seeing ghosts?" Thomas's father complained.

"I'm back from India, Father," Thomas said. "I thought you would have heard. I'm sorry to see you like this."

"Don't lie to me, I'm dying."

"I've seen other dying men, too," Thomas said. The man in front of him, though he still had a thread of life left, was fighting a losing battle.

"Have you then? Think that makes you a man?"

Thomas looked back to Timothy, who stepped out at the briefest signal. He probably didn't want to hear this conversation any more than Thomas wanted to be having it. There was something defeating about the whole situation. He wanted to rail at his father, but this near corpse of a man begged pity, even as he spat out his old venom with every bone-shaking cough.

"I'd had no intention of coming back," Thomas said.

"You were dead to me. Now I'm dying, and there's no one else to pass this wreckage on to."

"There's Nathan," Thomas reminded him.

"He's worse than I ever was," his father said

"Is he?" Thomas said.

"It's all yours now."

"Well, actually, it's Mother's, what's left of it," Thomas said. "Besides, you're not dead yet."

"Close enough. Your mother might be a baroness in her own right, but she's not man of the house. Never was, can't be." The speech was too much for his frail voice, and he collapsed into another fit of coughing.

Thomas reached for his hand again. This time, his father stiffened, but didn't draw away so quickly. His hand felt cold, even after Thomas's long ride from the village had left his own fingers nearly frostbitten. He just sat there, holding his father's hand by its icy fingertips. He seemed to be sleeping. A lone candle burned on the bedside table. It guttered as a draft blew in, and Thomas reached into the drawer below it for a replacement.

There were only three more candles. He set one in a spare candlestick and lit it from the old one, before it faded entirely away.

In the brief flare of light, his father's eyes opened again.

"You do look a bit like Thomas, but I don't see so well anymore."

"I'm sorry we parted so badly."

Thomas's father shook his head, ever so slightly, which set off another cough, but he swallowed before it took him away entirely. "No, don't be," he said. "I thought you had backbone. Misplaced backbone, but stomach. You'll have to do."

"I suppose I'll have to take that as a blessing."

The old man nodded, almost imperceptibly, and coughed again. When he'd stopped, he opened his eyes, looking straight at Thomas. "Go away. Let me die in peace. And... do something for this place."

"I'll do my best," Thomas said.

His father grunted. "Go," he said.

≈

In the morning, he found the old Lord Pently sleeping, attended by a quiet physician from a nearby town. "I'll call for you if he wakes," the doctor said.

"Shall I send for my mother?" Thomas said.

The doctor shook his head. "There won't be time for her to get here from London. And she knew, chose to go with that young widow instead," he said, scornful that she'd abandoned her husband in the end. Maybe the doctor couldn't see how that was for the best. Thomas suspected that his parents hadn't ever liked each other much.

"Call me if he wakes," Thomas said. He couldn't find fault with the doctor's treatment of the old Sir Pently. His father had been lucid last night, if not pleasant. He had laudanum, but not too much of it, so he was as comfortable as he could be. Between the consumption, the gout, and his long years of debauchery, it would have taken impossible feats to prolong the Sir Pently's life.

Thomas followed the dusty, once-familiar halls to the dining room. Like the rest of the house, he found the table and chairs draped in dust covers. Not sure what else to do, he rang the servants' bell. He waited. It seemed like an eternity before Betsy, the cook, burst through the servants' door, dusting flour from her hands and looking flustered.

"Sir Thomas!" she exclaimed. "We didn't think you'd be up for breakfast, not after your hard journey."

"I always rise early, at least, compared to Nate, and I imagine compared to my father," Thomas said.

The cook shuffled uncomfortably.

"It's a habit I got in India," he explained. "Always cooler in the mornings there. Would there be a bit of bread about? Maybe some tea?"

Betsy nodded, dusting the flour on her hands off onto her apron. "I'd think you'd want more of a proper breakfast than that, but we haven't got anything on hand. I just put a few loaves in the oven, for us, what servants are left. Didn't know what you'd be wanting. Mr. Fowles has gone into town for a chicken for tonight, Sir."

Thomas nodded. He knew that his arrival was a bit of a surprise, coming with so little forewarning, but hadn't expected the servants to be so visibly put out by his presence, nor that the larders would be so near to bare.

"Chicken. A chicken would be fine," Thomas said. "I'm quite used to ordinary food, common food these days. You don't need to put on full dinners for me. I could even eat in the kitchen, if that's easier." It was a concession he would not have thought to make, ever, as he was growing up, nor even when he was in India, and certainly not in London. Posing as a groom for the past few days, if only by implication, had changed his perspective a little, not to mention traveling alone from India to Gibraltar. He could tell that it would be a hardship for Tim and Betsy to serve formal meals, as well as providing broths and possets for his ailing father and feeding themselves.

"You would come to the kitchen?" Betsy gulped. Having swallowed the idea, she nodded. "Come on, then. At least it's warm, and I've got that bread to watch." She hurried away, as if half hoping he would change his mind and stay in the closed-up dining room. He lingered behind her, checking one of the drawers where the good silver had been kept. Some of it was still there. He wondered if the servants had absconded with it, or whether his relations had sold it off to pay their debts. He certainly hoped that the manager would arrive soon. If he had to extrapolate on his own, he'd guess that the house stood as well as it did only through force of habit, sheer inertia.

If the grand staircase had been dusty, the servants' stair between the dining room and kitchen was worse – not filthy, but with a deeper air of neglect. He wished that his mother had told him, but then wondered how much time she'd really spent here since Richard's death. It was as if the whole house had died with him... except, thankfully, the kitchen. Thomas opened the door into the cavernous old kitchen, built to serve a large, noble family, their guests, and a small army of servants and farm workers. A bright fire burned under the oven, and the central worktable gleamed, freshly scrubbed. A basket of eggs hung just inside the door, and a kettle whistled on the hearth.

Betsy didn't meet his eyes. "Here you are, Sir," she said, pulling out a stool. "I'll have tea for you directly. The bread won't be long, and Timmy's bringing butter and milk back with him. He won't be long."

"Thank you, Betsy."

"We're out of sugar, I'm afraid, but there's a bit of honey I was saving for the Sunday pudding, only I didn't know you were coming, Sir."

Thomas sipped his tea. It was bitter, and not very good tea, to begin with. "That's all right," he said. "I'll have this cup as is, and wait for the milk."

Betsy sighed with relief. "Good, thank you, Sir. I wouldn't know what to do for the pudding if I didn't have that honey."

"Listen, Betsy," Thomas said. "I know things must have been

hard here for a while, but I hope I can set things right."

She frowned, skeptical. "They weren't so bad when your brother Richard was here. I think the Sir Pently kept up appearances for his sake."

Thomas took another long sip of tea, trying to ignore the rank taste of something, maybe dung or bark, which smugglers must have cut into it. "But they were only keeping up appearances?" he thought aloud. "And Richard didn't notice." It was strange, to think of Richard as having flaws, but he'd always been so optimistic, so sunny, that it wasn't too much of a stretch to see that he might have simply ignored anything that didn't suit him.

Betsy turned away, discouraging further confidences. She'd been here when he was young, but, like Tim, hadn't been in her current post. She might have been one of the kitchen maids, he wasn't sure.

"Where did you come from, Betsy?"

She shook her head. "You ask your father that, if you want to know."

"So he gave you the post here?"

"And I won't get a reference for another," she said, "not from your mother, and not from him, neither." Betsy went to the door. "Thanks be to God!" she said. "There's young Tim with the milk and butter, and Nestor with him."

"I'm sorry I've pried," Thomas said, "but it seems to me you've kept the kitchen up, and that's something, with no one else here."

She ignored him, and sniffed the air. "That bread's done," she declared, and sprinted across to the oven.

Although the tea had been an abomination, Betsy's bread was delicious. Thomas allowed himself a breath of optimism, then asked Nestor to show him the account books.

❧

CHAPTER 16: RECKONINGS

Hyacinth and Maria walked to the Owens' cottage after breakfast to begin their tour of the land.

"It is a beautiful house," Maria said, looking back at Lindley Hall. It looked half golden in the morning sun, stretching up to greet the day.

Hyacinth shivered as her feet crunched over the frosty path. "It is," she said, "but it's so cold here."

"Not much colder than London," Maria said.

"Maybe not," Hyacinth said. "I wasn't ever out so early in London." The house – her house – was not particularly large, but it was bigger than Aunt Celia's London house, and had just as many servants. "I'm not sure I know what to do with all the staff," she said.

"What do you mean?" Maria said.

"It's a bit overwhelming. I was used to you and the housekeeper in Gibraltar, but it's so many people to get to know, and I don't know what they would think of having a school here," Hyacinth said. "It would be more work for them. I don't know."

Maria shrugged, and they walked on in silence until they reached the cottage, which lay just around a bend in the path from the hall.

"Hello!" Hyacinth called. She heard a clatter and a muffled conversation from inside the house. A moment later, a tall woman emerged from the house. She wore her chestnut hair pulled back into a severe bun and smiled broadly.

"Miss Grey!" She curtsied. "We've been expecting you! Do come in!"

Hyacinth took a deep breath and entered the small garden through a lacy cast-iron gate. Tidy rows of herbs stood here and there in mostly-bare beds, with hardly a weed in sight. She didn't know much about gardening, but this place was precisely laid out and obviously carefully tended. She hoped, no, felt sure, that she would like Mrs. Owen.

"It's my pleasure, Mrs. Owen," Hyacinth said. "Your garden must be beautiful in the spring."

"Oh, it is, but it's not mine!" she said, as she ushered them into a parlor just as tidy as the garden, and more colorful. "It's Mr. Owen's work, mostly. He was a farmer, before."

"Was he?" Hyacinth said.

Mrs. Owen nodded. "Had his own farm, twenty acres. Not much, but he must have kept it well." She sniffed, and pulled out her handkerchief.

"Had?" Hyacinth said.

"He had to leave it," Mrs. Owen said. "And though he misses it, I can't say I'm sorry, because I never would have met him otherwise."

Maria hovered on the doorstep, looking longingly at the garden. "Maria," Hyacinth said, "this is Mrs. Owen." The two of them curtsied to each other. "Maria came with me from Gibraltar. She's from Spain."

"*Buenos dias*," Mrs. Owen said.

Maria returned the greeting.

"I used to teach my pupils Spanish, as well as French," Mrs. Owen said to Hyacinth.

"Your pupils? Were you a governess?"

"Oh, no, only a village schoolmarm."

Hyacinth dared to hope. Maybe she wouldn't ruin this place, as she'd lost that necklace. "A schoolteacher. How wonderful!" she said. "Tell me, how did you come here, then?"

"Well, it's a long story," Mrs. Owen said. "I'd better get the tea first."

❧

After three days at home, Thomas knew that he could not flee back to India. There was simply too much to be done here, and no one but himself to do it. His father slipped deeper into his deathbed sleep. His eyes opened once or twice during Thomas's occasional hours of bedside vigil, but he did not speak again. He wrote to his mother, asking her to come home. She had grown up on the estate, and though his father had seized the reins some thirty years ago, and driven her away from the place in the decades since, she still knew the place better than anyone else in the family. He would want her help putting it back together, besides which, it was rightfully hers. He also sent instructions to his banker, telling him to release a certain large amount of funds to the Baroness of Lawton.

"There," he said to himself, "that should assuage her worries about my involvement in trade." Nestor, the manager, showed him the accounts. They were a tangle of atrocities, mismanagement, and poorly considered borrowings, but at least Nestor himself appeared to be honest. Thomas began to make arrangements to pay off some of the estate's debts, beginning with the servants' wages and the accounts with local establishments.

He surveyed the house and grounds, and rode out to the pastures to see the cattle and sheep. The land was... well, it was land. It was farmed land, and not wilderness, but beyond that he had no sense of whether it was well-tended or not. Perhaps he should visit some other estates in the neighborhood. With that thought, he set out on a fine morning with a hint of spring in the air, towards Lindley Hall. Polaris, bored of the stable yard and pasturing with cows and workhorses, seemed to enjoy the outing. As he rode through Grantley, the villagers tipped their hats to him. A little over an hour after he'd swung up into the saddle, he arrived at the turn to Lindley Hall.

As he rode through the gates and through the well-tended orchard, he admitted to himself that any comparison with Lawton would not be practical. To begin with, Lindley's income derived principally from its orchards, while Lawton, a much larger estate, grew grain and pastured cattle. Still, Lindley was in much better repair, judging by the state of its road alone. He hailed the first person he saw, a gardener, who was out in the orchards with a pruning saw.

"Good day," Thomas called cheerily, or as cheerily as he could manage.

"Good day to you, too, Sir," the man said, stone-faced. "May I help you?"

"Is Miss Grey at home?" he asked.

"I don't rightly know," the man said. He stepped in front of Polaris, blocking the way. "What's your business?"

Polaris tossed his head and made to step around the obstruction. Thomas patted him on the neck, soothing him.

"I'm Thomas Pently, of Lawton. I'm acquainted with Miss Grey, and wished to make a neighborly call."

The gardener narrowed his eyes. "We'll see," he said. "Follow me."

Thomas followed the man down the road. "I'm only just returned to Lawton," he said, after a while.

The man grunted.

"I've been attempting to settle any debts we have outstanding in the neighborhood," he said. The man only grunted again, and Thomas gave up trying to engage him in conversation. Soon, they reached a turning in the road, bringing the hall and its gardens into view. In the front garden, two women sat on a stone bench, talking. One of them was Hyacinth.

❧

Hyacinth immersed herself in getting to know the place, its

people, and its business. She spent most of her days with Mr. and Mrs. Owen, who taught her all about the estate, how the cider was made, and where they sold it. She learned that the hall and its orchards had been nearly abandoned before her grandmother acquired it. Mrs. Miller brought on all the staff herself. Hyacinth was just beginning to piece together their stories, and learned that each and every one of them was deeply, almost impossibly grateful for their post. All they knew about her was that she was her grandmother's heir, but they were eager to welcome her, and a little anxious. They wanted to stay, that much was clear.

One morning, she asked Mr. Owen outright how he'd come to lose his farm.

"I was a farmer, see," Mr. Owen said, "but there was a highwayman in the mountains near there, and someone, don't know who, don't rightly want to know, took it into their head that he looked like me. And so I was sentenced to hang."

"For nothing?" Hyacinth said.

Mr. Owen considered. "Well, someone thought I'd done something, and the judge agreed."

"So what happened?" Maria asked.

"I just slipped out of the jail that night. The watchman was drunk; they often are." He said it as if it were nothing, really, though it must have been terrifying. "But sometimes I think he wanted to let me go. I hid in the next village, first place I found, and that was the schoolhouse. Mrs. Owen's school house."

"Only I was Miss Nelly, then," Mrs. Owen said.

"So that's my story," Mr. Owen said. "And of course I had to change my name, but I'd much appreciate staying on, is all."

Hyacinth nodded. "Of course. I... I can't imagine. Of course you must stay." They'd reached the rose garden, barren now, but still a sunny place to sit.

"Thank you," Mr. Owen said, blushing. "I'll just go see how they're getting on in the house. Good day, ladies." He tipped his hat to Hyacinth and to his wife, who turned off into the garden.

"Is everyone here running from something like that?"

Hyacinth asked.

Mrs. Owen considered. "We all have different stories, and mine is probably the dullest of all. I only chose to go with a fugitive!"

"But it's so... so romantic," Hyacinth sighed, sitting down on their favorite bench. "I do hope they won't mind, having this school."

"I think there's a need for it," Mrs. Owen said, "and we all agree, here. It's only that some might be afraid of being found out, of someone coming for them, from the lives they escaped."

"Well, we must take care, then," Hyacinth said.

"Mrs. Miller was a grand lady, for us, but she never did mix much with the quality around these parts," Mrs. Owen said.

"Well, she had a past of her own," Hyacinth said.

Mrs. Owen nodded. "We always suspected as much. There was even a rumor that she won this house in a game of cards, but she told me herself that it was investments."

"That's what her banker said, too," Hyacinth said. She looked up at the house. "We must teach the girls maths. I don't know how my grandmother learned to keep her accounts so well, but it certainly stood her in good stead."

Mrs. Owen sighed. "I'm not so good with that, myself. I can do simple sums, but..."

"But I can teach a little, too, or I hope I can." She was about to tell Mrs. Owen of her lessons with George, but then she looked up. There was Thomas, sitting on his horse for all the world like a kind of general, or emperor. He tipped his hat to her, then handed his steed's reins to Matt and stepped into her rose garden.

"Who is that?" Mrs. Owen whispered.

"Thomas," Hyacinth said. She sounded like a lovestruck calf. She cleared her throat. "He's a Mr. Pently, or rather, a Sir Pently, or something like that. Lawton, across the valley, is his family estate, I believe."

Mrs. Owen frowned. "Mrs. Miller... Well, never mind. We'll talk about mathematics after dinner, I suppose. You'll want to keep Matt nearby, with a man like that around."

Mrs. Owen dusted off her skirts and hurried away before Thomas got halfway across the garden. Hyacinth wanted to run after her, but then there was Thomas, in her garden, and far, far sooner than she'd ever thought to see him again. She squared her shoulders.

"Miss Grey," he said, bowing as she approached.

"Thomas," she blushed. "I... I was just speaking with..." she gestured towards the retreating Mrs. Owen. "We were talking about the school, our idea for a school here. I didn't expect to see you here, not until years had passed. Why aren't you in London?" She gave a hasty curtsy, looking over her shoulder for Mrs. Owen, but her new friend had disappeared around the side of the house already.

"I'm sorry to have come at an awkward time," Thomas said.

"No, not at all," Hyacinth said. "It's just that I didn't expect you. I mean to say, I haven't had any callers yet. I suppose I should offer you tea."

"You don't need to, you know," Thomas said. He, too, looked over his shoulder. Matt stood beside Polaris holding the horse's reins and glaring at his owner. "I get the impression you don't get many visitors here."

"You're my first, my first visitor." Hyacinth blushed. "I'm not much of a hostess."

"Nor am I much of a guest. I should have known that you were only just getting settled in, here, and I should perhaps have sent my card, to ask if I might come." They stood in awkward silence for a moment. "I actually came to see the land," Thomas said. "Ours is in a state of neglect, I think, but I haven't seen a good, working estate in a long time, at least not in England. I don't know what to look for. I'd hoped to see how this place was run, because the folks in Grantley said it was a fine place. Besides, it offered a chance to see you again. I was worried, when I heard you'd left London."

He seemed taller than she remembered him, but also a little disheveled, as if he hadn't been sleeping well. "I arrived safely,"

Hyacinth said, "and I'm sure that Aunt Celia is half glad to be rid of me."

Thomas chuckled. It looked like the first time he'd smiled in a week. "I wouldn't be so sure about that. I think she enjoyed having the excuse to buy more gowns."

Hyacinth smiled ruefully. "Maybe so. She's probably practicing on poor Sophie, now." Thomas looked haggard, and she didn't want to think of Aunt Celia, or abandoning Sophie. "How are things, at your family's home?"

Thomas shook his head. "My father's on his deathbed. The staff have mostly abandoned the place for lack of pay, and... well, that's just the start of it."

"Oh," Hyacinth said.

"I'll salvage it," Thomas said. "It's still good land, I think, or the manager says it is, but it's a bit more of a job than I know how to do. Some of it, the accounts and all of that, I can manage, but the farming's a mystery to me. I've sent a letter to Mother, asking her to come home, but I have a feeling I'll be there for a while. At Lawton, I mean."

"So you're looking for help? Really?"

"I suppose I am." He seemed embarrassed.

"You told me a long time ago that you weren't raised to this, that you never expected to inherit," Hyacinth said.

"That much is true," Thomas said.

"And I don't know anything about farming, either, so I'm making this a school, because I do have at least some ideas about that. The staff here seem to like the idea well enough, even though it will make the place a lot less peaceful. I've been getting to know the place here, or at least trying to."

Thomas looked around. "And it's all new to you, but it's nearly as new to me. None of my childhood haunts look quite as I'd remembered them."

"No, I don't suppose they would," Hyacinth mused. "In any case, I won't be much good to you about the farming. Maybe Matt can show you the trees, while I go in to get tea."

Thomas reached for her hand. "I'd like you to come with me,

if you don't mind."

Across the hedge, Matt cleared his throat.

"No, I think I'll go in," Hyacinth said, "but I'll walk with you to the stables, first. Is it a terribly long ride from Lawton?" she asked as they approached Matt and Polaris.

"Not too long," Thomas said. "Only a bit more than an hour, with Polaris here." He patted the horse's neck affectionately and took the reins.

"Matt," Hyacinth said. "Would you be so good as to show Tho... Sir Pently some of the orchards? He's a friend of mine, from my journey back to England."

"Is he?" Matt said.

Thomas nodded. "And from London," he said. "I'd like to get some water for my horse, first."

Matt nodded and led them towards the stables.

"The folk in Grantley say the estate here is doing well, the orchards," Thomas said. "Lawton isn't at its best, and I'm grasping at ways to bring it back to itself."

"You won't do that with orchards, not there," Matt said.

"I don't plan to," Thomas said.

"So what do you come poking around ours for?" Matt said.

"I think he knows almost as little of farming as I do," Hyacinth said. "I wouldn't know the difference between what's needed in an orchard or what's needed in a wheat field, either." She looked up at Thomas. "I don't mean to insult you."

"No, it's all quite true," Thomas said. "I have no idea what a well-run farm looks like, or how far ours falls short, though I suspect it does fall short."

"Maybe I should go find Mr. Owen for you, as well," Hyacinth said. "I'll send him along after you, and meet you in the orchards."

❧

With that, Hyacinth rushed away. Perhaps he shouldn't have come, descending on her idyllic corner of the valley. It was so different from his family estate that it might as well have been on another continent. There was something about it that intrigued him, beyond the carefully tended orchards and, of course, Hyacinth herself. The people seemed even more suspicious of outsiders than country people usually were, but Thomas had the distinct impression that the gardener was only trying to protect Miss Grey, a sentiment he could only approve of.

Once they had Polaris comfortably settled, Thomas was led away from the house and into the orchards by the taciturn gardener. In short order, another man joined their party. Unlike the gardener, he touched his cap to Thomas.

"I'm Mr. Owen, sort of a manager of the farm here," he said. "I understand you're from Lawton."

"I am," Thomas said.

"Pity about that place. It was a fine property once, they say."

"I remember it in better days," Thomas said.

"You're not as old as that," Mr. Owen rejoined.

"No?" Thomas said. "I'm certain it was quite well-kept when I was a boy. At least, better than it is now."

Mr. Owen considered. "I suppose it might have been better then. I don't know. Wasn't here myself, but the folks in the village say it went into decline with the old Sir Pently, and it's never been right since."

Thomas scarcely remembered his grandfather. He had married late and was an old man when Thomas was born. "You're right; I'm not as old as all that. It's something the people in the village wouldn't have told me themselves."

"Why not?" Mr. Owen said.

Matt, the gardener, was trailing behind. "It's 'cause he's one of them," he interjected. "No one much likes them in these parts."

Thomas stopped to look at him. "It is my family. I left for ten years and had a few brushes with death in India, just to get away from them," he said. "But if I'm to live here – at Lawton, I mean – I intend to do something for the place."

"An admirable sentiment," Mr. Owen said. The gardener

looked skeptical.

There followed a moment of awkward silence. Mr. Owen regarded Thomas critically. They were closing ranks around their new mistress, as if there were some sort of unspoken agreement among the people of Lindley Hall, to keep themselves to themselves, and not to tolerate interlopers. Especially not interlopers from Lawton.

"So, would you show me the farm?" Thomas asked. He resisted the urge to look back towards the house. "Are these apple orchards, then, or cherries, or..."

Matt snorted. "You're not much of an Englishman if you don't know an apple tree when you see one," he said.

"I suppose I'm not," Thomas said. "But I'd better learn, hadn't I?"

❧

Hyacinth fairly ran into the house. She shut the door and leaned against it to take a deep, steadying breath. Her pulse pounded at her temples. She knew that she could build a life here, a good life here, the one she'd meant to live, but it would be far, far easier if he didn't come calling, reminding her of moonlit decks and hands clasped at the rail, in the night, or of dizzying dances and diamonds. She took one more deep breath... and opened her eyes to find Mrs. Owen peering at her from the library door, just a short way up the hall.

"You're in love," she said. "That complicates this matter of the school. I wish you'd told me."

"It changes nothing," Hyacinth said, trying to be resolute. Her voice shook, betraying her. "He has no intentions... I mean, not that he doesn't have intentions, it's only that I don't think we should. His family wouldn't like it. Nor would mine."

"Dear," Mrs. Owen said, drawing closer. "It doesn't matter what his family likes, or what your family likes, it's only what you and he would like. And even schoolmarms don't really want to be maidens all their lives. At least, I didn't."

Hyacinth blinked back tears. "It's very kind of you to say so, but..."

Mrs. Owen placed her hand over Hyacinth's. She wasn't a very old woman, but she wasn't young, either. She was a motherly age, comforting, but not too distant.

"I know my family must have raged when I ran away with a fugitive from justice," she said, "and I'm sure Mr. Owen's people would have torn their hair out to see him with a bluestocking like me, but we don't regret it, not for a moment."

Hyacinth sniffed. "That's... I don't know," she stammered. "Could you find Maria for me? I think we should put together some kind of luncheon for Sir Pently, and I don't have any idea where to begin."

"Don't worry," Mrs. Owen said. "I'll go speak to Sarah and find out what she has in the pantry, and Maria can help you dress. I always think that picnics are romantic, but it's chilly, now that the wind has picked up."

Hyacinth nodded, grateful to talk about something other than her illusory courtship. "This morning, Matt said we might have snow."

Mrs. Owen chuckled. "Yes, we might have snow. What about the yellow parlor? The room warms quickly, and yellow suits you. I'll see to the fire, and Sarah can send up tea and sandwiches, or whatever she has planned for your luncheon. Don't mind about the school. Love is..."

"I'm not giving up on the school, I'm not."

"Very well," Mrs. Owen said. "Why don't you wait in the library?"

"Yes, I think I will," Hyacinth said. "Or do you think I should go get dressed?"

"Of course, dear." Mrs. Owen winked merrily and strode off in the direction of the kitchen. Hyacinth collected herself and went upstairs.

Half an hour later, she sat in the yellow parlor, perched on the edge of a mustard-colored settee in a pale violet gown which Maria had packed for her, even though it was much too fine for travel and one of the ones that Aunt Celia had bought for her in

London. She heard them coming up the path before she saw them. Someone chuckled. Could it be Matt? He'd seemed quite hostile to Thomas when they set out.

The front door opened and she jumped to her feet, hurrying to meet the men in the hall.

"Do come in!" she said.

Thomas glanced around. Through his eyes, the house couldn't be very impressive, Hyacinth thought. Mr. Owen and Matt stood behind him. Mr. Owen coughed.

"I'm sorry," Hyacinth said, "you must come in, too."

"Not at all," said Mr. Owen. "I'll have my lunch at my own house."

"And I was just going to the kitchens, to see Molly," Matt said. With that, they hurried off, leaving Hyacinth and Thomas alone together, standing in the cool, dark hallway with its polished floors and dark drapes. The house seemed utterly silent. Hyacinth bit her lip.

"I've missed you," Thomas said.

"I've been very busy," Hyacinth said.

"Yes, I can see that. You've been settling in?"

"I have. Come, let's go into the parlor," Hyacinth said. She turned back down the corridor and led him to the yellow parlor. It was a pretty room, very feminine. She felt her grandmother's presence rather strongly there. Molly, one of the maids, said that Mrs. Miller had always taken her tea there. Also, a portrait of her in her later years hung over the mantel.

Thomas followed her in. "Was that your grandmother?" he asked. In the portrait, Hyacinth's grandmother wore silks and fur, and looked far more commanding than she had in portraits of her younger self.

Hyacinth nodded. "She commissioned that one herself. There are other portraits, but they belonged to her patrons."

"And you don't think much of her patrons?"

"No, not really."

Thomas circled the room and came to rest beside a chair. Hyacinth took one nearby, and they both sat, just a bit too far away from each other to touch.

"I wish I'd known her," Hyacinth said, "but I don't want to live like she did."

"I know. You've told me. You want to be independent."

Hyacinth nodded, avoiding looking at him.

"I couldn't be independent if I wanted to, not any more," Thomas said.

"No? Isn't having your own estate a kind of independence?" she asked.

"Maybe some day, but not until I get the estate back on its feet," he said. "And besides, it properly belongs to my mother – it's her title, you know."

"Is it?" Hyacinth said. "I didn't know that."

"No," Thomas said. "I think my father did everything he could to try to make her forget it, but it's too late for his regrets now. I don't think he'll live to see her again. It's a lonely place."

Hyacinth looked at him warily. He had that same lost look he'd had that night, on the *Whistler.* She reached for his hand, sitting on the edge of her chair, leaning towards him.

He looked up at her and closed his fingers around hers. Their eyes met, and he seemed about to say something, then leaned closer, his face almost touching hers.

There was a knock at the door. They sprang apart.

"Yes?" Hyacinth said.

Molly, the maid, entered. "It's the post, Miss," she said. "You've a letter from London." She walked briskly to Hyacinth's side, handed her the letter, and turned to go.

"Wait," Thomas said.

She ignored him. She kept her hair tucked into her cap, and there was never so much as a strand out of place, but when she reached the door, she turned a little, showing the side of her face. High cheekbones, and a frown.

"You look like Father," Thomas said. She paused. "I think you're my sister. Half sister. I'm sorry, I didn't realize it, that day in the woods."

"You left after that," Molly said. "We heard. Why?"

Thomas shrugged. "I thought you were his mistress. It's what any young man would think. But I suppose your mother was?"

Molly nodded. "She was, until... I don't know; maybe she still is." She closed the door to the hall, keeping her back to it. Now it was Hyacinth she ignored.

"She kept with him for years, even after the money ran out. Still keeps his accounts open at the tavern."

"She works at the tavern?"

"Always had to," Molly said. "Thanks to him."

"Is it Mary, there?"

Molly nodded.

"I met her when I came through, on my way home a few days ago. I'll settle the account there, just as soon as my funds get here from London."

"That's what he always said. Or when he won his next hand."

"Look," Thomas said. "I can't go back and... I'm not him, but I *can* pay the bills, and I will, and all the back wages. I didn't want to be anything like him. That's why I left."

"Should have stayed gone, then, and not come around here, either," Molly said. "If you'll excuse me?" She swept out of the room.

Thomas stood to follow her. "Hyacinth," he said, "I have to... I have to talk to my sister. I don't know her. What's her name?"

"It's Molly," Hyacinth said. "Her name is Molly. Go."

"I'll be right back," he said.

Hyacinth, feeling completely disoriented, set the letter on the table and walked over to the window. Thomas and Molly were outside, talking animatedly, arguing. They were nearly the same height, and her eyes matched his. She even had a shadow of that aristocratic nose. Molly didn't treat Thomas like the lord of the manor. She treated him like a man she'd had a grudge against all her life. She kept shaking her head. Thomas kept holding his hand out to her. Finally, after a few muffled exchanges, she shook it, and they walked together to the stables. Hyacinth brought her letter over to the window. The cook came in with tea and sandwiches, setting them down and leaving without a word.

Outside, a few snowflakes drifted down. Thomas re-appeared, leading Polaris. Polaris with Molly riding him, looking dazed yet pleased with herself. Thomas spoke to the horse, and patted him on the neck, then bowed ever so slightly. He sent Molly, the maid, on her way atop his prized horse.

Hyacinth glanced down at the letter at last. It was from Georgiana – she'd been expecting one from Aunt Celia, but nothing had arrived yet. She was just opening it when Thomas came back in. She half-rose to greet him, but he flopped down on the settee across from her.

"Father's dying. I thought she should see him, to say goodbye, or good riddance. She probably knew him better than I did." Thomas said. "I don't know why I came back here. Not here, to Lindley Hall, but to Lawton."

"Family obligation?" Hyacinth offered.

Thomas shook his head. "There's that, but mostly, I think it's that I failed so much in India."

"But you didn't," Hyacinth said. "You said you built a fortune."

"That's not what I mean," he said. "I mean... it was Sarita. I should have tried harder, tried to marry her. I don't think I'll ever have a mistress again. It's... Father didn't even pay his tavern bill, and yet Molly's mother was his mistress for years, along with who knows how many others. Including the cook at Lawton, I think, at least when she was younger. I don't want to be like that."

"But you weren't, not like that. You were loyal to your mistress, I think?" Hyacinth said.

"For a time, but... I have already forgotten so many little things about her, and now I don't think it would have lasted forever, not as we had it, not with the company closing ranks against the natives. I wouldn't have had the strength to stand up to it. I saw that, and whatever they might have said, I wasn't the first officer to duel. I could have stayed, but I needed to escape again. I'd failed, and my father's shadow was chasing me."

Hyacinth wanted to comfort him, but she knew nothing,

didn't know where to begin. Outside, the snowflakes thickened in the air.

"I got a letter from your cousin," she offered.

"From Georgiana?" he said, brightening. "Do read it. She writes excellent letters, sometimes."

Hyacinth broke the seal and unfolded it. "This one is very short, I'm afraid."

> *Dear Friend,*
>
> *I've engaged a Bow Street runner, recommended as one of the best of his profession. He has turned up nothing so far, but it has only been two days, and I hope to have better news to report soon. My cousin has set out for Lawton, so you may see him before I do again.*
>
> *The Baroness has declared that I am to go visiting with her, immediately, so I must go, but I will write you again as soon as I have any news from the runner, or from my own enquiries.*
>
> *Yours,*
>
> *Georgiana*

Thomas stared at the ceiling as she read, then blinked. "A Bow Street runner?" he said. "Why on earth have you and Georgiana hired a runner?"

ॐ

AMELIA SMITH

CHAPTER 17: DECLARATIONS

Have some tea," Hyacinth said. As she poured, he took one of the sandwiches from the tray that had appeared while he was outside arguing with his half sister. He had not thought of her much, since that day, but as soon as he'd seen her, he'd known who she was. She also appeared to be the only person at Lindley Hall with any connection to the local area.

Hyacinth sat across from him and took a sip of her own tea. "It's rather a common story," she said. "My necklace was stolen by a highwayman on our first day out of London. I was hoping that Georgiana would know if it might be possible to retrieve it."

"Probably not," Thomas said absently. "There are thousands of necklaces in England, and probably half of them have been stolen at some time or another."

"I know, but I have to try, and I wouldn't know where to begin. It must have been very valuable."

"It's only a..." Thomas suddenly remembered Hyacinth at the ball, with that impossibly large jewel resting on her breasts. "The one that you wore at the ball?"

Hyacinth nodded.

He cursed himself. "How? You must have reported it. Surely the local magistrate could have sent word to London?"

Hyacinth shook her head. "I told him I thought it was

priceless. He said that it was probably paste and wrote down its value as something like twenty pounds."

"Twenty pounds?" Thomas's voice rose. "He's a fool."

"He hadn't seen it," Hyacinth said.

"Do you have any idea how valuable that necklace is?" Thomas remembered half the ballroom watching it out of the corners of their eyes, with that loathsome man, Frank Churchill, coveting it, bald-faced. "Damn it!" Thomas jumped to his feet. "I must go. Georgiana can't manage this on her own."

Hyacinth looked puzzled. "You can't go to London. Your father is dying."

"I came this far. I can go to London," Thomas said. She looked strangely untroubled by the theft. "How can you just forget it?"

"I had no way of chasing after it," she said. "Besides, there was something about the highwayman – I thought he might be looking for me, for the necklace, in particular, and surely coming here, beginning my own life –"

"You say he was looking for you in particular?" Thomas demanded, his pulse racing. "Why? How?"

"It was just a feeling," she whispered. "The way he kept his eye on my reticule. I don't know. I had felt that there was someone following us. It frightened me. And then, when he came in with his pistol, I just... I just knew that was it, what I'd been dreading. After he left, after he stole the jewel, I didn't have that sense anymore. I felt safer. Oh, I know I should have left it in London, but we were all alive and he hadn't hurt anyone, and everyone said I should be glad he didn't... you know... take *me*."

Thomas knelt down and embraced her. "Yes. I'm glad, too. I should wish I had been there. I would have stopped him." She shook her head, and fumbled in her skirts until she found her handkerchief.

"I was frightened. I didn't tell anyone. I haven't told anyone. It's just that mostly I feel I should have kept it, kept better watch over it. It's only an ornament, but –"

"Shh," Thomas said, stroking her hair. "Don't say that. It's true, but it's not only an ornament. It was very important to someone, once, and it's extremely valuable, extremely valuable. Worth as much as this estate five times over, I'd say."

"Not to me," Hyacinth said, swallowing.

"Yes, but to the man who... Damn it!" Thomas looked up. "Damn it," he repeated. "Tell me about that highwayman. How tall was he? What did he wear?"

"Why?" Hyacinth asked.

"Just tell me." He got up, and paced the room as she talked, holding one of the sandwiches in his hand, half forgotten.

"He was small, not very small, but much shorter than you. His hand shook a little. And he was wearing a cotton coat, which I thought rather odd."

"And what did he say? Why do you think he was looking for you, again?"

"It was just the way he seemed to lose interest as soon as he saw the bag with the necklace in it. He didn't even look inside, though he must have felt its weight. He'd started at the other side of the carriage, demanding the contents of pockets and reticules, and went all the way around until he got to me. Maria was next, but he just left as soon as he'd passed me, without even stopping to demand the contents of her purse."

Thomas frowned. "I must go to London."

"But why? Why now?"

He wondered how much to tell her. There was no reason not to tell her all; there was so little to tell.

"There was a man in India, a Frank Churchill, who broke away from the Company to trade with the king of Sikkim. I believe he recognized your necklace from the descriptions of it – he thinks it's one which the Company, or one of their agents, stole from the Sikkimese some time ago. I saw him staring at you, at the ball. Well, he wasn't staring at you, only at your necklace. He even said to me that he thought it was Sikkimese, that it must be something called the Star of Kanchen, that the Company had lost a treaty over it."

"But why would he steal? Surely a gentleman who was

invited to that ball wouldn't be so desperate," Hyacinth said.

Thomas shook his head. "No, there's plenty of desperation in London ballrooms, even in the finest houses. You'd learn that if you stayed. In any case, Churchill is not a gentleman, not in any sense, not even by birth. He's a tradesman, through and through. All he seems to care for are profit and his own advantage. Though I don't know him well, I do know the covetous look he had when he saw you that night. I wouldn't put it past him to pose as a highwayman, and what kind of fool wears a cotton coat in the English winter, except maybe a fool who's been in the tropics too long?"

"You really think he was the highwayman?" Hyacinth said.

"I do. And I think he's going to take that necklace to India on the first ship he can get passage on. He was fairly bouncing away to the docks when I saw him last, just before I rode for home. I should have known!" He made a fist, and looked around for something to punch. Hyacinth had risen to her feet.

"But there was no way to know, and why was it so important?" Hyacinth said. "Was it stolen to begin with? And how did my grandmother come to get it?"

Thomas looked for his coat. Hyacinth followed him into the hall.

"The Company has stolen any number of things," he said as he strode towards the door. "It was one of the things I never quite made my peace with. I don't know the details, but I can find out." He found his coat and pulled it on. The servants were nowhere to be seen.

"Surely he will have sailed already?" Hyacinth said.

"Possibly," Thomas agreed, "but it only becomes likelier the longer I wait."

Hyacinth put her hand on his arm, stopping him. "Don't go," she said. Her eyes were beseeching, and very clear, clear still pools that he wished he could fall into. She was, despite her maid and the other servants in the house, quite alone here. She needed protection, protection from the likes of Mr. Churchill, who would only see her jewels or her fine estate, and want it for themselves.

"I don't want to leave you," he said sadly, "but I can fix this. If anyone can, I can. I don't know if anyone else in London knows enough about Churchill's plans, or has the authority to have him stopped."

"I don't care about the necklace," Hyacinth said. "I mean, if it was stolen to begin with, maybe my grandmother's patron left it with her merely to hide it. Maybe it's better off in India, or Sikkim."

"It may be better off there," Thomas said, "but not if it benefits that scoundrel!" He strode to the door, but paused before opening it. "I'm glad he didn't hurt you," he said, "but I have to go now. I have to set this right. When I come back, I'm never leaving you again. Ever."

Hyacinth's jaw dropped. Even with her mouth gaping open, she looked more beautiful than any woman he'd ever seen, anywhere. Then she flung herself at him and he was enveloped in violet silk and a gentle perfume of muguet and tea. She tipped her head back, and her lips parted again, this time in invitation. He took it. He took her mouth, her head, her body into his embrace and wanted to take her completely, but not here, not now. He kissed her, lips touching, then crushing, then just barely probing with his tongue until he opened his eyes. She was gazing at him again, in something like surrender. He broke away.

The cook, for only the cook could be so covered in flour, and brandishing a cleaver, appeared in the doorway along with that gardener, the manager, and two other maidservants.

"We'll not have none of that," said the cook, "even if you are our own Molly's long-lost brother. You'd best leave now, unless you intend to marry our Miss Grey."

"I do," Thomas said. "I do intend to marry her." He had not quite realized it until just then. He turned to Hyacinth. "If you'll have me?"

"I will," she promised. Then she backed away. "I'm not so sure about your family, though. And I want to stay here, living in my own house. You'll have to stay here too."

The prospect of living at Lindley Hall was certainly more cheerful than the idea of living at the derelict, haunted Lawton. "That is thoroughly agreeable to me, even if you do fill the place to the rafters with schoolgirls."

Hyacinth hugged him again. "You'll really help me with the school?" she asked.

Thomas considered. "I won't stand in your way, and I doubt you'll need my help. Besides, I'll have to spend a good deal of time at Lawton, even though it belongs to my mother by rights and she has a good bit of life in her yet."

The gardener harrumphed. "I'll just walk you in to the village, then, see that you have the banns read." He looked about him, as if searching for a cattle-prod to coax Thomas on his way, should he prove reluctant.

"In Grantley?" Thomas said. He looked at Hyacinth, who was at least as startled as he was. "I'd thought that maybe we'd marry in London, at Saint James. I was just going to ride there on... other business. I might as well."

The servants stepped closer, somewhat menacing in their unity. "You might skip out," the cook said. "We can't have that."

Hyacinth gasped. "Oh, no. I don't want a Society wedding. Unless you think we need to?"

"No," Thomas said. "We don't need to. Society can gossip in our absence." He exhaled. "Grantley it is, then."

"You'd best go, too, Miss," the cook said, "to be sure of him."

Hyacinth nodded. "I'll just change into my walking boots."

"And I'll get..." Thomas began. He muffled a curse. "I don't have Polaris. I meant to ride to London immediately."

"Well, you'll just have to wait for your sister to bring him back, then, won't you?" Hyacinth said. She squeezed Thomas's hand, then ran up to her room, taking the steps two at a time.

❧

By the time they reached the village church, Molly had ridden through on her way to Lawton, taking her mother with her to say their farewells to the dissolute and dying lord of the manor. The village was abuzz, almost as if they were expected. A crowd of curious onlookers followed them to the rectory, whispering amongst themselves.

Thomas and Hyacinth set a wedding date in the middle of March. They wrote letters to their relations in London, and Hyacinth wrote to her father in Gibraltar.

"Shall we wait for Molly to return?" Hyacinth asked, when their letters were sealed and waiting for the post.

"No," Thomas said. "Let's walk back home."

They spent the rest of the day together, talking about the future. By the time Molly returned to Lindley hall, dusk had settled over the valley, and Polaris was growing tired. Thomas would have to stay the night.

Hyacinth went down to the kitchen to discuss arrangements with Sarah.

"I'll put him in the brown bedroom. It's just upstairs from your grandmother's old room," Sarah said with a wink. Hyacinth looked at her dumbly. "So you can visit him if you like. Through the secret passage beside the chimney!" Sarah said, as if it were obvious to anyone. "You really are an innocent."

"But we're not married yet!" Hyacinth gasped.

Sarah rolled her eyes. "You're engaged. It's nearly as good, and we'll hunt him for a scoundrel if he cries off. Go on, have a bit of fun!"

Hyacinth felt quite out of her depth. "I'll consider that," she said.

❧

At dinner, Hyacinth sat at one end of a long table while Thomas sat at the far end, as if he were already her husband. Sarah had set out an admirable repast, centered around a roast goose, with apple pie from Lindley's own orchards. They spoke in pleasantries, but silences stretched between them.

"Are you quite certain?" Hyacinth asked him, after one long

pause.

Thomas's mouth was full. He finished chewing and swallowed before he answered. "About marrying you? I'm not sure I've ever been so certain about anything in my life."

"What if you want to go back to India?"

"You can come with me. I think Mrs. Owen is quite looking forward to having a school here, and she has the makings of a headmistress, if you ask me."

Hyacinth thought about that. "What do you know of headmistresses?"

"That they should be a bit like headmasters, and I knew the one at Eton, when I was a boy. She could stand up well enough to them, I think."

"To an Eton headmaster?" The thought was a bit dizzying. "That's high praise."

"We'll have time to see if she measures up, though I'd wager that she will." Thomas tucked back in to his dinner. "Your cook makes an excellent roast."

❧

That night, Hyacinth couldn't sleep. Outside, the snow clouds scattered and the stars shone through. The moon climbed up over the hills. Hyacinth lit a candle and took out one of her grandmother's journals, one from the time when she was in London, just before she became Bereford's mistress.

> *I cannot, I cannot, I cannot. He says he means to marry me, but why would he? He is a merchant's son, and wealthy enough to keep a wife, but not to keep a mistress, too, and he cannot really want me for a wife. Oh, how I long for him! But I cannot. I must go and find another patron before I am too old.*

There was a tear stain on the page. Hyacinth wondered if her grandmother had regretted that always. She wondered how her grandmother, having suffered so much at the hands of men, could still long for one, even knowing what they were like. She didn't know what they were like. Even Sarah's cheery, "Have a bit of fun," frightened her. She did long for Thomas, but beyond a kiss, what was it that she longed for?

She sat for a long time, holding the old leather-bound journal, its spine worn smooth by careful hands and time. An owl called out in the night. Hyacinth gathered a wrap around her and carried the candle to her grandmother's bedchamber.

It was easy enough to find the catch beside the fireplace, an irregular bit of molding shaped like a flattened rose. The panel swung out easily, revealing a dark stair climbing up, and descending in the opposite direction, towards the lake. She sheltered the candle's flame against the draught and took one tentative step up, then another and another, until she reached the next landing. The wall was smooth, no obvious catch. She felt around, searching for the way to open it, to enter Thomas's room. At the top, there was a gap with a loose bit of wood. She prodded it, but nothing happened. She ran her hand down the side, finding the hinges, then tried the other side, but again, there was nothing. Her heartbeat quickened as something scurried on the stair above. A rat? She fumbled along the wall.

She knocked the candle over.

She screamed.

"What in blazes?" Thomas's voice came from the other side of the wall, sleepy and half-aware.

"In here!" Hyacinth cried.

"Where?"

She could hear him scramble out of bed, the creak of the floorboards as his feet hit the floor, a muffled grunt as he stumbled. She knocked against the wall.

"Where are you?" he demanded.

"Here," Hyacinth called. "Inside the wall. Beside the fireplace. I can't find the catch."

"The catch?" Thomas said. "What are you doing in there?"

"Trying to come see you?" she said.

"That's charming, but would be much more charming if you weren't trapped in the wall."

The rat scuttled past her feet. Hyacinth shrieked.

"What is it?"

"A rat, I think," Hyacinth squeaked. "Just get me out of here. Look for a rose, or something, in the molding. The one downstairs works just by pushing it."

"I'm looking," Thomas said. There was a moment, a very long moment, of silence as he searched. "That's got to be it," he said. "Stand back!"

Hyacinth tripped, falling back straight onto the fallen candle, and its puddle of hot wax on the stone, which melted through her night rail, burning her posterior. She gasped.

Slowly, creakily, the panel swung open. She looked up at Thomas, silhouetted in moonlight.

He swept her into his arms, and muttered a tiny oath as the last of the candle's warmth curled the hair on his strong, bare arm. He carried her out of the secret passage and deposited her unceremoniously on the bed. He stood looking down at her.

"How did you come to be in the chimney?" he asked, looking into her eyes. He was naked, absolutely and completely naked, despite the cold.

"You see," Hyacinth blushed. She turned half away, hiding her face in shadow. "It's just that I'm not sure, about... about that thing. That we're supposed to get married first. Oh, I'm making a muddle of it."

He sat beside her. "You're afraid of it, of sex, so you go climbing in secret passageways?"

Hyacinth nodded. "It's ridiculous. Also I don't like rats. I especially don't like rats."

"You could have come in by the door."

"You probably locked it. And I wasn't sure I wanted anyone to know."

"They're all asleep, aren't they?" Thomas said. He stretched out beside her, every inch of his bare flesh. She'd never seen anything like him, his nakedness. Apart from prints of statues, and some antiquities here and there. But those weren't alive, and Thomas most definitely was – alive, that is, and the part between his legs larger than any on a statue, and getting larger by the heartbeat.

"Maybe I'd better go," she said.

"No, stay," he said. "Unless you don't want to."

"I do want to stay, but..."

"Don't be afraid," he said. "There's no need to be afraid. I haven't been with a woman in so long, I'm not sure I can remember what to do, myself."

"I can't believe that," Hyacinth said.

"Well, would you help me remember? Or rather, discover it all again?"

"I would, but..."

"But we won't... I'll be sure I don't get you with child, not yet."

Hyacinth gulped. "Yes, definitely not yet."

"I want to enjoy your company for myself, for a while," he said.

"So don't go to London?" she said. "You know, I want you to be safe, too."

He pulled away slightly and looked curiously at her. "That's a very dear thought, but I'm not a boy, and I don't like what that man has done. If anyone harms you, they must not escape."

"Still," she said, "I wouldn't like to see you harmed."

"I'm sure I won't be," Thomas said. "He's not that clever."

"Though he must be desperate," Hyacinth said.

Thomas shrugged. "I'll be back just as soon as I can, I promise," he said. He settled back on the coverlet and reached for her hand. "Now. How shall we begin?" he asked. Not waiting for an answer, he raised himself up on one elbow and leaned over to kiss her on the lips, before she could think of words to say, let alone speak. She tried to sit up, too, but he pushed her gently back down onto the bed. He loomed over her.

"Allow me," he said. She nodded. He kissed her again, then his mouth began a long journey down, tickling her jaw, lingering on her neck, her collarbone, slipping beneath her thin night rail and down to her breast. He looked up to her eyes again and she tried to speak, but something quickened in her heart, lower, in her belly and between her legs, and all she could do was to let out a tiny squeak. He pulled her up from the bed, pressing her against his long, hard self, and worked one hand under the hem of her night rail, feeling her legs, the whole, pale length of them, lifting the fabric up until he clasped her buttocks.

"Are you sure?"

She gulped and nodded.

"I don't know that I'll be able to stop myself. I want you."

"And I want you."

"I have from the first moment I saw you," he said.

"You intrigued me," she said.

"I hope I can do more than that." With one fluid motion, he undressed her, ripping the thin garment over her head and throwing it on the floor. His nakedness, now that she was naked too, seemed to take on more luster in the moonlight. Her nipples hardened as the air teased them, a draught blowing in from the window. Outside, an owl hooted.

"Let me see you," she said, getting up from the bed and leading him farther into the light.

He groaned. "I want to bury myself in you."

"Do." She drew him over to the window and touched him, as his lips had touched her, splaying her hands on his chest, so muscular, strong.

"Lower," he said.

Her hands fell, skimming over his midriff to the joint of his hips, where the sparse hairs grew into a thicket.

"Yes, there. Touch me."

And she did. Her fingertips reached his member, its surface velvety, surging up as she wrapped her hand around it.

He grunted, a primal sound, and flattened her against him. He picked her up and threw her on the bed, landing with a creak as the ropes strained beneath her. "Now," he said.

He took her mouth in his again while one hand pushed up between her thighs, parting her, dividing her, pushing into the soft, warm place between her thighs, grown slick with anticipation. His other hand released her head and teased one nipple. He looked into her eyes once more, and then bent down to kiss her neck. She almost screamed, but he muffled the sound with another kiss as the head of his erect member pushed against her.

"Go gently?" she said.

"I'm trying." He almost whimpered when he said it, and then... "Oh, god."

A sharp pain, over almost as soon as it had started, and he was inside her, sliding into her, taking her. She drew him in closer. "More," she said.

He nodded, and gave himself into her, more and more until they both erupted in ecstasy, dripping in perspiration, moonlight and winter air still teasing their bodies as they lay entwined.

&

Hyacinth awoke some time later to the sound of a distant bird. Along the southeastern horizon, the stars were winking out in the pre-dawn sky. Thomas slept beside her, looking oddly innocent and childlike in his repose. She considered stealing back to her own room – this time without any creeping in secret passages – but then decided against it. She roused him.

"I hope I don't wear you out before your ride," she said.

"Minx." He rolled her over so that she lay on top of him. "Just try. I don't mind at all."

Some time later, she heard a clatter from the kitchen.

"I'd better go back to my own room," she said.

"Until our wedding night?" he asked.

"Surely not that long?"

"I'll hurry back from London."

"Do. Do hurry." She tore herself away and reached her own chambers unobserved, so far as she could tell. Inside her own bedroom, the dawn light streamed in through the curtains. She pushed them aside to look out at the orchards, the bare-branched winter trees lacy in the blush of the rising sun. Turning back to her bed, she caught a glimpse of herself in the mirror, stealthy, disheveled, and, though she might not have thought it before, beautiful. She felt sure that the whole night's misadventures would be written large in every step she made, floating, as she felt, inches off the floor, and longing for him to be inside her, again and again.

❧

Thomas rode, impatient with the roads, the weather, even with Polaris, who trotted gamely on, swallowing the miles. Four days after leaving Lindley Hall, he trotted into London and straight to the East India Company offices, where he bullied his way into talking with a superior officer, a man who'd spent most of his career in the Subcontinent.

"Frank Churchill, you say?"

"Yes, Sir," Thomas answered. "I met him in Calcutta, then again in London, recently."

"And you say he married a Sikkimese princess?"

Thomas nodded.

"What, does he intend to bring this jewel back to his bride?"

"Only if it will secure him an advantageous private agreement with the king, I believe."

The man leaned back in his chair, scanning the papers on his desk as if they might tell him something of importance.

"And you want to return it to your own fiancée, I presume."

Thomas cleared his throat. "To be honest, I don't give a damn. We are well enough off without it, but I don't want that man to profit by it, by posing as a highwayman and frightening her."

There was a long pause. "We had always wondered what became of it."

"My fiancée inherited it from her grandmother, who was known as Mrs. Miller."

The man chuckled. "Mrs. Miller? The very beautiful Mrs. Miller?" He pulled a bell-string by his desk.

"There are several ships sailing in the coming fortnight. Mr.

Churchill may be aboard one of them. We'll have him searched, if we can."

"Thank you, Sir."

"And if this all turns out satisfactorily, we can see about revising your record."

"I don't think it would make much difference to me at this point."

"All the same, there's no need to be a martyr about it, and we must compensate you somehow."

Thomas shrugged. "And what will you do with the jewel?"

"I suppose we'll inform the Sikkimese consul, and work from there. We can see that it's returned to its rightful owners."

"I would like you to do that, as would my fiancée."

"Very well," the man said. A clerk appeared at the door. "See that you get the passenger lists for all our ships departing in the coming fortnight," he instructed. "Look for a Mr. Frank Churchill, and if he's still in London, have him detained and contact me immediately."

"Yes, Sir," the clerk said.

"And show this man to the door," he added, indicating Thomas.

"Good day, then," Thomas said. He walked out and rode back to Windcastle house, where he slept for two days straight, then rode again for home.

❧

EPILOGUE: A WEDDING

The morning of the wedding dawned clear and warm. Daffodils blanketed the hillsides and robins were building their nests.

Thomas woke in his mother's house. His father had died a week after his return from London, and just after his mother had arrived. She'd come in the carriage, to say a last farewell, and had begun to take the reins again on the estate. With most of the staff back in place, and a few extra men hired to repair the crumbling buildings, the place was coming back to life.

"It's a pity that Georgiana wouldn't come," his mother said, as they prepared to set out for the village.

"Well, someone has to stay with Lady Caroline," Thomas said.

His mother sniffed. "I don't see what good she'll do, though. She'll only terrify herself. She's not a married woman. She hasn't borne children. I ought to be there."

"You can go as soon as the priest says, 'man and wife,' if you like," Thomas said. "The carriage will be right there."

"Nonsense," his mother said. "You will need it to go to your wedding breakfast."

"We can walk, or you can leave us there on the way," Thomas said.

In the end, though, he knew that she would stay. Her affection for her childhood home had come back to life as she assumed control of the house once more. That included sacking the cook, but Thomas had quietly penned her a reference before she left in a flurry of the Baroness's long-suppressed rage.

❧

Hyacinth walked down from Lindley Hall with half the staff, while the others prepared the wedding breakfast. She'd sent word to Aunt Celia, but had not been entirely surprised when she did not arrive for the wedding. They had nearly reached the bridge when a carriage rattled down the road behind them.

Maria recognized it first. "Harold!" she called, and ran to meet him.

Harold drew back on the reins and the horses pushed back against the onrushing weight of the carriage, snorting. Before it had even come to a complete halt, the carriage door opened and George sprang out, followed by Sophie. Hyacinth ran to them and hugged them. She had her face tucked into the side of George's head when a once-familiar throat-clearing made her look up.

Captain Grey descended from the carriage, holding a pair of crutches in one hand.

"Father!" Hyacinth exclaimed. "What happened?"

He brushed off Aunt Celia and limped towards his daughter. "I caught a bit of shot in the foot, and they transferred me home. I only heard of all this," he said, gesturing at the crowd gathering in front of the church, "because I overheard your esteemed aunt bemoaning your fate to one of her cronies. She only told me that you'd gone into the country."

Aunt Celia bristled. "And so she had."

"Well, I'm glad you're all here." Hyacinth beamed at her father. "You may walk me to the altar."

"We'll see about that," he replied. He watched the Pently's carriage approach through narrowed eyes. "I don't like this business."

"You don't know him," Hyacinth said.

"I don't. And I don't like him forcing my hand like this, either."

The Pently carriage drew to a halt in front of the church. Hyacinth and her father, trailed by the rest of her party, walked towards it.

Thomas's mother descended first, looking every inch the Baroness. Thomas followed, seeking Hyacinth in the crowd. Their eyes met for a moment before Captain Grey stepped between them.

"A word, if you please," Captain Grey said.

Thomas nodded. "It would be my pleasure."

"I very much doubt that."

They walked towards each other like two men pacing the distance for pistols at dawn. A chilly breeze wafted in from the hills. Hyacinth looked for Maria, but she had disappeared with Harold, while Matt the gardener led the carriage horses to the stables at the village inn. Sophie and Aunt Celia stood looking somewhat lost while George scaled the village's best climbing tree.

"Don't rip your breeches!" Hyacinth chided.

"I don't know how you endured that boy," Aunt Celia said.

"Quite happily, most of the time," Hyacinth said. She took her cousin's arm, and coaxed her aunt along. "Shall we go into the church?"

❧

Thomas and Captain Grey walked into the graveyard beside the church until they were far enough from the others to talk privately.

"I don't know what you're about," Captain Grey said.

"Marrying your daughter, I hope," Thomas said.

"But why?"

"Because I love her."

"Hmph." Captain Grey leaned against a tree. "Not to spite your family?"

Thomas smiled. "That is only a convenient coincidence."

"And you'll make her a Duchess?"

Thomas looked back towards the road, where the rest of the

wedding party had been moments before. "I rather hope not."

Captain Grey raised his eyebrow skeptically.

"I preferred being Mr. Smithson, and I apologize for trying to buy your influence with the Pently name."

"A singularly bad strategic choice," Captain Grey commented.

"And why is that, exactly?"

Captain Grey looked away. "It was my sister. Your uncle compromised her, and of course paid none of the price, while she paid it all. Oh, I tried to make him pay, but I was a boy, and he was heir to a duchy."

"Was there a child?"

Captain Grey shook his head. "I don't know. I wasn't told."

"I see." Thomas walked away from the captain, from his future father-in-law, looking at the rows of untidy graves, the etched names and lichen-covered inscriptions. "Well, I can't say I have much to offer for that. I'm not fond of my uncle. I don't think anyone is."

Captain Grey grunted.

Thomas took a deep breath. "But today, I don't want to think of him. I just want to marry your daughter, and go to live with her at her house. She has plans to turn it into a school for impoverished girls, to save them from the streets."

"She has always wanted to help those less fortunate."

"I'll help her if I can, and someday, we might leave the school to others, and settle our family at Lawton, or at Windcastle, if need be. I am beyond glad that we met first as shipmates, and not as neighbors, though I'm glad now that our houses are so close to one another."

Captain Grey said nothing.

"May I have your daughter's hand in marriage?"

Captain Grey nodded. "If that's what she's chosen, you may. With my halfhearted blessing."

"I hope to turn that into a whole-hearted blessing by the time our first child is born."

Captain Grey's face fell. "Will that be soon?" he asked.

Thomas shuffled his feet. "Not too soon, no."

"Good. Because otherwise I might have to call you out, as I did your uncle."

"Very well. Shall we go back to the church?"

"Yes, let's get this all over with."

Although Captain Grey grumbled, he looked distinctly more cheerful, even joyful, by the time he reached the altar rail with his daughter on his arm.

૪

That night, Thomas and Hyacinth dined with Hyacinth's father, brother, aunt, and cousin, as well as Thomas's mother and a few distant cousins she'd summoned for the occasion. They were just rising from the table when a messenger arrived: Lady Caroline was recovering from childbirth, tired but well. She'd borne twins. Twin boys, small but hearty.

"One last toast!" Thomas said. "To an heir and a spare, and to Lady Caroline."

He turned to Hyacinth and kissed her right there, in front of everyone. "And to the life we want to live," he whispered.

"To our lives together," Hyacinth said.

"For a very long time." Thomas added.

They drank, then joined hands, turning to embrace their future.

The End

ABOUT THE AUTHOR

Amelia Smith lives in a small house in the woods with her husband, two children, one cat, and some poultry in the yard. She writes in a variety of genres and enjoys curling up on the sofa with a pot of tea, a plate of cookies, and a good historical romance.

If you've read this far, please let other readers – and the author – know what you think on Goodreads.com or at your online retailer.

Visit www.ameliasmith.net to find out more about the author and her work, or to join the mailing list, which will bring you news of new releases.

Thank you for reading!

CPSIA information can be obtained at www.ICGtesting.com
Printed in the USA
LVOW11s2133200815

450909LV00008B/951/P

9 781941 334010